TAKEN IN THE DARK

BOOKS BY PEGGY WEBB

LOGAN SISTERS THRILLER SERIES
Black Crow Cabin

THRILLERS
Snow Brides
Savage Beauty
The Ally
All the Lies
Just One Look

COZY MYSTERIES
A CHARMED CAT MYSTERY SERIES
Magnolia Wild Vanishes

SOUTHERN COUSINS MYSTERY SERIES
Jack Loves Callie Tender
Elvis and the Dearly Departed
Elvis and the Grateful Dead
Elvis and the Memphis Mambo Murders
Elvis and the Tropical Double Trouble
Elvis and the Blue Christmas Corpse
Elvis and the Bridegroom Stiffs
Elvis and the Buried Brides
Elvis and the Rock a Hula Baby Capers

Elvis and the Pink Cadillac Corpse
Elvis and the Blue Suede Bones
Elvis and the Devil in Disguise
Elvis and the Heartbreak Hotel Murders

PEGGY WEBB
TAKEN IN THE DARK

bookouture

Published by Bookouture in 2024

An imprint of Storyfire Ltd.
Carmelite House
50 Victoria Embankment
London EC4Y 0DZ

www.bookouture.com

Copyright © Peggy Webb, 2024

Peggy Webb has asserted her right to be identified as the author of this work.

All rights reserved. No part of this publication may be reproduced, stored in any retrieval system, or transmitted, in any form or by any means, electronic, mechanical, photocopying, recording or otherwise, without the prior written permission of the publishers.

ISBN: 978-1-83525-396-0
eBook ISBN: 978-1-83525-395-3

This book is a work of fiction. Names, characters, businesses, organizations, places and events other than those clearly in the public domain, are either the product of the author's imagination or are used fictitiously. Any resemblance to actual persons, living or dead, events or locales is entirely coincidental.

This book is dedicated to Vicki Hinze and Debra Webb—fierce warrior women, talented fellow authors, and the best, most loyal, most compassionate, and loving friends I have. I don't ever want to know what it's like to be without them.

PROLOGUE

THE COTTAGE | GULF BREEZE, FLORIDA

Blood. Everywhere.

Bile rose in her throat, and she bent over, heaving. Blood smears covered the front door of the cottage. So much blood that it pooled on the porch floor, trickled toward the steps. Even her pants were covered in it.

It looked like the scene of a slaughter.

Momentarily paralyzed, she stood amidst the carnage, her mind whirling with the image of a body, the life drained away. Terror slammed her like an avalanche, and she raced inside, screaming.

Frantic, she flipped on the lights. Where was it? She searched everywhere, tossing sofa cushions, overturning chairs, ransacking drawers, flinging open the door to the coat closet.

She found nothing. Only bloody footprints on the floor and crimson handprints on the sofa cushions.

She glimpsed toward the mirror, and a macabre sight stared back at her, a woman with blood in her hair. A woman with her eyes too bright, her cheeks and hands stained with scarlet. Horrified, she realized it was her.

The world threatened to go black, and she fought to remain

conscious. Had she been drugged? Was she hallucinating? She closed her eyes, hoping this was all a bad dream, that when she opened them, the cottage would be exactly as it should be.

But when she looked again, the blood was still there.

What had she done now?

ONE

THE TURNER HOUSE | PEAKE'S POINT | GULF BREEZE, FLORIDA

Two weeks earlier

Sunset transformed 3-Mile Bridge into a golden ribbon stretching from the city shoreline of Pensacola, Florida, across an endless sea shimmering with gilded whitecaps. If you were perched on the seawall that kept the bay from washing away the peninsular city of Gulf Breeze, watching a pod of dolphins frolicking in water painted rose gold by the dying day, you would hold your breath at the beauty of nature.

And if you were Jennifer Logan Turner, you would feel electrocuted.

Standing among the flower beds her husband Benjamin had created, clipping yellow hibiscus and pink azaleas to spread throughout her house, she put her hand over her heart to hold back a creeping sense of horror. It wasn't the water she feared. It was dozens of giant loggerhead sea turtles.

When sea creatures defy their natural laws, evil is not far behind them.

The warning from Jen's mother Delilah echoed through her

mind as if she were tuned to some mysterious, secret radio channel.

The sea turtles were lumbering onto the strip of white sand that served as a beach running the length of her backyard, dragging their 250-pound bulk in tank-like formation, the markings on their brown carapaces and leathery yellow skin lit up like a bonfire, inching toward her waterfront paradise. Intent on burning it down.

Loggerheads don't venture out of the sea in daylight. The females leave their warm water homes during high tide and move onto land at night, digging their nests and laying their eggs under cover of darkness, then slinging sand over the whole thing so the eggs remain hidden in the daylight hours when tourists and locals alike throng the beaches.

Although she'd seen them on the protected areas of Gulf Island National Seashore, this was the first time Jen had seen them near the mansions of Peake's Point.

Nature's messages are always delivered for a reason. Pay close attention.

As the loggerheads continued their slow march, Jen dropped her flower basket and hurried down the slope to get a closer look. The prehistoric creatures were fearsome, the largest hard-shell sea turtle in the world, their yellow necks turning this way and that, their eyes ringed with black like scavenging raccoons, like thieves wearing masks, like minions of every evil you could imagine. And they were moving slowly but irrevocably toward her house.

"I'm not going to have it. Do you hear me? There's a party going on tonight, and you are *not* invited."

Anybody else caught warning off sea turtles would be called unflattering names, perhaps considered a bit off their rocker. But not Dr. Jen Turner, the psychologist renowned for her straight talk and her success rate with her patients. Not the oldest daughter of Patrick Logan, a tough Irishman long gone from his ranch in Colorado, and Delilah Broussard, a former jazz singer infused with the blood of Creole parents and imprinted with the mysticism of her birthplace in the cypress swamps around New Orleans. Honey Island Swamp. A place Delilah wrapped up in secrets and stowed away so that neither her husband nor her children ever had a clue about her childhood. For all they knew, she was dropped into a bayou turned to green velvet by algae and fished out by sprites and faeries.

Jen possessed every bit of the courage and work ethic of her red-haired Irish ancestors. But with the identical wild black hair and dark eyes of her French/African American mother, she sometimes felt as if Delilah had not left this earth at all. She had simply taken up residence under Jen's own dusky skin.

Delilah, larger than life, changeable as a chameleon and as magical as the moon, had certainly imprinted all three of her daughters with her fearsome gift. Both Jen and her sister Rachel could read warning signs in the sights and scents of nature, while Annie, the youngest, could read the hidden world of dreams.

But for all the similarities between Delilah and her daughters, there was a notable difference. Where she had been secretive, they were forthcoming. Where she had been mercurial, they were steady. Where she had been unreliable and moody to the point of disappearing for days or months without any communication, they were safe ports in the storm for each other and for their families.

Thanks to the influence of the strong-willed, tough cowgirl rancher who had raised them, their indomitable grandmother, Victoria Logan, they were all fierce and courageous, willing to stand and fight to protect each other and their homes.

Now, facing the sea and the turtles that spit them out, Jen prepared to stand and fight.

Moving with purpose, she planted herself in front of the line of marching loggerheads, her jaw set, her red caftan blowing in the wind, and her gold bracelets jangling on her wrists as she motioned the invaders to turn around.

"*Shoo*! Get back in the sea where you belong. And take your warning with you. *Nothing* is going to mar this evening. Do you hear me?"

Later that evening, she and Benjamin were hosting a party to show off their new home in the private gated community of Peake's Point in Gulf Breeze, a sprawling dream of glass and stone that brought the world of sea and sand, palm trees and marine life, richly painted sunsets and vivid night skies right into their living room. With both the bay and the sound bracketing their house, everywhere they looked was water, a blue expanse sparkling under the sun, beckoning as if they might dive in and discover treasure. Even when it was moody and brooding during rain, crashing and threatening during storms, the water was magical, hiding secrets that made you itch with the mystery of it all.

They had discovered the house last fall after Jen's sister Rachel survived a personal nightmare in Colorado. Jen had said, "This is it," and Benjamin said, "I agree." The purchase of a home that held such promise had smoothed over Jen's lingering anxiety from her sister's kidnapping and somehow made her believe that nothing else bad could touch her family.

Prior to her kidnapping, the ever-practical Rachel had ignored all the warning signs, not only those she received but also those her two sisters had shared with her. But Jen had no intention of ignoring warnings. She would be hyper-vigilant this evening. Unlike Rachel, she wasn't in denial of the gift of seeing their Creole mother had passed along to her three daughters. Nor was she impulsive and sometimes lost in her artistic world like Annie, the youngest of the sisters. She was a lioness. A warrior ready to stand and fight for what was hers.

Her seven-thousand-square foot, two-story home with its spectacular views, a charming beach-style guest cottage, and indoor gym, spa, and swimming pool represented fifteen years of hard work and team effort between husband and wife. A dream come true. An earthly paradise.

Some people might call such a house a sign of ostentation or social climbing. She didn't care. She lived her life without worry of public opinion. To her, the house was an investment in their future, a fortress and a haven, a symbol that the Turners were firmly bound together—Jen, Benjamin, and their twins, Tommy and Marianne.

A family.

In the last six months, Jen's complete remodel of the main house and the guest house, plus Benjamin's attention to relining the pool, building a greenhouse, and upgrading the shrubs and flowers, had produced a showplace with lush gardens and welcoming spaces. She was going to let nothing mar her pleasure in showing off their new home to their friends and new neighbors in Peake's Point.

She particularly wanted to show off the gardens, which were so beautiful in April. They were more than Benjamin's pride and joy. They were a symbol of his and Jen's courtship, those lazy, halcyon days during their college years when love was going to last forever and the future was a rocket ride straight to the stars. He always came courting with a perfect hot-house rose or a single, fragrant gardenia from his wealthy Southern family's gardens. He even loved surprising her with a breathtaking wildflower he'd found by the side of the road.

She missed the unexpectedness and the thrill of it all. As she stood watching the sea turtles, wondering if they could ever recapture what they had once taken for granted, she saw the lead turtle head directly toward her. The creature came so close she could lean down to touch her.

Jen knew better. She had no intention of maiming a hand in those powerful snapping jaws.

"Go back where you came from," she said. "*Now!*"

TWO

"Are you talking to me?"

The female voice startled Jen so much that she threw her hands up, her gold bangle bracelets clashing together. A sound not unlike a tiny scream.

Her friend Sharon had sneaked up behind her, easy to do on a sandy spit of land. She looked impeccable, her black cocktail dress perfectly fitted to her slender body and short enough to show off her legs, her sleek honey-colored hair barely ruffling in the wind, and her high-heeled slingbacks dangling from her hand. She was in stark contrast to the bedraggled, terrified woman who had escaped to Jen's home in Gulf Breeze only a week ago.

"My goodness!" Jen put her hand over her heart. "I didn't hear you coming."

"I'm sorry." Sharon gave her friend a close quick hug that reminded Jen of their time together in college. So many years ago—and so many heartaches since then. Sharon leaned back with a smile, a look that transformed her from pretty to stunning.

Surely, it was the smile that had once attracted Jen's

husband, Benjamin, to Sharon. He had dated both of the friends in college. Jen's saving grace—that steady, reliable Benjamin had chosen her—had been Sharon's bad luck. Instead, she had gravitated toward the tall, muscular football star whose good looks and easy charm served to camouflage his penchant for violence.

"I wasn't talking to you. I was actually talking to the loggerheads." A little piece of Jen's heart broke as she linked arms with her battered friend.

"Is an alligator after them or something? Please tell me these awful-looking things don't usually come to your beach."

"It's okay. If you leave them alone, the sea turtles won't hurt you." The loggerheads were now crashing into each other in their confused exit back to the water. "Let's get you back to the house."

"Now you're singing my song." Sharon fell into step, relief at finally being safe evident in her loose gait and quick smile. "I just *love* it here. In spite of the water."

Jen squeezed her arm. "I'm glad you could come."

Sharon had been born in Eutaw, Alabama, a small landlocked city approximately two hundred miles north of Pensacola, Florida. She'd attended Tulane University in New Orleans with both Jen and Benjamin and had been exposed to both the massive Mississippi River that hugged the city and the Gulf of Mexico that spilled its pleasure boats, barges, tugs, and cruise ships into the Atlantic Ocean beyond. But Sharon, the music-loving, comfort-seeking fragile flower of red clay earth and tall pine trees, couldn't swim and was afraid of deep water. She was also leery of the aquatic creatures that thrived there. Though she adored the sun, she avoided beaches when she could.

It would be pointless for Jen to explain to her that alligators were usually only seen near Pensacola Pass where fresh water from four rivers poured into the salty bay—the Escambia, the

Black Water, the Shoal, and the Yellow Rivers. Sharon didn't care and didn't want to learn. Her sole interest was music. Her sole purpose, survival.

When Sharon finally fled a jealous husband addicted to alcohol and domestic brawls with flying fists, she had arrived at Jen's office last week battered, bruised, and terrified. Her biggest fear was that Matt Jones would come after her and kill her.

It wouldn't be the first time he'd tried. Over the course of their twelve-year marriage, he had put her in the hospital twice with ribs broken from the steel toe of his boot. And Jen couldn't even keep track of the number of times Sharon had called her sobbing about another fight, another beating.

If Sharon ran, her husband always found her. He lured her back with promises of better behavior and threats of fatal consequences. She always obeyed. Until a week ago.

And though therapy and safety had taken the edge off her anxiety, Sharon still wore the yellowing bruises and haunted look of a woman who might bolt at any minute.

Over the course of her career, Jen had counseled hundreds of women like her friend, broken into a million pieces by a horrible marriage and even worse luck. Those were the ones who survived. The ones who didn't became statistics, memories, and cause for regret.

Was the warning from sea turtles related to Matt and Sharon? If he was on her trail, how long before he brought evil right to Jen's front door? How long before her friend became a mere memory?

Not on my watch.

Jen's protective instincts rose to the surface. She'd always felt the need to shield her friend, even in college. She vowed to take care of Sharon and piece her back together. Both things she loved doing. And sometimes overdoing, according to Benjamin. Still, he hadn't complained when Sharon moved into their guest cottage.

Jen glanced back over her shoulder for one last look at the sea turtles. As their massive bulk slid into the sea, Delilah whispered to her.

One of nature's creatures behaving contrary to natural law is a warning to be careful. More than one is a trumpet call announcing that evil is already marching your way.

"Jen, I picked up the basket of flowers you dropped and told the maid to put them in vases all over the house." Sharon's voice pulled her out of the mists where past and present merged.

"Call her Nancy, please. She has taken care of the house and helped me with the twins since they were babies."

"I see. I've just been so upset lately I can hardly remember my own name."

"I know." Jen squeezed her hand. "You're doing good, kiddo."

"Hey, are you wearing that caftan to the party?"

"Yes. It's comfortable." If Jen were the kind of woman who worried about body image, she would mention that it covered a belly going soft and thighs jiggling with cellulite from years of sitting behind a desk. She had little time to head off to a gym after seeing patients all day, even with their new private gym at home. But she was strong and healthy. That was the important thing to her, and to Benjamin. Fortunately. "Is my husband home yet?"

"Oh, I almost forgot. That's why I braved the beach. Ben couldn't get you so he called me to say he would be late."

"Again?"

If she was a worrier, Jen might wonder why her husband spent more time at work lately than he did at home, why he left a message with Sharon instead of Nancy, and why her best friend was calling him Ben. The truth was that Benjamin knew she didn't drag her cell phone around like another appendage and check for missed calls and messages with the frequency of someone tethered to technology. Nor did she obsess over small things.

"He *adores* you," Sharon said with a smile. "I'm sure nothing inappropriate is going on. Don't worry."

"I never worry."

"Listen," Sharon said, "I know you're so laid-back you barely have a pulse. I just wanted to make sure you're okay, that's all. Even a psychiatrist needs a little pep talk about her husband every now and then."

"Psychologist."

"That's what I meant."

They topped the rise from bayside to lawn. Jen took the flagstone path around the house so she could check that Nancy had hung the festive spring wreath on the front door.

"Hold on a minute." Sharon came to a sudden halt and dusted sand from her feet.

Jen breathed in the beauty of the place she now called home. The sprawling stucco and glass Mediterranean-style house, the live oaks, long leaf pines, and cypress trees that afforded privacy on the two-acre lot, the flagstone patios meandering between wings, and the guest cottage tucked into a wall of spreading white oleander all glowed golden in the setting sun.

Delilah would have loved it. She had hated the dust and muss of the ranch, the frozen winters of Colorado, the feeling of being hemmed in by harsh, jagged mountains.

She had belonged in the Deep South, just as Jen did.

Years of undergraduate and graduate school in Louisiana followed by marriage and work that led Jen to Florida had turned her Southern, inside and out. Her speech was softer, slower, her dress casual bordering on Bohemian. She was more connected to the earth, the sky, the sea. Sometimes she felt as if her bones were made of coral, her soul made of star dust, and her skin molded from the rich, dark alluvial soil scooped from the earth where the rivers had overrun their banks and deposited silt from their riverbeds.

"There. That's done!" Sharon caught her arm for balance while she put on her strappy, impractical high heels. "Let's get you upstairs and make you gorgeous. You need a little makeup and something fancy to wear."

"I don't do *gorgeous*, and I'm not changing clothes."

Sharon chuckled. "Why am I not surprised? Will you at least put on some jewelry? That necklace Ben gave you for your fifteenth anniversary is outstanding."

"You're right. Of course, I should wear that."

It was a gold Byzantine chain with a hand-made medallion, the sun and moon molded in gold and studded with one single star made of ruby. A spectacular work of art. Jen seldom wore any jewelry except the gold bangle bracelets, which had belonged to her mother, but when she did, she preferred distinctive pieces. Benjamin knew her taste well.,

As she approached her front porch, she couldn't help but think of the recent changes in her husband's behavior, his many late nights at work and his strange reticence. And now he was going to be late for their party. It was almost as if he were disappearing before her very eyes.

She thought she knew him. Inside and out.

But did she?

THREE

Jen walked through the front doors with Sharon, and shock ricocheted through her.

Two omens in a row spell disaster.

The hibiscus and azaleas she had gathered from the garden were arranged in vases in the entry hall and on the mantel over the huge stone fireplace. They flanked the wall-to-wall, floor-to-ceiling windows and towered as a centerpiece on the table beyond the archway to the dining room. But mingled among the pink and yellow blossoms was the eerie glow of white oleander, its deadly leaves, stems, and flowers used to kill.

Never bring oleander into your house. It's poisonous, an invitation for trouble to come right through your front door.

Jen felt bloodless, glued to the floor. "Where did the oleander come from?"

"Which one are you talking about?" Sharon asked.

"The white flowers, Sharon. Why are they here?"

"Are you feeling okay? All the flowers were in the basket you left in the garden."

"I didn't cut any oleander." It had been planted by the

previous owner, and now she fervently wished she'd had her gardener Dal cut it all down before they moved in.

"You must have and just don't remember it."

"There was *no* white oleander in the basket."

Warnings bombarded Jen on all sides, followed by fear. She wrapped her arms around herself, expecting to be cocooned in safety by her home, comforted by the familiar objects around her—the massive chandelier over her polished dining room table, the rose- and peach-colored damask she had chosen so carefully for the coverings on the dining room chairs, the colors of the sea brought inside and splashed everywhere, in the turquoise chairs nooked near the bank of windows, the blue cushions thrown casually on her massive oyster-colored sectional sofa. Even in the blue eye shadow of the women in her favorite painting, Elegance II, an embellished serigraph on canvas, signed and numbered by the artist, Itzchak Tarkay. The eye shadow was his nod to the fierce courage of the Holocaust survivors, a narrative that infused Jen with hope.

Faced with the dreaded oleander, she struggled to find hope and even a modicum of peace. She, who had always believed herself to be as indestructible as her tough seventy-five-year-old grandmother, found herself unraveling.

"Oh, Jen." Sharon slid an arm around her shoulder. "You were so distraught when your sister was kidnapped, and you've been working non-stop since you got back from Colorado. Then I showed up at your front door. I think you've been under too much pressure. It's okay not to remember every little thing."

"I remember *perfectly*. I would *never* cut oleander for my house."

"Okay. I get it. Maybe Nancy decided to add a touch of white and cut it while we were on the beach. Why don't you sit down and let me get you a glass of water?"

Sharon was coddling her. Jen was the one always in charge, soothing hurt feelings, settling ruffled feathers, reassuring the needy and the fearful. She hated thinking of herself as either needy or fearful. Hated that her best friend, who faced a real and present danger, had discovered that her protector could crumble at the sight of a white flower.

She would ask Nancy about the oleander after the party. It was too late to do anything now, pluck out the offending flowers, deal with the mess that rearranging every bouquet would make, and question the woman who called herself Dr. Turner's Super Sidekick. In twenty minutes, her guests would start arriving. The early birds might even be here in ten.

"I'm okay," Jen said. "If you'll stay down here to greet the guests, I'm going to run upstairs to freshen up."

"Of course. But first I'll check with Nancy in the kitchen to make sure there's nothing in the food you're allergic to."

In spite of Sharon's eagerness to help, a shadow suddenly crossed her face, the ever-present fear that gave her the nightmares she shared with Jen.

"Don't worry about Matt surprising you." Jen gave Sharon's arm a squeeze. "He doesn't know our new address."

Not yet, anyhow, but evil was surely coming. Jen could see it in the signs, hear it in the wind, feel it in the shadows.

"And even if he did, he would never get past our security and staff."

She had never been more grateful for the security measures she and Benjamin had installed after her sister's kidnapping in Colorado. No one would ever be taken from her again. *No one!*

"I know. I *know*." Sharon hugged herself, hunching her shoulders and ducking her head as if she could make herself invisible, a posture Jen had seen on her patients too many times to count.

Jen reached for Sharon again and folded her into an embrace. A comforting touch was often worth more than hours of counseling.

"You're safe here. I want you to believe that."

FOUR

Jen said a silent plea that she could keep her promise to her friend, while Sharon drew a shuddering breath.

"I'm fine now, Jen. *Really.*" She managed a weak smile. "Go on upstairs. And don't forget to put on your necklace."

"I won't." She could almost feel the heavy gold lying against her skin, picture the smile on her husband's face when she showed up with his gift around her neck. *Dressing for guests.* The very ordinariness of the task restored Jen's confidence. She could face anything.

Can you?

Her mother, whispering from the past, reminding her of the gift that was always there, nudging and pushing, shouting and screaming. Stark evidence that Jen was... different. Whether she wanted to be or not, she couldn't ignore her intuition that something evil lurked in the shadows of the gathering darkness, that she was opening her doors to strangers, inviting the unknown right into the heart of her family.

"And a little lip gloss won't hurt!" Sharon called. The reminder brought back fond memories of their college days, the care she'd always taken with her appearance—unfortunately at the cost of paying attention to Matt's true character. He'd always been arrogant and self-centered.

"Okay."

That coaxed another smile from her friend. "Really?"

"You've convinced me, girlfriend." Jen gave a jaunty two-finger wave and headed toward the stairs, mistress of the mansion. In control of herself, the party, the food and wine, and even the conversation she would ensure flowed with the ease of a social event hosted by the legendary Gatsby.

The wind had picked up, and the branches of palm trees scratched against her window. In spite of sunset that laid streaks of orange and red, purple and gold, across the water, it looked forbidding in the creeping darkness. Wind and sea whispered that her idea of being in charge was as fictional as Gatsby.

But the mocking echo still followed her up the stairs.

Danger. Danger. Danger.

FIVE

Jen's daughter, Marianne, waylaid her on the way to her bedroom. With her long, gangly legs, it was obvious she would grow tall like her mother. Her dark hair and eyes and strong sense of self hinted that she might also be as fierce.

Marianne was holding her pet hamster. "Mom, can Bella Baby come to the party tonight?"

"Absolutely not."

"I'll hold onto her. I won't let her loose for one second."

"You know the rules, Marianne. Bella Baby is not allowed around guests. Not everybody appreciates animals the way you do."

Her teenage daughter stomped off without replying, her angry footsteps doing the talking for her.

Jen was glad to escape to her bedroom. Decorated in the soothing earth tones she and Benjamin preferred, it was her haven. She wished she could sink into the deep cushions of her favorite chair and simply *be*. It was arranged in the nook, cater-cornered with her husband's own chair beside the massive windows. The view of sunset-hued water, usually so calming, suddenly struck her as threatening, another omen that something terrible was waiting out there in the dark,

Why had she planned a party? She didn't even like them, not really.

She saw people every day at her office, hundreds of them over the course of a year, listened to their problems, searched for solutions, followed their progress, celebrated their successes, and mourned their failures. And now she had brought Sharon and her problems into both her office and her home.

Not that she minded. She was only doing what any good friend would do.

She had given Sharon a temporary job at her office as her personal assistant until she could save enough money to get her own place and have time to rebuild her reputation as a musician. Sharon's long-term plan was to get enough students to have her own music studio again, teaching voice and piano.

But of course, her immediate plan was to stay out of the clutches of a husband who was surely searching for her and would be eager to mete out a brutal form of justice. Jen had saved ninety-five percent of her patients who were victims exactly like Sharon. It was the five percent she couldn't save who left wounds on her heart.

Don't let Sharon be a wound on my heart.

Her words floated around the high ceiling, settled into the folds of the curtains open to the water, burrowed into the cushions in the chairs and on the bed, and settled like a promise in her soul.

Satisfied, Jen strode into her bathroom to rinse off the sand and apply a light coat of lip gloss. Then she took the black velvet jewelry box from the top drawer of her dressing table and opened the lid. Her necklace was missing, and in its place lay a folded piece of paper.

Had Benjamin left her a love note? He used to do it all the

time, before children and careers and life in general frayed the edges of their marriage.

Jen unfolded the paper:

> *Nothing you have belongs to you.*
> *You will lose it all.*
> *If you don't believe me, ask your husband.*
> *From, Invisible*

Jen felt lightning-struck. Images bombarded her of an enemy small enough to disappear behind trees, into closets, and under the stairs—someone clever enough to hide in plain sight so that no matter how hard she looked, she'd never see him. This was no prank. But if the note was meant to intimidate her, it failed. She prided herself on taking adversity in her stride.

Anybody could have put it there. She and Benjamin had a household staff and a large security staff, all with access to the house. And a catering crew had arrived an hour ago. Any one of them could have left this note. But why?

Even with premonitions of encroaching evil and warnings bombarding her on all sides, Jen refused to let fear take over. She could not allow the threatening message and her missing jewelry to ruin her evening. The necklace had to be around here somewhere. She had worn it to dinner last night with Benjamin, Sharon, and the twins, an early celebration of the completed renovation of their new home. She'd worn a simple red dress to showcase the necklace and a black wool shawl with pockets to ward off the chill of the April evening.

Any Floridian along the coast knows the beautiful warm days of spring cannot be trusted at night. Water is both capricious and secretive. It loves to stir up massive currents, turn into sudden squalls, foment killing hurricanes, snatch the unaware in riptides, spit out marine life that can turn deadly in a heartbeat, and swallow boats, houses, and people whole. The earth's rivers, bays, and oceans hid bones that would never be discovered.

The sea is a keeper of secrets.

She didn't need her mother Delilah to remind her of the grisly finds in the bay that made the news with depressing regularity. One of them had been a patient she couldn't save, murdered by a spouse and tossed into a watery grave. Though it *had* happened five years ago, Jen still mourned the loss... and her failure to prevent it.

Shaking off painful memories, she tucked the awful note back into the jewelry box then made a futile search of every drawer in her dressing table. Next, she marched out of the bathroom to look through the pockets of the shawl she'd worn last night.

Empty.

She pawed through the drawers in the nightstands that flanked the bed, turned over every piece of lingerie, every sock, and every sweater in the pullout drawers of her walk-in closet.

"Where *is* it?"

"Jen?" The intercom crackled to life, and Sharon's voice came through, loud and clear. "Maria Ramos has arrived."

If anybody was going to be early, it was bound to be her son's private swim coach. Didn't she always show up ten minutes early for Tommy's lessons, her swimsuit coverup gaped open just enough to show her perfect athlete's body? Three days a week, like clockwork she came, always asking about Benjamin.

Tommy, Marianne's no-nonsense, talkative twin brother, who was born old, reported Maria's every inquiry at the dinner table.

"It's *gross*, Dad. Like she's got a teenage crush on you or something."

Benjamin always laughed and pulled a lollipop from his

pocket. "She's probably just hoping for one of these. Everybody likes a treat and a kind gesture."

Tommy's response was always the same. He pushed his mop of curly hair out of his dark eyes and winked at Jen. "I remember from last time, Dad. Can I just get another swim coach?"

"She's the best. An Olympic bronze-medalist. Just be nice to her and learn what she has to teach."

"Aye, aye, Captain." Tommy saluted, all in good-natured fun. He seemed to have avoided the angst and rebellion that often accompanied a child's thirteenth birthday, unlike his twin sister, the drama queen of the family. Tommy was much more relaxed, less intense, the hint of red in his dark hair a sign that he got every bit of his charm from his Irish grandfather Patrick.

So far, the twins showed no signs of having inherited their mother's gift, which came as a relief to Jen. There was grace in not knowing events before they happened, freedom to live fully without looking over your shoulder. Children, in particular, shouldn't be weighted down with knowledge too heavy for them to bear.

Jen's gift—passed down from a mercurial mother born in the cradle of the Deep South among the mist-shrouded bayous of Louisiana and the colorful legends of the Creole—had manifested when she was only six. She'd been far too young to understand the full significance of what she was seeing: Earth's creatures behaving contrary to the laws of nature, their dark messages shivering her soul. By the time she was seven, she understood she was like her star-kissed mother, a vessel through which signs and warnings and predictions flowed, her gift of *seeing* as much a part of her as the color of her hair and eyes. She could never escape it, even if it meant seeing evil heading her way with the destructive force of a category five hurricane set to wipe the entire city of Gulf Breeze off the map—and her, along with it.

"Jen? Where'd you go?" Sharon's voice came through the intercom with a note of rising anxiety. "Is something wrong up there?"

"Everything is fine." Jen knew the note would only add to her broken friend's anxiety, and that was something Jen would *never* do. "I'll be right there."

Her ruby and gold necklace had to be somewhere in the house. She remembered taking it off last night and putting it in the velvet box...

Or had she? Had it slipped its clasp somewhere between the restaurant and home, and she hadn't even noticed?

She would ask Benjamin about it when she told him about the note. But first, she had to get through a party with the warning of sea turtles still echoing and the bad omen of oleander strewn throughout her house.

SIX

TURNER MEDICAL SOLUTIONS | DOWNTOWN GULF BREEZE, FLORIDA

Benjamin Turner was not a man who kept secrets. Especially not from his wife. But here he was, holed up in the conference room at Turner Medical Solutions, alone with the head of his legal department, Antonia Delgado, while Jen faced their party guests alone.

He should have stepped in and told his wife, "Let's forget it. Let's just enjoy our house with the kids and get to know our new neighbors gradually."

But, *no,* he went right along with the party plans, too exhausted to put up an argument, too stressed out to be more than a phantom in his own home.

He and Jen and the kids weren't alone in their home anymore. Sharon was in the guest house. Not that he minded. What kind of selfish person would he be if he didn't lend a helping hand to a friend in need?

She was more friends with Jen than with him, but he still had some fond memories of their days at Tulane. Simpler times. Hopeful times.

Today he was trying desperately to hold onto a tiny thread of hope. To not feel guilty that he was spending more time with

Antonia than with his own wife and kids. Antonia had the kind of charisma you couldn't ignore, eerily similar to Jen. With her long dark hair and big eyes, Antonia could almost be mistaken for a younger, shorter version of his wife, which did nothing to alleviate his guilt.

He should have found another solution to his problem. It shouldn't be necessary to take a route so clandestine he couldn't even tell his wife. But desperate men do desperate things.

No one could know. If word got out, he was ruined. He'd lose everything—his reputation, the company his father Kane had built and entrusted to him, the respect of his employees. Even his family.

And if Jen didn't leave him, she would lose respect for him. The idea sent a shiver down his soul. What was a man without the respect of the people he loved most?

For that matter, his own mother would view her only child as a loser. Marsha Turner was not the soft, motherly type. She was a woman of strong opinions, exacting standards, and expensive tastes. Benjamin was an old soul, born to please, naturally studious, and hard-working. And pleasing his mother had not been a problem. Until recently.

The good news was that his mother was spending the spring in Italy, rattling around with nobody except the staff and her best friend and fellow widow, Maxine Hudson, in the villa she and Benjamin's dad had purchased in Rome six years earlier, only months before Kane's death.

If Kane Turner were alive, Benjamin wouldn't be in this mess. Fortunately, his mother hadn't a clue what was happening back in the States. Particularly at Turner Medical Solutions.

"Is that all you need?" Antonia stood up and smoothed her skirt over her hips. She was shapely in all the right places. Despite being a high-powered lawyer in a position of authority, she wore clothes that called attention to her petite, athletic body, a choice that announced her streak of rebellion.

He felt a stab of remorse that he'd even noticed. "That's all for now, Antonia. But clear your calendar for tomorrow night."

"It's cleared all next week."

"Good. I can't emphasize enough that everything that takes place between us here in this board room is top secret."

"I understand."

"If word gets out..."

"It won't. Don't worry." She winked at him. Hardly the kind of behavior Kane would have permitted in the work environment. "You're protected under attorney-client privilege."

He had the grace to smile. Until Antonia came to work at Turner Medical Solutions, he had been the attorney in charge of the legal department. Kane had ensured that his son received the finest legal education money could buy by sending him to New Orleans to one of the only comparative law schools in the country. Because of Louisiana's mixed heritage and laws, Tulane's Juris Doctor program teaches both French/Napoleonic civil law and English common law. Kane had taken great pride in his son's legal expertise.

Sometimes Benjamin longed for the simpler days when he could hole up with law books and untangle the legal problems that came with every business. Give him a quiet place with a book of any kind, or a garden where he could work alone with shrubs and flowers, and he was happy.

Not that he was unhappy running the company. He'd been a contented CEO until last October. He knew to the day when his problems started. Only two days after Jen flew to Colorado. *Two days.* It seemed impossible to him that life could go from perfect to disastrous in just forty-eight hours.

"I'll see you at the party." Antonia slung her handbag over her shoulder.

"You go ahead. I don't want us to arrive at the same time."

"Good thinking."

After Antonia left, he turned the light off then sat in the

darkened room while the glow on his digital watch marked the time. He was drained, almost lethargic.

The sleeping pills could have something to do with his malaise. Until last October, he could fall asleep the minute his head hit the pillow and wake up energetic and excited to start the day. But since then, he fought his pillow and his sheets as if they had grown teeth and claws and were trying to tear him apart. Night after night it was the same.

Until Sharon came. The needy woman with an artist's temperament and a bag filled with sleeping pills. She was only too happy to share, one insomniac to another. They'd both been out walking the small private beach behind his house at midnight under a starless sky, hoping the wind and the cool night air would clear their heads to sleep.

He remembered the shivering, forlorn mess Sharon had been, pacing the sand with her thin pajamas whipping around her. She had screamed at his approach.

"It's okay, Sharon. It's me." He pulled off his windbreaker and put it over her shoulders. "Here. You're freezing."

"I thought you were Matt."

"I'm sorry, I didn't mean to scare you. What are you doing out here?"

"I couldn't sleep. What about you?"

"I couldn't sleep either." He fell into step beside her. "I thought Jen said you are afraid of the water."

"I used to be, but I sort of got over it. Don't tell her, please? I can't bear to let her see one more way that I'm this silly, messed-up weakling. She's so perfect and strong. She's a bit intimidating. You know?"

He understood. Almost too well. As much as he hated to admit it, Jen had always been the courageous, take-charge partner in their marriage.

That's why he had found it easy to promise Sharon he would keep her secret. He even used the excuse to himself that

Jen's strength of character justified asking Sharon to never mention the sleeping pills he'd borrowed that night.

They were over-the-counter, something he could easily buy for himself. But he hadn't, and he wouldn't, not in a city of just over six thousand where practically everybody would recognize the CEO of one of Gulf Breeze's largest companies. Anybody could see. Anybody could tell Jen.

His wife had always said crutches were for the weak.

Pride made him swear Sharon to secrecy. *Stupid* male pride.

He and Jen took a holistic approach to life, and set that example for Tommy and Marianne. Eat nutritious foods, get plenty of exercise, preferably outdoors—all that fresh air and sunshine, not to mention the ions coming off the salty sea. Talk out problems so you can sleep with a clear mind. Mental health and physical health are connected.

He and Jen agreed on the lifestyle. Adhered to it.

Until now. He was hiding borrowed pills that barely helped, from his own wife. Another breach of trust. The solid foundation he had always stood on was crumbling beneath his feet. He felt helpless and cowardly.

He didn't even walk over to the window to watch the sky. Normally, he enjoyed seeing the constellations on a clear night. This evening, all he could think about was how he had let Jen down, and whether he could ever make things right again. He felt like a man torn in half, grasping wildly at straws.

But then another thought came to him.

What if he ended it all?

SEVEN

THE TURNER HOUSE

If Jen ignored the oleander, she could pretend she was at an ordinary party.

She turned her attention back to her open house. Sharon had moved to the yellow baby grand and was pouring her heart and soul into the jazz standards she played while guests meandered through the house and spilled through glass doors onto the patios and outdoor spaces beyond, chatting with each other and admiring the views.

Even the twins were enjoying themselves. Though it was past their bedtime, Jen decided to let them stay and enjoy the party. But where was Benjamin? This was a small Southern town, and people would notice his absence and talk. For a businessman in his position, that kind of gossip was harmful.

Grabbing her phone from the pocket of her caftan, Jen hurried through the kitchen and ducked out the back door. Invigorated by the chill coming off the bay, she paced the flagstone path. There was a light out on the pole in front of the guest cottage which cast it in deep shadow. That was not safe for Sharon. As she punched her husband's number, she made a mental note to have the light replaced.

The ringtone went to voicemail.

"Benjamin, the party is in full swing, and people are beginning to notice your absence." That was her second unanswered call to him in the last two hours. Surely, he was not still working. Had he come home unnoticed? It would be easy to do in a house this huge.

For all Jen's independence and bravado, she was most comfortable with her family. And she wanted all of them with her tonight. With omens bombarding her at every turn and her necklace missing, she *needed* them now.

But Rachel and her children were on a honeymoon in Hawaii with her longtime friend and protector, Hank Carson, and her other sister, Annie, had an art show in Rome. The sisters' ever-cantankerous grandmother, Victoria Logan, said she'd stand out like a *prickly cactus among hot-house flowers in that highfaluting crowd.* Her words exactly.

When Jen had offered to buy Gran a ticket from Colorado, she said, "If I wanted a ticket, I'd buy it myself. Save your money. You might need it someday."

She had to smile thinking of her grandmother. Benjamin said she and Jen were two stubborn blocks carved off the same hardwood tree. He was probably right. She made one last futile attempt to reach him then went back inside to join her guests.

Sharon motioned from the piano. It didn't appear to be a distress signal, so Jen nabbed two glasses of champagne and joined her friend.

"The music is beautiful." She handed Sharon a champagne flute. "But I think it would be good for you to mingle."

"I prefer eavesdropping and watching from afar." Sharon moved to a quiet corner with her glass and put her small beaded purse on a side table, sinking onto the plush cushions of a turquoise chair. She made herself so small she seemed almost invisible. She was tucked in a nook away from the bank of windows, which was not surprising, as she had avoided being near windows since she had arrived.

Jen settled into the matching chair, reassured by the cool touch of her mother's gold bangle bracelets on her arm, grateful she and Benjamin hadn't skimped on comfort during their remodel. Her signature red caftan billowed around her, and she tucked her feet underneath the folds, pleased with herself for wearing sensible sandals instead of stilettos.

"Where's your necklace?" Sharon stared at Jen's neck as if she'd just lost the necklace, herself.

"It's somewhere around here, I'm sure."

"You've misplaced it!" Sharon gasped.

"No, not really... I don't know. Maybe. Do you remember if I was wearing it when we got home from the restaurant last night?"

"You definitely were."

"That's a relief. It will turn up somewhere, then." Jen leaned back and surveyed the room. "Have you seen Benjamin?"

"No, but his secretary got here twenty minutes ago and came over to the piano to introduce herself. I don't remember her name. April? Abby?"

"Antonia. She's head of his legal department."

"Whatever." Sharon waved a dismissive hand. "The way she's flirting with every wealthy husband in the room, I'd say she's a *gold-digger*. And she's not picky about who's married and who's not. Only two men came through that door without wedding rings, and she hasn't even glanced at them."

Jen never got upset when her husband talked to another woman. He was a businessman, after all, and a good one at that. Part of his job entailed being sociable. He'd been brought up among the glittering social set at his parents' parties. In fact, he enjoyed them so much, he'd made sure an active social life was part of their marriage.

Then why is he not here?

Flustered, Jen turned back to Sharon. "Antonia comes from a large, affectionate family. She's just friendly, that's all."

"And *young*. Not to mention *attractive*, if you like the athletic type. Plus, she mentions your husband every other breath. I'd watch my back around that one."

She could be right...

Jen's defense of Antonia rang hollow, especially in light of her husband's absence. Her own practice had taught her that a person's interior life is manifested in his actions. Her sense of unease grew.

Why all these late nights at work?

She pushed the thought aside. She was not the kind of woman who gossiped, or paid attention to rumors. Still, considering Sharon's trauma and precarious situation, she let her talk. If it helped take her mind off her own trouble, even better.

Antonia *was* having a good time. Jen could see how it would be easy to misinterpret her outgoing personality as flirtatious.

A whispering at the window caused Jen to peer anxiously toward the wide expanse of glass. The sound was ominous, as if the increased wind and darkness shivered at an approaching evil.

"Look!" Sharon set her champagne flute on the table. "There's Ben!"

Benjamin glanced in Jen's direction, and she motioned for him to come over. He headed her way, but Tommy's swim coach waylaid him. Maria Ramos hugged him a bit too long and clung to him like there was no tomorrow. Even Jen noticed.

"Talk about brazen!" Sharon said. "That woman is all over your husband. And don't you dare tell me that she's just being friendly. I have eyes."

So did Jen. Her husband was discreetly untangling himself from Maria's grasp.

"He can take care of himself," Jen said, hoping it was true.

"I wouldn't be too sure of that. It's the good ones like Ben that other women go after. Not the rotten apples like Matt. She's Tommy's swim coach, right?"

"Yes, she's great. Hard-working. Lovely and reliable..."

"Here like clockwork every week, ogling your husband?"

"No. You've got that wrong, Sharon."

"I saw it for myself, this past week. And I'm rarely wrong about other women. That's why I chose you as my best friend."

Some of the stress bearing down on Jen melted. Wasn't that always the way with good friends? For a moment, she considered confiding in Sharon about the note, but she seemed to be enjoying the party, and Jen didn't want to dampen her spirit.

She was about to suggest they grab some food from the buffet when the doorbell rang. Who could it be? Everyone she'd invited was already here. Ben glanced her way and mouthed, *I'll get it*.

He answered the door then headed Jen's way with a small gift box in his hands. A murmur of approval went through the party crowd, and they gravitated toward the corner of the room to see what was in the package.

Ben was smiling, and Jen felt its warmth all the way across the room. Was the gift from him? A surprise to make up for his unexplained absences and his distracted manner toward her?

"Special delivery for you." Benjamin handed her the box, and she untied the silver ribbon.

"I wonder who it's from?"

"I didn't see a card. It's probably inside."

Marianne bounced over and squeezed in between Maria Ramos and Antonia Delgado. "Mom! Who's sending you presents?"

"Let's find out." Jen opened the box and her world tilted sideways.

The package slid from her hands, and the contents hit the floor with a sickening plop. Marianne's hamster lay on the floor in a bloody heap, its head bludgeoned and its body stiff. A perky yellow bow was tied around its twisted neck with a note attached. All the signs had pointed to approaching evil, and here it was, lying right on her living room floor, threatening the ones she loved most.

She pushed against the terror clutching at her. *Not my family. Not while I have breath...*

The guests jumped backward, screeching, while some shielded their partners against their shoulders. Sharon fell against her chair in a frightened heap, Maria Ramos started praying in Spanish, and Marianne began screaming and wouldn't stop.

Jen held her daughter close while shock poured through the room like a tsunami. "Who would do this?" "Have you ever seen anything so sickening?" "I'm going to lose my canapes." "George, take me home."

"*Bella Baby!*" Marianne wailed, over and over. Jen's efforts at comforting her daughter failed. Benjamin called Nancy on the intercom, and she emerged from the kitchen, tucking Marianne into an embrace.

"Take her to her room and stay with her until I get there," Jen told her.

The dead hamster hit the party like a category five hurricane, sending the guests scurrying toward the safety of their own homes. In the midst of the mass exodus, Jen bent to read the note attached to the bow on the hamster's neck.

TIT for TAT —
You take from me.
I take from you.
Invisible

The name conjured up a terrifying vision of a dark void, lurking unseen, emptiness personified and vengeful. There was no mistaking the intent. The evil predicted by the signs had invaded Jen's home, and Invisible was taking things that belonged to her and her family. Cold fingers of fear gripped her. Her unknown enemy could take every possession she owned, but she would die before she'd let him lay a hand on her children.

Turning to her husband, she said quietly, "Have Clint take this out of here for fingerprints then join me at the door to say goodbye to our guests. We have to try and salvage the rest of the evening, and then I've got to talk to Marianne."

"Done." He went in the direction of the kitchen, and she turned to Sharon, who was as pale as a fading moon. "Are you okay?"

"I will be in a minute. Go smooth this over with your guests."

Jen was desperate to get to her children, especially Marianne. Her only consolation was that Nancy would mother them both until she could get there.

She headed toward her guests and made a special effort to engage the ones who hadn't already bolted in small talk that might help repair the social wounds inflicted by the bloody hamster. Benjamin joined her shortly. Anybody watching them chat with departing guests would have only seen an attractive couple in a home that screamed success and security.

They would never have noticed the turmoil boiling beneath Benjamin Turner's genial façade. Nor would they have seen the dark foreboding in Dr. Jennifer Turner's mind, the creeping terror that swept through her Creole blood like a river gone wild.

* * *

The housewarming party was memorable, but not in the way Jen had intended. As Antonia Delgado drove away, she wondered if the dead hamster was a symbol of the Turner marriage. An awful cosmic joke the universe had played on them.

The neighbors next door wondered if they had made a mistake in being excited when the CEO of Turner Medical Solutions and his brilliant wife, the psychologist Dr. Jennifer Turner, had moved in.

As old friends drove home across 3-Mile Bridge in the brooding night, they discussed the mutilated hamster as a sign the Turners should never have left Pensacola. "Moving upward is not always a good thing," some of them murmured. They congratulated themselves on the common sense that kept them safe in their houses in less prestigious neighborhoods.

Mario Ramos left with a heavy heart. She loved the Turner family, especially Ben and the children, and wondered who would have done such an awful thing to a kid's hamster. She was so caught up in the Turners' problems, she didn't notice when her car began to bump along the highway. When the bumping got so bad her purse slid off the seat, she felt the first fingers of fear. What was happening? This was a well-kept highway, and she had new tires.

When her tire blew, the explosion sounded like the end of the world. Her car careened across the highway. She fought with the steering wheel, only one thought in her head.

Tonight, I die.

EIGHT

All too aware of an evil plot unfolding outside the walls of her new home, Jen sat on her daughter's bed, holding her close.

"Why would anybody kill Bella Baby?" Marianne wailed. "Was it my fault?"

"It's not your fault. There are bad people in the world who do bad things without any reason whatsoever."

"Sometimes I get mad, and I act hateful."

"Anger is normal, and so is lashing out. But Bella Baby is not dead because of you."

"But who did it, Mom?"

"I don't know, but I intend to find out."

Jen stayed until her daughter had calmed down, and then she checked on Tommy before rejoining her husband. He was sitting in one of the turquoise chairs with Sharon, who wanted to know if Marianne was okay.

"She's resilient and strong. She'll be okay."

"That's a relief. I think I'll head back to the cottage."

"I'll walk you over," Benjamin said.

"I'll be fine." Sharon nervously opened then closed the clasp on her purse.

"You've got security guards posted. Right?"

"Yes," Jen told her. "At the front and back entrances and on the patios. We have security cameras there, as well. But there are none on the cottage, and there's a light out on the pathway in front. There are blind spots on the walkways, and it's impossible to see under the shadows of all those trees. You should take Benjamin with you."

"No, I'll be okay. If it makes you feel better, I'll call when I get to the cottage." Sharon leaned to kiss her cheek. "Take care and get some rest yourself. You look tired."

"I'm fine."

But was she? As Jen watched Sharon leave, she thought of the analogy she used with her patients. Taking care of problems is like picking up sticks. You keep adding to the load, unaware, until you finally buckle.

"I will not buckle," she said out loud.

"Talking to yourself?"

Turning to look at her husband, she noticed that Benjamin was only a ghost of the man she had married, the self-confident, take-charge man who had been her equal partner in every way. What was happening to him? He used to pick her up and whirl her around for no reason at all except the sheer joy of it. Where had that laughing man gone?

"Yes, but I really want to talk to you. Come with me." She led him upstairs and into her bathroom. "When I was getting dressed, I found a note in my jewelry box from someone calling himself Invisible." She opened the box, and was astonished to find it empty. "I left the note right here."

"Are you sure?"

"Of course I'm sure." But was she? She'd been upset about her necklace and the oleander and the sea turtles. "I can tell you exactly what it said. 'Nothing you have belongs to you. You will lose it all. If you don't believe me, ask your husband.' It was signed Invisible."

"Ask me about what?"

"I don't *know,* Benjamin." Jen couldn't stop her voice from rising. "*You* tell *me!*"

"We don't shout in this household."

"I'm not shouting. I'm being firm." Jen scrambled around in all the drawers in her dressing table. Lip gloss, hairpins, fingernail file, brush, comb, hair gel. But no note. "Someone was in my bathroom, and he left the note exactly as I told you."

"Okay, Jen. I believe you. It'll turn up. But let's go downstairs so Nancy can go home."

As they headed downstairs, Sharon sent a text on the burner phone she had been using since her flight from Alabama.

I'm here. All is well.

Relief washed over Jen, but it only served to take the edge off her anxiety. The constant threat of danger from Sharon's husband coupled with warnings from nature thrust her back to the tense days in Colorado after her sister disappeared. The terror of the unknown. The helpless feeling of wondering who the enemy was. The thickness of fear in the air. The feeling that any minute you might suffocate.

When she came home last fall, Benjamin took one look at her face and said, "I don't want you to ever have to worry about any of your family again. We'll get the best protection money can buy."

Looking back, the great irony was that he started drifting away shortly afterward.

When their head of security, Clint Brown, strode through the front door, Jen visibly relaxed. True to Benjamin's word, he was the best.

He reported that there had been no signs of intruders during the party, and no disturbances of any kind. Jen's macabre gift had been delivered by a large man wearing a cap who drove a white delivery van, but no one noticed or remembered if it had a logo on the side.

"So far, I've found no usable prints on the gift box, but I'll keep trying," he told them. "The security detail hired especially for the party has gone home, and the night shift on the regular security team is already in place."

She and Benjamin thanked him then went into the kitchen where Nancy Park bustled about stowing leftover food. When they walked in, her face was wreathed with smiles.

"I didn't pack up the sirloin because I knew the two of you would come in here acting like you were starving to death."

Benjamin wrapped her in a bear hug. "You're the best, Nancy. You know that, don't you?"

She removed the apron from her considerable girth and swatted him. "If you weren't so full of malarky, my man Dal would come at you with the hedge shears."

He laughed, the first genuine one Jen had heard from him in weeks, since Tommy told the tale of the swim coach's crush. Her heart broke a little remembering the way his laughter used to fill the whole house.

"Dal's so old he can't lop a hedge, let alone my head." Benjamin grabbed cutlery and dug into the steak. "Is he driving you home?"

"Yes, he's waiting for me in the greenhouse. He's been out there all evening puttering around, getting his garden tools organized for tomorrow."

The news didn't surprise Jen. Dal preferred the company of flowers over people. He was unsociable bordering on secretive. The exact opposite of his wife.

"Why don't you head on home? Jen and I can finish up in here."

Her husband's suggestion reminded her that was one of

things she loved most about him. His ability to surprise. The grass skirt he'd brought back from a business trip to Hawaii two years into their marriage still hung in her closet. Where was that whimsical, spontaneous man?

The bright lights in the ultra-modern steel-and-granite kitchen left no room for invention. They showed Benjamin, unusually haggard, and Nancy, unsoftened and true—the gray in her sparse brown hair, the map of years stamped on her face, the network of bulging veins in her legs and hands, and the pillowy contours of her short stocky frame—every inch beloved by the entire Turner family.

Jen's most trusted employee wouldn't be with her forever. She felt a rush of affection for Nancy tempered by the fear that had been trying to overtake her all evening.

"But before you go, can you tell me where you got the white oleander for the bouquets?"

"It was in the basket with the other flowers."

Nancy had never lied to her and had no reason to be lying now. Nor did Sharon. Still, Jen was certain she hadn't cut the oleander.

"You know I never put it in bouquets."

"I do," Nancy said. "That's why I was so surprised when I looked out the kitchen window and saw you out in the backyard cutting it."

The news torpedoed Jen. How could Nancy have possibly seen something she didn't do? Had her most trusted employee started lying? And for what purpose?

Suddenly, she remembered how Nancy complained about letting Sharon move into the guest house. She said it was asking for trouble and adding extra work for her. Was she still upset about that? Would she leave notes signed Invisible and kill Marianne's hamster to try and run Sharon off? Dal could have left the property and then come back, in disguise, to deliver it in a white van.

Or was Nancy simply showing signs of aging? Jen's own grandmother had become more cantankerous over the years. Even forgetful.

Benjamin bided his time while Nancy gathered her purse and sweater then headed out the door to join her husband. Jen could feel his tension, see his anxiety. He was far easier to read than some of her patients.

"What was that all about, Jen?"

"You know I *hate* oleander. I didn't cut it."

"Looks like you did and simply forgot." He didn't say it, but his implication was *like you forgot whether you received one note or two this evening.* "You've been forgetful lately and not quite yourself. Even the children have noticed."

The prickle of fear that had bothered her all evening began to magnify. She struggled to tamp it down. She could feel herself getting close to being the woman who picked up so many sticks she was about to fall under the load.

"How? What have they said?"

"Last week they asked me, what's wrong with Mom? You forgot to pick them up from a birthday party. Remember?"

"That was one time," she said. "And it was all a misunderstanding. We had an agreement that you would pick them up."

"Yes, but I couldn't because of a last-minute business crisis."

"And *I* was dealing with Sharon's crisis. You left the house without telling me."

"It was an emergency."

"Still, why didn't you tell me?" she said. "We don't do that kind of thing to each other."

"I sent you a message."

The scream pierced the night, ricocheted off the steel surfaces, and hung in the air like a witch suspended on a broom. Trapped in the spell, she and her husband froze, staring at each other in horror.

It ripped through them again, louder this time, closer.

Suddenly, the back door burst open and Sharon stumbled through. Her usually perfect hair was in disarray, her nightgown hung off one shoulder, and her bare feet were bloody.

"Help me!" she gasped before she collapsed.

NINE

Jen sat on the floor swabbing Sharon's head with a damp dish cloth and checking her pulse. In spite of her bloody feet and the trickle of blood on her face where she had hit her head on the corner of the cabinet when she fell, her pulse was steady.

Jen considered that a small miracle. Her own heart had almost stopped when she saw her friend's bloody condition. The predictions of sea turtles and oleander had come true—right there in her kitchen.

Benjamin was trying to be helpful, but he looked like he was slowly unraveling, kneeling on the other side of Sharon. His eyes were too bright, his face pinched.

"Do you think Sharon's husband found her and did this?" he said.

"Even if he did, I don't see how he could get past our security." She leaned in for a closer look. "I don't see any blood except on her feet."

"She has a few shallow cuts and scratches I can fix with a small bandage," he said, "but you never know when somebody is bleeding internally. Shall I call 911?"

Sweat beaded his face, and fear radiated off him in waves.

Her husband was falling apart before her eyes. And apparently, so was she.

"Let's wait. She's coming around." Jen leaned closer. "Sharon, can you hear me? You have to wake up."

Sharon came awake slowly, her eyelids blue-veined and her face colorless. She looked as fragile as a featherless baby bird.

She attempted to sit up, but fell backward. "Ouch!"

"Just lie there a minute," Jen said. "You came running through the back door, screaming. Then you fainted. What happened?"

Sharon's confusion immediately gave way to terror. "Matt's *here*! I'm going to die!" She managed to sit up, but then she fell against Benjamin, hysterical and incoherent.

"Sharon, listen to me. You need to tell us *exactly* what happened. Is Matt at the cottage?"

"I can't talk about it. It was too horrible..." She cowered against Benjamin, who wore the look of a man with his foot caught in a rabbit trap.

Jen's fear battled with her inner lioness. Delilah's oft-repeated mantra to her daughters swirled through her mind.

Never think of yourself as helpless, no matter what the circumstances.

"Benjamin, page security and have them check the property, starting with the cottage, inside and out."

Suddenly Benjamin was a man transformed, the one she had admired and loved for years, the take-charge man issuing orders to security while making certain all the doors and windows in the kitchen were locked. Like most men, he thrived on feeling needed and useful.

As soon as Jen got Sharon back on her feet, she was going to find out why her easy-going, always-reliable husband had spent the last few months turning into somebody she hardly knew.

She briskly patted Sharon's face. "Listen to me, this is important. When Matt came to the cottage, did he hurt you?"

"I was so scared, I just ran. I stepped on something sharp coming over here."

Had Matt really found Sharon, or had her own terror conjured him up while she was alone in the dark? It was not unusual for the victims of severe stress and trauma to imagine threats when there were none. Jen had seen it in her patients many times.

"It's easy to become afraid in the dark after you've suffered trauma," Jen told her. "You could have heard that big oleander scratching against the cottage window. Are you sure it was Matt?"

"Positive."

"Is he carrying a weapon? Where is he now?"

"I don't know. I didn't see him." Sharon's voice shook with fear, and she ducked her head. "He just slid a note under my door. It was so terrifying I ran straight here."

Alarm bells went off in her mind, and a chilling sense of dread swept through Jen. Trauma victims were unreliable witnesses. If Sharon had run straight out the door, she'd have encountered Matt. What happened in the gaps that were missing in her story?

Nothing good, that was certain.

Jen heard echoes of her mother's voice.

When you see quick results from nature's warnings, evil has no boundaries. Its tentacles are reaching into every corner of your life.

"What note?" Jen leaned close and brushed her friend's hair back from her face, trying to soothe away her terror.

The note Sharon pulled from her pocket was on ordinary lined notebook paper, the kind you could get at any drugstore or general store. Written in pencil, the bold message pierced Jen with the destructive force of a bullet.

BOO! THERE YOU ARE! YOU KNOW THE RULES!

"Matt's found her!" Jen gasped. She was struggling to remain strong for Sharon.

"Don't touch it." Benjamin grabbed a pair of kitchen tongs and dropped the note into a plastic bag. "I'm calling the police."

Sharon turned so pale she looked bloodless. "No! No cops or everybody dies. Those are Matt's rules. And he means them, too."

"I know Matt," Benjamin said. "Or *used* to. He's bluffing."

"No, he's not." Sharon had somehow dug deep within herself to find a remnant of the self-confident woman who once turned the heads of every man on campus at Tulane, including her fast-fisted husband. "He beat me black and blue with the regularity of the rising sun, and then threatened that if I didn't toe the line, he would kill my mother."

Her voice hitched, and she struggled to pull herself back together. "Mama is helpless in a nursing home. He said it would be worth the drive to Tupelo to put a pillow over her head and smother her. It was so awful. He would snap his fingers and tell me it would be just that quick and easy to get rid of her."

"That's outrageous." Jen knew Matt kept Sharon in line with threats, but it wasn't uncommon for wounded pride to prevent the abused from telling everything. When they spilled their deepest secrets, they felt powerless. Jen had heard this story so many times, women—and men—afraid to disobey abusive spouses for fear of consequences. "Have you talked to your sister recently? Is your mother okay?"

"I called Eleanor on a burner phone after I got here. Mama's fine. If Matt has been up there looking for me, my sister doesn't know about it. I don't know how he found me. But he's here now, and he's dangerous." Sharon lifted her chin, the gesture of defeated women everywhere attempting to show courage. "He wouldn't hesitate to put a bullet between the eyes of the two people he has always said got too big for their britches."

"He was talking about... us?" Benjamin's face reflected Jen's own shock.

"Yes. He always resented your success. And every time I showed a bit of spunk and defied him, he blamed Jen. He called her a bad influence."

Betrayal and accusation swirled around a kitchen already thick with the threat of evil. Disbelief held Jen and Benjamin in place.

The knock on the back door made them jump. Their head of security, Clint Brown, walked into the kitchen, his hand on his holster. Massive as a refrigerator, his skin gleaming with the sweat of exertion, he surveyed the room.

"Is everybody all right in here?" His question brought a sense of order into the kitchen.

"Not really," Benjamin said. "What's going on outside?"

"The cottage and the grounds are clear. There are no signs of forced entry anywhere. We even checked the beach to see if the intruder came by boat. The only thing we saw amiss was some broken glass on the path leading from the cottage to the kitchen. I'm going to take a closer look and I'll let you know if I see anything else."

"That must be where I cut my foot." Sharon sagged against the kitchen counter as if she were suddenly drained of all energy.

"You're staying in the main house tonight," Jen told her.

"I can't..."

"You *will*. You'll sleep in the room right next to ours. Get anything you need from my room—toiletries, robe, bedroom slippers. Benjamin will show you where to find them."

"Not a problem," he said.

"I'll see you in a little while, then." Jen watched him lead Sharon from the kitchen. She had a plan, and nothing was going to stop her.

Bad news floated around the kitchen like toxic gas, sent to

destroy them all. While she waited for Clint, Jen made a pot of coffee and tried to figure out *how* Matt could have found Sharon.

Sharon had escaped by telling him she was going to visit her sister Eleanor to help take care of their mom, whose health had suddenly taken a bad turn. Eleanor lived in Tupelo, Mississippi, a two-hour drive north of Eutaw, and she had made it very clear that Matt was not welcome in her home. Knowing his violent history, she would surely not have given him any information about Sharon,

Or would she? When people are threatened, they will do all sorts of things they would never dream of under ordinary circumstances. If Matt knew where Sharon was, he had likely written the threatening notes to Jen, as well. Through the years, anytime Sharon turned to Jen for help, he accused her of trying to take his wife from him.

By bringing Sharon into their home, Jen had called Armageddon onto their heads. She had put herself between a woman and a husband spurned, and in doing so, she had put her entire family at risk.

But just how far would Matt go? He had killed a pet hamster without remorse.

Was he capable of murder?

TEN
THE DIARY

Geniuses always have a plan.

Invisible had a plan, too, therefore Invisible was a genius. After years of feeling *unseen* and unappreciated, the feeling of power and imminent success was a bigger high than any combination of drinks or pills on the market.

Drunk on power, Invisible thought about each point already in the diary and the careful, purposeful way the first few had been carried out. The cardinal rule was USE MINIONS.

Like all geniuses, Invisible possessed considerable powers of persuasion. All sorts of things could be achieved with a combination of flattery and fear. Both were heady. And both were plentiful in the genius' arsenal of charms.

The entry that read BLUDGEON THE PET HAMSTER was particularly exciting to think about. No way was Invisible going to be deprived of that pleasure. No minions involved. The mere recall of the event was almost as delicious as doing the actual killing.

WHACK went the hammer. SQUEAL went the hamster. And all that beautiful blood came gushing out.

"Not quite dead yet? Oh, you poor dear."

The hammer came down again. Judiciously placed. Death would not be immediate. Watching the life slowly drain out of the wretched pet that got more love and attention than deprived people who were far more deserving had been a pleasure on par with winning a lottery. Not that Invisible had ever won any lotteries. Genius was the primary weapon in Invisible's arsenal. Everything coming down the pike would be earned, not won.

The death of the beloved pet was only the beginning. Invisible's lips curved into a secret smile about what the future held. Wouldn't everybody be surprised?

Horrified was more like it.

ELEVEN

THE TURNER HOUSE

Jen poured two cups of coffee then settled into the kitchen to talk with Clint. Long before she became a practicing psychologist, she had turned waiting into an art. All she had to do was follow the example of her mother. No restlessness. No sorting through the rubble of a problem-filled mind. No outer signs of a gifted soul so in tune with nature she could read every telling sign.

Her head of security had the same calm exterior, no matter what was happening. It was one of the many reasons Jen had hired him.

"Clint, could Matt Jones have come in with the rest of the party?"

"You can always fake an invitation. Or maybe he gave some plausible excuse for not having one. I checked the camera footage to see if I could spot him, but there are no cameras on the cottage."

She and Benjamin had deliberately left it free of camera scrutiny for the privacy of their guests.

"My children were either in the front room, or in the kitchen with Nancy the entire evening. Matt could have easily taken Marianne's hamster, sneaked off the property, and then returned in uniform to deliver it."

"If he was in the house, wouldn't Sharon have recognized him, even in disguise? A man his size is hard to mistake."

"He could easily have evaded her in a crowd that big and a house this size."

"He might have come in the delivery truck," Clint said. "But how did he kill the hamster, gift-wrap it, and then sneak around to deliver it at the front door? And what did he do with the truck all evening if he waited around to plant a note at Sharon's cottage? That's just not plausible."

"Unless he had an accomplice." Jen pushed her coffee cup aside. "I'm going to take a look around, and I want you with me."

"I don't advise it." Every fiber in Clint's body showed his disapproval.

It felt good to chuckle. When he disagreed with her, which was often, he puffed up like the Incredible Hulk until he was a massive tower of ebony muscle and scowling discontent.

"I know you don't, Clint. But you know me. I'm stubborn. I'm going to do it whether you stay with me or not."

"I'm not letting you out of my sight. You're so hard-headed, if you saw Matt Jones hightailing it across the bay in a boat you'd take out after him, swimming."

"You've got that right. I'm a better swimmer than Maria Ramos. I could have been an Olympic contender."

"Saints preserves us all!" he laughed.

Their easy camaraderie might fool others into thinking he didn't take his job seriously, but Jen knew better. He had been a detective for the Santa Rosa Sheriff's Department and served on the security detail for two recent governors. After she and Benjamin bought the house, she snagged him because he wanted to be out of the line of fire and not have to travel after his baby was born.

He held the door and they walked into the night, polished by the soft glow of moonlight and chilled by wind coming off the cooling currents of Pensacola Bay and Santa Rosa Sound. Surrounded by a cradle of water and the whispered secrets of the sea, Jen sought to regain the sense of optimism that had borne her toward the party that turned into a nightmare.

"Clint, how's the baby?" She thought with longing of Luther, his newborn son, innocent and trusting, totally dependent on his parents to keep him safe. Marianne's unraveling at the sight of her bloodied hamster loomed large.

How easy it is when they are small, and how hard when they get older.

"Kathleen is taking the sleepless nights in stride, but I may have to check myself into the hospital just to get some sleep."

"I remember how that feels. If you or Kathleen ever want to crash in one of my guestrooms, feel free."

The guardhouse had a breakroom with a sofa. Cots and bedding were stowed in the closet in case any of the security staff ever needed to stay overnight. But Clint felt like the brother Jen never had, and she viewed him as part of her extended family.

"You couldn't pry her away from Luther with a crowbar, but you might just see me with my toothbrush and pajamas."

Stars lit the flagstone path Sharon had taken earlier. The unaware might be fooled into thinking they walked an enchanted path, but Jen scanned the pavement with the vigilance of a woman both blessed and burdened with an unexplainable gift. The night had suddenly turned as quiet as the grave—no sounds of surf lapping the shore, no crickets chirping, no quiet stirring of leaves. The unusual stillness was nature's alarm bell.

There.

In the curve between house and cottage was a broken champagne flute. Clint leaned down to pick up a shard of glass still covered with blood.

"Here's where Sharon cut herself," he said. "Somebody must have broken a glass during the party."

Jen herself had been outside briefly while she tried to call Benjamin, but without camera coverage on the cottage, it would be impossible to tell who else had been here. The house was designed to bring nature inside and extend the comforts of the interior to the open patios and secluded courtyards outside so guests could flow seamlessly between the two. "I wonder who was out here?"

"The monitors in the guardhouse showed dozens on the grounds," he told her. "They were swarming in and out of the mansion like candidates at a political rally."

"Did you recognize anybody in particular?"

"Nancy came out, briefly. Tommy's swim coach was out here a couple of times, and so were Sharon and Benjamin's legal assistant. I saw Benjamin, of course. And you. Twice."

"I was only outside once tonight." She had made one call to her husband from inside the house.

"Unless I'm losing my eyesight, you were out here two times. In that red caftan, you're kind of hard to miss. The first time you were talking on the phone, and the second you were on the flagstone patch heading this way."

The chills that ran through Jen were not from the night air. Was it possible she had come outside twice tonight and didn't remember? If she kept getting these upsetting reports about her activities, she'd have to make an appointment with one of her colleagues.

But she still believed Matt had killed Marianne's hamster. Sharon's husband was a big man who had been a linebacker at Tulane, tall, heavily muscled with a thick neck and massive shoulders, and light-colored hair. Sharon said he now had a paunch belly and a receding hairline, but Clint had been right that his size would give him away.

"Did you see anyone here tonight who might have been Matt?" she asked him.

"No. And we were on the lookout for him all evening. But anybody who wants to move around without being noticed will find ways of doing it. As you know, the cameras don't cover every inch of the property." Clint eased ahead of her toward the guest cottage, its pale pink clapboard siding echoing the shadings of rose in the stone on their house and gleaming in the starlight that laid a silver path from the bay. "When we cleared the cottage, we left it just like Sharon did. I'm going in first."

The door stood slightly ajar, but it wasn't the sight of Clint drawing his gun before he entered that alarmed Jen. It was the ominous white glow from the oleander, hanging from the windowsills, the rooftop, and the trees, climbing over the porch railing and twining around the small Ionic columns that matched those in the gardens all around the main house.

Beware. Beware.

The warning from the poisonous white flower clanged so loudly Jen had to resist covering her ears. Oleander was *everywhere*. Multiplied a thousand times. The warnings bombarded her thick and fast, and she had to put her hand over her mouth so she could get through the door without choking.

This was why she had come. Not because she didn't trust Clint, but because her mother had equipped her to see things he could not. The other reason, of course, was that Jen was every bit as ornery as her grandmother. Victoria Logan always said, *if you want something done right, do it yourself.* A practice that was almost a religion to Jen, much to the dismay of her family.

Clint switched on the lights, and the room blazed to life, perfectly orderly and untouched. But then, according to Sharon, Matt hadn't come inside. He had moved around the property, practically invisible, only leaving behind a note.

"If she was fleeing for her life," Clint said, "I wonder why she turned off the lights when she left? Or was she here in the dark all the time?"

"She couldn't have been in the dark. She read the note he slipped under the door."

"I've heard of stranger things than flipping the light switch in a panic. People do all sorts of weird stuff when they're scared."

They walked through the rest of the rooms with Clint clearing each before he would let Jen enter. The cottage was exactly the way it had always been except for Sharon's belongings. Her clothes hung in the closet of the largest bedroom, and her suitcases sat in a neat row on the floor beneath. In the ensuite, a damp towel was folded neatly and hung over the towel rack. Sharon's cosmetic case sat in the corner of the dressing table, and the many products she had used recently were lined beside it, along with her comb and hairbrush.

Something in the brush caught Jen's attention. A single dark hair. Both Sharon and her husband had light hair. It must belong to Sharon's sister, Eleanor, who had probably used it on one of her many visits to Eutaw before their mother was transferred to a nursing home in Tupelo. Her hair was almost as dark as Jen's own.

Though everything appeared to be in place, Jen felt a creeping sense of unease. Evil had been here and left its mark, just as surely as Jen planned to leave her mark on the oleander. Tomorrow she would leave instructions with Dal to dig out the monstrous bush, no matter what he said.

"I've seen enough, Clint."

He escorted her back to the house and insisted on going inside to make sure no one was hiding there to launch a surprise attack.

Jen went straight to check on her children. In a room decorated with posters of champion swimmers and strewn with shirts, jeans, and tennis shoes, Tommy slept as only the innocent can, totally relaxed, his coltish legs and arms flung on top of the covers he'd kicked off. She kissed his forehead, brushed back a lock of hair, and went through the twin's dual ensuite to her daughter's room.

Marianne slept curled into a ball, as if she were protecting her dreams as staunchly as she fought for her independence and privacy. The glow of the nightlight showed her eyes still puffy from crying over her hamster.

"My fierce little girl," Jen whispered.

A sudden sense of dismay tugged at Jen. Marianne's schoolbooks lay in a pile beside her iPad, and her blue sweater was flung onto the flowered chintz window seat, her favorite place to curl up and read so she could face the water. Nothing to alarm. And yet, Jen had *every* reason to be terrified.

"*Where* are you?" Jen whispered. "*Who* are you?"

There was no answer except the distant sound of a boat whistle, far across the bay and the crashing of waves against the shore—the massive Atlantic Ocean pouring into Pensacola Bay, its alchemy of currents and evaporation creating weather and eco-systems and food sources, the sound of it almost imperceptible because of its constancy.

Its mere presence was balm to Jen's soul. She stood there, soaking it up, then leaned down to kiss her daughter's cheek. "Dream big."

By the time she went to bed, Benjamin was flat on his back, snoring loud enough to rattle windows. They were slightly ajar, as they often were in spring and fall, to let in the fresh ocean breeze, and the curtains were open. Jen left them that way. Both she and her husband enjoyed the spectacular play of stars and moon in the heavens and the occasional comet blazing across the night sky.

She went down the hall and opened the door to the adjacent guestroom. Sharon was curled into a little ball, her bandaged foot sticking out from the covers. She was sleeping so quietly Jen had to walk inside and bend over the bed to tell if she was breathing.

"Sleep tight, my friend," Jen whispered.

Satisfied, she finally crawled into her own bed, careful not to wake her husband, though lately that hadn't been a problem. Recently, Benjamin could sleep through a tornado.

She envied that. She chased sleep with the futility of a racehorse running dead last in the Kentucky Derby but still harboring the dream of winning. Too much had happened in one day. She was just drifting off when she startled awake.

Someone was watching.

Daring not to make a sound, she lay in the dark peering into the shadows of her room. *There.* Movement by the window. The flutter of giant wings. A strange, guttural cry.

Two great blue herons glided by, side by side, on wings wider than an eagle's. Each great blue has a wingspan of a mind-boggling seven feet. Standing, the herons are four feet tall. Massive birds, that are even more impressive in flight.

They soared past Jen's window, their blue-gray feathers darkened by night, their long necks tucked into an S-curve, their long legs and the black plumes that ran from their eyes to the back of the head flying out behind them. Their massive wings blocked light and created enormous shadows in her bedroom. As soon as they passed her window, they turned and came back. Once, twice, three times. Ever circling. An anomaly. A sure sign.

When one of nature's creatures behaves in an extraordinary way, it's a warning. When two are involved, it's a certainty. Trouble is already on your doorstep.

She didn't need Delilah to interpret the omen of the great blues. Somewhere, something dark and destructive was watching, waiting for her to let her guard down.

She got out of bed and closed the curtains. But even then,

she could still see the birds' silhouettes, gliding back and forth across her window.

I won't let you win.

Filled with determination, Jen closed her eyes. But when sleep finally claimed her, she was under the ominous shadow of wings.

TWELVE

Dawn colored the sky outside Benjamin's bedroom window, jarring him awake with the horrible knowledge that last night's housewarming party had added complications to a life that was already coming apart at the seams. Careful not to wake Jen, he eased out of bed and put on jeans and a tee shirt.

He usually enjoyed the early morning hours before Nancy and Dal arrived and his family woke up. But today, he struggled to think of anything to be happy about. Still, he soldiered on. Hadn't his father drilled that into him?

He made coffee the way he liked it, with chicory, a taste he had acquired in New Orleans. Then he turned the volume on the wall-hung TV down low, and divided his attention between the remarkable sunrise beyond the kitchen window and the morning news show. John Bailey, a Gulf Breeze television favorite, stood on the parkway beneath the leaping marlin on the iconic Pensacola Beach sign, giving his morning report.

With the sun beaming down on locals and tourists whizzing along the beach road, it could be an ordinary day in one of the world's sunniest and most popular playgrounds. Only, it *wasn't*.

"Late last night a blue Toyota Camry went off the road here

at one of our most famous landmarks," the reporter said, confirming Benjamin's assessment that everything, everywhere, was flying off the rails.

A photo of the crushed Toyota filled the screen, and he set his coffee cup on the table. Could it be *her* car? It just didn't seem possible.

"A blowout spun the car off the road. And if it wasn't for the thick cover of shrubbery, the driver would have crashed into the sign. There was no evidence of foul play, but police are still investigating the accident." Another photograph flashed onto the screen. "The driver, Maria Ramos, is listed in fair condition at the local hospital."

"Impossible." Benjamin's hand shook as he picked up his coffee cup. *How could this awful thing happen to a nice woman like Maria?* Disaster had set a straight course toward his family and his friends, and just would not veer.

"Did he say Maria Ramos? *Our* Maria?"

Jen had sneaked up behind him. She did that a lot lately. She was already dressed for work, her red suit a power statement, her ever-present gold bracelets clicking together in a tune he'd recently dubbed as *I'm the boss*.

It was the tragedy in her face that gave him pause. Instant shame rushed through him. This was the woman he swore would always be his sun and his moon. He'd sworn to protect her from everything, even devastating news such as Maria's accident.

"He did, Jen, but don't worry. She's alive. In fair condition, the reporter said."

No need to mention foul play. They had had enough foul play of their own to fell an elephant.

"That's *horrible*. Poor Maria! I'll stop by the hospital to check on her this morning when I do clinicals."

They stared at each other, stricken, as if the bad luck from their party had somehow rubbed off on Maria and caused her to crash into the leaping marlin sign. Finally, he broke the silence.

"Tell her not to worry. Consider this sick leave with pay. I know she needs the money."

"She does... and I will." Jen visibly pulled herself together. It was remarkable to see his wife gathering courage the way a hurricane gathers strength from the warm waters of the Gulf.

On the mornings she saw patients at the hospital—which was three times a week—she always left the house before he did, dropping the children off at school on her way to work.

Now, she put a bagel in the toaster and poured her coffee, her usual routine in a day that was anything *but*. Benjamin's whole life was flowing down the drain, disappearing before his eyes.

Even the sound of his children did nothing to relieve his gloom. They stormed toward the kitchen with energy only seen in teenagers and comets. Bursting through the door, Tommy and Marianne jostled each other to see who could be first to get to the cabinet holding three kinds of cereal, all of them guaranteed heart-healthy and vitamin-packed.

After the fiasco of the dead hamster, he was astonished to see Marianne make such a comeback. She was tough, like her mother. Benjamin was ashamed at how much the admission plummeted his self-esteem. What sort of monster was he becoming?

Marianne grabbed the Cheerios box before Tommy could get his hands on it and dumped the cereal into a stoneware bowl.

She gave a little screech then yelled, "Mom!" in the accusatory tone of teens everywhere who believe their mothers have lost all reason.

Lying in the bowl among the toasted oats was Jen's gold and ruby necklace, a shocking sight. He watched in horror as Jen dropped her cup, her face a mask of the same confusion he felt.

Coffee spattered her shoes, and Tommy jumped out of the way to protect his new sports Adidas.

Benjamin snatched up the necklace. It had cost a fortune. He had spent precious time he couldn't afford to waste personally searching for the exact gift Jen would treasure, or so he had thought.

"Jen, how did it get *there*?"

"I don't know…"

Any other time, the note of sorrow in her voice would have moved him to reassurances and hugs, like any good husband. But though he searched for those finer qualities in himself today, he came up lacking.

Another horrible thought came to him. His wife had seemed unusually forgetful lately. Had *she* tossed it in the cereal box?

He had to tamp down his dismay before he could even speak. "Jen, what on earth is happening here?"

She stood among shards of her coffee cup, her brow furrowed, while the twins stared at her, speechless. And no wonder. Jen was the unflappable parent who took everything in stride, the one they counted on to keep their schedules straight and make them obey rules they pretended to hate. Before Sharon came, she had always been the reliable one.

"I'm so glad you found that," Sharon said as she swept through the door, limping only slightly, and wearing Jen's pink fuzzy slippers and robe, which was slightly too long for her. "Jen was distraught when she discovered she'd misplaced it."

"She dropped it in the cereal box." Benjamin stared at his wife, gut-punched. He knew she hadn't been herself lately, but he would never have guessed she'd do something so careless.

"I did *not*."

"Maybe it slipped off your neck and dropped into the box?" Sharon suggested. "When we got back two nights ago, you came in here. Remember?"

"Yes, you did," Benjamin said. It had been early when they got home, and they all came inside the house to finish the conversation they'd started at the restaurant. Something about a Mardi Gras party at Tulane. He had too many problems on his mind to recall the details. Enough to drive any man half-crazy. But he *did* remember Jen coming into the kitchen.

"I came to make a cup of tea, and I didn't go near the cereal."

Jen looked so distressed he finally managed to slide his arm around her and dredge up a shred of affection that was paltry compared to the wealth of love and joy that had been their hallmark since the day they married. Regret filled him. "Sweetheart, why don't you call your secretary and have him reschedule your appointments? You've been working non-stop lately, and you could use a day off."

"I don't need a day off."

"That's actually a good idea." When Sharon came over to put a hand on his wife's shoulder, she saw the mess of broken pottery and black coffee. Her face registered the same dismay Benjamin was feeling. "I'll just clean up this little accident then head to the office. I can reschedule your patients then come back here, and we can both have a girls' day out. Everything's going to be all right, Jen."

"Absolutely not." Jen turned to the children. "Tommy, you won't have private swim lessons for a while. I'll explain in the car. Marianne, don't make any after-school plans with your friends. Your math tutor will be here at four."

"Do I have to?" Marianne pouted. "Can't I have a day off? My hamster was *murdered*."

"No days off and no excuses like that bogus stomachache last time. Finish your cereal while I get the coffee off my shoes. We leave in five minutes."

Jen left the kitchen, then backtracked, snatched her necklace from his hands and stormed out. The loud staccato rhythm of her high heels on the stairs announced her turmoil.

Benjamin's heart sank. The storm brewing in his house was on a collision course with the tornado already tearing him apart. He could feel the approach of cataclysmic destruction.

And he didn't know if any of them would survive it.

THIRTEEN

"Jen's okay. And everything is going to be all right." Sharon patted his arm then started cleaning up the mess his wife had made.

"I hope so." If a woman being chased by a crazed husband could believe that, so could he. Benjamin grabbed some paper towels and knelt to help her. "How's your foot?"

"Almost perfect." Sharon tossed the debris into the trash can then flashed her beauty queen smile. It was heady stuff that any man with a pulse would notice. "I'm going to the cottage now to get dressed for work."

"I'll walk you over." He wouldn't be leaving for work for another forty-five minutes, a respite he needed. Once Jen and the twins were out of the house, he could breathe again. A troubling reality, but true.

"I'll be okay. You and Jen have done more than enough."

"I insist."

He wished his children a good day at school then stepped outside with the trepidation of a man walking through a mine field. Spring in Gulf Breeze had to be one of the most glorious sights a man could hope to see, everything green and blooming, emerald waters stretching endlessly toward the horizon, marine birds carrying on their graceful aerial dances. The flower beds he had so carefully designed and cultivated with Dal's help were particularly stunning, a rainbow of color, a perfumery of scent.

Ben should have been content, even happy. Instead, he slouched along wondering what disaster would befall him next. If he weren't married to a psychologist, he might go in search of one.

Lost in his own misery, he was blindsided when Sharon cried out, "Oh, no!"

"What?"

The scene before him emerged slowly, as if he were just waking from a bad dream. The sun was spotlighting Sharon's horrified face. Her little black hatchback car was sitting lopsided in the driveway, one tire flat.

"They were *fine* last night. Matt did this. I *know* he did." Sharon's voice rose a few decibels.

"We don't know that for sure..."

Benjamin squatted to inspect the flat tire, but it was impossible to tell without removing it if she had punctured the treads by driving over a nail, or whether someone with a vendetta had taken a sharp object and punctured the sidewall.

Maria Ramos' car had also been parked at his house last night. Maybe Matt had punctured her tire to make it look like both cars had picked up a nail in the driveway? A small puncture would make a slow leak that Maria wouldn't have noticed until the changing pressure caused a blowout that could have easily killed her.

Murder.

The word whispered through his mind while Sharon dissolved into hysterics.

"*I* know it for sure! He wouldn't just leave a note for me. He would show me that he's in control." Sharon's shoulders began to heave. "What will he do next?"

When she burst into tears, Benjamin patted her shoulder with the awkwardness of a man flummoxed by a woman and wishing he were on another planet. He was relieved when her sobs turned to sniffles.

"Maybe we should call the police."

"*No*! He'll kill me!"

That was exactly the response he had expected from her. "We'll hire a private detective to investigate, then. Matt will never know."

"Yes, he will. He has a cousin in this area. Near Pensacola, I think. He's mean as a rattlesnake."

"Maybe that's how Matt found you?"

"Probably. He's watching me, itching for me to give him cause to drive up to Tupelo and put a pillow over Mama's head. *Promise* you won't hire a private eye."

"All right. No private detective. I'll just beef up security around the house."

"Thanks, Ben. I hate to ask one more thing, but can you help me change the tire?"

"I'm going to call the garage to tow your car. Then they can find out whether the leak is coming from the treads or the sidewall." The treads were protected by a steel band, and most deliberate slashes were made in the thinner sidewall. "If it's in the sidewall, it won't prove Matt slashed your tire, but at least we'll have a better idea of what he's capable of."

"But how will I get to work? Is there a good cab company here?"

"Why don't you stay here today and try to rest? You've had a hard time, lately. Nancy and Dal will be here, and I'll get Clint to post a security detail on you today."

"Please, no. That's not necessary. I can't abandon Jen. She

has a heavy patient load today, and I can't let her down. She needs me."

Sharon was a good friend to Jen. How did his wife get all the luck, while he was left to clean up every mess? "Okay, you can ride with me."

"Can I? That would be wonderful."

"It's no problem, Jen's office is not far from mine. It's easy to swing by and drop you off."

But nothing felt easy anymore.

Sharon was disturbingly beautiful and sweet. Needy and grateful. Being in close quarters with her would be torture, a man lost in the Sahara suddenly confronted with a cool oasis.

As soon as she was out of sight, Ben scanned the area for nails or bits of broken glass. There was nothing to indicate her slashed tire was an accident. Not that he was surprised. Dal was rigorous about keeping up the grounds. Nothing that threatened his standard of perfection escaped his notice.

Benjamin walked back to the house, feeling like a fraud. Sharon behaved as if he were some kind of hero. For calling the garage. For offering her a lift. For little things so ordinary other women took them for granted.

For a moment, her opinion buoyed him up. Then reality hit. He wished he could take the morning and throw it into the bay like a rotten fish. He wished he could take his whole life and press a reset button.

What would Jen do if she knew what he was really thinking? What if she caught on that he was putting on an act?

FOURTEEN

GULF BREEZE HOSPITAL | DOWNTOWN GULF BREEZE, FLORIDA

Jen finished her clinicals at Gulf Breeze Hospital then went to Maria Ramos' room. The TV was blaring, and she was pale against the sheets, her right arm in a cast, her eyes black and blue, her face covered with cuts. Still, the monitors above her bed showed the almost perfect pulse and blood pressure of a young woman who spent hours in the water, swimming with a vigor that rivaled dolphins.

But Jen knew looks could deceive. News reports on the radio told that Maria's airbag didn't deploy, and she wasn't wearing her seat belt. On impact, her head crashed into the windshield. Her charts showed she had a concussion that would need time to heal. Fortunately, she had escaped other internal injury.

If the shrubbery around the Pensacola Beach sign hadn't stopped the momentum of her car, Maria would almost certainly be dead, a horror foretold to Jen by sea turtles and giant blue herons.

"Dr. Turner? I didn't expect you to come."

"Of course I came. You're an important part of our community as well as Tommy's coach."

"He's a great swimmer, a real natural. I expect to be out of here in a couple of days, and I can resume his private lessons."

Jen spotted the fake optimism for what it really was, a desperate hope that what she said would be true. Maria was a woman of modest means who needed every penny she earned and could ill afford a long recovery that would drain her bank account.

"You just concentrate on getting well. Consider this a paid sick leave."

Tears sprang to Maria's eyes. "I couldn't accept that..."

"Yes, you can. Benjamin and I are happy to do it." A quick glance at the wall clock told Jen she had only a few minutes before she had to get to her office. "Do you have any idea what caused your blowout? Worn-out tires? Driving off-road where you might have picked up a nail?"

"I got a new set of tires two weeks ago, and I haven't been anywhere except at home, the school, and your house. That tire should never have blown. I think somebody *did* this to me."

All the signs said so. Jen tamped down her growing intuition that the danger around her was spreading beyond her family to everybody who even came close to her. Who would be next? *And why?*

"I'm sure the police will find out. Don't worry about a thing. If you need me, just call." A scene from the party came to her. Maria and her husband. "Or call Benjamin."

That coaxed a smile from Maria. Was Sharon right that the swim coach had more than a friendly interest in her husband? Jen hated that the idea even popped into her mind. Nothing in her professional experience indicated that Maria was a husband-stealer. And in spite of nature's warnings—and Sharon's—Jen had the feeling the problem didn't stem from Maria, but had *targeted* her instead.

As she turned to leave, Maria called out. "Please wait. This is embarrassing, but I want you to know, I flirt with everybody, even Mr. Turner. That's just the way I am. It's not personal, and I don't mean any harm."

"Thanks for telling me." Both astonished and bemused by the confession, Jen placed a business card on the bedside table. "If you want to talk, I can help you with that impulse. Take care."

Women of low self-esteem often sought validation through inappropriate and risky behavior. But was Maria telling the truth?

The sudden appearance of a seagull beating its wings against the window across from Maria's bed riveted Jen. *Bizarre behavior from a creature far from its habitat is a clear warning that all is not as it seems.* Delilah's warning from the grave sent shivers through her as she hurried off to her car.

She had the sensation she was walking in quicksand. The more she tried to move forward, the more she was tugged down into a mire so dark, so frightening, she might never find her way out.

The sudden flash of dark wings in the sky sounded an otherworldly warning. The great blue heron belonged on the beach, *never* in a crowded hospital parking lot. Fear shivered through her.

"Who's there?" Jen called, but no one answered.

Through she searched in all directions, she saw nothing. Still, she *knew,* she could *see.*

Someone or *something* was watching her. And it was pure evil.

FIFTEEN

THE DIARY

Invisible opened the diary and crossed the item off the list.

ELIMINATE MARIA RAMOS.

She had been in the way. People who stood in the way had to go. That's all there was to it.

Elimination could mean all sorts of things—causing accidents, creating so much chaos everything just fell apart on its own, even death. Preferably death. But broken to pieces in a hospital would do for Maria.

Invisible was not a monster. Oh no, Invisible was a genius with a plan. That's all. A perfectly respectable human being who had better sense than to telegraph every thought to the unsuspecting public.

Invisible never acted on impulse, either. Every step of the plan was carefully calculated. Invisible had an eye on the end game.

Ink flowed onto paper as Invisible wrote in the day planner.

EVERYTHING I WANT IS MINE.

The words were positive, but they were not strong enough. Invisible scratched through the notation and made a new one.

TAKE WHAT IS MINE.

There. That was better. It was a promise. And a promise made with full intention could not be broken.

Of course, achieving that meant one more thing. Invisible wrote:

ELIMINATE EVERYBODY WHO GETS IN MY WAY.

Invisible closed the diary, feeling powerful. There was so much more to do.

SIXTEEN

JEN'S MEDICAL OFFICE COMPLEX | DOWNTOWN GULF BREEZE, FLORIDA

When Jen walked into her office, she could suddenly breathe again. This was her world. Except for the occasional omen that revealed itself as a seagull bashing the window or a line of ants suddenly appearing on the pristine Formica cabinet top around the cookie jar in the breakroom, nothing happened here that she couldn't control.

Larry Brent, her secretary, friend, and jack-of-all trades, flashed a winning smile so like her sister Annie's, Jen wanted to hug him. His deep, copper-colored hair and his talent with people also reminded her of her sister. Both of them could charm their way out of a pit of crocodiles.

"Right on schedule, as usual. Your first patient will be here in five minutes, Doc."

"Great." Jen's gold bracelets slid along her arms as she brushed her hair back from her face. She felt as if she'd already run a twenty-six-mile marathon, and she'd barely started her day. "Where's Sharon?" She was usually at her desk in the small office opposite the reception enclosure. But today her door hung open and her office was empty.

"In the breakroom, stowing her things. She got here a little late. That lunatic husband of hers slashed her tires."

A chill ran through Jen. "How did that happen?"

"She discovered it this morning. Mr. Turner thinks he must have done it during the party. He brought Sharon to work."

It came as no surprise that Larry's bad news was punctuated with a tapping at the office window. A seagull, who should have been nowhere near the commercial medical complex of hospital and doctors' offices, had landed on the windowsill and was rapping at the glass with his beak as if his sole purpose was to get inside.

Nature's creatures know when something bad is afoot.

Jen hadn't been bombarded with so many signs since her sister Rachel vanished. A dizzy spell hit her, and she had to lean against the wall.

Larry raced over and steadied her. "Are you all right?"

"I'm fine. Too much to do, too little sleep."

Or was it something else? A sedative dropped into her coffee at the hospital this morning? A narcotic crushed into the icing on the petit fours at the party? It could have been meant for either of them. It seemed Sharon's husband would stop at nothing.

Jen was a strong woman in excellent health, a stranger to fatigue and vertigo, forgetfulness and fear. Strong enough to take care of herself, her family, and Sharon, too. Only the gullible would call the numerous strange events of the last two days coincidental. And she was far from gullible.

Are you? Her mother's voice, a sharp reminder to be ever-vigilant.

"Can I get you anything?" Larry hovered, anxious. Did he think she was losing her grip, too?

"No, I'll grab water and coffee in the breakroom."

"There are fresh muffins, too. Don't worry. I know not to get the ones with blueberries."

Jen took pride in schooling her emotions, but obviously Larry had picked up on the stress that had her wound as tightly as a piano wire.

"Good. The last thing I need is an allergic reaction."

The breakroom was at the back of her suite of offices, separated from the reception area, Sharon's office, and the large office where Jen consulted with her patients by a long hallway painted beach blue. A color that lifted her spirits. It reminded her of days spent with Benjamin and the children romping in the waves and building castles with the famous white sand on Pensacola Beach.

Sharon stood with her back to the door, stowing her jacket and purse in the locker they all shared. When she heard Jen, she turned around, her hand over her heart, the wariness of the abused stamped on her face.

"I'm sorry, Sharon. I didn't mean to startle you."

"No, that's all right. It has been a horrible morning. Ben drove me to work."

"Larry told me." Jen put her own purse in the locker and poured herself a cup of coffee, a routine she loved. A signal she would soon be in her office offering hope to the defeated and the broken. "How are you doing?"

"I'm a nervous wreck."

"Of course you are. That's a normal reaction." Jen motioned to a chair. "Sit down and let's chat a while."

"Are you sure you have time?"

"For you? *Always*." Jen took a sip of her coffee. "You know you'll be safe in our house for as long as you need to stay there. We'll do everything possible to keep Matt away. If you see anything that worries you—no matter how small it may seem—come straight to me."

"You're so good—and so strong. I wish I could be more like you."

"You just concentrate on being the best *you* possible. Agreed?"

Sharon gave her a small, grateful smile. "Maybe we can have lunch together today, just the two us? I need some girl time."

"You've got it! We'll go to Shaggy's. You'll love their seafood tacos."

When Jen got back to her office, she settled into her chair to enjoy the rest of her coffee. Shades of sky and earth on her walls and in her comfortable chairs created a haven for her as well as her patients, while the water fountain, koi pond, and flower beds in the private walled patio outside the window soothed the soul.

The garden resurrected visions of oleander shouting its ominous message all over her house and overtaking the guest cottage. In the chaos of her morning, she had forgotten to tell Dal to cut it. She sent him a text message.

Dal, dig up the oleander around the cottage today. It's taking over.

His message came flying back.

Dr. Turner, it's in bloom.

She tamped down her irritation. This wasn't the first time Dal had questioned her authority over the gardens. Additionally, he insisted on addressing her and Benjamin formally, no matter what they told him. Though Dal had only started working for them after they bought the new house, Jen suspected he would never drop the formalities, never become like family to them as his wife Nancy had.

Dig it up, anyway. I want it out of there.

Did Mr. Turner say I should take out the oleander? He's in charge of the gardens.

She tapped a furious response.

Just do it, Dal.

Her hand hovered briefly over the message then she punched *Send*. That should be enough for him.

Any other time she might have explained that it wasn't Benjamin's house and grounds. The property belonged to *both* of them. And they never countermanded each other. She could have added that she would explain to her husband this evening that the oleander was overtaking the cottage and had to be cut back for her peace of mind. No matter what time of year it was.

But Jen was fresh out of diplomacy. She was a quart low on generosity. Troubles besieged her at every turn. Authority was authority. The boss was the boss. *Period*.

She tossed her phone aside and opened the folder Larry had placed on the table beside her chair. The patient's name leaped out at her.

Jackson Markle. Histrionic personality disorder. Uncooperative. Tendency toward violence. Extreme paranoia. When he decided Jen was among the many women trying to harm him, she recommended a male colleague.

Larry's voice came over the intercom. "Jackson Markle is here."

"He's no longer my patient."

"I thought so, too, but his name is in the book."

"Maybe Sharon made the appointment. She wouldn't have known better. We'll sort this out later." She hesitated a moment, uncertain and doubting her own judgment. Something as foreign to her as if she'd suddenly grown horns. "Send him in, but be ready to come into my office immediately if I punch the intercom."

"Do you want me to tell him you had an emergency, and he'll have to see his regular doctor?"

"No, he's volatile. We can't risk setting him off. Go ahead and send him back."

Jen heard Jackson Markle coming. His shoes slapped the hardwood floor in the hallway, emphasizing his rage.

When he came through the door, he chained whatever beast raged inside him and took his seat in the chair opposite hers. A bottle of water and a box of tissues lay on the table beside him.

"What brings you here today, Jackson?"

"You know." Even though the temperature in the room was a comfortable seventy degrees, he was sweating, a sure sign of discomfort.

She waited for him to elaborate. But the silence stretched past the comfort zone and inched toward danger.

"I don't know, Jackson. Do you want to tell me?"

"Do you want to tell me?" He mimicked her perfectly.

Chills went through Jen. His face, tight as a fist, set off alarms. Briefly, she considered summoning Larry.

"Take your time," she said. "It's sometimes hard to talk about the things that make us sad or hurt or angry."

His predatory gaze reminded her of a shark waiting to strike.

Keep going. You can do this. You're trained for this.

"There is a bottle of water beside you," she added. "You can drink that if you like."

"Are you trying to poison me?"

He jumped out of his chair so fast, Jen thought he was going to attack. Silence screamed around the room while he stood too close and glared at her, still as a gathering storm.

"It's okay, Jackson. The bottle has never been opened. There is nothing inside except water."

Suddenly he lifted his heavy chair as if it weighed no more than a newborn. Before she could get her hand on the intercom button, the chair whizzed past her head, missing it by inches. It crashed against the wall behind her then clattered to the floor.

Everything else happened so fast she couldn't put the pieces together. Jackson's contorted face and balled fists. Sharon's screams. Footsteps pounding. Larry yelling, "*Call security!*"

The door burst open, and her fit and furious secretary made a flying tackle that sent Jackson crashing to the floor.

By the time the security officer for their building arrived and hauled him off, Sharon had insisted on tucking Jen into a blanket from the supply closet, and Larry had put the closed sign on their front door without even asking her opinion.

Every fiber in her revolted at being seen as helpless, at sitting cozy in a blanket while the two of them carried on a conversation as if she might be losing her mind. Still, she was truly scared.

Larry righted the chair Jackson had thrown, and Sharon sank into it as if her legs would no longer hold her. And why not? She was the target of an unpredictable and dangerous spouse.

What about you?

Jen catalogued the recent bizarre happenings and the avalanche of omens. Was Sharon the target, or was she?

Sharon glanced around the room as if she might discover enemies in every corner. Then she folded her hands in her lap and dug deep into herself for composure.

"You're doing good, kiddo," Jen told her.

"I'm not worried about myself. It's *you*." Sharon turned to Larry. "What will Jen's other patients do when they see the closed sign?"

"Her next one won't be here for another forty-five minutes," he said. "I'll turn it around long before then. Right now, I want to get to the bottom of why Jackson Markle was here in the first place. I know *I* didn't make the appointment."

"Neither did I," Sharon said. "When I organized the case files, I saw a sticker that said his case was closed. Besides, I immediately recognized the name. Jackson Markle is Matt's cousin."

The news sucked some of the air out of Jen. Was that relationship why Jackson had come to her in the first place, thinking she might be so unprofessional as to reveal something about her friend Sharon that he could report to Matt? It certainly seemed a likely motive for today's explosion.

"Could your husband have sent him to do this?" Larry asked.

"Possibly... But I would *never* have made an appointment for him. If I had known he was coming, I wouldn't even be in the office. He *despises* me, and the feeling is mutual." Sharon exchanged a worried glance with Larry, and Jen's apprehension ratcheted up a notch. "Jen, could you have made it yourself?"

"No, that's not possible."

"You sometimes do that," Larry told her. "And you've been so busy for the last few months it wouldn't surprise me if you simply forgot. You're human, too, Doc."

Jen's chill had nothing to do with Jackson's outburst, and everything to do with her creeping self-doubt. She tried to find her inner warrior, but discovered she had vanished and was somewhere searching for doughnuts. Sugar and grease to make her feel better.

A sound shot Jen out of her chair, her heart hammering. Was Jackson back? Was *he* Invisible, tracking her wherever she went?

The sound came again, soft and stealthy, like a rush of wings. Her hand over her heart, Jen moved toward her window and saw a colony of seagulls going mad, circling and screaming as if the very devil himself were after them.

If nature goes crazy, take heed and take cover. Danger is all around you.

What would Invisible take from her next?

SEVENTEEN

SHAGGY'S WATERFRONT BAR AND GRILL | ON LITTLE SABINE BAY IN GULF BREEZE

Sharon was enchanted the minute she laid eyes on Shaggy's. With Little Sabine Bay sparkling behind it and signs announcing it was family and dog friendly, it was just the kind of place she'd always imagined coming with a family of her own. She could breathe here. *Unwind.* The rustic interior had an island vibe that made her long for the kind of life Jen had.

Her euphoria took her through one of the best meals she could remember and a lovely, meandering conversation that steered clear of problems and focused on shared happy memories. It was wonderful... until it all fell apart.

Watching Jen unravel was like seeing a horror movie.

Sharon could hardly believe her eyes. Perched on a bar stool, she marveled that a quiet lunch at the popular waterfront restaurant intended to take her mind off Matt, and Jen's off the horrible scene in her office, might just prove to be her undoing.

Remnants of shrimp and crab claws lay in their plates, evidence of a meal they had enjoyed. Across the table, Jen pawed through her purse, getting more anxious by the minute.

"What's wrong?" It alarmed Sharon to see her unflappable friend losing control.

"I can't find my wallet."

"It has to be in your purse."

"That's just the thing. It's *not*."

"Did you switch purses and forget to transfer it?"

"I *never* switch purses, Sharon. I'm not a *fashionista*!"

Jen didn't snap at people. She was always even-tempered, calm, often maddeningly so. And yet, there she sat, her eyes too bright and her wild hair slipping its French twist and flying around her head like so many snakes on Medusa. Her face was turning so red Sharon thought she might have a stroke.

It happened to women their age. More often than she'd like to think about. And the Jackson Markle incident had been enough to topple even a strong woman like Jen.

"Everything's going to be okay." Sharon smiled, hoping for one in return, a sign Jen was as strong as she had always believed her to be. "Isn't that what you always say to me?"

Suddenly, Jen paled and snatched her hand out of her purse as if it contained a snake.

Now what? The way disaster was piling up, both of them were going to be in need of a good stiff drink when they got home.

"Jen, what is it?"

Jen pulled a note from her purse and placed it on the table.

Tit for Tat.
Invisible.

"I've taken nothing from anyone! What does this person want? And who is it, anyway?"

"Calm down." Sharon wadded the note up and tucked it out of sight in her own purse. She was no psychologist like her friend, but her mother had always said, *Out of sight, out of mind*. "We're not going to let this maniac ruin our lunch. Okay?"

"Okay."

"Good. Hand your purse to me, and I'll look for your wallet."

"Check and see if my EpiPen is in there, too." Jen passed the bag across the table.

It was designer, *of course* it was. The real thing. Kate Spade. A brand that made Sharon salivate every time she saw a display of purses. She couldn't even afford one at a mark-down price. And Matt would have killed her if she had charged one to their credit card.

It didn't take much for Matt to want to kill her anyway. He was stingy with her, but the sky was the limit when it came to his habits—gambling, drinking, shooting pool, *you name it*. He never skimped on himself. She mentally patted herself on the back for finally deciding she would no longer be his punching bag.

She caressed the leather on Jen's purse then started a systematic search, opening zippered pockets, digging into the corners past car keys, lip gloss, and a case for Jen's sunglasses—also designer. Tiffany. For a woman who cared nothing for fashion, her friend spared no expense on having the best and most expensive of everything.

"The EpiPen is here, but the wallet isn't." Just as Sharon had expected. And her friend, her rock, was crumbling before her very eyes.

"It *has* to be." Jen waved the ticket for their lunch as if she were trying to hail a lifeboat leaving the *Titanic* without her.

Sharon could have cried for her.

Their young server hurried over, her platinum ponytail bouncing. She hovered over Jen, anxious.

"Dr. Turner, is everything all right. Can I get you anything? Refill your tea?"

Sharon was not surprised to see Jen singled out for personal attention. She and her husband were both well-known and admired. Sharon had suspected it from their phone conversations through the years, but a week here confirmed her opinion. Jen was one of the lucky ones. Good practice, beautiful home, fabulous husband, and the kind of great children that would have been hers if she hadn't married a loser.

And now it all seemed to be slipping through Jen's fingers. She sat there, speechless, her face burning with embarrassment.

"We're okay here." Sharon smiled at the waitress and waited for her to disappear, then reached for her friend's hand. "Listen to me." How many times had she heard Jen say that to her? "This is not a problem. I'll pay for the meal."

"No credit cards. Matt can track them."

"That's moot, since he's already in Gulf Breeze." She shivered, and resisted the urge to duck her head for the blow she knew was coming. Would she ever get over that reaction to the mere mention of his name? "But don't worry, I have cash."

"I'll pay you back," Jen said. "You need to save every penny so you can build a good life for yourself here, or wherever you want to go."

"I think I'll stay here, close to you."

That response put color back into Jen's face. *Good.* They had to get through the rest of the day, and Sharon didn't relish the idea of having to call Ben to say his wife had snapped at work. After all the Turners had done for her, the least she could do was make sure Jen's descent into madness happened in the privacy of their own home.

As they left the restaurant, she studied Jen's face, her body language. Was she really losing control? Nearing a total breakdown? Sharon had never been good in emergencies, but she wondered whether she ought to call somebody now. Ben or even that gargoyle of a housekeeper, Nancy.

It seemed impossible that someone so strong could fall apart. Jen had the good fortune to be raised by a hard-working, sensible rancher and a mother so formidable and stunningly beautiful she might have descended from an unknown island of warrior women like Wonder Woman. Add a no-nonsense, doting grandmother to the mix, and Jen had a gene pool that almost guaranteed she would have a life that others envied.

Sharon's gene pool was so shallow, her resources so small, it was a miracle she ever got out of small-town Eutaw, Alabama. Her mother, God love her, had done the best she could. But what sort of life can a woman who works at a dry cleaners make for her two daughters if her husband flits from one menial job to the next and drinks up every penny he earns? The only way the poor soul ever got out of her impoverished life in Eutaw was propped on pillows in the backseat of her older daughter Eleanor's car, heading north to a nursing home she could only afford because Eleanor was secretary to the home's director.

After all her mama had sacrificed so Sharon could have a better life, she turned around and married a man just like her daddy. *Try to figure that out.*

Of course, Jen did. Years ago. She had the degree for it. She said women from backgrounds like Sharon's often chose a spouse similar to a broken parent in an attempt to repair a relationship that still haunted them. But Sharon didn't believe life was that complicated. Some people were just born to have bad luck.

After she and Jen drove back to the office and plunged into the afternoon's work, she thought of the first time she'd met Jen's parents. It was on Christmas break from Tulane. She had been bug-eyed at the idea of spending the holidays at the Logan ranch. She'd spent the entire flight asking Jen questions and imagining her parents as some kind of royalty.

Patrick and Delilah Logan had paid for her ticket. And they had exceeded every one of her fantasies. A coat of arms hung on the wall in their entrance hall, the real deal, not some fake you could buy on Amazon and pretend it had been in your family for generations. Jen's coat of arms meant valor or some such exalted term, which seemed perfectly appropriate for a tight-knit family so full of life and possibility.

Beside the coat of arms were all those family portraits, painted in oil. Jen's grandparents and her daddy as a little boy, riding horses that were housed in the stables out back. Delilah Broussard Logan, her portrait so magnificent it made her look like royalty. Sharon wouldn't have been surprised to see the portrait hanging in Buckingham Palace.

Of all Jen's relatives, her mother Delilah was the one who fascinated her most. She was goddess-like. Impressive and intimidating. Wonderful and awful at the same time, and Sharon wanted to be just like her.

Unfortunately, that was the only time she ever got to see Jen's mother. Shortly after that visit, Delilah and Patrick had been killed in a car wreck. Anything else she could learn about Delilah had to come from conversations with Jen. One of the most fascinating things, of course, was Delilah's *gift*.

"Sharon?" Larry was standing beside her desk. She hadn't heard him coming, a sign she should be more vigilant. "I'm heading home. Jen's still in with a patient. Do you need a ride?"

"No. I'll stay and go home with Jen."

"That's a good idea. She's had a hard day."

He didn't know the half of it. With Jackson Markle breathing down her neck, Sharon felt as if she'd been thrust right back into the hellish nightmare of her life. Add the disaster swirling around Jen, and everywhere Sharon looked, there was a Boogie Man.

Her instincts yelled *run and hide*. The problem was, she didn't know a single place that was safe.

EIGHTEEN

JEN'S MEDICAL OFFICE COMPLEX

When Sharon left the building with Jen, dark clouds scudded across the sky, and the slight drop in temperature suggested a chilly spring rain was on its way. Across the street, a figure leaned against the trunk of a massive magnolia tree, hunched into a jacket exactly like the one Jackson Markle had worn to his appointment. Why was Matt's cousin still lurking around the office? He was a powder keg, waiting to explode. He should have been long gone from the premises.

Sharon shivered, then glanced to see if Jen had noticed him.

She was pulling her red suit jacket closer, oblivious to everything except the change in weather. She looked only slightly better than she had at lunch. Sharon didn't know how she had managed to counsel patients all afternoon.

Poor Jen.

"Do you want me to drive?" She would love to know what it felt like to drive a white Mercedes with leather seats that smelled like expensive boots. She might even pretend, for just a moment, that it was hers.

"No, I can do it."

Jen didn't look like she could shoo a squirrel off her lawn, let alone navigate the late afternoon traffic and find her way home. Sharon slid into the passenger side of the car and watched her friend turn on the heat.

She even tapped the climate app on the console that blasted heat through the seats. Sharon got so hot she wondered if her skirt would catch fire.

She turned to study Jen as they drove the short distance home. Her knuckles were white on the wheel, her teeth were clenched, and her hair looked like she had styled it with a mixer. She had removed the combs holding her French twist in place and apparently tried to re-style it before she left the office.

"Jen, as soon as we get home, let's fix a drink, sit by the pool, and relax."

"It's going to rain."

"The pool is indoors."

The look on Jen's face told Sharon that she had forgotten. Sharon understood all too well how unrelenting stress can take a toll, how you feel as if little pieces of yourself are disappearing, how you despair that you will ever find a way out.

Jen needed help as much as Sharon did. That much was evident. What was not obvious was her capacity for endurance. Their history proved she was a courageous woman who would fight for herself, her home, and her family. But for how long?

Sharon owed it to Jen to watch over her. It was a sacred duty of friendship, and she was the perfect friend. If anybody in this world knew how to keep going in the middle of a nightmare, it was her.

As they neared Peake's Point, she noticed a black SUV following too close.

"Jen, we've got a tail."

"What?"

Of course, Jen wouldn't have a clue. She wasn't a TV junkie like Sharon. She had probably never watched a single episode of *S.W.A.T.* or *Law and Order*.

"That black SUV hugging your tailpipe is exactly like the car Matt drives, and the driver looks like him." Of course, Jackson was about the same size and drove the same kind of car. He imitated his cousin with the dedication of the obsessed.

"Oh, no!" Jen stomped on the accelerator. The Mercedes lunged ahead then began to wobble and weave. She clutched the steering wheel like there was no tomorrow.

Sharon reached over and steadied the wheel. "It's okay. Slow down. Matt already knows where you live, and he's too cowardly to follow us through the security gates in broad daylight."

"Sorry." Jen eased off the gas pedal, and the car corrected course. Any car except the heavy Mercedes would have been upside down in the ditch.

"It's okay." Sharon rubbed her friend's shoulder, and patted her arm. "He's just trying to scare us."

"It worked."

"Yes, it did." Sharon glanced back to see the SUV turning in to a gas station. "He's turned off. He's not following us home."

Jen blew out a shaky breath, but she white-knuckled the steering wheel all the way to her ritzy neighborhood. She glanced at the cottage, then tightened her mouth and stormed toward the house.

Nancy met them at the door, her arms crossed over her chest, her mouth drawn into a thin line. She looked like a gargoyle with a big streak of mean. It was a mystery to Sharon why Jen had such a high opinion of this woman.

"I was hoping you would get here sooner." Nancy practically snarled the words. If it were left up to Sharon, she'd fire her. "Marianne walked out on her math lesson, and the tutor stomped out of the house. I was left to deal with it."

Jen looked as if she'd been slapped. "Is Benjamin not home?"

"Not yet. If the last few months are any evidence, he won't be here for another two or three hours. If then."

"Where's Marianne?"

"In her room. *Pouting.* I talked to her about showing disrespect to her math teacher, and she's mad at me." Nancy crossed her arms over her chest. "She said I should be nicer to her because she's still upset over Bella Baby."

"I'll take care of it. But first, tell me why the oleander is still there. I told Dal to cut it."

"Dal says he'll cut it when Mr. Benjamin says so."

Her face fiery red, Jen headed toward the children's wing so fast she left Sharon and Nancy in the foyer with their heads spinning.

Nancy pursed her lips, a move that deepened the lines already there. "I meant to talk to her about her wallet."

Tension sizzled through Sharon. The day's events swirled through her mind, each one more horrible than the one before. She struggled to compartmentalize.

Focus.

"What about her wallet?"

"I found it in the laundry room," Nancy said.

Of course she did. Wasn't she all over this house all the time, acting as if she owned it?

"What a relief." *There, now.* Sharon smiled at Nancy in a way that said *we are such good friends I can keep your secrets.* Years of living with Matt provided a graduate course in hiding her true feelings. "Jen's been searching for it. Was it in one of her pockets?"

"No. It was tucked behind a bottle of bleach. Maybe you can give it to her and tell her you found it on the hall table or something."

"The truth has to come from you. The one thing Jen will never abide is lying. I wouldn't want you to lose your job."

"She wouldn't fire me over that. We've been through *everything* together."

"I'm sure you have." Sharon would never tolerate somebody like this hateful, ugly woman in her house. The fact that she was here just showcased Jen's generous heart.

"Besides all that," Nancy added, "I wouldn't know how to tell her. She hasn't been herself lately. She texted Dal to cut the oleander, but he ran his own nursery for years. He knows more about gardening than Jen ever will."

"She's losing her grip, Nancy, and she needs all of us to help prevent a complete breakdown. That's exactly why you have to tell her the truth. She needs to know she can count on the people around her to be completely honest."

Hadn't Jen always said that to Sharon? *Surround yourself with people you trust.*

NINETEEN
THE TURNER HOUSE

After speaking to Marianne, Jen stormed toward her bedroom in a move so uncharacteristic, she wondered if she had been given something mind-altering. Maybe a drug had been slipped into her food at the restaurant? It could have been anybody, someone in the kitchen, or one of the waitresses. Even one of the patrons passing by as her food tray was delivered.

Jen had been in practice for years. Some of her patients didn't like her, and they had large families who could have taken up a vendetta. Still, the idea that she had enemies who actually sought to *harm* her and her family was foreign. Even her house was beginning to feel like enemy territory.

After years of helping others regain control of their lives, she realized her own was slipping away. No matter how strong you are, or how well your profession prepares you to face problems, nothing can arm you against a bombardment of threats so frightening you feel as if an unknown evil force has seized you and won't let go until you are totally broken—or dead.

Jen was *terrified*. Even worse, she felt helpless. If she knew Invisible's identity, she could fight back. But how do you fight someone you can't see?

She thought of her mother, of the way Delilah could always vanish into her own mind then later explain that she could envision the bayous of her childhood so vividly she could transport herself there.

Everything is so green there, the trees, the water, even the creatures hiding in its cool depths. I find peace there.

Jen tried to find comfort in memories of her childhood, of her mother's musical voice telling of Spanish moss dripping from cypress trees whose roots looked like knees rising out of the green water, of mist that hung over the bayou, lending an air of mystery and romance to a Creole culture slowly vanishing from the land that spawned their legends and color, their stories and songs.

But bits and pieces of Nancy's conversation smashed the wall of her temporary peace, her accusations hammering at Jen as she walked away. *Stressed out. Losing touch. Need help.*

All of it was about her. All of it portrayed her as teetering on the brink of madness.

She'd thrown up her hands and bolted, leaving Nancy and Sharon with their astonished expressions and wrong opinions. Leaving her daughter in her room, still pouting and defensive of her rudeness in walking out on the math tutor. Leaving her son to his own devices, probably in the pool or the workout room. Leaving her husband with his clandestine activities at his office. Or wherever he was.

Jen didn't know anymore. She couldn't be certain of anything, or anybody.

The quiet haven of her bedroom welcomed her, the plush pillows, the weight of the covers as she crawled into bed, the soft light from the overcast sky filtering through her windows, the constant dance of water beyond. She closed her eyes and imagined herself standing at the window of her grandmother's kitchen in Colorado, smelling gingerbread in the oven, and listening to the sound of wind singing through the birch trees. She dreamed of the hayloft at the ranch, the sweet smell of clover hay, the warm breath of horses hoping you'd open the stall door and let them race across lush pastures surrounded by mountains that kept watch over everything in the canyons below.

Her longing for Victoria was visceral. She needed to hear her voice. See the world through her sharp blues eyes that missed nothing.

Suddenly the light came on, and Sharon was standing over her, pulling back the covers.

"Jen? Are you okay?"

"I wish everybody would quit asking me that. I get tired, too, just like an ordinary person."

Sharon sat down on the edge of her bed. "You're in bed with your suit on."

"I'm well aware of that." But she hadn't been. Not really. And that scared her as much as the dead hamster in her house and the misplaced objects. "I took off my shoes."

"Okay, that's fine." Sharon's expression said that she meant the exact opposite.

"I don't need your *permission*." Jen glared at her. "And don't you dare tell me I'm under stress. I know that, too."

Sharon stared at her a while, flummoxed, and then she burst out laughing. "Now, *that's* the Jen I know and love."

Relief washed through her. *See.* She was not losing one bit of herself. Except for a little unexplained dizzy spell—and losing stuff here and there—she was the same strong woman she'd always been. She sat up, plumped the pillows behind her, and tucked her legs up to give her friend more room.

"I always tell my patients to walk away if a situation escalates beyond their comfort level. To stop further engagement. I took my own advice with Nancy. How did she seem after I left?"

"Miffed. And that's putting it mildly. She found your wallet in the laundry room."

"The *laundry* room?" Jen couldn't even remember the last time she was there.

"Yes. I told her to tell you about it, but I'm not sure she will. Do you trust her?"

"I always have. But the things that have happened lately make me wonder. She put the oleander in the bouquets. My necklace was in the kitchen, and now... my wallet in the laundry room. That's her domain. Dal was supposedly in the greenhouse all evening the night of the party. He could have delivered the box with Marianne's butchered hamster."

"But she seems devoted to you and Ben and the children."

"People change. She has complete access to this house, and we've had our disagreements through the years. She might even be the one calling herself Invisible."

"You think she's doing these things out of revenge?"

"I don't know. She could even be taking revenge on her husband's behalf. Dal is so strange and withdrawn, I never know what he's thinking. But I'm not going to accuse her unless I have proof." A massive fatigue overtook her. "Sharon, do you feel like having dinner with Benjamin and the twins this evening? I really need some time alone."

"I'll be glad to. You know I'll do anything for you."

"And stay here again tonight. With Matt lurking around, plus his cousin on the rampage, I'm afraid for you to be alone in the cottage."

"I won't argue with that."

"Good." In spite of Jen's determination to remain strong, she could feel evil pulsing around her, gathering somewhere in the darkness like an electrical storm. "Just one more thing. Can you leave the lights on? I don't want to be in the dark right now."

TWENTY

Jen woke to the sound of laughter drifting up the stairs. She sat up in bed, her head throbbing, the sleeves of her suit jacket restricting her arms. She'd fallen asleep in her suit, the jacket still buttoned and pinching her waist. A quick glance at her watch told her that she had been asleep for two hours, which was unheard of for her. She hated the idea of being considered lazy. Or even worse, *incapacitated*.

Holding her head, she rolled out of bed. The red suit was a favorite of hers, and now it was a mess. *She* was a mess.

In the bathroom, she turned on the water and considered getting in the shower, clothes and all. She could imagine what her husband would say to that. And Sharon. The twins, too.

She stripped and dropped her clothes onto the floor then stepped under the blast of hot water to lather up. Her shampoo and body wash both smelled like magnolias, a scent that always reminded her of Delilah. She sank onto the pull-down shower seat she rarely used, bent over, propped her elbows on her knees, and let the soapy water cascade all over her.

"*Jen!*"

Startled, she jumped up and nearly fell on the slippery tiles.

Benjamin shouted her name again then opened the shower door. He stood in the bathroom on her crumpled clothes. "What on earth are you doing?"

"Taking a shower."

"In your bra and panties?"

She was suddenly and painfully aware of the wet elastic cutting into her waist, the soggy lace straps digging into her shoulders.

"There's nothing wrong with that." Stricken, she knew there was *everything* wrong with *not knowing* you were doing it. Was she losing her mind? "I just didn't feel like taking them off. What are you doing here?"

Quick irritation crossed his face. "For one thing, I *live* here."

"We don't do *snarky* in this house."

"Well, *we* don't usually leave our handbag and our cell phone on the hall table. I had to leave in the middle of dinner to bring them to you."

When she saw the items in his hands, she realized she hadn't even noticed them when he opened the shower door.

"Why didn't you bring them upstairs when you got home?"

"I thought you were coming right down until Sharon informed me you wouldn't be joining your family for dinner. Then I got sidetracked, until your phone started ringing."

Did being sidetracked mean whooping it up at the dinner table without even bothering to check on his wife? The Benjamin of old would have *immediately* checked on the well-being of his entire family the minute he came through the door. He had *always* put her and the children first. Besides all that, he knew she disliked taking phone calls in the evening. It was family time. At least, it had been until she started disintegrating like a carboard box left in the rain.

"Jen," his face gentled. "I don't like for us to be this way."

"I don't either."

He reached toward her then changed his mind. "The call was from Annie. I knew you'd want to know."

He turned and walked out.

Jen's *thank you* died on her lips. The brief fantasy of them in the shower together, making up for his late hours and her recent absent-minded ways, vanished in the steam that fogged up the mirrors.

TWENTY-ONE

Wrapping herself in a bathrobe, Jen hurried into the bedroom. Benjamin had tossed her phone and her handbag onto the nightstand by her side of the bed.

A glance at her watch told her it was two a.m. in Italy. That could mean only one thing. She punched in her sister's number, and Annie answered on the first ring.

"Jen? I had a terrible dream."

"I know you did, that's why I'm calling you back in the middle of the night."

Delilah Broussard had passed the gift of *seeing* to each of her daughters. Prescient dreams to Annie, warning scents without a source coming out of the blue to Rachel, and Mother Nature's creatures gone berserk to Jen. Of the three Logan sisters, only Jen and Annie embraced their gift. Rachel acknowledged hers grudgingly, but mostly she wanted to forget about it and live a normal life, free of knowledge that could drive you crazy if you let it.

"Stay away from the water." Though Annie was thousands of miles away, she transmitted her fear as if she were sitting in Jen's bedroom.

"That's impossible. I'm *surrounded* by it. I'm in my new house in Gulf Breeze. Remember?"

"Of course, I do, but your life is in great danger."

Jen sank to the edge of her bed, both chilled and afraid. Annie was no alarmist. She never shared a dream unless she was certain it was a manifestation of her gift, a foretelling, a warning as clear to her is if their mother had written it in lights across a dark sky. Her dream about their sister Rachel being in danger in the woods had come true in spades.

"What do you see?" Jen asked her.

"There are several dark figures around you. Male and female."

"Who are they?"

"I can't see their faces. But their intentions are clear. I see secrets. Harm. And death. There's blood in the water."

"*Mine?*" Jen shivered. Had all warnings been pointing toward her instead of Sharon?

"I don't know, Jen, but it's connected to you. Tomorrow, I'm booking a flight to America."

"I don't want to take you from your painting. Don't you have another art show coming up soon?"

"Yes, but I've already finished most of the watercolors. I nearly lost Rachel. I'm not about to lose you. I can't sit over here in Assisi like a prima donna. You need family."

Annie not only had prescient dreams, but she also had an uncanny ability to divine what you were thinking. Her gifts coupled with her compassion made her the kind of sister you want in your corner when you're in the ring fighting against an enemy you can't see.

Still, it took years for Annie to build her reputation as a significant watercolorist. Art is a demanding mistress, and its admirers even more so. An artist who quits the scene risks being forgotten. Jen had no intention of being the architect of her sister's professional downfall.

"Don't risk your career, Annie. Stay in Italy. I'll call Gran. She's rattling around the house all by herself with nothing to do except talk to the dog. And he's so old he can't half hear."

"She won't come. You can't pry her away from that ranch."

"I can."

"I'd like to know how. I've been trying for years to get her to spend some time abroad with me."

"After I talk to her, she'll come. If nothing else, then out of curiosity."

Annie's laughter carried the music of bells and the quiet beauty of starlight. "The day Victoria Logan leaves that ranch is the day the earth stands still."

"Get ready for the earth to stand still."

Even after Jen said goodbye to her sister, she could still feel her presence, lingering in the room—the fading melody of a favorite song, the remembered taste of fine wine, the faint echo of a childhood spent in both the shadow and the sunshine of a larger-than-life mother. Jen had been born with an old soul. Though she appeared to be the toughest, most-focused of the three Logan sisters, she had an Achilles heel. Her deep love for her Logan family. Such a strong bond left her vulnerable. Even needy. Especially when life spiraled out of control.

As the oldest of the three girls, she had taken on a motherly role early in their childhood. Delilah was both a doting, loving mother, and a distant phantom, often lost in her own world of dark broodings and deep mystery, borne off both mentally and physically by her unbreakable ties to the Broussard family she kept hidden from her entire family. When she traveled back to the bayous of her childhood, she never took family with her. When she returned, she never spoke of what had happened or who she had seen. Her daughters' only glimpse of her childhood was in Delilah's descriptions of the land—never her family, her friends, or her reasons for leaving it all behind.

Though Jen's sisters were almost grown when their parents

were killed, she continued being their substitute mother. It was more than a role to her, it was imbedded in her DNA, carved into the Jungian jungle of her psyche.

Maybe that's why she and Victoria often clashed. She and her grandmother were unconsciously at war over the matriarchy of the family.

Outside Jen's window thunder rolled and a streak of lightning blazed through the sky, the gloom of the evening turning into a full-fledged thunderstorm. The sound effects were perfect for Jen's own dark mood.

Quickly, she punched in their grandmother's number.

Victoria Logan answered with, "It's about time you called."

"Hello to you, too, Gran. What's going on at the ranch?"

"How long since you noticed? We haven't been a working ranch in so many years I'm growing moss out here. I can't stand to sit still and do nothing."

In her ranching days, Victoria had herded cattle with the best of the cowboys. Even at seventy-five, she was never idle. She stayed active with a circle of friends who were almost her equal on the cantankerous scale. She involved herself in civic life and in the school activities of Rachel and the children, who lived on the ranch with her. Jen couldn't even picture her energetic, feisty grandmother attempting to live a life of leisure.

"That old lady act doesn't fool me, Gran. When is Rachel coming back from her honeymoon?"

"Tomorrow. Out here, spring break is almost over, and she and the kids have to get back into the classroom. I don't know how she and Hank are ever going to enjoy married life with me around all the time, sticking my nose into their business." Sam howled in the background, and Victoria chuckled. "The dog agrees with me. What's going on with you?"

"Sharon's hiding out here from her abusive husband, and everybody around me seems to think I'm losing my mind. But I'm not, and I don't intend to. I'm... I'm great."

"That's not what Annie said. She's driving me crazy. She thinks you're in some kind of danger. She wants me to come running and bail you out. I told her if there was anybody in my family who can take care of herself, it's my only ornery granddaughter."

It felt so good to hear someone who thought of her as competent and dependable, she sat in silence a while, basking in the feeling.

"Jen? You're never at a loss for words. What's wrong?"

"Just some weird things happening around my house. Nothing I can't handle."

"Sounds like you've got some skunks that need cleaning out. That's my specialty. I'm packing my bag and heading your way. I'll be there in three days."

The relief that flooded through Jen astonished her. "You don't have to do that... but if you want to come, I'll send you a plane ticket."

"I'm driving."

"That's *fourteen hundred* miles! You can't possibly drive your old wreck of a pickup that far. And at your age."

"I'm old, not dead. I can drive better than those young whippersnappers on the road who think they own both coasts of the U. S. of A. and everything in between. Hank got his favorite new grandmother-in-law a wedding gift, a brand new Dodge Ram 2500. I aim to drive it, and you might as well not try to stop me."

"I won't. I'm glad you're coming. Call me every day from the road and let me know where you are. Don't exhaust yourself driving long hours, and don't stay in cheap hotels. Pick something nice. And safe. I'll pay for everything... "

Jen paused to marshal her thoughts. "It really is a long way from Manitou Springs to Gulf Breeze. Take as much time as you need. Do some sightseeing along the way. You deserve a little time to yourself without trying to take care of us three girls."

"Jen?"

"Oh, wait a minute... pack for spring in the Deep South. You'll need shorts and tee shirts during the day but winds coming off the water can make it so chilly at night you need a light jacket. Bring a swimsuit, too. I have an indoor pool. And don't forget your cell phone charger."

"Are you finished?"

"I meant every word I said."

"So do I. And here it is. My truck is red. You'll see me coming. Bye."

Of course she would! Who could miss a bright red Dodge Ram with an engine that rattled the windowpanes?

Jen felt the first glimmer of hope since she saw the loggerheads. Having the no-nonsense, indomitable Victoria Logan in her house would be better than consulting any of the best psychologists she knew. Gran didn't tolerate foolishness and weakness. She despised pretty little lies and hunted down deceit with the commitment of a search and rescue dog looking for bodies.

If anybody could get to the bottom of the strange events happening in Jen's new home, it would be Gran.

Moving with renewed vigor and purpose, Jen washed her face, brushed her hair, and pulled on jogging pants and a sweatshirt. Holing up in her room was not her style. She had things to do, secrets to uncover. She had all of Victoria's spirit and intolerance for lies, and at least half of her ability to sniff out the liars.

Starting now.

TWENTY-TWO

As far as Sharon was concerned, she was having the best evening she could remember since she was in college.

This is the way an evening at home should be.

Great company, great house—and best of all, freedom from abuse. Any little thing at all could turn Matt into a battering ram, and her, the target.

In her days at Tulane, she thought the world outside the protected campus was waiting for her to make a mark. She pictured her future as a shining, straight road to success and happiness. While that illusion had shattered long ago, Sharon was finally catching a glimpse of how good life could be. *Her* life.

Forget the rain lashing the windows to the drumbeat of thunder. The water cascading over stone walls and into the indoor pool glowed yellow in lights designed to mimic the sun. With Tommy and Marianne frolicking in the pool, sleek as seals, she and Ben enjoyed an after-dinner drink. Laughter filled the room. Joy. Hope.

Fear, which had been Sharon's constant companion for years, dissolved in the party-like atmosphere. She imagined all this was hers—the smart and lively teenagers, the kind-hearted and successful husband, the house straight from the pages of *Architectural Digest*. Her need for heavy makeup to cover bruises was gone. The lies she used to explain her crutches and her arm slings had vanished.

She pictured herself leading this life. She had talent. Of course she did. Her mother had been musical. And her degree guaranteed a certain level of skill on the keyboard and in the choir. She would be sought after to sit on the symphony board, the community concert association. She would be asked to chair events at the twins' school.

She would be respected. Admired. *Beloved*.

If all *this* were hers.

Unbidden, Sharon's last day in Alabama came to her, as clear as the water in Jen's fancy indoor pool. She was standing in the kitchen making breakfast, sausages sizzling in the skillet, biscuits rising in the oven. She had taken eggs from the refrigerator and broken them into a bowl while the sun poured through the kitchen window, buttery yellow and warm, promising the kind of balmy spring day you can only experience in the Deep South.

The sunshine even held the promise that today might be different. Her husband might get out of bed in a good mood, and she might get through a day unscathed.

"Sharon!" Matt roared into the kitchen, half-dressed, his shirt hanging open over his boxer shorts and two socks in his hands, one navy blue, the other black. He shook the mismatched socks at her. "How many times have I told you to match my socks? Huh? How many?"

"It's dark in the laundry room, and the colors are so close I didn't notice. You never fixed the light fixture out there."

"So it's *my* fault, is it?"

He knocked the bowl from her hand and egg spattered all over the floor. The first blow spun her around, and the second sent her sprawling into the slick mess of eggs. She drew herself into a fetal position, knowing what came next. When he kicked her, she felt lucky. Thanks to his anger over mismatched socks, he wasn't wearing his steel-toed boots. He kicked her again.

"Stop!" She held up her hands. "Please don't do this!"

"You think you can tell *me* what to do? Is that what you're trying to say, Sharon?"

"No, I just mean you'll be sorry."

She meant to add, *you always are,* but she had no breath left for it. He started kicking her again and kept on until he wore himself out.

"Now, get up and clean up this mess. I don't want to see it here when I come home. I'll have breakfast at McDonald's."

Sharon shivered at her memories. When she had straggled into Gulf Breeze like a whipped dog left out in a storm, Jen sat with her all night assuring her that she didn't have to live in defeat, she could heal and put the past behind her, she should envision a better life for herself, and work hard to make it come true.

"The human spirit is tough and resilient, Sharon," her friend had told her. "You are strong. You will do more than survive; you will blossom and shine. Dream big."

Sharon was doing exactly that. Following Jen's wise counsel. Sitting in Jen's amazing pool room, picturing herself in a good life. She felt such a sparkle of satisfaction, it was a wonder she didn't stand out like a Fourth of July celebration with fireworks.

Ben glanced her way. He noticed. *Of course* he did. He was a kind and observant man, always had been.

"Nice evening," he said.

"Very. You deserve more evenings like this, Ben."

"So do you."

He *appreciated* her. Such a stark contrast from Matt. Sharon had kept herself in shape. Didn't all former beauty queens? Still, she *almost* wished she'd let herself age gracefully like Jen. Her friend was comfortable in her own skin, and maybe that's why she had everything a woman could desire, while Sharon was still hoping for some kind of miracle.

Growing up, the only thing Sharon had that couldn't be ripped away were her looks and her personality. They were her ticket out of poverty and a future of drudgery. When she was eighteen, she found a sponsor for the local beauty pageant that led her all the way to being first runner-up to Miss Alabama. With the title came a scholarship to Tulane.

In spite of all Matt did to tear her down, Sharon still had her looks. And she intended to keep them. Maybe Jen was right about the human spirit, but Sharon didn't intend to rely on something she couldn't see. She could see how she looked—and how men looked at her. Including Jen's husband.

Jen deserves more loyalty than that.

If Jen wasn't careful, she was going to lose her good man. He was already straining at the marriage leash in ways that were perfectly obvious to Sharon.

She had already warned Jen once. She'd have to do it again, more vigorously this time. Friends deserved the truth from each other. And Sharon prided herself on being a good friend. A wonderful friend, really. Willing to go the extra mile. To set things right when she got the opportunity.

She glanced at Jen's unhappy and beleaguered partner. *Poor man.* She felt sorry for him, too.

Sharon's hard-knock, bad-luck life had taught her to look for—and seize—every opportunity. It never hurt to butter up the people providing free room and board.

"That's sweet of you to say, Ben. You are so generous to allow me to stay here. Jen, too, of course. That goes without saying."

"Yes. Well...." His slight hesitation was a big clue to her. Uncertainty clung to him as if it were the scent of another woman's perfume. "When everything sorts itself out, Jen and I will have quiet evenings like this again."

"Of *course* you will, Ben."

Like men everywhere who have just told a lie, Ben studied his drink as if it contained the secret to world peace. He didn't believe *anything* would sort itself out. Besides that, he wore the uncomfortable look of the guilty. Just what was he guilty of?

Sharon owed it to Jen to find out. *Just not tonight.* The evening was too perfect to spoil it with accusations.

She and Ben were in a side-by-side chaise longue, designed for two. And what were good friends for if they couldn't offer comfort when it was needed most?

She reached over to pat his hand, and he surprised her by hanging on as if he were sinking at sea and she was the only lifeboat. "I can't tell you how much that means to me, Sharon."

Was that a loaded statement, or what? The big tell was that he still clung to her hand. Sharon was on a highwire, doing a balancing act. Her only hope was that she wouldn't fall.

"Things are going to get better." She hoped she struck just the right note—a woman with the good sense to convert a past romantic attachment to friendship. "I *promise* you that I will do everything I can to help Jen."

"Help me do what?"

"*Jen!*" Sharon leaped up like somebody shot, dropping Ben's hand.

TWENTY-THREE

There Jen stood. Towering in the archway like a goddess. Hair darker than midnight framed a stunning face that was the exact replica of Delilah Broussard in the oil painting that hung in Jen's childhood home. She was fully in command. Invincible.

Even the baggy sweatpants and shirt Jen wore did nothing to diminish the impact she made. She'd piled on those gold bangle bracelets. Power pulsed around her like jagged lightning ripping the night sky. It was moments like this when Jen made Sharon feel like a toad. Inadequate. Undeserving. Feelings she'd fought against her whole life.

"Hey, Jen. I thought you were in for the night." Sharon hopped off the chaise-for-two and sat in a poolside chair nearby. *Of course* she did. The chaise was meant for husband and wife. Designed that way. A symbol. She just thanked her lucky stars Jen wasn't the suspicious type. She could have exploded when she saw how Ben was hanging onto Sharon's hand. And then where would she be?

Without a best friend, that's where.

"We didn't hear you coming," she added.

Had Ben? He looked just as surprised as she was. And not too happy.

The house might look a paradise, but the two living here as husband and wife were not in the middle of a dream. It appeared Jen needed her help in more ways than one.

Jen joined them at the side of the pool, but she didn't sit in the chair Sharon had vacated. She stood over them so they would have to look up to her. It was an old trick Sharon had learned a long time ago. You can't fool a woman who grew up the hard way. She knows every ploy to make herself look more powerful than she is.

She catalogued the shadows under Jen's eyes and the hint of lines around her mouth, evidence of a clenched jaw. Jen wasn't towering, she was teetering on the edge of a breakdown. It showed in her voice when she shouted the twins' names.

"Come out of the pool. You shouldn't be in the water when there's lightning."

Tommy climbed right out, but Marianne remained in the middle of the pool. "Dad let us swim. Why do you have to spoil everything?"

Jen shot her husband the look of wives everywhere who want to make a husband squirm. Sharon saw the way Ben's face turned red, the careful way he set down his glass then glanced from his wife to his daughter. The weighted silence even made Sharon uncomfortable.

Finally, he said, "Marianne, don't talk to your mother that way. She's right. I should have had you and Tommy out of the pool twenty minutes ago."

Marianne made a big to-do of getting out, and then she stomped over to grab her towel off the chair beside Sharon.

Sharon winked at the angry teenager and mouthed *it's okay*, which brought a smile from the kid. *Good.* Sharon knew what it was like to feel helpless. And wronged. A feeling of power surged through her. She would have been a good mother. She still could be if she got the chance.

When, not if.

She was learning from the master—her friend, Jen. *Think positive. Be smart. Be fearless.*

After the twins left, taking the easy laughter and sense of fun with them, the storm outside the windows seemed to have come right into the room. The chill and grayness of the night seeped through Sharon, and she shivered.

Ben shot her a sympathetic look that clearly showed he felt the same sense of despair. His look also said *help me*.

And she knew just how to do that. "Jen, why don't you sit down and relax while I make us all a cup of tea?"

"That sounds wonderful," Jen said, sinking into the chaise beside her husband.

"I'll help," Ben said. "Jen loves chai."

He popped out the chaise, relief written all over his face. *Good.* Sharon had a Ph.D. in the art of reading men, and Jen's husband was providing her with ample opportunity.

"Great." Sharon refrained from smiling and linking arms with him, ordinary things friends do. "Then you can show me how to make it."

Tea had always been Jen's drink of choice. Sharon learned the reason when she visited the ranch so many years ago. Tea was a charming and comforting ritual in Jen's family, passed down from Delilah Broussard, that beautiful magnolia nurtured in a city steeped with the history of both the Spanish and the French and flavored with the rich heritage of the Creole. New Orleans. Aptly dubbed the City of Romance.

When Sharon and Ben came back with the tea, Jen was exactly where they had left her, sitting in her lonely chaise, staring at the storm beyond the window, brooding. Sharon passed the beautiful china cup to her friend. Limoges, a French design. What else would someone of Jen's heritage and wealth have?

"Thanks, Sharon. But I should be taking care of you, not the other way around."

"Nonsense. I'm getting stronger every day, thanks to you."

And Jen was getting weaker. Anybody with common sense could see it. If she kept declining, there would be no going back. It was hard to watch. Really.

The compartment in Sharon's mind reserved for friendship found Jen's downward spiral shocking. The compartment labeled survivor prompted her to brush back her unexpected tears.

No time for that. Much left to do.

Suddenly, Jen set her cup down and glanced at her husband, still standing, looking lost and uncertain.

"Benjamin, where's your cup? Aren't you having tea with us?" Jen aimed her questions at him like darts to a bull's eye.

He actually flinched. Sharon knew that feeling all too well. Jen was going down a dangerous path.

"I have to go back to the office. There's some work I need to finish."

There's nothing that telegraphs feelings as dramatically as the hollow echo of a departing husband's footsteps on the tile floors of a cavernous room with great acoustics. Sharon felt sorry for Jen as she watched Ben all the way out the door. Then she slumped deeper into the lounge designed for two, defeat in every line of her body.

"That went well."

"Don't beat yourself up, Jen. He's tired, the kids are grumpy, and you've had an extremely hard day."

"You're right," Jen said. "Gran's coming."

"*Here?*" Sharon almost dropped her expensive teacup on the tile floor. Victoria Logan was as durable as Pikes Peak that towered over her ranch. And just as formidable. "When?"

"She'll be here in three days. She's driving."

Of course she was. The old woman could drive a Conestoga wagon through an ice-covered mountain pass if she decided to. As much as Sharon admired her, she didn't relish the idea of having Victoria poking around in her business. She was on a good track, thanks to Jen. But how long could she maintain her course with Jen's grandmother nosing around and making her opinion known about every little thing?

Jen and her sisters respected the woman. Admired her. Idolized her, almost. Victoria could change everything.

So could Matt. Sharon had to stay focused. *That's all*.

"That's good news, Jen. I hope your grandmother can help take the pressure off you."

"I can cope with stress, but I need some answers."

"Who can blame you? If you don't mind lending me your car, I'll drive to Ben's office right now and find out what he's up to while you stay with the children."

"You can use my car any time you need to. The keys are always in my purse. But Turner Medical Solutions is a very demanding business. They've been working on a new design for the robots used in surgical procedures. That requires vigilance and Benjamin's full attention."

"If you ask me, *April* is the one requiring his attention." How Sharon wished she could help her friend understand the dangers of another woman on the make!

"Antonia," Jen said. She gulped her tea, something she never did. She was rattled. Also foreign to her nature.

"Whatever. She's like dangling bait in front of a hungry fish. You're just too trusting to see it."

"Benjamin and I don't keep secrets from each other."

Oh, Jen. For someone who knew much about almost everything, she was surprisingly naïve about the man she'd married. Sharon reached for her hand, a comfort for both of them.

"I disagree. He has already been at work more than the

normal eight-hour day. How many hours does it take to check on robots? And who does it this time of night, anyhow? Jen, listen to me. Something fishy is going on with your husband. I wouldn't be saying these things if I were not your best friend."

"I know. And I appreciate your honesty."

Jen took another big swig of tea, a sure sign of turmoil. She was the lady who always sipped, the woman who was so precise and organized about everything, she could walk blindfolded through her house and put her hands on every item she owned. Until bad luck found her.

Join the club, my friend.

TWENTY-FOUR

"I don't want to talk about Benjamin," Jen said. "I want to talk about your sister Eleanor. Have you spoken to her lately?"

Sharon was taken aback by the change of subject. The last thing she wanted to do was dredge up her *other* life.

"Only once, when I first got here. She promised to call me if Matt showed up, and she hasn't. That means he hasn't been to Tupelo since I left, and both Eleanor and Mama are safe."

"It could also mean he scared her so badly, she's afraid to call. He had to find out from somebody where you are, and I think it was your sister. If she told him where you are, she might be able to tell us other things about him, like where he's staying and what he's planning."

Nothing, Sharon sincerely hoped. But then there were her slit tires, and Jackson Markle snooping around.

"Okay, Jen. I'll call her. You're working yourself into a dither." She was *sincerely* worried about Jen's state of mind. "Finish your tea."

Sharon punched in her sister's number and put the cell on speaker.

Eleanor was slow coming to the phone. *And why not?* Her

boss was the director of the nursing home, but the nitty-gritty workings of it all fell to his underpaid, overworked secretary. She always complained about being exhausted at the end of the day.

"Hello. Sharon, is that you?" Eleanor sounded groggy. Or was she just being cautious? Scared? Sharon had warned her that Matt was capable of murder. Had even threatened it before.

"Yes. I'm here with Jen. You're on speaker. How are you and Mama?"

"We're fine. Aunt Cill drove up for a visit, and that perked her up." Priscilla, her mother's sister, still lived in Pine Hill, the tiny south Alabama town where they were born. When Sharon was a child, they visited Aunt Cill often, but she hadn't seen her in years.

"Oh, I'm jealous." Out of the blue, Sharon remembered their little playhouse in the woods in Pine Hill. Memories of the sun filtering through pine needles and oak leaves made her long for a past where an impoverished little girl could sit high in a tree, close to the sky, and dream of something better. "How is she doing?"

"Great. She's always been stronger than Mama, but don't you worry. Mama's health is good, better than when she was in Eutaw, Sharon."

Her sister didn't mean that as an accusation. Of course, she didn't. Eleanor wasn't like that. She was simply blunt that way.

"I'm glad to hear you and Mama are doing well. I wanted to ask, have you seen Matt, or heard anything from him?"

"No... Not directly."

Chills went through Sharon. Was this her worst nightmare coming true? "What do you mean? Has he sent somebody to threaten you and Mama?"

"No. But a friend of his from work called me. Somebody named Billy Rakestraw, I believe. He was looking for Matt, and

I was the other number in his contacts list. He said he called you first, but you didn't answer."

"Of course I didn't answer, Eleanor. My cell's in Eutaw. What did Billy say about Matt?'

"He said he hadn't been at work for a while."

"Is that all? Matt misses work all the time with his drinking binges. His uncle owns the lumber yard where he works, so he knows he won't get fired. I don't know what he did in the week after I left, but he's down here in Florida now. Harassing me so I'll come home and be his punching bag again."

"You be careful, Sharon."

"I will. Jen and her husband are taking good care of me." She ended the call and pocketed her burner phone. "Well, that answered your question."

"Yes, it did." Jen set her tea on the table then rubbed her eyes and leaned her head against the back of her chair. She looked clammy and unnaturally pale.

Sharon jumped out of her chair and put her hand on Jen's forehead. "What's wrong?"

"Another dizzy spell, that's all."

"Lean on me, I'll get you back to bed."

"I don't need to go to bed. It's probably a simple allergic reaction to something I ate or drank. Lately, I haven't been careful."

In spite of her seemingly perfect health, Jen had many allergies that could be triggered by something as simple as blueberries. She never made a big issue of her problem, and in fact, tried very hard to hide it. Of course, Sharon knew. Ben did, too, and probably everybody responsible for taking care of this household.

"You should be taking better care of yourself, Jen. Everybody depends on you. Including me."

"I know." Jen twisted to reach for her tea and almost toppled from her chair.

"I'm helping you upstairs, and I don't want to hear a word of argument."

Jen was unsteady, and taller than Sharon by a good three inches. She was puffing when she finally got Jen tucked into bed.

"Do you want me to help you into your nightgown?"

"No, I'm fine."

But Jen wasn't fine. Any fool could see. Sharon tucked the covers around her then got a damp washcloth from the bathroom and bathed her face. Jen was asleep by the time she leaned down to kiss her on the forehead.

Jen's cell lay on the bedside table. Had she really talked to Victoria Logan, or was that a hopeful fantasy conjured up by a mind rapidly coming unhinged? Everybody in the house deserved to know the truth.

Her phone lit up at Sharon's touch. Jen hadn't locked it. Of course, she hadn't. She was in her own home with only family and her dearest friend nearby.

Sharon began her search. Sure enough, Jen's latest call was to her grandmother, but that still didn't mean the woman was driving to Florida. Further research showed a call with her sister Annie.

"Please tell me she's not coming, too." Sharon muttered under her breath as she continued mining Jen's phone.

Annie, the youngest of the Logan girls, was a force of nature. And just as unpredictable. Sharon had met her only once, on the long-ago trip to Colorado, but she had never forgotten her. Of the three Logan girls, Annie was the one who had inherited Delilah's ability to take your breath away. She had an aura about her, a magical presence, as if being close to her might snatch you up in a spell you could never undo, no matter how hard you tried.

If Annie Logan showed up here, Sharon was leaving. *Period. End of story.* Since Jen was such an unreliable source,

Sharon would have to enlist Ben's help in trying to ensure that the unpredictable artist didn't come here.

There were too many complications in Jen's life already. She needed peace and quiet. Sharon simply wouldn't allow the baby sister to fly in and upset her even more.

Ben was smart. He would take Sharon's side on this.

She nabbed the keys to the Mercedes from Jen's purse. She had much to do, and Jen had given her permission.

"Sleep tight, my friend," she whispered, then tiptoed from the room.

TWENTY-FIVE
TURNER MEDICAL SOLUTIONS

The complex that housed Turner Medical Solutions looked as substantial as the man who had built it—Ben's father, Kane Turner.

Sharon had met him only once, but the impression he made stuck with her even as she parked Jen's expensive car in the shadow of one of the massive live oak trees bordering the parking lot. Big, bold, brash. Self-confidence oozed from him like syrup from sugar cane.

Ben had been just like him, back in those college days when life was good and Sharon was dating one of Tulane's most sought-after young men. *Yes.* She had dated Ben first. It was nothing serious. Just the campus beauty and the wealthy hunk gravitating toward each other as surely as a sunflower seeks the sun.

Ben had taken her to a posh Christmas party at his home, and Sharon had seen a glimpse of what her future might hold. Jen had been at the party, escorted by Ben's best friend. Matt had been there, too. One of the football stars invited because Kane was a huge fan of the sport.

The party changed everything. Sharon gravitated toward

Matt, moth to flame, and Ben had spent most of the evening in the corner talking to Sharon's best friend, Jen.

Shaking herself from her memories, she wiped at her foggy windows while the car idled.

Life is a trickster. Start thinking you've won the jackpot, and it will unveil the ticking timebomb in your hands.

Sharon was finished with timebombs. The survivor in her finally left her abuser and was fixing everything that had gone wrong in her life. *Nobody* was going to stop her.

The storm had passed, but mist still swirled close to the ground. She powered down the car window to get a better look at the two people showcased in a second-floor window of the office building. Ben and Antonia Delgado. That woman was a manhunter. Husband snatcher. Gold-digger.

Sharon didn't care what Jen said about her husband's relationship with his own personal legal eagle. There was the evidence, right before her eyes. The two were standing so close they appeared to be kissing. Were they? With the curtains open and the lights on, Ben knew better than that.

Besides, how could he stand the Delgado woman? She was as fake as the fur coat Sharon had to have in spite of the fact that Alabama rarely got two days in a row cold enough to wear it. In addition, Ben's cute patootie was shorter than Sharon by a good inch and a half. If Antonia let herself go and started putting on weight, she would look like a dumpling.

Sharon wished she'd brought her binoculars, but they were in Eutaw. Of course they were. She couldn't think of everything. After what had happened in that house of horrors she'd called home for twelve years, it's a wonder she had one brain cell to rub against the other. She barely had any grit left. It's a wonder Matt hadn't stomped it out, shouted it out. *Take your pick.*

She shut off the motor and shifted in her seat to get a better view. She should have parked closer. Antonia's and Ben's cars were way on the other side of the huge parking lot. No one would have noticed. Why would they? The two beyond the window were so involved with each other, they wouldn't see a hurricane coming. They were standing too close to be discussing robots. From Sharon's vantage point, Ben was far more interested in his sweet young thing's killer body than work of any kind.

Rage ripped through Sharon with the force of a tornado that sent the residents of Eutaw fleeing to shelters every spring. Was Ben doing all those horrible things to get rid of his wife so he could have the strumpet in his office? No woman should have to put up with that kind of sneaky behavior.

"How dare you do this, Ben!" Sharon was so outraged, she was shouting. "Think of your children!"

They would be devastated if Ben brought in a woman only slightly more than twice her children's age to take Jen's place. Sharon had to do something. For everybody's sake.

She grabbed her phone, punched in his number, and listened to the ring tone.

The two figures jumped apart like they'd been shot. Sharon had a fit of wicked glee as she watched Ben scrambling to find his phone.

Jen would be heartbroken when she heard about this. She might try to act superhuman, but in this case, she would be just like the rest of her kind. Defeat was the nature of spurned women everywhere. And fury.

"Sharon?" Ben sounded harried. "What's wrong?"

Don't get me started.

"*Everything.*" The hitch in Sharon's voice was real. The least little thing triggered memories no woman should have to bear. She proceeded to tell him about Jen's latest dizzy spell. "It's the second today. The first was at the office, and it was just horrible."

Sharon went into detail about the chaos at the office, her

voice rising and falling like the finest symphony, designed to mesmerize. Every musician who follows music notations understands the importance of pitch and rhythm. When she finished her story, Ben groaned, a guilty man, caught red-handed, feeling remorse.

"Why didn't she tell me?" he said.

"You know how she's been lately. But don't worry. I got her back into bed. She's fine now. But she really needs her rest."

"Thanks. I'll sleep in one of the guest rooms tonight, so I won't disturb her."

"I think that would be best." Sharon watched Ben plop into a chair, while Antonia appeared to be gathering her jacket and purse. "I can wait up for you, if you need to talk? Maybe have a cup of hot tea or hot chocolate? Something warm and soothing."

"Tea would be good... Hold on a minute."

"Of course." She felt a gleeful satisfaction that he and Antonia appeared to be saying goodbye. Discreet, this time. No standing close. No linked hands and lingering caresses.

Mission accomplished!

Ben didn't come back on the phone until Antonia walked out the door. *Of course not.* Besotted men did foolish things.

Deep down, she knew Ben was a good man. He just needed Sharon to guide him back onto that path. He and Jen would both be so grateful.

"Sharon, if you have any more of those sleeping pills to spare, I could surely use some."

There. That was better. More like the old Ben she knew.

"Of course I'll share. That's what friends are for."

"Thanks. I have a few things to finish up, but I'll see you in a bit."

"Perfect. I'll be in the kitchen with the kettle hot."

Sharon felt good. Triumphant, really. How many years had it been since she'd felt this good having a conversation with a man? Any man.

See! That's how life should be.

She sat in Jen's luxury car until Ben's secret woman exited the building and drove out of the parking lot. Sharon vibrated with triumph. She never wanted to lose the feeling.

Didn't intend to. *Ever*.

TWENTY-SIX

THE TURNER HOUSE

The next morning, it came as no surprise to anyone that Jen didn't feel like getting out of bed. Certainly not to Sharon, her best friend.

So sad. Jen lying there in her wrinkled sweat suit and pants, her hair a tangled jumble of curls, her hands shaky.

Sharon had been to the cottage early to take care of business, which included putting on a fitted blue suit tailored to emphasize how well she kept her body. She had made sure her hair and makeup were both perfect. A stark contrast to Jen, who looked as if she had just tumbled down a laundry chute. The friend side of Sharon wanted to cry. Instead, the efficient new Sharon she was becoming leaned over Jen and pulled the sheet over the whole mess.

"Don't you worry about a thing. I'm taking care of everything. Ben's getting the children ready for school, and I'll help Larry reschedule all your patients."

"No... I need to be there."

Jen's protest was weaker than Sharon expected. The side of her that always put her best friend first was horrified.

"You need to rest. Nancy's already here, making chicken

soup especially for you. I heard Ben giving her explicit instructions."

Jen flinched at the idea of being cared for. Hadn't Sharon been in her shoes many times?

Poor Sharon. In the hospital again. Recovering from another beating she's trying to pass off as a fall down the steep back steps to her house.

Jen didn't know how lucky she was. She had grown up privileged, she had a great-paying job, and her husband still took care of her, even while he was pulling away from the marriage like a fast tug leaving harbor. And she had Nancy who, in spite of the dowdy woman's sneaky ways, would be at Jen's beck and call to bring homemade soup and hot tea, and every other little thing her heart desired.

Not to mention that Jen had a friend determined to pay her back for years of rescue and rehabilitation. Now, it was Sharon's turn to be the strong one. She hoped Jen was grateful.

It took the kind of courage Delilah Broussard had to bounce back from so many beatings and take charge of a house this size —not to mention a family with children going through their terrible teens. Sharon was really proud of herself. *Delilah* would have been proud.

"Jen, when you're stronger, I have something to tell you."

"I'm under *siege* here. Tell me." Jen's eyes were too bright, even feverish. Sharon reached for her hand and felt her pulse.

"You know when I took your car last night? I *saw* them together."

"Who? For Pete's sake, Sharon, spit it out!"

"Okay then. I think Ben is seeing Antonia Delgado."

"That's impossible! He would *never* cheat on me."

"I saw them canoodling at his office, brazen as you please." Jen looked as pained as if she'd been doused with gasoline and set on fire. It couldn't be helped. The only way to protect her was to tell the truth. Sharon adjusted the covers over her friend, then patted her hand. "I broke them apart with a phone call. He'll think twice before he does that again. Especially with the lights on and the curtains open."

"I just can't believe it! How could I have been so wrong about him?" Jen looked close to tears. "I *hate* being this weak. And *gullible*. How could I have not known?"

"I understand what it feels like. But don't you worry about a thing. I've got your back."

"I can't thank you enough. But with Matt in Gulf Breeze looking for you, you can't carry this burden, too." Jen tried to lift herself off the bed, but a dizzy spell sank her like a wrecked ship. She took a deep breath and wiped the sweat beading her face. "Have you heard anything else from him?"

"No. But I was in the cottage this morning only long enough to grab clean clothes and make a call to Eleanor." Sharon shuddered, thinking of the dark corners. "I was in and out so fast, I didn't even turn on the lights." Except those on her makeup mirror, of course. There was never an excuse for letting your looks go.

"Good for you. Clint is the best at what he does. I don't think Matt will slip through security again."

"I hope not." Sharon shivered, and her last day in Alabama bloomed in her mind—colors, sights, sounds, even the song that was playing, Matt's favorite country western ballad by the iconic Tammy Wynette. "Stand By Your Man." Tammy Wynette was dead—as well as dead wrong—and Sharon was no longer in Alabama. She was never going to listen to that song again. And she certainly was not going to ruin this day thinking about her husband. Sharon shoved her husband into the dark basement of her psyche where he belonged. "Maybe you should let Clint follow Ben. See what he can find out."

"*No!*" Jen's protest was that of a wronged wife in denial.

The intercom crackled.

"Jen?" When Ben called her name, she turned another shade of pale. "Is Sharon still upstairs with you?"

"Yes." The effort of speaking in her normal, authoritative voice made Jen sweat even more. Or was it the knowledge of what he was doing with another woman? "Tell Marianne that if she's rude to her math tutor again this afternoon, we will take away her cell phone."

"Don't worry. I'm taking care of everything." Ben's voice was filled with the tension of a man hiding a big secret, and a husband who despised being bossed around. "The garage just called about Sharon's tire. It looks like the sidewall was punctured by a small, sharp object. Something like an ice pick."

"That's not news to me," Sharon said. "It sounds *exactly* like something Matt would do."

"Benjamin, listen." Jen made a Herculean effort to sit up. Sharon helped by stacking pillows against her back. "This could mean that Maria's tire was also deliberately punctured. But a blowout would make that impossible for a forensic team to discover. The police need to know."

"*No!*" Fear ripped through Sharon—and horrible memories of Matt's abuse and threats. "No cops. *Please!*"

"Maria was seriously injured when she hit the Pensacola Beach sign," Jen told her. "She could have died. If someone tampered with her tires, that makes him a criminal."

"Please don't tell. If Matt finds out we went to the cops, he'll *kill* me! He'll kill us all!"

"Sharon's right." Ben's response tamped down the fear rampaging through her. "I'll think of another way to let the police know without involving her. Agreed?"

Finally, Jen said, "Agreed." But she didn't look too happy about it, even when her husband said he would see her that evening.

Sharon leaned down to adjust the pillows. "Do you want the curtains open before I go?"

Jen nodded *yes,* too tuckered out from a mere conversation to say anything else.

Sharon trotted over to open the curtains, then screeched and fell backward into a chair. Two giant birds were flapping around out there, glaring through the window with eyes that looked pure evil.

"Close the curtains!" Jen yelled. "*Quick!*" She was as pale as her sheets.

Was she having some kind of hallucination? Sharon heaved herself out of the chair and rushed to her side. "What's wrong? What were those horrible creatures?"

"Great blue herons. They won't hurt you."

But if they were harmless, then why was Jen scared out of her mind?

Sharon glanced at her watch. It was hard to be indispensable to a friend who had tumbled off her pedestal, but it was rewarding to be the cog that kept the wheels of her family turning.

"I have to go," she said. The kids had to be at school, Ben had to be at work, and she had to dash back to the cottage because she had left her phone there. She glanced at the curtains. The massive birds were still out there, their shadows floating across the curtains like a horror movie. She was relieved she wasn't the one left in bed to watch. "Are you okay?"

"Yes!" Jen's stinger was on full display. Was she rallying this fast?

Sharon told her to take care of herself and get plenty of rest, then headed downstairs. Mornings were always a busy time in the Turner household, and it was up to her to see that everything went according to plan.

It was only when she got back to her cottage that she figured out blue herons were somehow part of that quirk Jen always called her *gift*. Was there no end to the things she considered mystical and somehow prescient? Jen didn't talk about it much, never had. But Sharon, being a close insider and a true-blue confidante, was one of the few people who knew.

Ben certainly knew. Sharon wondered if Nancy did. And that strange little husband of hers, Dal Park. Pronounced *Pock*. Such a brooding man. Vengeful, too. He'd been so mad when Jen texted him to cut down the oleander that he'd ignored her.

Sharon would have handled Dal differently. Probably better than Jen. She sometimes came across as brash and bossy. Not a good look, in Sharon's book.

When she finally climbed into the car with Ben and the children, she congratulated herself on her ease in stepping into Jen's shoes. Wasn't that what best friends did? She knew she was only playing a role. *Of course*, she did. But it was a role she enjoyed. And she was giving an Oscar-worthy performance.

She leaned against the seat and planned how she and the children would make cookies this evening. Everyone would be so happy. With the possible exception of her dear friend.

Poor Jen.

She looked so helpless. But was it real?

TWENTY-SEVEN

THE DIARY

Invisible was having a good day. Everything was going according to plan, except for one new flea in the ointment.

ELIMINATE THE NEW THREAT

That was the latest entry in the day planner. By defying the rules of society, the new threat was vulnerable to all sorts of attacks. Taking her out would be easier than killing that stupid hamster. And even more fun.

There would be no blood involved. At least, not for now. Nothing was off the table for Invisible. Murder. Almost murder. Accidental death. Faked suicide. The options were all so deliciously appealing. Nothing was sweeter than a win earned the hard way. The more brutal the means, the more satisfying the reward.

And Invisible would be satisfied. Nothing else would do. In the end, Invisible would be completely triumphant, enemies scattered to the four winds. Vanquished. Or annihilated.

There were many exciting ways to do it. As always, Invisible preferred inflicting a slow death. The joy of planning. The suffering was *so* satisfying to watch. Balm to a tortured soul.

Strike out tortured. Invisible was not tortured. Invisible had the power to grant life or death.

Invisible would soon own the world.

TWENTY-EIGHT

ANTONIA'S APARTMENT | DOWNTOWN GULF BREEZE, FLORIDA

Antonia Delgado went running every morning at five, no matter the weather or the season. Physical fitness was almost a religion to her. Now, more than ever before.

She was in love with her boss. She hadn't meant for it to happen, had fought against it for a long time, almost from the moment she was hired. But there was Benjamin Turner, as splendid as any of the men in her large, beloved Sicilian family, and just as imposing. The only difference was the clipped speech of her Newark, New Jersey relatives and Benjamin's soft and appealing drawl.

Antonia let herself back into her apartment. The polished surfaces created a perfect backdrop for the clean, modern lines of her furniture. It was posh by any standards, the envy of all her cousins back home.

"Hello, home. Here I am!"

For the most part, she was happy here. Through the years, she had dated several men hoping to take her mind off Benjamin, mostly young executives with great potential. But none of them had lasted. All of them paled beside Benjamin.

Every day she was in close contact with the man she

wanted. At first, without any hope—or intention—of ever having him. But lately, Jennifer Turner appeared to be sinking into some sort of dark night of the soul. Recently, Antonia had allowed her hopes to grow. She had even talked herself into crossing the line to try and take another woman's husband. Didn't the circumstances justify such a move? Happy marriages failed. Divorce happened. Judging by events of the last few months, the Turners were surely heading to the divorce court.

But that didn't mean the unhappy husband had to remain that way forever. It didn't mean he had to see his future as bleak. Antonia could give him a reason to be optimistic. Happy, even.

The prize could be hers. And didn't she deserve it?

Shucking her sports clothes, she studied her body with a critical eye, looking for any signs that she needed to add more lunges to her workout, lift more weights. Assured that she was still fit—and more than young enough to bear children, hopefully Benjamin's—she headed to the shower.

Yes. She wanted to have children with him. *Yes,* she loved him. But she didn't want his mansion or need the prestige of being with a powerful man in Gulf Breeze society. She was simply a woman in love.

The thing is, would he ever love her back. *Could* he?

The bathroom tiles were cool against her bare feet. She was reaching to turn on the shower when her cell rang. Number unknown.

Antonia's first instinct was to ignore the call. Her second almost panicked her. She had many beloved relatives back home, some of them flighty, the kind who constantly lost car keys and cell phones and even dogs. One cousin was famous in the family for taking his German shepherd to the park for a walk then leaving without him. Fortunately, the dog would grab his own leash in his mouth, trot back home, and slide through the doggie door to wait for Jimmy Delgado to return.

Or it could be her aging Aunt Gloriana, always burning her soup and losing her head scarf. A heart attack, maybe, and Antonia's was the only number she remembered to call.

"Hello," Antonia said, but there was nothing on the other end except the sound of heavy breathing. "Aunt Gloriana, is that you? Are you all right?"

"I'm not your aunt, you flagrant *home-wrecker*!"

The caller was female, her voice vaguely familiar, a sort of husky, rich timbre. Antonia resisted her impulse to end the call. But the attorney in her wanted answers.

"Who is this?" she asked. Obviously, the caller was hiding her identity behind a phone that couldn't be traced.

"Someone who will be your worst enemy if you don't leave Benjamin Turner alone."

"Jen?" The laughter from the other end of the line caused goosebumps on Antonia's arms. She rallied quickly. A family trait. "Whoever you are, you should know that I don't frighten easily, and I don't run scared."

"Big talk from a gold-digger."

Antonia retreated into stubborn silence. She refused to dignify this coward's remark.

"Cat got your tongue, *slut*?"

"Keep talking," Antonia told her anonymous caller. "I'll find out who you are, and I won't rest until I have my revenge."

There was dead silence on the other end of the line. *Good.* No Delgado worthy of the name would retreat from a coward who wouldn't even use her own name. Antonia was more than worthy. She was proud. Fierce. Unbowed and unafraid.

The caller must have Antonia mixed up with the unfortunate Maria Ramos, so obviously after Benjamin she didn't bother to be subtle. Her indiscretion had almost gotten her killed. Benjamin said she was getting out of the hospital today and would soon be back at his house, giving private swim lessons to his son Tommy. The boy was a real sweetheart, lively and personable. Antonia would enjoy being his stepmom.

Someday. Maybe sooner than she had dreamed.

Benjamin had told her, "I'll be glad when Maria is back. The twins are taking Jen's... *problems* hard. They need something in their lives to go back to normal. Even if it's only swim lessons."

Benjamin was a good father, protective, just the kind of man Antonia's family-loving heart desired. He would fit in well with the aunts, uncles, and cousins. Her dad, an engineer who had always wanted to be a gardener, would adore Benjamin, and her mom would outdo herself cooking dishes from old family recipes to fatten him up. She thought everybody needed more flesh on their bones, including Antonia.

"Have another cannoli," she'd say, passing the tray of Sicilian delicacies. "You're nothing but a rack of bones!"

Antonia got nostalgic just thinking about her family. Maybe she would stop at the bakery on the way to the office and pick up a box of pastries, enough for everybody in the office. She and Ben could share a delicacy at morning break. Something cream-filled. Decadent. Suggestive.

Or maybe she would save the pastries for a late-night work session. She had been stretching them out far longer than the problem warranted. Her conscience twinged her, but her practical side said you have to take bold measures to achieve desired results.

She waited for the other person to end the call, and then she showered and dressed in the most provocative suit she owned that she could pass off as office attire. She would never have the kind of looks that turned heads, but she prided herself on staying fit so she could do all the things she loved—play tennis, shoot hoops with the cousins, play shortstop at the spontaneous Delgado family baseball games.

She'd seen the way Benjamin checked her out. The look of pure longing, so much more dangerous to a wife than just lust.

Fired up with a new agenda, Antonia vowed to show everybody a thing or two about being a true Delgado. She was from tough, never-give-up stock. Starting right now, the old rules were out the door.

Nothing was off limits.

TWENTY-NINE

Sunset streamed through Antonia's kitchen window, its beauty erasing her anger at the threatening phone call and camouflaging the forces of evil swirling through the city that would not leave the Turners or anyone who knew them untouched.

She stood barefoot in the colored patch of light unaware of anything except the feeling of success. The pastries she'd carried to the office this morning had worked their magic, clouded her vision, fooled her into thinking her life was normal.

The cowardly phone call had only solidified her determination to win the man of her dreams, no matter who tried to stand in the way.

"You haven't seen anything yet, Benjamin Turner."

Her kitchen was filled with the aroma of fine Italian cooking. She came from a long line of fabulous cooks, many of them renowned chefs and owners of upscale restaurants. She sang as she stirred Italian wedding soup in a pot, did a little jig as she tasted it.

"Perfection!"

Wouldn't Ben be surprised to see her? Shocked, even. It would make a great story to tell at family weddings. Especially, if Antonia achieved her goal and got to invite them to her own wedding.

She ladled soup into a carry-out dish, a beautiful pottery design that fit perfectly into a wire holder. She would leave the dish behind, which would entail another trip to pick it up.

She left the soup cooling on the kitchen counter then went into her bedroom. Her suit from this morning still lay across the bed. *Ah, glorious, sexy suit.* Benjamin had noticed. How could he not? When he told her about Jen's latest malady, home in bed, unable to go to work, Antonia had leaned over him and been rewarded with the rush of color to his face. Embarrassment at his own lust. His flush deepened when she rubbed his shoulders and let her hand briefly caress his cheek.

He'd leaned into the caress. She *knew* he had.

What the man didn't know was that his wife wasn't too sick to make threatening phone calls. Everyone had a dark side, but Jen's was over the top.

What about your dark side?

For a moment, Antonia's conscience gave her pause, but she pushed it aside and selected a yellow strapless sundress with a top that was barely there. Without the office staff to worry about, she could dress for pure seduction and douse herself with the sweetest fragrance she knew. *Gardenia.* She wanted to associate herself in Benjamin's mind with the flowers he loved to tend.

Benjamin tending *her*. Anything worth having was worth fighting for.

Antonia hummed as she climbed into her car and drove to the mansion on Peake's Point. Would Benjamin meet her at the door? He had gone home early this afternoon to check on his wife.

She could hardly wait to see the look on his face. Would he be pleased? Excited?

She rang the bell, then waited, barely breathing. That's what love did to a woman.

Suddenly, it struck her with the shock of cold water dumped into her face that she—the woman who wanted to make a positive impact with her career—had become a walking cliché. She almost turned and left.

But the door was opening... and there stood that wretched woman. Sharon "Miss Alabama" Jones. The scheming beauty who had insinuated herself into the Turners' lives and was living in their guest cottage.

Antonia felt a quick stab of remorse at her uncharitable thoughts. The woman had left an abusive husband. Something no woman should have to endure. Benjamin hadn't shared details, only that she was Jen's best friend, and they had taken her in. She was a good musician, too. Everybody in Antonia's family loved music. If she tried, she might even become friends with this unfortunate woman.

She put a smile on her face. "Hi. I'm..."

"I know who you are. We weren't expecting *you*, April."

Antonia's gracious thoughts vanished, and her hot temper rose. That woman *deliberately* got her name wrong. *Every* time. She battled the urge to pour Italian wedding soup over the smirking woman's head and watch meatballs get tangled in her bleached-blond hair.

"Benjamin told me Jen is sick. I brought soup. It's an old family recipe." The woman still blocked the doorway. Undeterred, Antonia pushed her way inside.

Nobody speaking in that breathy, little-girl voice was going to get the best of her. Was this crazed woman doing a poor imitation of the iconic Marilyn Monroe, or was she naturally foolish? She certainly appeared bright enough to remember Antonia's name.

"Where's Benjamin?" Antonia asked.

She didn't intend to spend all day in the hall with this

bimbo. Or was Sharon putting on an act? Some women were cagey enough to hide their true nature by playing dumb.

"Ben's in his home office." Sharon treated her to another self-confident smirk. "He said he had *lots* of work to do."

"Good. I'm here to help him."

"He said he didn't want to be disturbed unless it's an emergency."

"I *work* with him." Antonia thrust the soup into Sharon's hand. "Take this into the kitchen. I'll find my way back."

Antonia had gone over every inch of the blueprints for this house with Benjamin when he was planning his greenhouse and his gardens. She had a photographic memory and could navigate this house as if she'd been here a million times. Plus, the housewarming party had given her a great opportunity to explore, undetected.

His office was downstairs, on the back of the house overlooking Pensacola Bay, sparkling like a blue jewel shot through with pink and gold by the setting sun. There was even a pod of dolphins playing so close to the shore you could see the light glint off their silvery backs as they leaped through the waves.

Benjamin's office door stood open. A good omen. Framed by the spectacular view, he was the most appealing man Antonia had ever seen, boyishly handsome, the touch of silver in his hair and the laugh lines fanning out from his eyes only adding to his appeal.

He hadn't yet seen her. She composed herself to still her racing pulse and tame the color she knew flamed her cheeks.

"Knock, knock!" she said.

He glanced up at her, and his face bloomed with joy. *See!* Antonia practically floated into the office and around the desk. She leaned over to hug him, felt the tremble in his arms as he hugged her back, exulted when he hung on a little longer than mere friendship would demand.

Triumphant, she swanned to the chair in front of his desk

and crossed her legs so her tight skirt rode up her legs past the point of decency. He noticed, and stared. Then he cleared his throat and glanced at the sunset turning the bay into a watercolor painting.

"What brings you here, Antonia?" He glanced at the open door. Was he thinking of closing it? What would happen if he did?

"I brought soup for Jen. You said she was sick."

"That's kind of you. But I don't think it's a good idea for you to be here. Especially right now. Sharon is here, and Jen's not herself."

"Actually, I came to tell you something about Jen, something I think you need to know."

"Just a minute." Benjamin closed the door then settled behind his desk. "Make this quick, Antonia. So much is happening, I don't want to make things more complicated than they already are."

"I understand." *Poor darling*. Next time, she would have to be more careful. She was no Maria Ramos. And she surely was not that transparent wolf-in-sheep's-clothing she'd sent to the kitchen with soup. "Jen called me."

"When?"

"This morning, before I left for work. There's so much going on at the office, I didn't want to tell you there and get us off track. But it was pretty awful."

"What did she say?"

Antonia told him, verbatim. Not a nasty comment or threat left unsaid.

Disbelief flooded his face, then horror. "Are you *sure* it was Jen?"

"Almost. She never identified herself, and she was calling from an unknown number, but her voice had that same distinctive tone as Jen."

Were those footsteps outside the door? The soft rustlings of someone eavesdropping?

Benjamin heard it, too. He hurried around his desk and pulled Antonia out of her chair. "Thanks for telling me." He drew her in for a quick hug before letting go.

The hug felt impersonal, rushed. When he opened the door, disappointment washed through Antonia. Then resolve. Sharon Jones was rapidly disappearing down the hall. She ducked through a doorway out of sight.

Antonia was relieved to see the last of her. She risked one last look at Benjamin. "I'll see you in the morning," she whispered, and then she hurried out of that house of secrets and intrigue.

When she got into her car, she felt as if she'd run—and won—some kind of marathon. She sat a moment, savoring her victory. Finally, she shook her fist in the direction of everybody holed up behind the walls of that mansion, leading the seemingly perfect life.

She never backed down from a challenge.

Never.

THIRTY
THE TURNER HOUSE

Time blurred. The past and the present merged and played through Jen's head like a movie with a plot half-forgotten. Was she in the library at Tulane, the smell of books everywhere, the silence echoing as she crammed for an exam? Or was she in the attic at the ranch house, going through old trunks with Rachel and Annie, wearing Delilah's sequined and feathered costumes from her days as a jazz singer?

No. The feathers were birds, outside her window. The great blues, haunting her new home in Gulf Breeze as if they had a right to be there, starlight scattered across their wings like sequins.

Trouble is already at your door... already at your door...

Jen covered her ears to shut out the sound of Delilah's warning. She closed her eyes, but it didn't stop the room from spinning, the nausea from threatening to spill over onto the pajamas she was wearing.

She didn't remember putting them on. She didn't even recognize them as belonging to her. And the pants were too short. Were they Sharon's? Jen had vague memories of her friend drifting in and out, a phantom, a beautiful mirage, always kind and thoughtful.

The herons passed by her window again, moonlight turning them silver and laying a bright path across the floor beside Jen's and Benjamin's chairs.

She was in her own bedroom. How long had she been there?

Her memory came in snatches—hot soup, Nancy, cold compresses, Sharon, questions, disjointed words. *Eat this... drink this... let me help you...no, you can't...calm down. Ben, hot tea, oleander, Dal.* Had Dal been in her bedroom?

The birds were still there, their wings covering her with shadows. Jen tried to scoot to the other side of the bed, but she fell backward onto the pillows. Exhausted. Her eyes heavy, her mind foggy.

The hands on the bedside clock pointed to three. The wee, small hours of morning. Like the song. *No. Not a song.* A nightmare. A horror show she couldn't stop watching.

"Jen."

The voice came out of the dark, out of nowhere. Jen was alone in her room. No one sat in the chairs coupled beneath the window. No one hovered over the bed with a steaming bowl of soup. No one appeared from the ensuite holding a cold bath cloth for her aching head.

"Who's there?" Jen's own voice was barely more than a whisper. Squeaky with disuse.

"Jen... Jen... Jen."

The voice was female. Authoritative. Familiar. Jen pressed her hands over her temples, trying to concentrate.

"Who is that?" *There.* That was better. Stronger. Jen clung to her small burst of strength. "Why are you doing this to me? What do you want?"

"Benjamin... Benjamin..."

Jen knew that voice. Female. The bright edge and arrogance of youth. The slight Italian accent.

"Antonia Delgado, what are you doing in my house?"

The whisper came back, less distinct, but more chilling. "I want you gone."

"I have news for you. I'm not going anywhere. I'm dizzy, not dead. Do you understand?"

She waited for the reply, but there was nothing except the eerie silence of a dark room surveilled by prophetic birds.

She shook her fist at the great blues. "You won't beat me. None of you will!"

Jen turned her back to the windows and lifted herself off the pillows. It took Herculean effort, but didn't most things worth having require that kind of work? She sat on the edge of the bed until the room stopped spinning.

Something white on the bedside table caught her eye. She switched on the light and reached for the note.

Tit for Tat...
You can't have it all.
I take what's mine.
No matter who has to be eliminated.
Invisible

Horror sent Jen crashing back onto the bed. She closed her eyes to center herself, but then she began to drift. Suddenly, Jen jerked. Had she dozed off?

Determined to find out what was happening, she rose like a phoenix from the ashes. She pushed forward. *One step. Two.* And then she toppled.

The crash sent Sharon and Benjamin running, their footsteps pounding from opposite directions. They were shouting. Snapping on the overhead lights. And looking stricken.

Both were in their nightclothes. Both stared at her as if she had landed on the floor in an alien spacecraft. Even Nancy barreled into her room in gown and robe. What was she doing here? Had Benjamin asked her to spend the night?

"Jen!" Benjamin knelt beside her and began to feel for broken bones while Nancy raced into the bathroom for a cold cloth to put on her head. "What on earth are you doing?"

"Antonia Delgado is in this house, and I plan to find out why!"

Her husband and Sharon exchanged a look that clearly said they thought she had lost all control of her mind.

"Nobody's here in this house but the family and Sharon and me," Nancy said as she swabbed Jen's face.

Sharon knelt beside Benjamin. "Nancy's right. No one is in this house except us and the children. It's three o'clock in the morning."

"I have eyes, Sharon. I can read a clock. Antonia's *here*. I heard her voice, and she left a note."

"Sweetheart," Benjamin said. "Listen to me. No one else is here."

Her husband was not using the term as an endearment. He was using it to placate. Jen knew the difference, and it made her furious.

"She *is*. The note's right there." She pointed, but the note was gone. What was happening? "I *heard* her." Had she? Doubt began to creep in, bare his ugly face. "She was calling my name. Yours, too, Benjamin. Didn't you hear her?"

"No, sweetheart, I did not. Let's get you back in bed."

"I. Am. Not. Going. Back. To. *Bed*! Help me up and prove to me that Antonia Delgado is not in my house."

"All right," he said. "Don't upset yourself."

"I'm not upset." Suddenly, Jen made another horrible discovery. "Where are my gold bracelets?" They were her only heritage from the mother she never really knew. "Who *took* them?"

"*Nobody*. I moved them for safekeeping." Benjamin retrieved them from a drawer of the bedside table and shot Sharon another of those loaded looks. *My wife is losing it. Help me.*

Jen wanted to slap him, an urge as unfamiliar to her as the overwhelming weakness and confusion that turned her mind and body to rubbish. As the two of them helped her off the floor, she gritted her teeth against the need to jerk away and search the house for herself.

Suddenly, she realized the impossibility of searching the entire house. It would take hours for her to creep along, supported by Sharon and Benjamin. That kind of search would be as foolish as trying to see the entire Metropolitan Museum of Art in New York in an hour.

Besides that, she felt wobbly. She was likely to fall again, taking one or both of them down with her.

"Antonia has to be close," she told them. "She was whispering, and I *heard* her. Why don't we just check the bathroom and see if she's there?" She glanced around her bedroom. "And maybe the closets."

She sounded paranoid. And why not? She was acting like so many of the patients she'd counseled through the years.

Nancy shot her a look of pity. "Why don't I just go and take a look downstairs for you?"

"That's a good idea, Nancy," Sharon told her. "We'll take care of everything here."

Embarrassment washed through Jen that she had three adults trying to take care of her in the middle of the night. As she crept along, supported on both sides, she asked her husband, "How long have I been in bed?"

"It doesn't matter." Why was her husband not telling her the truth? He was treating her like a child. "You were sick, and you needed rest. Victoria should be here tomorrow evening."

Gran! On the road alone, driving, and Jen hadn't even called her.

"Have you talked to her?" she asked.

"No. I tried calling, but you know your grandmother. She didn't answer. She sent a text this morning that said, 'Fit as a fiddle. See you tomorrow whenever I get there.'"

Ever since the sea turtles came ashore with their warning, Jen had seen herself as vulnerable. Weakened by cracks formed when an avalanche of unexplained and awful events descended on her. How many times had she told her patients, "Don't be hard on yourself. Repeated stress takes a toll on everybody."

Antonia was not hiding in Jen's bathroom or her closet. Benjamin and Sharon had not heard voices whispering in the night. Nancy called on the intercom to say there was no one downstairs except the twins, safe in their beds.

After half an hour of searching her bedroom and even the two guest bedrooms where Sharon and Benjamin were sleeping, Jen's longing for her family was so visceral she could almost taste her grandmother's homemade chicken and dumplings, see her wringing the neck of the hen she'd put in the pot.

Victoria Logan was a five-star general—and she was coming tomorrow. Jen could hardly wait. Her life was in such turmoil, she knew only one true thing.

The repeated warnings from nature were real. Someone, somewhere was trying to kill her.

THIRTY-ONE
TURNER MEDICAL SOLUTIONS

Benjamin left the Turner building early for the first time in weeks, if not months. As he drove home, he searched for a tiny shred of optimism, but found very little worth celebrating. He tried whistling to boost his spirits, but the absurdity of it all rendered him tight-lipped and grim-faced. Jen had turned into his biggest problem.

Despite her late-night rally and search for Antonia, she had not been able to go to work again today. Unheard of for his take-charge wife.

Fortunately, Sharon's husband had not been back to their house since the night of the party, and her self-confidence was returning, a glimmer of hope in Benjamin's upside-down life. If they were lucky, Matt wouldn't be back. Probably, all the security around Benjamin's house had scared him off.

Sharon was picking up the children at school so he could concentrate on the monumental problems at work.

Little did she know. Little did anybody know. Especially, his wife.

Still, he and Antonia had used the extra time wisely. They had come up with a plan that might fix everything. Well, almost everything. Benjamin still hadn't figured what he was going to do about a marriage falling apart and a wife he no longer knew. That, alone, was enough to break his heart. The larger-than-life, seemingly invincible woman he'd married was slowly disintegrating.

Even Antonia's sharp legal mind couldn't solve that one. Benjamin felt guilty and disloyal, asking Antonia's advice about Jen. Since all his problems started, he had come to depend on his legal eagle too much. She was like a breath of fresh air, and she occupied far too much of his time. Even worse, she took up far too much of his mind. When he wasn't with her, he was thinking about her.

When all this was over—if it ever was—he needed to seek help. He needed to make changes, both professional and personal. The idea of continuing along his current path made him shudder. He had become weak, needy, vulnerable. He was not the kind of man who fantasized about other women, and certainly not the kind who engaged in clandestine behavior. He was failing the twins. And Jen.

What on earth was he going to do about her?

His wife refused to see a doctor. How like her. Independent to a fault. Even deserving of the label her own grandmother had pinned on her. *Ornery.*

But most troubling was Jen's mental decline. Her forgetfulness, and the denial of things she had obviously done, as well as the accusations.

Ben's better nature mocked him. He was making excuses for himself. But at the moment, he had no energy to change.

As he let himself into the house, he put the dilemma of his wife out of his mind. Laughter came from the kitchen, Sharon and the twins, probably planning some new adventure together. She was good with kids. Should have had some of her own. Probably would have if she hadn't been married to Matt.

It wasn't too late for her to start over. She was still young enough to have children. And she was beautiful, amazingly so. Sharon looked very much like the lovely girl he had dated. Briefly. He reminded himself that Jen had been the only woman for him.

Was she still? It was a question that haunted him.

He hurried upstairs, eager to see his wife. Talk to her. Clear the air. Maybe even share his long-kept secret with her.

He hurried into the spare bedroom that now felt like his. Was he going to let that happen, move all his things in? He didn't know. It had become a haven for him, a place where he could be truly himself. No one there to ask questions. No one to tempt him. No one there to guess he was hiding something.

It felt good to shower and change into clean clothes, a ritual shucking of his problems and becoming a new man. Clean. Honest.

He grabbed his dirty clothes to put in the hamper in the ensuite to the main bedroom. Jen was sitting in her chair by the window. An improvement.

"Hello, you," she said.

"Hello, yourself." He gave her a smile. A genuine one. Maybe things were looking up on the home front. Maybe everything was salvageable. He lifted his hand carrying dirty laundry. "Be right back."

The wicker hamper in the ensuite was temporary. The chute to the laundry room downstairs by the kitchen was one of the handful of small upgrades that had not yet been completed.

Jen's wrinkled jogging pants lay on top of a nearly overflowing hamper. He reached in to tamp her clothes down and make room for his. His fingers encountered something hard. And sharp.

"What in the world?" He felt into the deep pockets of Jen's pants, and his heart almost stopped. He could barely believe what he was seeing, even after he held it in his hand.

Thunderstruck, he went into their bedroom, holding the object in his outstretched hand.

"Do you want to tell me the meaning of this, Jen?"

When she saw the ice pick, she shrank into her chair, her face ashen. "What are you doing with that?"

"I might ask you the same thing. It was in the pocket of your jogging pants."

"It couldn't possibly have been there."

"It was." He resisted the urge to stalk closer, shake the ice pick in her face. How dare she do something like this and then try to hide the evidence in the laundry hamper? "How did it get there? And why?"

"*I* didn't put it there. That much I know." Two red spots bloomed on her cheeks. Guilt?

Benjamin felt gut-punched. What had his life become? He'd only turned his back for a moment. A mere few months. It seemed impossible that a dream could so quickly become ashes.

"You don't believe me." His wife sounded desperate. And why not? She was neglecting her husband, her practice, her children. Doing truly bizarre things. Who knew what she was capable of?

"How can I?"

"I'll bet Nancy put the ice pick in the hamper. She put my necklace in the cereal, my billfold in the laundry room, and lied about seeing me clipping oleander. She probably killed Marianne's hamster, too. She must be mad at me about something."

"How can you say that? She adores you and the children. She's been loyal for years."

"I don't know." Jen raked her wild mass of tangled curls back from her face. Had she even brushed her hair today? "I can't prove Nancy did anything. Maybe... it was Antonia. When she was here last night. Or Dal. He's here all the time, slithering in and out..."

This was over the top for Jen. Unlike anything she'd ever

done or said. The woman he had married always dominated every room. She walked in, and you couldn't take your eyes off her. But her appeal was more than skin deep, more than her striking beauty. Jen had a brilliant mind. She could hold you spellbound in any conversation. She could juggle work and play, home life and civic duty, and make it look easy.

What had happened to his wife? Where had that amazing woman gone?

He studied her closely. Her eyes were too bright, her pupils slightly dilated, and her skin ashen. He should insist she see a doctor.

When?

Benjamin hated that little voice in his head. Without warning, his own problems expanded until he thought his mind might explode. He couldn't sleep. He barely had time to eat. And then there was Antonia, suddenly transformed from his reliable employee to his greatest temptation... if he didn't count Sharon.

He hadn't meant for any of it to happen. Was he giving off signals? Was he in some kind of middle-aged crisis? What was wrong with him? Maybe he had gone crazy, and he was the one leaving notes signed Invisible and doing unspeakable things, like killing his daughter's hamster, and trying to kill Maria.

He didn't possess enough backbone to confess to his wife what was going on at work. That surely wasn't normal. Nor was his ambivalence about *how* he could change the current, wretched course of his life.

"Ben, say *something*!"

How could he hope to have the energy to engage in an argument with Jen that he would surely lose? Maybe Victoria could convince her to get medical help. Maybe *he* needed medical help.

"You think I'm losing my mind, don't you?" she said.

Judging by her actions, what else was he supposed to think?

"Let's not jump to conclusions. These are all good, loyal people you're accusing."

"I'm not accusing. I'm merely suggesting alternatives to your theory that *I* hid the ice pick." She narrowed her eyes at him. "Maybe *you* did it. Maybe you did everything. Hid my billfold, arranged for Nancy or Dal to put oleander all over the house. Took my necklace to make me think I was the one who put it in the cereal box."

When illusions shatter, they make a tiny pop like silver striking the rim of a crystal champagne flute. The shards rain around you, imbed in your heart, and pierce your mind so it's hard to remember the dream you once had and impossible to think of a way to get it all back.

Ben stood among the shards, his intentions evaporating like smoke in a strong wind.

"Jen, if you really thought that was true, you wouldn't still be in this house. Let's just forget all this and try to move forward without any more drama. Okay?"

He left her sitting in her chair while he marched out with only one purpose. To put the ice pick back in the kitchen before anybody else even knew it was missing. Sometimes, the only way you can get through a crisis is to cover it up and pretend it never happened.

Fortunately, Sharon and the children had left the kitchen, and Nancy was in the pantry, humming as she selected food for the company dinner. He slid the ice pick back in the drawer where it belonged. Nobody would ever know it had been missing.

All that would change when Victoria got here. She was an astute woman, far more alert than most women her age.

She would be here this evening. Nobody had a clue exactly when she would arrive. He could see why Jen was so stubborn. She was exactly like her grandmother. If the sharp-eyed matriarch of the Logan family weren't such an independent woman, he would know her arrival time and have his act prepared. Benjamin Turner, successful CEO, great father, and good husband.

Instead, here he was, accused of trying to drive his wife crazy, under attack at work, and teetering on the brink of a breakdown, himself. He thanked his lucky stars he had Antonia and Sharon.

And plenty of sleeping pills, which were his *current* favorite method of escape. Perhaps even his backup plan.

How easy it would be to end it all with a simple overdose.

THIRTY-TWO

THE TURNER HOUSE

Jen knew her grandmother was there before she saw her. The roar of that powerful diesel engine. She stood at her bedroom window watching the driveway for the first sign of Victoria Logan.

There.

Headlights slicing the darkness, the fire-engine red Ram mega cab pickup coming closer by the minute, plowing forward like Hannibal crossing the Alps with his elephants.

Relief washed through Jen. If anybody could get to the bottom of her problems, it was Gran.

She parked by a magnolia tree. The door flung open and the power side running board deployed. Out stepped Victoria in full, authentic western garb, turquoise colored cowboy boots and all. She settled her well-worn Stetson back on her head, spotted Jen at the upstairs window, and pumped her fist. Then she strode toward the house like a woman twenty years younger.

The troops had arrived.

Jen punched the intercom button. "Benjamin, Gran is here! Send Sharon up to help me dress for dinner."

"I don't think that's a good idea. You're still weak."

"I'm coming down for dinner whether you like it or not, with or without Sharon's help."

"Okay, okay. Don't get upset. I'll send Sharon. She can bring you some tea to calm your nerves."

"Fine."

Why bother protesting that she didn't need her nerves calmed? Nobody believed anything Jen said. Not anymore.

She made her way to the closet, hanging onto the furniture as she went. She would wear her red caftan, her gold bracelets. A statement. *I'm back.* It was easy to get into. She would put it on herself if she weren't afraid of teetering off-balance and falling.

But where was Sharon? Holding her caftan in one hand and stretching the other out for balance, Jen made her way to her bedroom door. Voices drifted up the stairs. Gran and Sharon.

"Ben had to take a call from work, and Jen is upstairs. I was just going up there to take her tea and help her dress."

"Help her dress?" Victoria bellowed. "*Poppycock*! My granddaughter is strong as an ox."

"I'm afraid she's not. If you'll wait down here, I'll go up and help her."

"I'll go upstairs and see for myself."

"Well... great," Sharon said. "Here, take the tea."

"You can drink it yourself. Tea my hind *foot*." Victoria's boots sounded like war drums as she clattered up the stairs, grumbling every step of the way. "Jen! This house is big enough for everybody in the state of Colorado. Where are you?"

"In here, Gran."

When her grandmother topped the stairs, Jen almost cried. She loved every wrinkle in her face, the faded blue eyes, the stubborn set of her mouth, the cropped gray hair sticking up all over her head where she had removed her cowboy hat.

"You look like *death*. What have they done to you?" Gran

sailed her hat onto the bed then swept forward and wrapped Jen into a tight hug that was almost her undoing.

You never know how much you need someone until you're drowning and they pluck you out of the deep water.

"Oh, Gran! I'm *so* glad you're here." Jen had to work extra hard to control the quaver in her voice.

"I'm glad to see you, too."

Victoria, the woman who had held a ranch and her whole family together after the death of her husband, her son, and her daughter-in-law, clung to Jen longer than she normally would. She'd always considered her oldest granddaughter to be the strongest.

Finally, she leaned back to study her with those piercing eyes that never missed a trick.

"The world must be coming to an end. You barely tolerate my bossy ways, and I ignore yours. What's all this nonsense about you needing help to dress yourself?"

"The short version is everybody thinks I'm losing my mind, and everything I eat is making me sick."

Gran shut the door and led her to the chairs by the window. "First off, I will take over the cooking."

"Nancy won't like it." Jen was grateful to settle into the plush chair and lean her head back.

"She can get over herself." Victoria surveyed the room, taking in its large scale and grand view, noting the king-sized bed. "How come only one side of the bed has been slept in?"

"Since all this trouble started, Benjamin is using one of the guest bedrooms."

"So that's the way it is with you two?"

"It's only temporary... I think."

"I'm sleeping in here with you."

"We have plenty of bedrooms. Nancy prepared one for you on the first floor, so you won't have to climb the stairs."

Her sister Rachel had long ago converted the playroom

downstairs at the ranch house into a bedroom so Victoria wouldn't have to climb stairs. Years always took a toll, no matter how young her grandmother looked and acted.

"I've got two good legs!" Victoria's protest said she would brook no argument. "And I'm not leaving your side. That bed is big enough for two elephants with room left over for a hippopotamus."

"You snore." It felt good to argue with Gran. *Great,* even. Normal.

"And you need help. Starting with the bed. If I'd had a bed like that, Finn never would have found me in the acre of sheets. Your father never would have been born, and then there would no ornery granddaughter who needed rescuing."

"My bed is the least of my worries."

"I know that, hon." Victoria studied Jen once more. "Let me catch my breath a minute, and then we'll go downstairs and start straightening out this mess you're in."

Gran leaned her head against the back of the chair. In repose, she showed the fatigue and stress of a fourteen-hundred-mile drive. Jen found it remarkable that she could even do it.

"Why don't you just rest this evening, Gran? I'll have Nancy bring our dinner up here. We don't have to go downstairs."

"We do. I want to eat with my great-grandkids."

Guilt slashed Jen. The twins were at that dangerous age, still children but harboring the belief that being thirteen gave them the right to independence and rebellion. They needed her firm hand and level head, especially since Benjamin had become an absentee father. What would her children have done without Sharon to take up the slack? For that matter, what would she have done without her friend?

"I've neglected them recently. I'm an awful mother."

"You are no such thing. Everybody needs help once in a while."

"I'm the one who *provides* help." Her weakness threatened to swamp her. "I *hate* this."

"It's going to be okay, Jen. I'm here now."

She felt ten years old again, and comforted by the tough-minded woman who could take care of everything, even a cougar that came down the mountain to threaten three little girls playing in the backyard. One well-placed blast of the shotgun Victoria called Old Betsy had sent the ghost cat racing back up the mountain.

"Thank you, Gran. For everything."

"*Pshaw*." Victoria waved her gratitude aside as if losing her son and daughter-in-law then raising three lively and fiercely independent granddaughters had been nothing more complicated than folding laundry. She studied Jen for a long time. "How long has it been since you've seen your doctor?"

"I had my annual exam last month. He said I was in tip-top condition. There's absolutely no reason I can think of to be dizzy and so weak."

"That's what I thought. Who do you think is doing this to you?"

Hearing her grandmother confirm what Jen had believed all along was better than any medicine she could imagine. Renewed confidence pulsed through her. Strength. Determination.

"It could be anybody... a disgruntled former patient like Matt's cousin or an angry family member of the ones I failed. Then there's Matt himself, Sharon's husband. He's in Gulf Breeze, on the rampage. But the most likely candidate is someone with easy access to this house. Nancy or her husband Dal. Benjamin's legal assistant Antonia comes and goes at all hours. I even suspect Benjamin."

"I always liked that man."

"I did, too." Did she still love her husband? She felt her grandmother's scrutiny and shrugged. Victoria was wondering the same thing. Jen knew her well. "I'm losing my ability to be decisive. And I'm afraid I'm even losing him."

"You've lost nothing you can't get back. That's what the enemy wants you to think, Jen."

"That's just the thing. I don't know the identity of my enemy."

"Could it be Sharon?"

"Absolutely *not*. I'm surprised you even asked that. We've been best friends almost forever, and she's taking care of me like a sister."

"I know, and I *like* her, always have. But people change..."

"You're playing devil's advocate, Gran. I know how cagey you are. You don't fool me for a minute."

"We'll find out the truth soon enough. I didn't make this long trip for nothing." Victoria heaved herself out of the chair. "Let's get ourselves presentable then go downstairs and show this bunch a thing or two. Nobody gets the best of a Logan."

THIRTY-THREE
THE DIARY

There was a complication in the plan, and Invisible hadn't decided how to handle it. But one thing was certain—complications had to be dealt with.

A push down the staircase would do. Simple and easy.

But wait, someone could be watching. *No, no.* That wouldn't work.

Pills would do the trick, but there was always trace evidence of an overdose.

Invisible's preferred method would be a hammer. A blow to the head like Invisible had done with the hamster would be satisfying and extremely effective. But the new complication was fierce. What if she fought back?

No. There had to be another way.

For once, Invisible had the luxury to sit and think without the risk of anybody seeing the diary. Nobody could know its secrets. Invisible's master plan depended on the element of surprise.

A brilliant thought occurred. Not unusual for a genius. Invisible knew exactly how to take care of the problem.

Pen flew over paper, and a new notation appeared in the day planner.

GET RID OF THE OLD LADY

THIRTY-FOUR

Sharon could hardly believe her eyes.

Even though Jen was pale, she looked like the queen of a small country. Sitting under the chandelier at the shining mahogany table for twelve in her dining room, she appeared to be wearing a crown. Or a halo, *for Pete's sake*. She wore her red caftan—what else—and the gold bangle bracelets she was never without. How could this be the same woman who couldn't get out of bed for nearly a week? That kind of determination was remarkable.

Marianne squealed with excitement to see her mother, and Tommy, who wore his heart on his sleeve, yelled, "Mom!" and jumped out of his chair to hug her. Even Ben perked up with his wife at the table.

This is how a real family should look.

"Sharon," Jen said. "I can't thank you enough for taking care of my family while I was sick."

She acted as if her problems were all past tense. As if Victoria Logan was some kind of magic pill that had cured her on the spot. Sharon knew better. Her best friend self easily saw beneath Jen's façade.

"That's what friends are for, Jen. I will *always* be here for you, looking out for you."

Ben gave Sharon a gracious nod and a big smile of gratitude, but she couldn't say the same for Jen's grandmother. She treated Sharon to an unwavering scrutiny that made her uncomfortable. The old lady was one tough bird. Skeptical. Unwilling to make any concessions until she figured things out for herself.

Sharon admired her. She had from the first moment she'd met her. The years hadn't changed Victoria much. She'd never been a beauty, but she had the same imposing presence of the mountains that had always been her home. The same quality of permanence, endurance. Majesty, even.

It wouldn't do to make an enemy of her.

"Mrs. Logan, I'm so glad you're here." She beamed a look in the old lady's direction that was grateful and sincere but stopped just short of being a beauty queen smile.

"Please, call me Victoria."

"Great, *Victoria*. I'm going to do everything I can to help you take care of Jen and her family. If you need anything, just let me know."

The old lady pursed her lips, as if she had to think about it. Sharon tamped down her irritation. She had come a long way from that beat-up woman who escaped from Alabama. It wouldn't do to ruin everything now.

"That's a nice offer, but I aim to take care of my granddaughter myself. I may be old, but I'm not ready to be put out to pasture yet." The twins giggled, and Victoria winked at them. "Isn't that right?"

"Right on, Gran." Tommy, sitting on Victoria's left, gave her a high five. "You're like Rooster Cogburn in the movie *True Grit*."

"But without the alcohol." She winked at her great-grandson again.

"Yeah, but you sure can ride a horse!" Tommy turned to his dad. "Can I have a horse?"

"Son, let's get through the rest of the year on the swim team before we start talking about a horse. Your swim teacher will be back on Monday."

So, the lusty teacher had called Ben. Of course she had.

Tommy groaned, and Jen said, "So soon? That's great news."

Sharon didn't know what was so great about this perfect house suddenly being overrun with people. She wouldn't have a minute to grab a peaceful cup of tea with Jen. And forget about those fun times with the twins, making cookies in the kitchen, and seeing Ben smile when he followed the scent of cinnamon and vanilla.

Conversation swirled around Sharon, normal dinner-table topics that families talk about, and she was suddenly transported back to her last day in Alabama.

She had planned the meal so carefully…

THIRTY-FIVE

SHARON'S HOUSE | EUTAW, ALABAMA

Weeks earlier

Sharon got up off the egg-smeared floor and tested herself. She hurt everywhere, but no bones appeared to be broken. She shot a furtive glance through the kitchen door in the direction of their bedroom as if Matt might reappear any minute to finish the beating he couldn't complete without his steel-toed boots.

She could hear his electric razor, the closet door banging open then shut as he grabbed his work clothes. He whistled as he dressed.

Whistled. As if beating his wife was something to celebrate.

She grabbed paper towels to wipe up most of the eggs, then filled a bucket with soapy water to mop up the rest. She cringed when he headed back to the kitchen, didn't dare look him in the eye, shivered at the idea that he had come back to finish what he started.

He stood in the doorway so long she wanted to scream. She could *feel* him towering there, a malevolent presence, a rattlesnake poised to strike at the least provocation.

Mop. Mop. Scrub. Scrub.

Sharon never looked up. Finally, he turned and walked out. She didn't catch a normal breath until she heard the front door slam. Then she didn't allow herself to sink into a straight-backed chair until the sound of his truck engine was nothing but a faint echo, going on down the road. Away from her.

Good riddance.

Sharon sat in her chair, listless. *What next?* How long could she repeat this same old pattern?

She got her cell phone and called the only person she trusted, the one who would know.

Jen answered on the first ring. She always did when she saw Sharon's number.

"Sharon, what's wrong?"

Sharon burst into tears. When had her name become synonymous with trouble? She spilled the morning's events between sobs.

"Listen to me," Jen said. "You have to get away. I'm going to give you the name of the nearest shelter for battered women. They will protect you. They know how."

Sharon had considered and rejected that idea dozens of times. Matt would find her and make her pay. No doubt about it. Silent, she clung to the phone, her lifeline to Jen.

"Sharon, are you hearing me? You can't keep enduring this. You're going to die or end up crippled for life. The abuse *has* to end."

"I know. But a shelter is out of the question..."

"You can't continue on this path. You *have* to do *something*."

She couldn't muster the energy to get out of her chair. Doing anything seemed as impossible to her as jumping over the moon.

"Sharon, are you there?"

"I'm... here."

"Come and stay with me. Drive directly to my office in Gulf Breeze." Jen laid out the ruse of Sharon pretending to care for her ailing mother at Eleanor's house. It was a logical plan, typical of the most logical woman she knew. "This will give us time to think of a permanent solution, one that works for you, okay?"

It might work. Sharon grabbed the slender thread of hope with the desperation of a woman in the midst of a storm, teetering on a broken bridge above an angry river filled with hungry alligators.

"Okay, Jen. I'll do it."

"Good for you. We'll make this work."

Of course Jen would. Her plan was perfect.

Almost.

Sharon had only a few hours to get ready for her escape. Matt would come home with flowers, probably daisies because they were cheaper than roses, and he had spent all his money on whiskey. Or gambling. Depending on how low he was on cash, he might just come home with a king-sized candy bar, Hershey's chocolate, her favorite.

He would be full of apologies and empty promises. She would serve his favorite supper—fried chicken and homemade biscuits—and pretend to believe him. They would live under the new truce for a few days, long enough for her bruises to fade, before he would explode and cover her with fresh ones. It struck her with awful clarity that the only thing she knew of love was pain.

He might kill her next time. She had been broken so many times, it wouldn't take much to finish her off.

"Not this time, mister," she muttered to herself.

Energized, she walked through her house, telling it goodbye. Then she went into the bedroom she shared with the monster to pack her bags.

The song "What a Difference a Day Makes" came to her mind. A day. A week. Twelve years.

On her wedding day, she thought she had hit the jackpot. Matt was not only a handsome athlete, well-known, but almost famous from the records he had set in college football. Even better, he was as eager to get her out of Eutaw as she was to leave.

Though the small Alabama town seemed as dry and dusty as the woods and sloping hills that held it a prisoner of loblolly pines and red clay, two rivers flowed beyond the city's boundaries—the Tombigbee and the Black Warrior. When she and Matt found the small cottage hidden among cypress and blackjack oaks on the outskirts of town, they were ecstatic. It was only fifteen minutes from town, but it appeared as remote as the wilds of Alaska.

For Sharon, the one downside of the house was the Tombigbee River, flowing right past her back door. But Matt, an avid fisherman, said the river made the house perfect. Not only did it have access to a public boat dock nearby, but it had a private dock in the backwaters of the river.

Sharon was surprised at how much she enjoyed sitting on her back deck reading and catching a cool breeze off the water. Breezes were hard to come by in the smothering, sticky heat of the Deep South. She never learned to fish—she couldn't abide the thought. But in the halcyon days of their marriage, Matt taught her to swim.

"You can't live by the water and be afraid of it," he said. "Come on, baby. You're going to love it."

Sharon had never learned to love it. Never would. But she and the river were now on friendly terms. They understood each other.

As she packed her suitcase, she glanced at the main channel of the river outside her window. The water looked beautiful in the sunlight. Peaceful. Inviting. Wasn't that always the way of life? If you only look at the surface, you will never know what lies beneath.

Sharon had made an art of presenting a beautiful façade. This evening, when Matt came home, she would play that role to the hilt.

He would never guess that she was leaving and never coming back...

THIRTY-SIX

THE TURNER HOUSE

Present

"Sharon. Are you all right? You've barely touched your dinner."

Jen's voice brought her back from the horrible life she once had to the present where light from the chandelier turned the dining room into a fairy-tale setting, and the night beyond the window turned the bay into an endless sea of darkness.

How like Jen to rise up from a sickbed and start taking care of others. The best and dearest friend side of Sharon applauded her strength and tenacity. Her victim side worried that all was not as it seemed.

"I was just thinking about Matt," she said, "and I lost my appetite."

"Who wouldn't?" Victoria all but bellowed. "That man is a *snake*. I'd like to shake some sense into him..."

"He's dangerous," Sharon told her. "You should be careful while you're here, Victoria. How long are you staying?" That sounded too blunt. The public Sharon was embarrassed.

"Long enough to straighten everybody out." The old lady's

eyes twinkled, but she didn't fool Sharon. Victoria's steel backbone was on full display.

"That's *great*." Sharon knew how to play this game. She was an expert. Really. "We're all happy to see you. Especially the twins." She shot a conspiratorial look toward Jen's son, the talkative one. "Isn't that right, Tommy?"

"Yep. Maybe she can convince Mom and Dad to buy me a horse? I bet you could even teach me to ride, huh, Gran?"

"Son, we will not involve your grandmother in the horse discussion." Ben was firm, but kind. His hallmark traits. So different from Matt. Sharon smiled her approval at him, and he smiled back. He was on her side all the way. Being validated felt so good, Sharon ate a fried chicken wing.

Nancy had done a wonderful job cooking, but she couldn't cook half as well as Sharon. The fried chicken she had served for her last meal in Eutaw mellowed Matt so much he acted normal. *Almost.*

Victoria's voice pulled her back from her memories.

"Tommy, I can still sit a horse with the best of them. Come to the ranch this summer for a long visit, and we'll ride the best horses in Colorado. Your new uncle, Hank, bought back some of the ranch land we had to sell, and before the wedding he bought Rachel and the kids the finest Appaloosa you'll ever see."

It was obvious that nobody told Victoria what she could and could not do. Not even Ben. The friend of the family side of Sharon admired her spunk. Even wanted to emulate it.

But the victim was wary. She covered her fear by nibbling on a biscuit. Not homemade. Not even close. You'd think Nancy would learn to make biscuits, or that Jen would demand it. After all, this was the Deep South. Synonymous with great biscuits and gravy.

"I was thinking we could all go to the beach tomorrow?" Jen said.

Her suggestion came out of the blue. Jen was trying too

hard to make things as normal as possible for her kids in the midst of chaos. She barely looked strong enough to sit at the table, let alone play on the beach. Sharon was so shocked she lost her appetite for biscuits.

Ben's face was a map of concern and something else. Dismay? Panic? "Are you up to that, sweetheart?"

"I certainly am." Jen glared at her husband, daring him to defy her. "The weather is supposed to be beautiful. Gran can relax after that brutal drive, and it will do us all good to get some sunshine and romp around in the sand. We can pack a picnic and act like any other normal family on a weekend outing."

What a dig. Ben's face flushed, and Jen's jaw clenched. Sharon would certainly have handled that differently.

She always used finesse with Matt. It was the only way to coax him into an occasional good mood. That and fried chicken. A picnic suited him even better. Sharon's last meal with him had been a picnic.

"I think I'll stay here," Sharon said. Ben noticed how she supported him. Of course he did. "It will give me a chance to practice the piano. I used to play every day."

"I wouldn't hear of going off and leaving you alone!" Jen was stubborn that way. "I forgot you don't enjoy the water. We can go somewhere else, maybe into Pensacola to tour the Blue Angels Museum on the Naval base, or over near the Flora-Bama line to play miniature golf?"

"I want to go to the *beach*." Marianne shot her mother a defiant look then turned to Sharon. "Please come, Aunt Sharon. Please, please, *please*."

Jen's dismay showed. In her absence, her daughter had bestowed on Sharon the next best title to mother. Naturally, Jen was shocked. But the title made Sharon feel needed. Important. Even necessary. Emotions that had been denied her for years.

"You've talked me into going, Marianne. I think the

sunshine will do us all some good. You can ride in my car and make sure I take the right road."

"Deal!" Marianne leaned across the table and gave her a high five.

Excitement circulated around the table, and everybody started talking at once, making plans for special treats and favorite beach towels, beach chairs and a portable beach tent. Victoria said her cowboy hat would be all the sun shield she needed.

Tommy glanced at his dad. "Can you set up the volleyball net on the beach?"

Before Ben could answer, his cell phone rang. He glanced at the screen, and his entire attitude changed.

"I have to take this," he said, then hurried from the table.

Jen turned to watch him leave. "He never takes phone calls during dinner."

That's exactly what Sharon thought. The silence following Ben's departure was explosive. Nobody said anything. Nobody even pretended to eat.

Just before the tension became unbearable, Ben came back to the table. Well, *slinked back* would be a better description.

"That was the office. I'm afraid I have to work tomorrow."

"The *office?*" Jen's face flushed with anger and her voice dripped with disbelief and betrayal. "Did you say the *office?* Don't you mean *Antonia?*"

Jen was losing it. Everybody noticed, especially Ben. He reminded Sharon of a pot, slowly boiling over. The friend side of her had tried to help Jen with her marriage, but it was too late now. Far, far too late.

The survivor in her pushed back her plate. "I'm sure Ben will join us at the beach when he can." He looked as if he'd been reprieved from the gallows. "If you'll excuse me, I'll head to the cottage and dig out my swimsuit and suntan lotion for tomorrow."

"With Matt still hanging around, you shouldn't be in the dark alone, Sharon," Ben said. "I'll go with you."

Her ploy worked. Of course it did. Ben felt rescued, and everybody at the table could breathe again.

See all the good things I do for Jen.

"I'm fine, Ben. Stay with your family."

"Go with her, Benjamin." That was Jen for you. Always the caretaker, even when she was obviously still seething. "Sharon, it will be chilly at the beach. If you don't have a windbreaker, you can borrow one of mine. And don't you even think about staying in the cottage tonight. I want you under this roof until that man quits stalking you and slinks back home where he belongs."

That's how easy it was to head out the door with Ben. Sharon would make one more attempt to talk some sense into Jen about the dangers of bossing her husband around and sending him off with another woman. Jen was just lucky the other woman had her best interests at heart. *Always*.

Sharon left the table with Ben following. He didn't take her arm until they were outside and around the corner of the house. His grandmother-in-law had watched him like a hawk all evening.

Sharon wouldn't put it past Victoria to still be standing at the kitchen window, staring.

THIRTY-SEVEN

THE COTTAGE | GULF BREEZE, FLORIDA

As Sharon headed to the cottage with Ben, she was glad to escape Victoria's scrutiny. The old woman was far more inquisitive and cantankerous than she remembered. And far more likely to come gunning for *anybody* she perceived as a threat to Jen.

The night was one of those picture-perfect evenings. The sky was lit by starlight, the water lapping softly at the shore. The moon painting a silver path over the bay. Even the few blooms left on the butchered oleander glowed in the dark. Tropical. Mysterious.

Still... none of it made Jen's war-hawk of a grandmother any less intimidating.

Sharon inched closer to Ben, as if he offered protection from his own grandmother-in-law. He didn't let go of her arm until they reached the cottage door.

"Thanks for the escort, Ben. I'll be okay now."

"I'm coming inside to make sure Matt's not lurking behind the doors."

A horrible thought. Would the mention of his name always make her cringe?

Except for the two of them turning on lights as they walked from room to room, the cottage was empty. Ben wanted to stay and escort her back, but Sharon finally convinced him that the security guards were on the job, and Matt hadn't tried to sneak onto the property in days.

She had to have a minute to herself. She needed to process the turn of events—Victoria's arrival, Jen's remarkable recovery, the imminent return of the sexy swim coach, and even the new aggressiveness of Ben's legal assistant. That ploy with the soup, and now this bogus work on Saturday. Who did that Antonia creature think she was fooling? She was worse than Maria Ramos. More subtle. Smarter. And both of them were trying to take Jen's husband.

How was Sharon possibly going to take care of her friend with a whole menagerie hovering nearby? Still, hadn't she handled worse?

Sharon dug out her swimsuit and coverup, found a favorite rosy lipstick she'd left on the dressing table, a smaller purse and a big tote. She was very fond of purses and totes, and had brought four from Eutaw, purchased secretly over the course of two years with cash siphoned from the food budget. Not designer bags like Jen had, but knockoffs good enough to fool most anybody. Who knew when she would get to go back to Alabama to collect the rest of her belongings?

Thinking of Alabama brought back an avalanche of memories so horrifying, she had to sit down a minute, just to catch her breath. She had known running away would be complicated, but she never imagined anything like *this*.

Shortly, her cell phone beeped. An incoming message. From Matt. Of course it was.

But *wait*. How did he get the number to her burner phone?

Never mind. The message was already there. It leaped out at her, as scary as if Matt himself had walked through the door with his fists already balled.

Don't think you can win, Sharon. You WILL come home, even if I have to haul you back from that over-the-top house by the hair of your head. NOBODY can stop me. Certainly not that wimp Benjamin and his overbearing wife. What a joke!

Sharon's first impulse was to fire back an answer. Then Jen's wise counsel played through her head.

"Don't ever respond to a bully, even to say leave me alone. Cowards want a reaction. Any kind of reaction. It makes them feel powerful. Ignore them. Don't give them any power."

She held onto her cell tightly. What would he do if she didn't respond?

His second text wasn't long coming.

I know this game you're playing, Sharon. Hard to get. Right? Don't make me laugh. I'm a patient man. I'll just bide my time until I'm ready, then I'll catch you out somewhere without your two watchdogs. When I'm done with you, you'll be sorry you ever left our happy home.

She stared at the message, dumbfounded. Was it possible Matt's cousin somehow sneaked down the hall to the breakroom that day in Jen's office and got her phone number while Sharon was busy in her office? It would be easy to do if he pretended to go to the restroom down that hall.

The mere sight of Matt's name made the cottage feel invaded, unsafe. Sharon gathered her belongings and hurried back to the safety of the house.

What would Jen say when she saw the text? What would she and Ben do?

Sharon was glad her friend had recovered enough to understand the danger posed by Matt's text. Having Jen on her side had always felt like having Wonder Woman as a bodyguard.

She *needed* Wonder Woman. The amazing Dr. Jennifer

Turner was the engine that drove Sharon's train. She was the engine that drove the train for everybody in her family. Including Ben. He just didn't know it yet.

He needed time to find out.

Sharon let herself in the back door. She could hear faint echoes coming from the pool room, the twins' laughter mingled with Victoria's chuckle and Ben's deep bass voice. Was Jen with them?

Sharon checked the rooms downstairs then went far enough down the hall to see into the pool room without being seen. *Yes.* There she was, sitting in a chair beside her grandmother. Ben had the chaise-for-two all to himself.

Victoria held her phone up so everybody could hear Rachel and her family talking on speakerphone, retelling everything they did on their honeymoon and asking a million questions about Jen's health. Of course, they were all on speakerphone. The Logans were a close-knit family. The only thing Jen loved more than seeing them was talking to them.

Sharon decided to keep Matt's text to herself until the time was right. He'd said he was biding his time. There was no need to spoil everybody's evening.

Her best friend self was extremely pleased as she slid back down the hall and up the stairs. She took great care of Jen. Besides, it would be pleasant to have the rest of the evening to herself. She could read. And refine her plans for the future.

Wouldn't everybody be surprised when they saw the old, battered Sharon finally taking charge of her own destiny?

Shocked, even.

THIRTY-EIGHT
ANTONIA'S APARTMENT

Antonia curled into the plump red and purple pillows on her cream-colored sofa, wearing a yellow silk teddy and her favorite perfume. Gardenia. *Benjamin's* favorite perfume. Since she'd fallen in love with a forbidden man, she always wore silk lingerie and perfume to bed, just in case he popped by. It could happen. They were working together so much they were a team. Almost like husband and wife. Wouldn't it be wonderful when Benjamin shared her bed with her?

She smiled, thinking of his eagerness earlier in the evening when she called to tell him they needed to work tomorrow. Fortunately, in legal matters, there was always a new angle that needed to be explored.

She knew just the outfit she would wear. Short, tight black shirt she could use to her advantage. Red silk tank top, one strap slipping down her shoulder, the vee-neck barely covering a black lace bra. Matching red linen jacket she could shuck off the minute she was past the security cameras and safely inside the conference room.

She sent Benjamin a text.

I can't wait to see you tomorrow. You're going to love what I've come up with.

She added a heart emoji, then deleted it. Subtlety worked best. She wasn't like the blatantly obvious Maria Ramos. And she certainly was not like that transparent beauty-queen-victim, Sharon.

Her phone pinged. She had an incoming text. Ben? As eager as she was?

The name that popped onto the screen shocked her.

Stop chasing my husband or I will kill you.

She had Jen now. A murder threat in writing! And she'd even sent it from her own phone.

Antonia refrained from answering. Never put anything in writing that you don't want the rest of the world to see. Never leave a paper trail.

Boy, was Jen leaving a paper trail. It was unlike her. Or so Antonia had thought.

Maybe she didn't know Benjamin's wife, after all.

Maria Ramos' blowout had happened after she left Jen's party. To all appearances, Jen had slit the tire. It was unfortunate that Ben had to worry over the tire because he was trying to cover for his wife. Slitting a tire was easy for a woman to do if she made the slash on the tire wall.

Antonia didn't come from a big, boisterous Sicilian family for nothing. They taught her a little bit of everything—how to fillet a fish, spray paint graffiti on an enemy's garage door, strip the net with a basketball, cook Sicilian dishes like a gourmet chef, change the oil and the tires on her car, and pick a lock. Any lock. She saved a screenshot of the text.

Jen had no idea who she was messing with.

THIRTY-NINE

THE TURNER HOUSE

The start of a new day should have been a relief to Benjamin. Except, it wasn't.

With his family preparing to go to the beach, it could have been any normal Saturday morning. His children's excited voices rang throughout the first floor, Nancy hummed as she prepared a picnic, and Jen appeared to be her normal, take-charge self, enjoying a morning cup of coffee. Energy and optimism poured through him, and he told himself that his life could be salvaged.

Then reality hit. His home was a war zone.

A scream ripped through the house.

"Gran!" Jen slammed her cup onto the cabinet and took off running with Nancy right behind her. Benjamin dropped his briefcase and went after them.

What he saw struck terror to his soul. Victoria was in the middle of the staircase, doubled over, and a section of the collapsed railing lay on an Oriental rug on the first floor. Just when he thought things couldn't get worse, they did.

Jen took the stairs two at a time, in a panic. "Gran, are you okay?" She sank beside her grandmother and started fussing over her like the loving mother she had always been. To *everybody* in her family.

His own anxiety felt like a grizzly bear clawing at him. Victoria was either paralyzed with fear or had collapsed with a heart attack. Benjamin caught up to them and reached for her hand to take her pulse.

His grandmother-in-law jerked it back and shot upright. "I'm just catching my breath, that's all. If I hadn't been spry as a monkey, I'd have plunged to the floor below when the railing gave way. Somebody tried to *kill* me."

"Victoria, I'm sure that's not true." Ben hated these kinds of histrionics, and was surprised to see them in his grandmother-in-law.

"Of course it is. I'm the only one in this house old enough to *need* the railing. Somebody tampered with it."

"I'll check with the builders to see what's going on," he said. "Do you need to get checked out by a doctor?"

"I don't have time for that nonsense. I've got to get our picnic ready for the beach."

Nancy bowed up like a frog. The kitchen was her domain, and Victoria had been bossing her around ever since she got there, saying she was going to make sure every bite Jen ate was safe.

"Maybe we should cancel the trip to the beach so you can rest and we can get to the bottom of this." Jen didn't sound like the unsinkable woman he had married, the one who would swim an ocean filled with sharks to protect her family.

Did she buy into the story that somebody had tried to kill Victoria and make it look like an accident? How had his family life sunk this low?

"*Pshaw*. You rest if you want to. I'm going to the beach with my great-grandkids."

There was no use arguing with her. She was the most stubborn woman Benjamin had ever known. Everybody went back into the kitchen, and Victoria got on Nancy's last nerve overseeing everything that went into the picnic hamper. His housekeeper went into one of her dark moods. Dal was already in a foul mood, out in the greenhouse still fuming about having to cut the oleander. He had complained to Benjamin again first thing that morning. Did he need to find a new gardener, in addition to fixing everything else that was wrong?

If he lost Dal, he would surely lose Nancy, which was an unthinkable situation.

Then there was Sharon. She had shown him Matt's threatening texts, early this morning while the two of them were in the kitchen having a quiet cup of coffee before the rest of the family woke up. He didn't have a clue what he was going to do about Matt.

Ben's life wasn't normal at all. It was falling to pieces. And here he was, grabbing his briefcase, heading to the office when he should have been taking his kids to the beach and fixing whatever was wrong with his marriage.

Jen stood at the kitchen counter, making herself a second cup of coffee. She jumped when he put his hand on her shoulder, actually *jumped*.

"As soon as I finish at the office, I'll join you at the beach."

"Whatever, Benjamin."

He'd struck a wound to her heart. He *knew* it. He could see it in the slump of her shoulders and the defeat in her face. The load of guilt he'd carried for months grew even heavier.

His wife didn't even turn around. Ben dithered, trying to decide whether to kiss her on the cheek or just walk out, which was obviously what she wanted.

"I'm glad to see you're feeling better, Jen. This evening, let's find a quiet corner and talk. Okay?"

She remained quiet for so long, he almost walked off. Finally, she angled her head so she could see him.

"I think we should, Benjamin. Gran's right. That staircase was solid."

"Maybe not..."

"The builders would never have left it that way."

She had turned her attention back to her coffee. Dismissing him. She did a lot of that lately. *Fine.* At least she was willing to talk to him this evening. But was he going to tell her the truth? That was the question he couldn't answer.

He left without kissing her. Not that it mattered. Nobody was paying him attention, anyhow.

* * *

It was a relief to get to the office later that morning. Antonia was already there, waiting in the conference room. She was a breath of fresh air, wearing red.

Jen's color.

Benjamin wouldn't think about that right now. He set his briefcase on the table and settled into a chair. Then he let himself simply breathe.

Antonia came up behind him and massaged his shoulders. He let that happen, too. Even leaned into her touch.

"Hard morning?"

"*Umm-humm.*" He felt like a traitor admitting even that much. Still, he was only human.

Antonia slid into the chair beside him. The sweet fragrance of gardenias washed over him. If he closed his eyes, he could imagine himself standing among his flowerbeds, feeling the sunshine on his face.

He glanced in her direction. Her legs were shapely, her hand soft as she placed it over his. She would be so easy to love. Why had no man already snatched her up?

"I hate to be the one to add more bad news," she said slowly.

"What's wrong, Antonia? I'm always here to help."

Are you? What about your own family?

He was a man divided. It was anybody's guess which side of him would win.

Antonia pulled out her phone and showed him a screenshot. He was so horrified by the text, he barely heard her explaining when the text was sent and why it was so serious.

Jen had lost it. Slashing tires with ice picks and threatening murder? She was into criminal activity now. Punishable by law.

What was he going to do about her? If she kept on this track she would end up in jail or an institution for the mentally ill.

The idea of a life without Jen seemed impossible. It suddenly dawned on him that she was at the center of everything, his marriage, his family, his social life, his standing in the community.

What would he ever do without her? She was irreplaceable.

Or is she?

"Benjamin." Antonia's voice called him back to the matter at hand. "Forget the text. I can handle it. We have bigger things to do."

"That's a fact."

"I've come up with a solution."

"If you have, you're a genius, and I'm eternally grateful." He took his notepad from the briefcase and clicked his pen. "Let's hear it."

"It's called the poison pill."

FORTY

THE DIARY

Invisible wasn't done yet. Not by a long shot. The latest item in the day planner screamed boldness. It telegraphed success.

THE FIRST HORROR. BLOOD.

Advance planning for the first horror had started three days ago. The results would be stunning. Invisible's excitement grew. The first horror required a useful minion. Invisible might even say a useful idiot.

Smiling, Invisible sent the minion a text message with final instructions. Not a single detail was left to chance. The first horror would be happening today, and it had to be perfect.

Invisible put pen to paper once more and wrote:

THE SECOND HORROR. DEATH.

As details spilled onto the paper, Invisible realized the second horror could be the winning event. The enemy vanquished forever. Game over. Winner take all.

But the wise always had a backup plan. Invisible wrote:

THE THIRD HORROR. ICING ON THE CAKE!

This one would be easy. The details were so delicious, Invisible decided to carry it through, regardless. It would definitely be a perfect building block to the future.

See, the thing about creating a master plan by a genius is that it ensured Invisible would eventually triumph. The plan was already working like magic.

Just a few more turns of the screw, and Invisible would have everything.

FORTY-ONE
GULF BREEZE, FLORIDA

Jen navigated the weekend traffic on the highway to Pensacola Beach with the jubilation of a prisoner fresh out of jail.

Gran, who had announced she would ride shotgun, sat in the passenger seat wearing cotton slacks rolled to midcalf, a green cotton tee shirt that proclaimed *Pikes Peak or Bust,* and the only sunhat she would hear of, her battered Stetson. Her cowboy boots were missing. Before they left home, Jen had spent five minutes convincing her a pair of borrowed flipflops was the only footgear that would be suitable for the beach.

"Reckon Sharon will get lost back there?" Gran pulled down the sunshade on her side of the car and peered in the mirror, angling her head to see the road behind her.

"It's impossible. We're on a small peninsula and will be crossing the only bridge from Gulf Breeze to an even smaller island." The Santa Rosa, a nod to Florida's Spanish heritage. "Even if she makes a wrong turn, Tommy and Marianne can guide her to the beach."

Sharon was following them with the twins and everything they needed for their day at Pensacola Beach except the folding chairs and the cooler with their food and drinks, which had been loaded into Jen's much larger trunk.

"I didn't expect to see her doing so well," Gran said thoughtfully.

"Sharon is far stronger than people give her credit for. Smarter, too. I'm really happy for the progress she has made."

As Jen turned at the Pensacola Beach sign, Victoria displayed the excitement of tourists from everywhere, awestruck by the view. Sky and sea merging into an endless panorama of such breathtaking size and beauty it took your breath away. Though she had visited Florida a few times through the years, she retained a childlike wonder of the visitors' paradise.

"It's spectacular here, Jen. No wonder you love it so much."

"It's home to me now."

"Lots of water."

It felt liberating to laugh. They were crossing the Bob Sikes Bridge, with nothing to see except the vast expanse of blue sky and water, the whole thing overlaid with gold from a sun that seemed to be apologizing for the dark days Jen had spent in bed.

The question was, what had put her there? And who? Nancy, Dal, Antonia, and Benjamin had easy access to her. Any one of them could have done it, and all seemed to have motive. The heartbreak was in thinking her husband might be trying to get rid of her without the legal entanglements of a divorce that would end up costing him a fortune.

As if Gran were reading her mind, she said, "Annie's worried about you. She called me every day while I was on the road."

"How is she?"

"Who knows? All she wanted to talk about was her nightmares."

Jen's senses went on full alert. Gran had never believed in Annie's dreams. For that matter, she had dismissed Rachel's mysterious scents and Jen's own visions from nature as nonsense. Still, she had never forbidden them to talk about it, or tried to discourage them from honing their unusual talents.

"What did she say?"

"The usual poppycock."

"I'm serious, Gran. I need to know every single detail. And don't tell me you don't remember. You're sharper than most forty-year-olds I know."

"She said the water has brought enemies to you, closer than you think, and that you are in grave and imminent danger."

"Are you sure she wasn't talking about *Sharon* being in danger?"

"No. She specifically said it was you. Annie's worried half to death, especially since you haven't answered any of her calls lately."

"I couldn't." It scared Jen that she had been too sick to know her sister called. "Then I never even thought to check my messages after you got here."

"That's all right. I don't like talking on the phone, either. After I finally talked to your husband, I called Annie and Rachel to let them know you were in bed sick."

"That's good."

The lie soured in Jen's mouth. Nothing was good. Not anymore. Even the view outside her car had become depressing. After they crossed the bridge, sunshine and sparkling water gave way to stunted trees, scrub brush, and swampy patches of dank water that would be more suitable for burying a body or encountering a viper than for enjoying a carefree weekend.

She was glad to make the turn into the beach-side parking lot where the sea spread out before her, so vast the changing shades of blue seemed to go on forever. As she searched for a parking spot, she powered down her window so she could hear the familiar language of water—the joyful cresting of waves followed by their greedy lapping at the shore and quiet sighing as they settled into the sand. Add the songs and sighs of terns busy among the sea oats in the sand dunes and the raucous calling of seagulls wheeling above the water, their white wings blinding in the sun, and the beach was nature's most beautiful symphony.

Beloved by Jen.

Not surprisingly the lot was full of cars, and the beach beyond teemed with people enjoying the sun. Beach umbrellas sprouted along the sand like colored mushrooms. Families clustered around coolers and beach chairs, built castles in the sand, and waded the shallows in their search for seashells. It was exactly the sort of return to normalcy she needed.

Sharon pulled into the parking lot beside her, and the twins barreled out, racing each other to see who could get to the water first. Why spoil their fun by calling them back to help tote beach gear? Over the past few days, Jen's mothering expertise had shrunk from a perfect ten to almost zero. She had no desire to repeat that abysmal performance.

Tommy and Marianne splashed in the shallows with the joyful abandon of teenagers enjoying a weekend break from school. Occasionally, they found a treasure in the sand then bent their heads together to share the wonder.

Jen almost teared up, remembering her closeness with her own sisters that had carried from childhood into their adult years. She sent a prayer winging upward that the same would be true of her children.

"Gran!" Marianne called. "Come see! I found a sand dollar!"

Victoria hesitated, her habit of duty so ingrained, she couldn't bring herself to walk away from a trunkful of beach paraphernalia without helping unload it.

"Go join the twins," Jen said. Victoria deserved time to forget about problems and spend a grandmother's limitless love in a setting designed to wash away doubt and fear. "Sharon and

I can handle this. You might find some seashells to take back to Rachel's kids."

Victoria settled her hat on her head and strode off, an authentic cowgirl undeterred by age and sand. Would Jen be that lively at her age? Would she even live that long?

She searched the sand and sky for signs. *Nothing*. Relief washed through her, and she shook off the dark mood that had threatened ever since Gran told her about Annie's latest dream.

"I see an empty spot on the beach close to the twins," Sharon said. "You want me to take the chairs over there?"

"That'd be great." Jen slung her tote over her arm then followed with the cooler.

It took another trip to the car before she could finally settle into a beach chair beside Sharon, who looked like old Hollywood glamor in her one-piece blue swimsuit and rhinestone-studded sunglasses. Jen searched for signs that her friend was distressed by the endless vista of water, but she seemed to be blossoming on the beach.

Something felt off. Why would a battered woman afraid of the water pack glamorous beach attire? "Are you doing okay, Sharon?"

"Yes, I am." Sharon lifted her sunglasses and winked. "I might just become a beach bunny."

"I think that's beach *bum*."

"Whatever."

Just be glad she's having a good time. One less thing to worry about.

Jen dug into her tote for her sunglasses. She was *certain* she had put them in. She never went anywhere without them. Why would she in Gulf Breeze? Besides that, she loved the frames—dark tortoiseshell with an edging of the signature Tiffany blue.

"Sharon, did you see me put my sunglasses in my tote?"

"Yes, you did it when we were in the kitchen."

"I thought so." Jen took everything out of the tote and

placed the items on a beach towel. But the leather sunglasses case was nowhere to be found. She squinted across the bright water. "I wouldn't possibly have come to the beach without sunglasses."

"Maybe you took them out and forgot?"

Jen bit back her retort. She was done with defending herself. Tired of being seen as someone who left a trail of abandoned jewelry and wallets and sunglasses behind her. Sick of being seen as weak. Needy.

"Never mind," she said. "If the sun gets too bright, I'll put up the umbrella. Let's just enjoy the day."

"Oh, I couldn't agree more."

"Aunt Sharon," Marianne called out. "Come join us."

It didn't escape Jen that her own daughter didn't ask her to join them. She had some major work to do to restore the easy relationships she had somehow let slip through her fingers.

"Go ahead, Sharon. I brought a book to read."

"You sure?" Concern was too mild to describe the way Sharon looked at her. Pity was the word.

"Absolutely. I'm just going to take it easy today."

Jen hated being the object of pity, despised being seen as weak and needy. As she repositioned her chair so the sun wouldn't put a glare on the page, she told herself to buck up. Then she opened her book and tried to get lost in the thriller that would soon become a movie.

The laughter of her children drifted around her, and the tranquility of sun and sea. In spite of her surroundings, Jen couldn't shake her fear, and the awful premonition that someone was watching. Someone was waiting. Someone bent on harm.

FORTY-TWO
PENSACOLA BEACH

Sitting on the warm sand with waves singing their endless lullaby and the burning blue bowl of sky overhead, Jen should have found a moment of peace. But she had brought her fear with her to the beach. Clutching her book tightly, largely unread, and with beachgoers all around her unpacking picnic lunches, she scanned the parking lot and a stretch of beach as far as she could see. *Again.* It felt like the thousandth time.

Where is Benjamin?

Logic and her professional training told her there could be several explanations, including emergencies at work. But fear knows no logic. Suspicion does not bow to reason.

He's seeing Antonia Delgado.

Sharon's warning slammed through her, and she fought the urge to run down the beach screaming. The primal scream was known to relieve tension.

If only this were just tension.

Was her husband's affair motivated by love for Antonia, or did he have a more sinister one?

Driving her crazy.

It was a lightbulb moment. All the signs pointed in that direction.

But why? What does he have to gain? And, if not Benjamin, then who?

Jen shaded her eyes and searched in all directions. She had the creepy feeling of being *watched*. Was it Invisible? She could *not* shake the conviction that evil had followed her all the way to one of her most peaceful places in the world—the beach.

Her family was happy without him today, but Jen couldn't get her grandmother's narrow escape on the staircase out of her mind. Horrible things were happening with too much regularity to be dismissed as a string of bad luck.

Who was after her and her family?

Jen glanced at her grandmother, stretched on her towel underneath the beach umbrella, taking a nap. Later, she would swear that she had done no such thing, but her snoring was so loud a couple of kids building a sandcastle nearby were giggling. The twins and Sharon were playing a lively game of beach volleyball with some teenagers from down the beach.

Her family was safe for now, but how long could Jen keep them that way? She turned back to her book and felt the crawl of time, the sun's rays moving along her arms, her shadow on the sand shifting.

When her phone pinged with an incoming text, she jumped as if pirates had stormed the beach for the sole purpose of kidnaping her and her entire family. With her heart hammering, she glanced at the screen to see it was from Benjamin.

> *This is taking longer than I thought. It looks like I won't get to the beach until late. I'll take us all out to supper when I get there. Pick a seafood place with picnic tables outside. It's a nice day, and we can all enjoy the weather.*

Why even bother to make the beach drive? YOU pick the place, and we'll meet you there... unless you're all tied up with her.

Before she hit send, she got her brain back and erased the whole thing. Her next message read:

That's fine. We'll see you soon.

Frustrated, angry, confused, she dropped her cell phone back into her tote. She was tired of reading, tired of squinting into the sun, tired of everything. With a wave toward Sharon and the twins, she took off running down the beach in the opposite direction. She had to have some time to herself to think.

Three minutes later, her run became a walk, and not even a fast one at that. How quickly a body can betray you. A few days in bed, and here she was, winded and sweating.

"I will not quit," she said to herself.

Jen soldiered on until she was out of her family's sight, and then she collapsed onto the sand, panting for breath. A couple of least terns wheeled in the air above her, their tiny white wings beating so close to her head, she could see their beady, evil little eyes glaring at her from knobby black heads that made it look like they were wearing masks.

She glanced around to see if she could spot any sand dunes covered with sea oats. The least tern, a migratory shore bird, preferred the cover of the pale golden-brown wheat-like plant for their nests. All along Pensacola Beach, signs warned swimmers away from the sand dunes that were protected nesting areas of the terns. There was nothing on this part of the beach as far as Jen could see except white sand abloom with colored swimsuits and umbrellas.

She waved her hands at the small birds. "*Shoo.* Go away. I'm not disturbing your nests. Not even close."

They flew off while she fought for recovery on the sand like a beached dolphin, wounded in too many ways to move. The deepest wound of all was her husband. His accusations. The way he studied her when he thought she wasn't looking, as if she were an alien who had landed in his life from another planet.

But was he trying to kill her? Was he even capable of such a thing?

Every fiber in her being screamed *no*. Her training said the evidence and his background did not support that theory. She wouldn't let him near the children if she believed he was capable of murder. Nothing in his history or his psyche said Benjamin would ever resort to violence.

Then, who in her circle would? And what if she was wrong about her husband?

People snapped. Look at her, a wad of uncertainty, hiding from her family on the beach.

Suddenly, a cacophony of shrill cries filled the air. The terns were back, and they had brought all their friends. Dozens of them, whirling around her, flapping and screeching.

What was this?

When you are in great danger, nature delivers the message in a way you cannot ignore.

As if Delilah had telegraphed the same message to the birds, they plunged toward Jen, shrieking. She crossed her arms over her head and bent double, her face almost in the sand.

The innocent appearance of the birds didn't fool her. The least tern is known as the little striker. Threaten them or their nests, and they will divebomb you in the same way they plunge out of the sky and into the water to spear small prey.

Though she posed no threat to them or their nests, the terns continued their attack.

"What am I? A movie star on the set of *The Birds*?"

They could peck her eyes out. Slash her hands and arms.

Draw blood. Tear her flesh. This large number could even kill her.

She cowered on the sand. How could such small birds hold her hostage? She peered under her arms to see if help was nearby. There was no one. Not even a lone beachcomber walking his dog.

One of the terns dived close enough to tear her arm. Rage filled her, along with a determination so great, she rose like a phoenix from the ashes.

"I'm no cringing coward." She whirled round and round in the sand, arms pinwheeling and hair flying. "*Shoo*... Go away... Leave me alone."

Miraculously, the little strikers shot upward with the same energy and sense of purpose they had used to divebomb her.

"Good riddance!"

Jen shaded her eyes until her latest bad omen was out of sight, then she walked down the beach to find her family. She was going home. Sharon could stay with Gran and the twins until Benjamin came. And if he never showed up, Sharon could load up and drive them all home in her car.

Jen refused to endure. One. Single. Other. Solitary. Thing.

After she explained her plans and said goodbye to her family, she headed to her car, but her feeling of empowerment evaporated.

Was that someone skulking near a black vehicle? Jackson Markle!

She ducked into her car and held onto the steering wheel until she could stop shaking. Her former patient had already tried to intimidate her. What would he do next?

What if it's not even him? What if it's someone you never imagined as your enemy?

Jen shook off her fear and made herself get moving. But her gift warned her the road home was leading her to a terror worse than any she had known.

FORTY-THREE

THE TURNER HOUSE

Alone.

How long had it been since Jen had the house all to herself? Relief flooded her as surely as sand from the beach washed down the shower drain. She leaned against the tiles while the hot water soothed away the trauma of terns and the avalanche of recent disturbing events.

She lingered under the hot water, fell into the blessed quietness of being alone without any possibility of someone waylaying her with questions and demands and accusations. Finally, she put a small bandage on her arm, dressed in comfortable sweats and went downstairs to make herself a cup of tea. She would make green tea chai, her favorite.

The sight of her sunglasses on the bar stopped Jen. Alongside them was a note from Nancy.

Jen, I left a big pot of soup in the refrigerator. Your grandmother said she was going to do all the cooking, but the last time I checked, that was part of my job.

The snarky tone didn't escape Jen. Nor did the fact that

Nancy was miffed at Victoria. Another problem that needed solving. Maybe she'd just let Benjamin do it. If she could ever get him to stay home long enough. She turned her attention back to the note.

After you left for the beach, I found your sunglasses in the cookie jar.

Jen crumpled the paper and tossed it into the wastebasket. She wished people would stop acting as if she were losing her mind. "Nothing is wrong with me."

Obviously, Nancy had put the sunglasses in the cookie jar. If she were that disgruntled, why wouldn't she just come and talk to Jen?

Or maybe it was Dal. He was still furious about the slaughter of oleander that wasn't even his. His antisocial behavior could be a cover for a hidden agenda.

Then there was Antonia. Whispering around Jen's house at night, poking into corners under the guise of bringing Italian soup. For all Jen knew, her husband might have even given a house key to his legal eagle. Was she his mistress, too?

Maybe Benjamin was the one gaslighting her? In the blink of an eye, he had changed from attentive husband to disgruntled, absentee spouse.

Horrible thought.

But the terns' warning had been so clear. What was she missing?

Sharon in her glamorous beach attire.

Jen rammed her sunglasses on, stormed out the kitchen door, and gulped down air as if she were oxygen-deprived. The sunset was fading into shadows, and the lanterns along the flagstone path appeared dim because of her dark lenses. Still, she wore the sunglasses out of sheer stubbornness. And frustration. And uncertainty.

She had every right to her feelings. Didn't she always say that to her patients? There was no one around to see her except Clint, who would be somewhere on the property, possibly in the guardhouse, the lone weekend security detail, and he would never criticize her. Still, she didn't care who saw her or what they thought. This was *her* house, *her* property. She was *not* losing her grip. She was being her usual, ornery self.

She strode along the flagstone path, and a sudden movement near the cottage caught her eye. A figure racing in the direction of the beach. Male? It was hard to tell in the fading light, and he was wearing black pants and hoodie. Jen reached for her cell phone then realized she'd left it in the house, still in her beach bag.

"*Stop!*" She chased after him, but was quickly overtaken by Clint, pounding ahead of her.

"I've got this!" he yelled over his shoulder.

The camera on the path to the beach must have detected the intruder. Jen sank onto the cottage steps and whipped off her sunglasses.

Blood. Everywhere.

Bile rose in her throat, and she bent over, heaving. Blood smears covered the front door of the cottage. So much blood that it pooled on the porch floor, trickled toward the steps, and dampened the seat of her sweatpants.

Horrified, she jumped up and stared. Her cottage looked like the scene of a slaughter. Was this Annie's warning coming true?

Blood in the water.

The truth slammed Jen like an avalanche. "*Sharon!*"

She tried to skirt the blood as she raced into the cottage. While she was in the house showering, had Matt taken Sharon from the beach and brought her back here to kill her?

Jen flipped on the cottage lights, still screaming her friend's name. The front room appeared untouched. She raced around, searching behind the sofa and chairs, tossing sofa cushions, flinging open the door to the coat closet.

Blood. On the floor. On the sofa cushions.

Scarlet stains marred the colors of sun and sea Jen had brought inside the cottage. What was she missing? She tore around the room again, panicked, and then she regained her senses. The blood was hers. She had tracked it in on her shoes and her hands when she opened the blood-smeared door.

What had she done? This was a crime scene, and she was destroying evidence. Until recently, she had never acted in this rash manner. Was she getting early-onset Alzheimer's?

"I've got him!"

Clint's yell came from the direction of the beach. Torn between fear for Sharon and a need for answers, she headed toward the water.

The intruder's hoodie had been jerked off, and Clint was frog-marching him back to the house. He was a big man, similar in size to Sharon's husband, with the same sandy-colored hair. As they came closer, Jen recoiled. Clint stopped short of her, a deliberate move so the culprit in his grip couldn't touch her, even if he tried.

"He came by boat," Clint said. "It's hidden around the curve of the bay in some bushy overgrowth. He probably came up to the cottage by sneaking through the bushes. If he hadn't taken the path back to the beach, I might never have seen him."

"It's Matt's cousin." Jen noticed blood spatters on his shoes and the hem of his pants. "Jackson Markle. A former patient. He hates me so much, I should have guessed he'd do something like this. Call 911. There's blood everywhere at the cottage. I think he killed Sharon."

"No! Wait!" Jackson's panic showed in a voice that wobbled and a face stamped with sheer terror. "It's not like that!"

"Give me one good reason why I shouldn't deliver you to the cops in handcuffs?" Clint's booming voice rang with unmistakable authority and more than a little hint of dire consequences. He had zero tolerance for criminals, and the size to back up any claim he made.

"I never killed anybody! I *swear*. I was pranking you, that's all. Just pranking!"

Jen tempered the hope that swept through her. Jackson could be lying. He'd done it many times in her office. If she had her cell phone, she could call Sharon to make sure she was still at the beach.

"Are you telling me Sharon's alive?"

"Yes!' Jackson looked both shaken and defiant. "She's as alive as you and me unless she had a sudden heart attack or got hit by a truck or something."

"Then why is blood all over my cottage?"

"I smeared it there, but that's all I did. This is not about you, Dr. Turner. It's about *Sharon*."

"Why? She has never done a single, harmful thing to you."

"I hate her guts. That's why. But I would never kill her. Me and Matt were going to be buddies forever, bum around seeing the world together. And then *she* came along and messed up everything, including my cousin's life."

If Jen hadn't been so busy dealing with omens and false accusations, she might have guessed Matt would use his cousin to do his dirty work.

"So, Matt also put you up to that little performance you gave in my office?"

"He told me to harass you at work and tail you home so you would stay out of his business and Sharon would come back home where she belongs. When that didn't work, he told me to put a scare in both of you with the blood."

Clint tightened his hold on Jackson. "Where did all that blood come from, Markle?"

"I work in a meat processing plant over in Pensacola. Locals call it the slaughterhouse. Getting plenty of blood is no problem for me."

The puzzle pieces were dropping into place. If Jen had stayed on Pensacola Beach that evening and Jackson Markle hadn't taken the beach path, he might have gotten away with smearing blood all over the cottage front porch, and Sharon would have been the one to find it.

It was impossible for Clint to see everything and be everywhere on this large estate at once. She made a mental note to install more cameras on the property and to beef up the security detail.

"Did you also slide that note under Sharon's door and rip her tire with an ice pick?" she asked.

"No. Matt must have done those. He likes to handle things by himself, but when he needs help, I'm his man."

"I'll just bet you are." Jen couldn't keep the sarcasm from her voice. "It takes some big man to kill a child's hamster then deliver it to the door all wrapped up in a pretty package."

His face paled. "Is that what was in the box? I delivered it, but I didn't kill it."

"Then who did?"

"Matt."

"Where is he?" Clint asked the same thing Jen was thinking.

"I don't know."

"Don't lie to me," Clint said. "My job is to protect this family, and I'm running out of patience with you. You don't want to be anywhere near me when that happens. Do you understand?"

"I'm not lying, I swear! He's holed up somewhere. That's all I know. I'm just doing what he asked me to do."

"I don't believe you," Jen said. "You've left nasty notes all over my house and done all these things on your own because you hate Sharon and me. Isn't that right?"

"You're got the hatred part right, but I don't know anything about any notes. That must be Matt's doings. If your guard will let me get to my cell phone, I can prove everything I've done was Matt's idea."

Clint kept a tight hold on the culprit while he retrieved his phone. Two of the text messages from Matt instructed Jackson how to create havoc at Jen's office and spread blood around the cottage. A third told him to get a panel truck to make a special delivery at Jen's address at 10:30 p.m. on the night of the party. The rest of the text read:

> *No earlier. Wait until the party is in full swing. You'll find the package underneath the white oleander bush beside the cottage. I broke the outdoor light so no one will see you, but wear your baseball cap low to cover your face.*

But it was the fourth message that curdled Jen's blood.

> *Don't get caught, and don't let them call the cops. If they do, Sharon will be the first to die, and I'll name YOU as my accomplice. Then I'll kill the twins so the rich witch who is hiding my wife knows what it's like to lose someone she loves. Next, I'll kill the privileged, money-bags husband, and then I'll knock off the old granny she dotes on. By the time I kill Dr. Turner, she will be begging me to put her out of her misery.*

All the warnings in nature had been pointing to this one moment, and the awful certainty that she could lose her entire family. Jen dug deep into herself for courage and took a step toward Jackson Markle, then a second. She kept moving forward until she was close enough to see the evil in his eyes, feel the hatred tainting the air around him.

"Yes, this rich witch has enough money to hire an army of bodyguards to keep you away. Now, listen carefully because I'm only going to say this once. If you *ever* come near Sharon or any of my family again, I will kill you. Then I'll call the cops myself and say I shot an intruder." The silence on the beach became electric. There was hardly even the sound of breathing. "Nod your head if you understand?"

After a small eternity, Jackson nodded his head. Jen knew body language. Jackson fully understood that his cowardice was no match for her courage. He would not be back, no matter how many texts he got from his wife-beating cousin.

"You can let him go now," she told Clint. "Stay here and watch until he gets into his boat and heads back to the hole he crawled out of."

"I don't advise that," Clint told her. "We need to turn him over to the law and file charges. Trespassing, vandalism, and destruction of property."

"You saw Matt's threats."

"Jen, people like Matt and this scumbag are cowards and bullies. They count on victims believing their threats so they can get away with their criminal activities. Let's put this one away, and let the law go after Sharon's husband. She can get a protective order, and we can beef up security."

Clint believed in Occam's razor, the simple solution that cuts through speculations and imaginings. But psychology had taught Jen to look beyond the obvious. If Clint was wrong, she would lose everybody she loved.

"I can't take that risk. Get him off my property." She glared up at Jackson and pointed a finger at his chest. "I meant *every* word I said. Come back here, and you are *dead*."

She wheeled around, marched back to the house, and sent a text to Sharon explaining what had happened. Jen ended it with reassurances.

All is well. No cops involved. Don't worry about a thing. I'm going to have Clint install a security camera outside the cottage.

Sharon sent a quick reply, and relief swept through Jen. She grabbed cleaning supplies then hurried back to the cottage to wash up the blood. All the lights were on, transforming the cottage and the white oleander spilling around it to a macabre, bloodstained jewel in the gathering darkness. A scattering of stars piercing the inky sky added to the surreal appearance.

Clint was still there, just coming out the front door. "There's no sign that anyone has been in there except Sharon. And you. I put the pillows back and wiped up the blood smears."

"I don't know what I'd do without you."

"You don't ever have to find out."

"Thanks, Clint. We would have already caught Jackson, and probably Matt, too, if we had a camera on the cottage. Can you take care of that Monday?"

"Yes. I'll add a few more for the other blinds spots, too." He reached for the mop and bucket. "I'll clean up this mess. You can go on back to the house and rest."

Was that his way of saying she looked tired? Sick? On her last leg?

"I'm staying," she said. "I need to be busy."

"Judging by this mess, that won't be a problem."

Blood was everywhere on the porch. Within ten minutes, Jen's clothes looked like she'd had a bloodbath. She probably even had streaks of blood on her cheeks where she kept raking her hair out of her eyes.

When the car came up the driveway, Jen was on her knees, scrubbing a particularly stubborn spot with a wire brush. She didn't turn to look. It would be Sharon or Ben, returning with Gran and the twins, or someone on the security staff. Everybody in the family or who worked with the family had security clearance to get through the gates.

"Jen?"

That voice!

Electrified, she stood up to face the stunning woman standing beside a baby-blue convertible, her hair the deepest mahogany shot through with red that glowed under the stars like fire, her blue-green eyes as mesmerizing and changeable as the sea.

"*Annie!*" Propelled by a storm of conflicting emotions, Jen flew off the porch and stopped short of throwing her arms around her sister. "I can't believe it's you."

"I wanted to surprise you." Annie stepped back and stared at the bloodstains covering her sister. "Oh, Jen, what have they done to you?"

FORTY-FOUR

PENSACOLA BEACH

Sharon read the text message from Jen with growing apprehension. The horror show at the mansion seemed never-ending. It was enough to make her wonder just exactly how safe she was.

Still, she felt a sort of grim satisfaction at the outcome of today's incident. Matt's foolish cousin had dumped blood all over Jen's cottage, but her security guard caught him. *Of course he did.* Jackson Markle didn't have sense enough to come in out of the rain, as her mama used to say.

Deeply grateful to Jen for not calling the cops, she shot back a quick text.

> *I'm glad you are okay and that you caught the skunk. I am fine. Everybody's fine. I promise you I won't mention a word about the blood.*

Why on earth would she? Didn't Jen know Sharon was as protective of the children as she was? Why burden Tommy and Marianne with adult problems? Teenagers dealt with enough angst of their own.

She had a Ph.D. in brave fronts. *Fronts of all kinds, really.* Arranging her face into a smile that would fool even the most discerning, she got back to dinner with the family. They were all here, including Ben. When he'd arrived at the beach earlier, he seemed relieved that his wife had left, a bad sign for Jen, but one that didn't surprise Sharon in the least.

The best friend side of her pitied Jen, but the survivor in her exulted to be part of this lively family group, sitting at a picnic table on a little plank porch attached to one of the many food trucks near the beach, eating fried shrimp and oysters with a side of fried onion rings served in paper trays. Everybody in the group, including Victoria, had sandy feet, wind-blown hair, and sunburned cheeks. They had never looked happier—with the possible exception of Victoria.

Sharon congratulated herself that she had once more risen like a phoenix from the ashes of the latest disaster—a lesson taught the hard way by her anvil-handed man—and was right in the middle of the whole thing, the happiness, the beach-glow look, the seafood supper where the only music was laughter and water lapping at the shore.

There had been water lapping at the shore during her last supper in Alabama. The music had been Tammy Wynette, wailing through the boombox. And the only happiness had been the kind you had to keep secret if you didn't want your neck twisted in two, or your jaw broken.

Lap. Lap. Lap.

The sound of water brought it all back. Sharon fought against the pull of her memories, but it was no use...

* * *

That fateful day in Eutaw, she decided to turn her last supper with Matt into a picnic. It was one of his favorite things to do, and would put him in a mellow mood, receptive to the idea that she had to drive up to Tupelo for an unspecified time to take care of her mother.

She considered spreading a cloth on the table on the deck, but rejected the idea as too complicated. Mosquitoes were out and about. She hated the pesky insects, and so did Matt. Nothing would spoil his mood quicker than having a mosquito buzzing around his head. He would just as likely slap her as the bug.

The only place that would work for this picnic was Matt's boat. Out in the middle of the river where breezes off the water would ensure no insects bothered them. It would be peaceful under the moonlight. Private. *Perfect*.

When Matt wasn't out on the river fishing, the boat was always there, moored in their backyard on the backchannel of the Tombigbee, hidden from any neighbors that might get too nosey about what was going on at the Jones household. Sharon had learned the hard way that the home she treasured for its privacy also afforded the opportunity for her husband to treat her any way he pleased, anytime he chose, and nobody would ever know.

Today that would end and the tables would turn.

She peered out every window in her house to make sure Matt hadn't somehow sneaked back and hidden outside. He could be behind any of those trees or bushes at that very moment, spying on her through a set of binoculars. He was capable.

She searched for any hint of movement or the glint of sunlight on binocular lens, and then she sent him a text.

Have a good day at work, sweetheart. I'm planning a nice surprise for your supper. Love you much!

Her phone pinged with his reply.

Now, that's what a man likes to hear. A wife who knows how to appreciate a good husband. Wear something frilly for me, baby.

The idea made her want to hit something *hard*. Sharon marched into their bedroom, took the pair of pinking shears and cut up every pair of frilly underwear she owned. Black lace. Sheer pink silk. Flaming red satin with matching ribbons. Rainbow-colored shreds fell into the wastebasket. When she finished, she carried the hateful scraps to the back deck, dumped them into the barbecue grill, and poured in exactly the right amount of fire-starter. Oh, she knew how to barbecue. Of course she did. Her ribs were the talk of Eutaw, and her chicken wings the pride of north Alabama.

Wait till they got a gander at her barbecued panties.

She marched into the kitchen and got some sauce just on general principle. Then she sprinkled it liberally over the lingerie. Sweet tomato barbecue sauce with honey and vinegar. The choice had its own irony. She lit the match and stepped back to admire the flames.

She was done being a punching bag, and she for sure was no longer a clone of Stand-By-Your-Man Wynette.

Every frilly thing Matt would never see again went up in flames. She stood there until the whole conglomeration was nothing but blackened cinders. Then she cleaned the grill in case he checked when he came home. You could never predict him. She wasn't going to leave a single detail to chance.

Nothing was going to ruin her plans...

FORTY-FIVE

"Aunt Sharon?"

Sharon came out of her reverie. Marianne was tugging the sleeve of the windbreaker Jen had left on the beach for Sharon. "What do you think?"

About what? While she'd been down nightmare lane, the family had discussed something that went right over her head. Of course, she wouldn't admit it. Jen was the forgetful one now. Sharon was the steady center this family revolved around. She would do anything for her best friend, even give up the time she could have spent rebuilding her music career.

"Sweetie, why don't you give me your opinion first?" She winked, and the teenager flashed a smile exactly like her daddy's. Marianne was going to grow up to be a very fine young lady, savvy and self-confident. Sharon would teach her how to play piano.

"Tommy wants to take Mom a milkshake with pralines, but I don't know what kind of nuts they put in it. Mom can't eat peanuts. I think vanilla would be best."

"Pralines are made with pecans, but I agree with you. We don't want to take any chances. Let's go with vanilla." Sharon smiled at Ben and as an afterthought, turned to include Victoria. "Don't the two of you agree?"

"Add chocolate syrup with a cherry on top!" Victoria made her opinion sound like law. "Jen always liked that."

"Agreed." Ben looked ten years younger in the glow of moonlight and the electric lights strung around the food truck and the porch.

Totally relaxed, he was a different person from the one Sharon saw at home. This Ben was the charming law student from Tulane, the most desirable bachelor on campus, the one who could always make you laugh, but at the same time always be counted on to take good care of you.

They spent the next half hour taking pictures against the backdrop of a tropical paradise, buying Jen's milkshake, and deciding how they would divide themselves between Sharon's car and Ben's. The twins opted to ride with her, while Victoria said she would ride with her grandson-in-law.

Perfect.

"You go first so I can make sure you get home safely," Ben said.

His thoughtfulness moved her to tears. She would have hugged him if Victoria hadn't been standing there, watching her. Always watching.

With the radio playing love songs and starlight washing both sea and sky with silver, Sharon had a blissful drive home in the company of Ben's children. They made her feel loved and appreciated, validation she'd been missing almost from the day she said *I do* to the wife-beater wearing the mask of a loving husband. The kind of love she felt in that car with Marianne and Tommy was worth fighting for.

Suddenly "Moon River," a romantic ballad she loved, was interrupted by warnings of a hurricane brewing off the coast of Florida.

"If it doesn't veer, it's likely to make landfall in Gulf Breeze," the announcer said.

Sharon switched the radio off. The last thing she wanted was news of more disaster. Those slow-moving walls of wind and water took *days* to make up their minds which way to go. They were as unpredictable as Matt. And, *boy,* did she know how to survive that storm!

Satisfied that she *knew* what she was doing and *nothing* could stop her now—not even a monster storm—she chatted with the twins about the details of their day, what they loved, what they hated. There was no middle ground with teenagers. She imagined what it would be like if they were hers. The confessions they would make at bedtime when darkness made sharing intimate details easy, the hugs they would share, the dreams. Even the fears.

Kids got scared, too. How well Sharon knew. If she was a mother... *when* she was mother... she would be the kind her children could always count on.

"Aunt Sharon," Marianne screeched. "There's the gate!"

She almost missed it. She made a slight correction then wheeled her car down the driveway. The front porch was lit up like Christmas. When Sharon saw who was standing there, she became a party balloon with all the air leaking out.

Annie. The most beautiful woman in the world. And the most dangerous.

Everybody knew Jen was the smartest woman in every room. Fiercely courageous and independent. What you saw was what you got. But nobody saw Annie coming. Her keen intelligence and savage cunning were hidden under the soft, feminine exterior of an absent-minded, flighty artist. Underestimate her at your own peril.

Sharon had no intention of doing so. Obviously, the baby-blue convertible belonged to her. *Correction.* To the rental company she'd used at the airport. How like her to choose a car that screamed frivolous and fun-loving. In that car, Annie would be a Bengal tigress masquerading as a Persian kitten.

Not a lioness. Lions will warn you before they attack. A tiger never does. Make a tigress mad, and she will watch you for weeks, biding her time until she can eviscerate you with one slice of her claws.

Only this one didn't want your innards. She wanted your soul. That was Annie.

How Sharon knew, she couldn't exactly say. Jen used to laugh when she told the stories of her baby sister's escapades, stories that slowly built Annie to legendary status in Sharon's mind. But the proof was in recognition. One kindred soul to another. Artists took chances, ignored boundaries, embraced a wild sort of freedom in real life as well as art. You could no more predict the behavior of an artist than you could predict the exact path of a hurricane. Sharon saw something of herself in Annie, and it terrified her.

If it were left up to her, she would drive off and not look back. She'd stay out of sight until Annie left so she would never get a chance to excavate Sharon's soul with her particular form of magic.

But Sharon had no choice. The twins bounced up and down with excitement, waving and calling.

"Aunt Annie! Aunt Annie!"

She parked the car, and they barreled out, racing toward her nemesis. She sat behind the wheel as long as she could without being obvious.

Just as Ben pulled into the driveway behind her, Jen walked to Sharon's car and opened the driver's door.

"Are you all right?" Jen's face was a map of concern. She was going to get wrinkles frowning like that. "I hope the beach trip wasn't too much for you."

"No. It was very nice. I was enjoying it until I read what happened here. That was *awful*. Are you okay?"

"I am now, but it was truly terrifying. I thought you might be dead." Jen linked arms with her. "You won't believe who showed up while you were gone."

"I see her." Sharon forced some enthusiasm into her voice. "Did you know she was coming?"

"No." Jen made a sweeping gesture and set her gold bangle bracelets tinkling. "I would have talked her out of it. She didn't need to make a trip from Italy because of me."

Jen was dressed in her red caftan. What else? She looked relaxed, almost her old self. An almost impossible feat considering that, only hours ago, Matt's cousin had tried to turn her cottage into a slaughterhouse.

See. That was the kind of magic Annie had. She could stare at you with those ocean eyes until the best you had inside floated up to the surface.

Or the worst.

Jen bore Sharon along like a clipper ship with red sails, and thankfully, she didn't have to make conversation. Jen's family loved reunions. Always had. They moved inside as one unit, still talking and laughing and hugging each other.

And Annie was drinking the milkshake. Of course she was.

The best friend side of Sharon was thrilled to be even a small part of the Logan and Turner family circles, but the survivor side of her withdrew into a private shell. The victim in her hated surprises, felt threatened by them.

She settled into a turquoise chair in the corner and curled herself into a small question mark. What was she to do *now*?

Annie would take charge. She always did. Funny, how Jen never noticed that.

Jen came over to sit in the matching chair beside her and squeeze her hand. "You're quiet. Are you sure you're okay?"

"Yes. Just unwinding... and processing."

"I'm glad you didn't see the mess at the cottage, but I don't think you have to worry about Jackson coming back. I have some reservations about not bringing in the law, but Clint will be taking care of extra security. We're putting a camera directly on the cottage front door. That ought to keep Matt and Jackson both away."

The beauty of true friendship brought tears to Sharon's eyes. *What would she do without Jen?*

"Thank you," she whispered. "For everything."

"This will all be over soon, Sharon. We will outlast Matt. He'll give up and walk away, and eventually you and I will be able to do whatever we please without looking over our shoulder."

It *had* to be over soon. With Annie in town, there was no predicting what would happen next.

She was over by the baby grand now with the twins and Victoria, playing one of Sharon's favorite songs, "Somewhere Over the Rainbow." She played almost as well as Sharon herself. Was there nothing Annie couldn't or wouldn't do? That was only one of the many frightening things about her.

The music wound through the room like snake oil. Was Sharon the only one who saw through Annie's manipulative charm?

Besotted and oblivious, Victoria and the twins chatted with the artist/siren about a welcome party they were planning in her honor. Tomorrow, of all things. Didn't Annie always move at the speed of a runaway train barreling down the track where you were tied to the rails and pinned under the headlights?

Everything was coming unraveled. Sharon didn't know what she was going to do. But she had come too far to back down now.

Tommy separated himself from the group and trotted over to Jen. "Mom, can we have a party for Aunt Annie?"

Jen's smile collapsed as she struggled to balance the needs of her children with her own. *Constant upheaval always takes a huge toll.* If anybody knew that, it was Sharon.

The dearest friend side of her rushed to Jen's rescue. "I'll help Tommy and Marianne with all the legwork. You can just sit back and relax."

"Then, let's do it," Jen said.

"Cool!" Tommy gave them both a high five then hurried back to the piano to spread the good news to the rest of the family.

It felt good to simply sit in the corner and watch from afar. Sharon was used to watching the wonderful lives of others from a distance, but she couldn't imagine what her best friend must be feeling. Finally, Jen shrugged her shoulders as if she were casting off some heavy burden.

"Everything looks normal, doesn't it, Sharon?"

"Looks can deceive." Any black-and-blue woman who ever believed in contriteness and regret from a fast-fisted man understands the truth of that adage.

Jen leaned closer and lowered her voice. "I don't want you to worry, Sharon. With our new security measures in place, the bloodbath at the cottage will be the last chance Jackson ever gets to come near us again."

"I hope so."

Was the party a perfect way to spit in the eye of fate, move beyond chaos, and step into a better future? For all of them?

Who do you think you're kidding?

Something more dangerous than a hurricane was heading Sharon's way. She could feel it in bones that had been broken so many times they could predict her future with the accuracy of hurricane hunters flying into the eye the storm.

FORTY-SIX

THE TURNER HOUSE

Benjamin couldn't sleep, even with the pills guaranteed to provide a full night's rest. His latest stand-off with Jen over the beach outing and the breach of security that resulted in a bloodbath at the cottage added to a list of problems that seemed insurmountable. If his problems didn't destroy him, the hurricane bearing down on Gulf Breeze would.

If it didn't change course, they'd have to evacuate. What a nightmare that would be, especially with so many people in the house.

Not that he minded Sharon or Jen's family. In fact, just the opposite. They were all good people, and Annie was especially charming, easy to please. Everybody loved her. Particularly the twins. She had brought them Pinocchio puppets from Assisi then spent an hour showing them how to put on a show.

Tommy and Marianne were planning to do another show tomorrow at the ice cream party for Annie. A surprise. Earlier in the evening, they had sworn Benjamin to secrecy.

The puppet show wouldn't be the only surprise. Antonia was coming to the party. When he went outside to bring Annie's bags in, Antonia had sent a text that she needed to see him. She said it was an emergency. What could he do but invite her? His other choice was unthinkable. Meet her at the office and miss the party.

Maybe that's why he couldn't sleep...

He glanced at the clock. Two a.m. He slipped out of bed and into the hall, careful not to wake anyone. Sharon's bedroom was shut tight with no light showing around the door. So was Jen's.

Separate rooms! He'd lost count of how long. Almost since Sharon arrived. How could two people once so in love have come to this?

Once?

Was he *still* in love? Benjamin didn't know his own mind anymore.

The guest bedroom that was now Annie's showed light filtering under the closed door. *No surprise there.* It would be mid-morning in Italy. Not easy to make that massive time adjustment.

Without turning on lights, he headed toward the kitchen. Moonlight poured through the glass windows downstairs, and the sky looked as if someone had covered it with a net of stars. It seemed impossible that a hurricane was brewing out in the ocean. But wasn't that always the way? The awful surprise of a storm that snatched lives and houses and whole towns, destroying everything in its path with the carelessness of capricious nature bent on showing man that he was not in charge of anything.

Usually, Benjamin loved this time of night, alone in the dark with no expectations. But tonight, something awful was afoot. It stirred through his house like the ghost of everything he'd lost—and stood to lose if he couldn't stop the personal storm tearing through his family and his business.

A cup of hot chocolate was just what he needed. He would add a dash of hot pepper and some cinnamon. An old Mayan recipe Jen had taught him. She had taught him so many things, introduced him to a fascinating world seen through her eyes.

What was he going to do about her?

Wait.

There were voices, coming from the kitchen. Jen's voice. And Annie's. As he came closer, he realized they were murmuring about Nancy.

This couldn't be good. She was a faithful employee. Jen's suspicions were way off base. He would put a stop to it.

Suddenly, he heard his name, and his march came to a halt. He ducked into the shadows. *Eavesdropping.* A reprehensible pastime. A few months ago, he would have joined them, confident his name would only be linked with good news.

"Benjamin is so secretive, I don't even know if he still *wants* to be my husband. Oh, Annie, I feel like a traitor telling you all this."

"Don't. I didn't come all the way across the ocean to see a performance of the Turners' perfect life. My dreams tell me otherwise. But I don't know how to help you if you don't tell me everything."

Annie had always liked Benjamin. And she never judged people by what anyone else said, even Jen. Still, it was awful to cower in the dark listening to his wife recount his disappearances, his accusations, and his obsession with Antonia. It was terrifying to see himself through Jen's eyes. It was also telling that Jen conveniently left off any confessions about her threats to Antonia.

In the kitchen, their voices, so much alike, blended like music, like a symphony they had learned long ago at the feet of their mother. Though Delilah had been dead years before he married Jen, she had been an ever-present mystery in his marriage.

Delilah had left gaps in Jen's history that no one in the family could fill. Was that why she needed her family so? Was that why such a strong woman had crumbled so easily over a missing necklace, a slashed tire?

He remained hidden as the conversation in the kitchen continued.

"I *will* get to the bottom of all these strange events," Annie told Jen firmly.

"I think I'm dealing with more than one dangerous adversary. I don't want you nosing around, getting hurt."

"Nosing around is not my style. I think we should hire a top-notch private investigator. The sooner, the better. Maybe your security guard Clint can recommend someone."

"Even better, he can do it." Benjamin could hear that the strength and resolve were back in Jen's voice. "He was once a detective. If anyone can help solve this puzzle, it's Clint. I don't know why I didn't think of this sooner."

"When you're in the middle of a war, you can only think about ducking."

Benjamin broke out in a cold sweat. Why would his wife want a private eye uncovering her dirty little secrets? He sneaked from his hiding place and back up the stairs.

This had gone too far. Something had to be done about Jen.

FORTY-SEVEN
THE TURNER HOUSE

Antonia should never have come to this party. And she should never have called Benjamin with yet another trumped-up meeting. She knew it the minute she stepped foot onto his front porch and heard the laughter. Her presence in there would be as destructive as the hurricane barreling their way.

She couldn't go in. No way! Ducking behind a large urn holding some exotic-looking greenery, she stared through the large windows. It was like watching a movie everybody said you would love, but you couldn't make yourself feel anything except numbness.

The sight of Jen's family punched her right in the gut. Just the blow she deserved for chasing after a married man. Ben had told her to expect his sister-in-law Annie, who was about her age, and Jen's grandmother, Victoria. But hearing about them did nothing to prepare her for the impact they had on her. They were both larger-than-life, charming, it seemed, and interesting in the way of Antonia's own large and beloved family. Especially Annie, the artist.

Antonia cowered behind the urn, observing them from afar. Annie threw back her head when she laughed, and Victoria

Logan trotted around in cowboy boots like she owned all of Gulf Breeze and the whole state of Florida, too. That was exactly the kind of confidence Antonia's own Mimi possessed, the grandmother by which all others were measured.

The family scene shifted, with the twins and their dad moving in the direction of the kitchen, then Benjamin returning to speak briefly to Annie. Seeing him join his wife at the ceiling-to-floor windows would have hurt, except for one thing. The Turners were two wooden carvings. Expressionless. Unhappiness personified.

Antonia was both overjoyed and dismayed. What was happening to her? She was turning into the kind of woman she hated.

"Enough of this," she muttered to herself.

She often gave herself these pep talks aloud. It propelled her out of her hiding place, and she punched the doorbell.

Suddenly, Annie was there, opening the door, towering over her by a good five inches, her hair shooting sparks everywhere the light hit. And those eyes. Antonia couldn't look away. Slowly, she tumbled into the center of a blue-green vortex.

"Hi. You must be Antonia? Welcome to my party." She held the door wide.

"Call me Toni." Only her family called her Toni, but she felt as if she had known Annie forever. Was it because she'd lived in Italy where some of the Delgado family still resided? "I'm actually a party-crasher. I apologize for that."

"No need. Both Benjamin and Jen have told me what an asset you are to the company."

Yes. She would have done exactly that. Antonia cut her glance in Jen's direction. She was obviously not happy with the uninvited guest. For that matter, neither was Benjamin. Misery dripped from those two like poison from a rattlesnake's fangs.

Annie's laughter was like music. "Don't mind them. My sister has had a rough time lately, and apparently, so has my brother-in-law. Join me in the kitchen, Toni. The twins are in there driving Nancy crazy. We'll rescue her."

"Great." She fell into step beside Annie. Anything to get away from Jen. Was it possible Benjamin's wife would make good on her threat and try to kill her while she was here?

Oh, help. What had she done? Remorse swept through her. Her grandmother would be disappointed in her.

The beauty queen, Almost Miss Alabama, was in the kitchen with the housekeeper and the twins. The look she gave Antonia was that of a cobra.

"*April*, how nice to see you."

You're going to pretend you don't know my name? AGAIN?

Toni was so mad she couldn't react, but Annie corrected Cobra Sharon so smoothly you would never notice the steel in her backbone unless you were from a family who prided themselves on indestructible backbones. Next, Annie inspected the boxes of ice cream spread out on the bar, along with every silver dish containing ice cream toppings.

"I checked the ice cream boxes and the toppings myself, Aunt Annie," Marianne said. "Daddy helped me. We wanted to make sure there were no peanuts or anything else Mom is allergic to."

"Great job, you guys." While Annie hugged her niece and nephew, she studied Toni as if she could see into her soul.

Remorse flooded her. Soul-searing and bitter. And more despair than a heart should hold. In loving Benjamin, in wanting him, what was she doing to his family, especially his children?

As if Annie had read her mind, she handed her two bowls of toppings. "Toni, do you mind taking these into the dining room?"

"I'll be glad to help."

It gave her something to do besides be miserable. The room was huge, the table massive. Made for this large family. Toni had no trouble picturing the Turners seated at each end, presiding over this lively group.

They were very much like her own family, except taller. Jen and Annie were regal, five foot nine if they were an inch, with Annie slightly taller. The height Antonia had always aspired to be. She felt Hobbit-like. A shrimp. A toad aspiring to be a princess. Why, oh why had she never tried to be friends with Jen instead of trying to steal her husband?

Was loneliness her excuse? Culture shock? Moving from New Jersey into an apartment and a job so far from home, with a lifestyle as different from her own as if she had landed on the moon?

She glanced around her as if she were seeing Benjamin's family for the first time. The twins, who had obviously planned the party, took over as hosts. Marianne took center stage, as bold as both her mother and her aunt, to announce there would be a puppet show after dessert. Tommy followed with the announcement, "Let's eat ice cream! Everybody scoop your own and pick your own toppings!"

There was a general rush to the table. Antonia got lost in the crush. She couldn't even find Benjamin among all those tall women. *Gorgeous, too.* Toni hated jealousy, particularly in her own self, but wouldn't it be nice if some of those good looks could have been passed around, say, up to New Jersey when she came squalling into the world.

Now would be a good time to leave, she thought. She was here on a bogus excuse, anyhow. What did she think she was going to do? Get whisked off to her boss's office and pretend he was hers while the whole family was down the hall celebrating the return of a rarely seen relative? Pull off some kind of magic to make her boss realize she was the woman he needed, the one he couldn't live without?

She felt guilty, and slightly delusional, emotions as foreign to the no-nonsense lawyer as her recent activities had been. The come-hither outfits and blatantly sexual behavior in the office. Why on earth had she abandoned all common sense and her principles, too?

The housekeeper Nancy scurried back and forth between the dining room and the kitchen, while the beauty queen Sharon made herself indispensable at the ice cream table. She really was very pretty in a fragile, needy way that had its own kind of appeal.

Antonia skirted around the edges of the crowd. Distance gave her breathing room, a better perspective. The interesting grandmother in her cowboy boots was keeping an eagle eye on Jen. The twins in jeans and tee shirts emblazoned with *Gulf Breeze Bait and Tackle Shop* were pigging out on ice cream.

And there was Benjamin. *Finally*. Had he slipped out earlier to get some breathing room? He looked so deeply worried he didn't even glance her way.

Maybe it was for the best. Was he feeling as guilty as she was? And where was Jen? She was wearing red, easy to spot, a vivid silk tank top with white linen slacks. She was nowhere to be seen. Antonia felt a frisson of fear. Was Benjamin's wife really capable of making good on her threat?

Suddenly Antonia spotted her, hurrying out of the room, her face as crumpled as a discarded napkin. What was up with that?

She had no intention of sticking around to find out. Desperately wishing she had never come, she set down her ice cream dish, angled around the table and toward the massive front room, an open space that suddenly seemed as vast as the Sahara.

She felt exposed. Vulnerable. As if her whole constructed world was about to collapse.

She was almost to the door when Annie's voice rang out.

"Call 911! Jen's not breathing!"

FORTY-EIGHT

Galvanized by Annie's scream, Benjamin raced in that direction. He found his sister-in-law at the top of the stairs, bending over Jen.

"Where's her EpiPen?" Annie was on the edge of panic, unusual for his sister-in-law. She was a laid-back artist with the easy charm of angels.

"What?" His own terror nearly blinded him. All he could see was his wife crumpled, her face ashen.

"Benjamin, listen to me. Get her EpiPen. I don't know where she keeps it!"

Reality came to him in bits and pieces. Jen's severe allergic reactions. The epinephrine she always kept in her purse. He raced into the bedroom, jerked open her purse, and dumped the contents on the bed.

Nothing.

"Hurry!" Annie yelled. "We're losing her!"

He frantically searched the drawers in the bedside table. His children's voices filtered into the bedroom, as well as Victoria's and Sharon's. Terrified. Tearful.

Where is it?

Annie's voice, soothing, keeping them back in case Jen tried to catch a breath, get some air. There would be no more breathing unless he could find her EpiPen. He was near tears.

He pawed through the drawers, unhinged at the possibility of losing Jen.

"Ben?" It was Sharon, standing in the doorway cool and collected. A godsend. A blessed angel. "I think I know where she keeps it."

He wanted to grovel. Kiss her feet.

He raced after her into the ensuite. She went straight to Jen's dressing table and jerked open the drawer.

"It's here," Sharon said, then stepped aside as he grabbed the life-saving device.

But was she too late?

FORTY-NINE
GULF BREEZE HOSPITAL

Benjamin was living his worst nightmare.

He didn't know if Jen would live or die, and the weather news drifting from the radio in the waiting room down the hall warned of the massive hurricane building in the Atlantic, its gale-force winds and towering waves already pounding the coast of Cuba, building in intensity as it moved relentlessly toward the Gulf of Mexico.

If it kept its current path, it would veer in the direction of the Florida Panhandle, its destructive eye turned toward Gulf Breeze. Depending on the speed it was traveling, and the whim of the monstrous storm itself, it would be here within days. He could get caught between getting his children out to safety or sheltering in the hospital if Jen was still here.

If she lives...

It seemed impossible the sun should be beaming into this hospital room. But wasn't that the way of any disaster? Outward signs led you to believe you were safe until the destruction was upon you.

Jen lay so still and pale, as if Death already sat on her chest. He could hardly bear to look at his wife, and yet he couldn't turn away. It was a relief to see the door open to admit a doctor. Young, energetic, capable-looking. The kind of doctor who inspired confidence. "Anaphylactic shock," he said. According to his nametag, he was Dr. Chris Reeder.

The family was gathered around Benjamin at the hospital—his children, still crying; Victoria, looking grim; and Sharon, his rock. Everyone was there except Annie, who had stayed behind at the house. For what purpose, he couldn't imagine. Thankfully, Antonia had slipped out sometime during the trauma, making one less problem to deal with.

"We don't know yet what caused it," Dr. Reeder said, "but we are *very* lucky you got the epinephrine into her in time."

Relief washed through Benjamin.

"When can I go home?"

That was Jen for you. Rising up from her deathbed with the fierceness of a mama eagle, wings outspread and talons bared. She was a fighter. Something he had always loved about her. How could he have forgotten that?

"Dr. Turner, right now you probably think you have come through this unscathed, and we suspect that's true. But we are going to keep you overnight, just to make certain you're okay. I've ordered some tests to check for internal damage."

"In that case, I'm staying, too." Victoria plopped into a chair by Jen's bed. "You might as well order me a cot."

"Gran, you don't have to..."

"Save your breath," she told Jen. "I'm not leaving this room unless somebody drags me out. And then they'd better brace for a fight."

Dr. Reeder chuckled. He might not find her so amusing if he had to deal with the fallout from her bossy ways. Victoria and Nancy were like two stubborn old hens in Benjamin's kitchen, feathers ruffled and sharp beaks ready to peck each other's eyes out.

Still, he was grateful Jen would have company. Her

behavior of the last few days made it obvious she didn't want him at her bedside.

"I'll order a cot for this evening." The doctor turned his attention to Jen. "Dr. Turner, you can rest assured we will take good care of you and your family. The lab techs will be up shortly to take you down for lab work and X-ray. We will have results for you as soon as we can."

When Dr. Reeder left the room, Sharon hurried to Jen's beside. Considering her own situation, she had held up well through this ordeal, but Benjamin could see visible signs that she was cracking. In the car coming over, the breathy Marilyn Monroe voice she had cultivated so carefully during their Tulane days wavered between Hollywood chic and backwoods twang. One false eyelash had come loose and hung slightly askew over her left eye as if she were being attacked by a giant spider, and a spot of ice cream topping marred the front of her pink blouse.

She would be mortified if she knew. That's how meticulous Sharon was. As soon as he got the chance, he would take Marianne aside and tell her to take her adopted aunt into the ladies' room so she could fix herself up. Presenting a beautiful image had always been important to her, even in college. She seemed even more obsessed with appearances since she'd escaped to their cottage.

People under stress did all sorts of things to cope. He had to look no further than himself to understand that truth. He supposed Sharon coped with her own private horror story by presenting a perfect public façade.

When he thought about it, wasn't that better than what he had been doing?

Sharon leaned over to smooth Jen's mass of tangled curls. "I'm so sorry this happened to you." Her voice hitched. "I would rather it be me in this bed instead of you."

"Don't cry, Sharon. I'm going to be all right."

"I can stay with you, too. I don't even need a cot. I'll sleep in the chair."

"No," Jen said. "Honestly, I'm fine."

"Are you sure? Can I get you anything? Do anything for you?"

"Just help Benjamin take care of the children. Okay?"

Jen sent him a look that was clearly an appeal for help. After all these months, being needed by her was so shocking he almost missed the signal. He gave her a thumbs-up.

"Sharon, let's take the children downstairs to the cafeteria and get something to eat while we wait. We've had nothing much today except ice cream." Victoria's stare bored into him. Pierced by guilt, he hurried to his wife's side and took her hand. "I'm glad you're okay. I should have been more watchful."

His wife didn't say anything. Did she think he had engineered this catastrophe? He knew the ice cream was fine. He'd checked the boxes. There had been at least a dozen toppings, but nothing there that Jen couldn't eat.

"I'm going to be fine," Jen told him. "There's no need to hang around the hospital. I'll call you if the tests show anything amiss. I don't want Tommy and Marianne cooped up here. Get out in the sunshine so they can enjoy the rest of their weekend. Take Sharon with you and find a fun place to eat. Take everybody fishing."

Tommy perked up. "Can we, Dad? We haven't fished in forever. I'll bet Aunt Sharon would like it."

Sharon's face didn't say *eager to fish,* but as she turned to him, her attitude did. "I don't know one end of a fishing pole from the other, but I'm willing to learn."

"Cool!"

Benjamin felt better already. The Gulf Breeze Bait and Tackle Shop was open twenty-four/seven. Why not in this tourist town surrounded by water? Maybe this awful day was salvageable, after all.

For that matter, maybe his whole life could be saved.

After all, there was still his and Antonia's poison pill.

FIFTY

THE TURNER HOUSE

Annie stood in the dining room alone among the clutter of dirty dishes, melting ice cream, and scattered toppings, her feet bare against the vibrations of her sister's house. Every house has a story to tell, and Jen's more than most.

But this story was dense with layers, twisted with contradictions, heavy with the weight of love, guilt, and fear that had conceived it. Annie could feel the story's heartbreak and pain, its longing and uncertainty, its mad descent into evil.

"*Where* are you?" she whispered. "*Who* are you?"

The room remained as quiet as the ancient catacombs in Rome, as tightly closed as the crypts that held the secrets of the past. There was no use chasing a story that didn't want to be found.

Annie opened her eyes and moved about the room, careful not to touch any of the plates and dishes. She considered this the scene of a crime. It *was* the scene of a crime. In her *sister's* house. The horror of it would overwhelm her if she'd let it.

Someone who knew of Jen's allergies had tried to kill her sister. If Annie hadn't noticed her missing from the party and hurried off to find her, Jen would now be dead. If Sharon hadn't found the EpiPen, if Ben hadn't popped the shot into her thigh, if it had been a moment later, Jen would be in a morgue instead of a hospital room.

Gran had called from the hospital as soon as she had news.

"It's anaphylactic shock. They've got her downstairs now doing more tests, and she's mad as spit that she can't go home. We'll get the skunk who did this. Jen's going to call you. She said don't let anybody touch a thing in the dining and living rooms."

"I'm on it, Gran."

The minute the ambulance had left the driveway, Nancy marched into the dining room with a large tray and an even larger intent to collect dirty dishes and tidy up. Going up against her had been like climbing the Dolomites without any gear. It had taken Annie fifteen minutes of diplomacy, sugar-coated compliments, and tearful gratitude to get Nancy Park to leave the house without washing, moping, and dusting every inch of the crime scene. The effort had been more exhausting than smiling through her nervous energy all evening as art patrons and critics viewed her latest watercolor collection at a gallery in Rome.

But exhaustion was nothing compared to her fear. Hatred swirled around the chandelier, wrapped its ugly tentacles around the polished mahogany legs of the dining room chairs and threatened to smother her. Annie stood her ground, feet firmly planted, chin thrust at a stubborn angle. *Whoever you are, I won't let you win.*

The dining room held a puzzle she couldn't solve until after she talked with her sister. But there were other things she could investigate while she had the house to herself, starting with Nancy's domain.

Jen's longtime housekeeper and nanny had her own cubby near the kitchen where she kept a gray sweater, a pair of rain-boots, and a battered straw tote with *Florida* embroidered in pink on the side. Annie found a pair of thin surgical rubber gloves in one of the kitchen drawers and systematically went through Nancy's pockets. She found wadded tissues, a pencil stub, a tube of ChapStick, and a blue bead that might have come off a piece of jewelry. She inspected the sweater and found a dark stain on the left sleeve, damp and obviously still fresh, but nothing that would mark her as the person who had tried to kill Jen.

Still, the answer to a puzzle was not always obvious. Annie checked Nancy's rainboots. The soles had no clumps of mud, and the sides were clean, indicating that she probably had not used them in a while or, if she had, she had wiped them clean.

Next, Annie searched through the laundry room. This was where someone hid Jen's wallet. She found nothing except a neat row of cleaning products and a stack of clean laundry.

Benjamin. The word whispered through Annie's mind.

It was more than strange that he didn't know where to find Jen's EpiPen. Who wouldn't know where to locate his wife's life-saving device? And then, there were all the suspicious activities Jen had told her about revolving around the office and his legal assistant. Jen hoped the rumors about Toni weren't true. She liked her straightforward manner and the uncomplicated way she fit into her own skin. Under other circumstances, they might have been friends.

Still wearing the skin-tight rubber gloves, Annie made her way down the hall to her brother-in-law's office and picked the lock with her hairpin. When you live by yourself and have nobody to call when you lock yourself out of your tiny villa, you are forced to learn all sorts of skills.

Benjamin kept the usual items in his desk drawers. Nothing there to see. No secret files on Jen. No hidden letters from lovers. No diary confessing that he wanted to do away with his wife.

Annie moved to the more interesting bookshelves. He kept

memorabilia here, framed photos, water globes from places he and Jen had visited, a tattered old teddy bear he had won for Jen at a carnival in New Orleans on their first date. Funny that it was here, and not in Jen's office.

She picked up the bear and felt the lump in its back. The seam in the back had been split, the two sides held together with stick-on Velcro, easy to get at any Walmart or variety store. Annie reached inside and pulled out a bottle of sleeping pills. Like most over-the-counter sleep aids, it had a cutesy name, Sleep Tight, and it was chock full of diphenhydramine, an antihistamine as toxic to Jen as poison.

How easy for Benjamin to empty the contents of a few capsules into the tea Jen loved, then stand back to watch his wife reel with dizziness, nausea, headache, and confusion, to see her take to her bed, unable to work, incapable of even picking up her phone to take a call from Italy.

Fury instantly shot through Annie. She made herself breathe deeply to the count of eight, inhale calm, blow out anger. Then she took several pictures of the pill bottle against the backdrop of Benjamin's bookcase and the teddy bear with the tell-tale Velcro opening.

Who went to such lengths to hide sleeping pills unless he had a dark motive?

But wait. What if someone else hid the pills in his office to implicate him? In this huge house with staff and security guards coming and going at all hours, not to mention the tutor, the swim coach, and a vast assortment of guests, it would be easy to slip into Benjamin's office and plant a pill bottle.

Annie's cell phone rang. *Jen.*

FIFTY-ONE

"Listen, Annie, I don't know how much time I have before they whisk me off for more tests. Did you secure the scene?"

Annie was so relieved to hear her sister's voice she had to overcome her emotions before she could speak rationally.

"It took a *Herculean* effort to keep Nancy from cleaning, but I did it."

"Good. I ate nothing at the party but vanilla ice cream with chocolate topping. It would be hard to mix something into vanilla without detection. The toxin had to be in the topping. Probably blueberry juice or syrup? Blueberries and peanuts are the only two foods that are this toxic to me. It would be easy to hide in chocolate, and hard to detect by taste."

"Did you notice anything when you ate it?"

"I thought the chocolate tasted a little off, but nothing to be alarmed about. And then my tongue started swelling and my throat closing, and I knew I was in trouble. Call Clint and have him bag the bowl of chocolate topping, and my dish, too. He'll know what to do."

"Where did you leave it?"

"I had it in my hand when I started up the stairs to get my

EpiPen. You'll find it on the flower stand at the bottom of the staircase. Search the kitchen and see if you find any blueberry syrup. If Clint can find fingerprints, we'll know the culprit."

"Unfortunately, I strongly suspect... Benjamin." Annie felt awful as she told her sister what she had found. "It would have been so easy for him to make you sick by dumping diphenhydramine into your tea, and then trying to finish the job with blueberries. I'm so sorry, Jen."

"Don't be. You're doing what any loving family member would do. I want you to pick me up after I'm dismissed tomorrow, and tell Clint I'll want him to set up a guard outside my bedroom door. At this point, I don't trust anybody except you, Gran, Sharon, and the twins."

"We'll find the culprit. A Logan never gives up. *Hoc majorum virtus*. This is the valor of my ancestors." Annie had seen the Logan family coat of arms and motto every day of her childhood, hanging on the wall at the ranch house. Valor was part of her DNA, the beginning chapter of her history, the blood promise of her future.

"Yes, we will. See you tomorrow, Annie."

Purpose and progress always invigorated Annie. After talking to her sister, she could now add hope to her arsenal. There was *no way* this fierce team of Logans could be defeated. *None!*

After she hung up, Annie called Clint Brown, a man who, according to Jen, epitomized the valor of their own family. The evening she had arrived and met him at the bloody porch, her own impression of him was a man devoted to family and friends and dedicated to justice. She gave him a run-down of events.

"I'll be there in ten minutes," he said. "Don't touch any of the dishes."

True to his word, the Hulk-sized security guard arrived in exactly ten minutes. His aura was so strong, Annie immediately knew a true thing about him: he was a man with a divided heart. It was both fierce and soft.

"Annie, it's good to see you again. I just wish it was under happier circumstances." His handshake was firm, his smile sincere. "I sent Jen a text to let her know I will personally guard her. She's a great woman and a generous employer. One of a kind. She's also my friend. Nobody gets to her without going through me."

"I can breathe easier knowing you'll keep my sister safe. Jen said I could count on you."

"Let's get to work then, and find that blueberry toxin."

When Annie found the bottle in the trash, she was livid. Here was the proof someone who knew Jen's allergies had deliberately targeted her.

Wild blueberry juice concentrate. A little would go a long way. All natural, no additives. Just pure poison for Jen.

It was in the bag Nancy had already closed with ties and set beside the back door. Except for Annie's intervention, it would already have been hauled off in the back of Dal's truck to the recycling bins.

Annie stared at the bottle while emotions swamped her. "The murder weapon," she whispered.

"Almost." Clint carefully bagged and tagged the bottle. "It will take a while to get prints, and then we won't have much to go on unless the culprit is already in the system."

"Probably not. Only those at the party had access to Jen today. And any number of them could have hidden the blueberry juice in the trash. But Nancy was so eager to clean up after the party, I had to argue with her."

"The proof will be in the prints. I'll dust every ice cream dish. Can you identify where each of the suspects left their dishes?"

"Unfortunately, no."

"Then I need prints from personal items of the other adults at the party to create a match. Can you walk me through that?"

She showed him items in Nancy's sweater pocket first. He found a usable print on the ChapStick. The hairbrushes and water glasses in Benjamin's and Sharon's bathrooms yielded clear prints.

"We can find Dal's prints in the greenhouse, and probably Benjamin's, too. But the only thing I can identify as being touched by Antonia Delgado are the dishes of caramel sauce and M&Ms I handed to her, and all the prints on them won't be hers. Or even mine. Anybody here could have touched the topping dishes, including Jen." She glanced at her watch. "We need to hurry. Ben and Sharon and the children could be back any time. I don't want to further upset the children, and I don't want Benjamin and Sharon to know what we're doing."

"Got it. Let's go to the greenhouse, then. If I can get Dal's, an unknown print on the blueberry juice would probably point to the Delgado woman. Can you think of anyone else who might have slipped inside to put a lethal dose of blueberries in the chocolate topping?"

"Sharon's husband. One of Jen's patients. Or even a business rival of Benjamin's who might be trying to get to him through Jen. The possibilities are almost endless." The scope of it almost took Annie's breath away.

I refuse to be intimidated. Or defeated.

"Let's deal with what we know." Clint led the way out the back door.

The greenhouse bombarded her with a profusion of color, scent, and impressions. Its story was so loud and clear, it swept Annie into its midst, bore her upward on a whirlwind that was part of what she had come to know as a waking dream. Love was here, utter devotion to the beauty and healing of nature. The air was iridescent with it, and perfumed with a heady mix of scents that made hatred impossible under a glass ceiling open to sun and sky.

"There." Clint picked up a trowel. "That looks promising."

As if she were seeing him from a distance, Clint walked about among the gardener's tools, dusting for fingerprints, nodding his approval, talking to no one in particular, certainly not Annie, who was oblivious to everything except the story of her waking dream, whispering in her ear.

Underneath the surface of color and light lay a wisp of darkness, swirling slowly, biding its time. Boiling resentment. Deep disappointment. Seething discontent.

But was it Benjamin's or Dal's? Under cover of night, alone in the kitchen with Jen, her sister had told her that Nancy claimed a back injury had caused Dal to close his flower shop and nursery, sell all his greenhouses and the landscape business he had built from scratch. The truth was more complicated. When one of his biggest customers accused him of padding his invoice, Dal, an expert in Taekwondo, the ancient martial art of his Korean homeland, had almost killed him with his bare hands and feet.

A man capable of flying into a killing rage because of an invoice operated on a very short fuse.

"That wraps it up," Clint said. "I took several prints to be sure I got a clear one for Dal." He scanned the area for any details they might have missed, then led her from the greenhouse. "You should know I strongly advised Jen to call law enforcement."

"She's made up her mind, and there's no use trying to make her change it."

"I won't."

"It's more complicated than her trying to protect her friend. I think she wants the matter kept private to protect the children. In case Benjamin is the culprit."

"I understand," he said. "When I find out something, I'll call you or Jen."

After he left, she hurried into the house to clean up the party dishes. She had just put away the last dish and put tea in the pot to steep when she saw headlights coming up the driveway.

Marianne and Tommy burst into the house first, both seeking reassurances and hugs from their aunt. Benjamin came into the kitchen next, subdued, and Sharon appeared almost shell-shocked. She wore a pinched expression, and she was missing the animation she always worked so hard to project.

"What a day!" She sounded like a woman waking from a bad dream. "I just can't believe it."

"I've made tea," Annie told Sharon. "Why don't you sit down and have a cup with me?"

Jen's friend stared at her for a moment as if Annie might have just floated into the kitchen on a broomstick. Then she batted at her hair which hung in salt-encrusted tangles. They had been to the beach then. Jen had said they might go fishing.

"I have... lots of things to do for Jen." Sharon wandered off toward the back door, then caught herself and turned to head upstairs.

Benjamin turned to his daughter. "Marianne, follow her and make sure she's all right. Okay?"

"Sure. Do we have to go to school tomorrow?"

"Of course you do."

"I thought after what happened with Mom, we might get to stay home... and help."

"The best way to help your mom is to do your homework, go to school, and do your best. Tommy, that includes you, too."

The twins hurried out, Marianne rolling her eyes and Tommy grinning. Benjamin watched his children go, and then slumped into a chair.

"I guess that leaves the two of us," he said. "I could use a cup of tea. Do you mind fixing it? I don't seem to have the energy."

"Coming right up."

Was his lack of energy from defeat or guilt? Or both? Annie busied herself with mugs, cream, and sugar, then sat in a chair across the table from her brother-in-law and searched his face for clues to his heart.

"Do you love my sister, Benjamin?"

He squirmed and glanced at the clock on the wall before he could look her in the eye. "What kind of question is that?"

"The question of someone who hasn't been home often enough, and returns to find her beloved sister has deteriorated from the most capable woman I know to a bloodstained, uncertain woman who is the target of a killer."

"You think *I* did this to Jen?"

Annie treated him to such prolonged, silent scrutiny that he squirmed in his chair. Still, she said nothing, simply gave him the space to let his true feelings emerge. Fear flickered across his face, then outrage, then self-pity.

"*Did* you?" She never backed down from a challenge when one of her family was under siege. Jen was engaged in all-out war with an enemy no one could unmask.

I plan to. Annie wouldn't stop till she did.

Benjamin set his mug on the table, then pushed back his chair.

"I'm surprised you even asked. And disappointed. I thought you knew me better than that." He stood up, hesitant. Second-guessing himself. "Jen sent a text to say you are picking her up tomorrow. I guess that says it all."

Annie watched him leave the room. Then she cupped her hands around her mug and let the warmth soak in.

"Not quite," she said.

FIFTY-TWO

THE TURNER HOUSE

Sharon's room—well, actually, the guest bedroom she'd been assigned in Jen's house—was designed for comfort and beauty. The dusty rose color of the walls encouraged relaxation, and repeated in more vivid shades in the plush cushions on the bed and in the chair beside the window overlooking the water. The curtains and even the paintings on the wall contained splashes of yellow, the exact color of the buttercups that sprang up everywhere in March and April, reminding Sharon of the home she'd left behind in Alabama, it's red clay hills awash with yellow in the spring. Not only buttercups but wild Carolina jasmine hanging from the trees and hillsides abloom with golden forsythia.

Still, she couldn't sleep. Her sleeping pills were in the cottage, and she'd had no chance to get them without Annie seeing. And watching with those unsettling, laser-beam eyes. And wondering what she was doing.

Then there was Ben, who would have insisted on walking her over. The blood on the cottage front porch had spooked everybody. And, of course, Jen's brush with death.

Sharon shivered as if death had breathed down her own neck. What a nightmare!

It was the water doing this to her. Water everywhere you looked. Blindingly blue in the daytime under the relentless Florida sun, nowhere to turn without seeing it, no place to go without crossing it. Metallic and cold-looking at night under the moon, shading to a black void in the distance that could swallow you whole, make you vanish so completely you'd never be found.

There was no escaping it. Why had Jen, a rancher's daughter, chosen a house in such a threatening location? One hurricane would wipe it off the map. Especially the one headed their way. One encounter with a shark in the water would leave you crippled for life. Or dead.

As if a magnet were pulling her, Sharon turned to stare out the massive windows. The moon laid a streak of silver across the bay that seemed to go on forever. An endless highway to perdition. To the nightmare that haunted Sharon's waking hours as well as her restless nights.

The moon had been bright on that last day in Eutaw, as well. An omen. A good luck sign. Or so she had thought.

She followed the pull of the moon across Jen's impossibly beautiful guest bedroom—done in shades of rose and gold—and stood at the window, ghost-like in a white satin gown, arms wrapped around herself for protection.

Memories poured in with the moonlight...

FIFTY-THREE

SHARON'S HOUSE

"Sharon? Baby? I'm home!" Matt called to her in a sing-song voice. A man confident of getting away scot-free with his brutality.

She quivered like a whipped dog expecting his next kick to the ribs. A glance in the mirror over her dressing table showed a white-faced, terrified woman. Sharon grabbed blush to put color in her cheeks, slashed on some berry red lipstick, then walked out to give the performance of her life.

"Sweetheart," she said. "How *wonderful* to see you."

Sharon didn't imitate his sing-song greeting. She used her voice like the finest violin, the music of it so hypnotic even a man of Matt's suspicious nature fell under its spell. Her secret was in mimicking the breathy quality of her favorite movie icon, Marilyn Monroe, a flawed woman who, nonetheless, knew how to use her looks to her advantage.

He reached for her, and she stood on tiptoe to endure his sloppy kiss. He had been drinking, so no surprise there. After one of their little misunderstandings, as he called them, he always stopped by a bar on the way home to load himself up with liquid courage.

Matt was as predictable as the rising sun. For once, it would work to Sharon's advantage.

"I made your favorite meal."

"Baby, if you tell me it's something besides fried chicken, I'm gonna die on the spot."

"It's fried chicken with *all* your favorite trimmings." She took his hand and reeled off the list as she led him into the kitchen. "Potatoes and gravy, sweetcorn, fried okra, and pineapple upside-down cake for dessert."

"That's my girl. Sharon, when you try, you sure know how to keep a man happy."

When she *tried*? If that were true, she would be in a picture-perfect marriage, and Matt, the scumbag, would be in hog heaven, as her mama used to say.

"Oh, I'm going to try *real* hard this evening, sweetheart. We're having a picnic at your favorite spot."

"The river?"

"Right smack dab in the middle of it with our old friend, Robert Mondavi." She held up two bottles of his favorite cabernet sauvignon, then stuffed the wine bottles into the picnic basket along with dinner. "If you'll grab the boom box, we'll have a private concert by Tammy Wynette."

"Mrs. Jones, are you planning to *sheduce* me?" His slur of seduce showed just what kind of condition he was in.

Getting him down the steps, across the backyard, around the curve of backwater, and into the boat took Herculean effort and more grit than Sharon knew she had. The trees were thick in this corner of their yard, and they cast shadows across the now-dark river that made it look forbidding.

For an instant, terror seized Sharon, and she froze. She couldn't get into the boat. She couldn't motor out into a river that could turn monstrous in a heartbeat. She could die out there. If the river didn't turn against her, Matt could. He had done it too often for her to expect he would remain in a jovial mood for the rest of the evening.

Anything could go wrong. Anything could happen out there in the dark, just the two of them in the middle of an unpredictable river...

* * *

Sharon shivered, returning to the present. She was cold. The silvery bay beyond the windows in Jen's mansion looked frozen, as if it had locked its secrets beneath the water and dared her to come find them.

She turned from the window then climbed into bed and lay under the covers, still trembling. With Jen gone, everything seemed so wrong. Threatening.

"Oh, please, please be all right, Jen," she whispered.

What if the tests showed something awful? And what if Jen never recovered?

FIFTY-FOUR

THE TURNER HOUSE

The morning brought no relief to Sharon. She crept into the gorgeous ensuite bathroom like an old lady Victoria's age but without her spunk. It was all she could do to make herself presentable enough to face the Turner family.

All of them. Especially Annie, the wild tigress parading as a house cat.

She was in the kitchen, taking up all the air. Her claws sheathed. Sharon felt immediately diminished beside her. Too short. Too colorless. Too unsophisticated.

The TV blared with the latest news of the path that awful hurricane was taking. Everybody was watching. Riveted. Beyond the window, the sun was shining on the bay, but the water looked gray and restless, like an angry giant awakening, getting ready to vent its rage.

Sharon didn't want to be hemmed in by two bodies of water when gale-force winds, clocking in at two hundred miles an hour, sent the water in forty-foot-high waves to destroy everything in its path.

How long before it would get here? Three days? Six? Hurricanes were always terrifyingly unpredictable. Underestimate one, and you were *doomed*...

The twins dawdled over their breakfast, under the TV's spell. And Annie's, too. It would be impossible to get them to school on time. The mighty, glorious artist wasn't going to take them. *Of course not.* She was heading to the hospital to bring Jen home.

That meant Sharon would have to rush through her morning like her hair was on fire. Hurry with breakfast, hurry getting dressed, hurry into the school office and explain the twins were tardy because of a family emergency.

Plus, Ben was in a foul mood, possibly because his wife had made it clear he wasn't welcome in her hospital room. Everything was left up to Sharon.

Anything is better than my life in Eutaw. This, too, shall pass.

That was going to be her new mantra. She could do this. She was smart. She was capable. Didn't Jen always tell her that?

Sharon reminded the twins they needed to leave for school in ten minutes, and they were amiable about it. *See.* Everything was going according to plan until Ben reminded Tommy that Maria Ramos would be there at four for his swim lesson.

The bombshell gold-digger with the killer body. Was that woman made of Play-Doh? Smash it any way possible, and it bounced right back.

Oh, well. Sharon couldn't think about the Olympic swimmer right now. The dreadful Nancy Park just came through the door. When she spotted Jen's sister, her lips pursed as if she had been eating bitter persimmons. It seemed the hateful old gargoyle saw right through Annie's doting aunt act to the fearful magician who lurked beneath the surface.

Sharon *could not wait* for Annie to go home.

But the next best thing was escaping the house. Finally, in the car with the twins, she could breathe again. She deposited them at school, trotted inside to explain why they were tardy, and then drove to Jen's office. By the time Sharon parked her car in the slot designated for employees and stepped into a blast of muggy heat, she already felt like she'd been going all day. She didn't need a weather report to tell her the heat index was high today, and the amount of humidity even higher, a combination guaranteed to make a lady sweat. She hated that.

She stripped off her jacket in the parking lot to catch a breeze, then hurried toward Jen's office. Larry was already there, enjoying his morning coffee and the morning news on the TV with the volume turned low while he pored through Jen's appointment book.

"Morning, Larry. I see you're multi-tasking."

"Don't you know it." He looked up and his smile froze. "Are you okay?"

Alarm skittered through her. "What do you mean?"

"Well, your shoes are mismatched, your blouse is buttoned wrong, and your hair has this thingy..." He gestured toward his own head, speechless, it seemed.

Sharon looked down to see she was wearing one black pump and one navy. Mortified, she raced down the hall to view herself in the bathroom mirror. The blue faux-silk blouse she had chosen so carefully to match her eyes was hanging crooked like some cheap thing off the bargain table in a dollar store. Her fingers shook as she rebuttoned it. Her only saving grace was that her jacket would have covered it when she went into the office at school that morning.

There was nothing wrong with her hair. It looked fine. Perfect, even. Until she turned her head and saw the curler from her set of hot rollers still hanging in a clump on the side of her head.

Oh, well. It could have been worse. Larry could have seen a gray hair. It wouldn't surprise her. She'd had more than enough trauma to turn her prematurely gray.

There was nothing she could do about the shoes, short of going home to change and facing Annie. *Awful thought*. She made repairs, stowed her purse and jacket in the breakroom, and headed back to the reception area.

Larry still had the TV going. The meteorologist pointed to a weather map tracking the hurricane, still too far away from Gulf Breeze for them to even smell a sniffle of rain. Then an earnest-looking reporter announced a prison break in Atmore, Alabama, with such a funereal air Sharon wondered if he knew the female prisoner personally.

Next, the scene of a wrecked town flashed onto the screen with the word TUPELO underneath. Sharon nearly had a heart attack.

"The tornado that swept through Tupelo, Mississippi, last night left a path of destruction up Highway 45 north toward the Barnes Crossing Mall. Six people were injured, and numerous houses and businesses demolished."

Sharon jerked her cell phone from her pocket while the reporter showed a group of police cars and a coroner's van that had converged at the scene of another disaster.

"Before dawn this morning, a local fisherman discovered a body snagged in some brush..."

Larry snapped off the TV. "Sharon, you look like you've seen a ghost. What's wrong?"

"My sister and my mother live in Tupelo. I've got to call them and see if they're okay."

"You poor thing. Let me get you some coffee." Larry whizzed by while Sharon listened to the busy signal from Eleanor's phone.

"Come on, come on... Pick up." The horrifying image of Eleanor's house and the care home blown to bits by tornadic winds while her sister and her mama lay buried under the rubble almost buckled her knees.

Larry took her arm and led her to the chair in her office. "Here." He thrust the coffee cup into her hands. "Drink this."

Her hands trembled as she ended the busy signal and took the coffee. Black dots danced before her eyes. Horrible images. Her sister and her mama, staring sightlessly at the sky while the escaped convict stole her mother's wedding band, and the gory find of the fisherman did a gleeful, macabre death dance among the debris that had once been Eleanor's home.

It felt like Armageddon. The end of life as Sharon knew it.

FIFTY-FIVE
GULF BREEZE HOSPITAL

Jen waited under the hospital's awning in a wheelchair she didn't need, her grandmother standing at her side. When Annie drove up in her rented convertible with the top down, her face alight with relief, Jen felt such a vaulting sense of love for her family she could have danced her way across the parking lot.

Suddenly, a colony of seagulls wheeled across the sky, leaving a trail of sorrow and heartbreak. Their message was sobering and unmistakable to Jen.

The worst is yet to come. Delilah, whispering to her from the grave.

"Would you look at that!" Gran was trotting along beside the wheelchair with the spryness of a young-at-heart woman whose family loved and needed her. "Finn used to drive me around in a convertible. Those were some of the best days of my life."

Annie burst out laughing. "Brace yourself, Gran. Today is going to be another one of your best days."

"Why is that, dear heart-of-mine?"

Annie held up a finger, then waited until the nurse had loaded Jen into the car and headed back inside the hospital.

"Because today, we're going to find out who has been trying to ruin Jen's life."

"Brava, Annie! You bet we will." Jen applauded as Annie navigated the car down the hospital's exit ramp. "First stop, Benjamin's office. I have a few things to say to him."

Gran stuck two fingers in her mouth and gave the piercing whistle she used to call up her cow dogs. "It's about high time."

"Which way, Jen?" her sister said.

"Pull over and let me drive, Annie. It'll be faster."

"Absolutely not! Your job is to rest and give directions, and mine is to run the show."

Jen spouted off directions, and Annie tore out like the car had wings and the highway patrol wore blinders. She winked at Jen. "If I get a ticket, you can pay for it."

"It will be worth every penny. Somebody's trying to kill me, and I don't have time to play nice." She whipped out her phone to send a text to her husband. She had no intention of starting a serious discussion with an ambush.

I'm out of the hospital, and I'm heading your way. Clear your calendar. We have a lot to talk about. I need answers.

His response was a thumbs-up emoji. Jen didn't try to read anything into it. Nothing good ever came from a meeting when one person had already decided the outcome.

Annie parked the car in the section reserved for employees. "Do you want me to come with you, Jen?"

"No. I don't want Benjamin to feel double-teamed. Why don't you take Gran to the company cafeteria downstairs for lunch? She didn't eat breakfast at the hospital."

"You bet your boots, I didn't. The coffee was awful, and the pancakes were so thin I could see right through them."

Annie winked, then leaned in to hug her. "I'm so glad I got my sister back alive."

"That makes two of us."

"We'll be in the cafeteria when you need us. *Hoc majorum virtus*, Jen."

With Annie's reminder to take courage from their family's coat of arms, Jen headed toward her husband's office.

* * *

Annie and Victoria followed the smell of Southern cooking to the company's restaurant and settled into a quiet alcove with a cup of tea. For a moment, the steam swirling around the teapot took on the sinister appearance of a rattlesnake.

Annie shivered. She needed no voice from the past to interpret her brief glimpse of another waking dream.

Her sister was going to need more than a family logo to survive what lay ahead. Danger was waiting to sink its fangs into Jen, and next time, she might not survive the deadly venom.

FIFTY-SIX

BENJAMIN'S OFFICE | TURNER MEDICAL SOLUTIONS

Jen settled into a chair opposite Benjamin's desk, an act that should have been as natural as breathing. Except it wasn't. The tension between them was so thick, she felt as if she had entered a dangerous foreign territory without a map.

She had never been more grateful to have Annie and Gran waiting for her in the cafeteria. She even viewed Annie's rental as a sort of getaway car. *From her own husband!* She'd never expected her marriage would come to this—an ugly stand-off, no quarter given, no love in the room.

At least, not that she could feel. She squeezed her hands together, holding in her emotions as if they were a runaway horse.

Instead of moving to sit beside her, Benjamin remained barricaded behind his desk, his coffee cup on a trivet bearing the company logo. It was both a power play and protection. If they were in her office, she would have done the same thing.

"I don't suppose you want coffee?" he asked.

"No. Until I know my enemy, I won't drink or eat anything unless I know *who* prepared it." She felt like one of her own patients, heartbroken and tragic, her husband, her rock, now being viewed as the enemy. She thought of the box of tissues she kept on hand in her office, such a casual thing, it seemed. And yet, she now saw that box as her patients must see it, a symbol of their own failure.

"Fair enough. You look better, though. How are you feeling?"

Like a stranger. Jen felt like crying, but she wouldn't. Not in front of him.

"Healthier than I have all week. The IV fluids helped flush out the toxins." *Courage. Go straight for the jugular.* "Are you the one who put them in my food?"

His face! Was that guilt or sorrow or regret—or all three? Jen's own mixed emotions were heavy, almost unbearable. She knew how she looked, cool, composed; but it was a lie. She was flying apart, sitting in a chair.

"No. I would never do anything to harm my wife and the mother of my children. Believe me, Jen. I want to get to the bottom of this mystery as much as you do. It's time for us to level with each other."

"Are you kidding me?" She clenched her teeth. She was so mad, she wouldn't be surprised if her hair caught fire. "There is no *us* to come clean. *You're* the one who makes every excuse not to come home. *You're* the one with all the secrets."

He didn't bother denying it. His face turned red, and he got that little tick in his jaw she used to think was part of his manly charm.

Say something! She wanted to shout at him. *Scream.* But she was, after all, a respected psychologist and a pure-bred lady, to boot, descended straight from that magnificent magnolia of New Orleans who could melt a man—any man—with one look.

At the moment, Jen couldn't melt an ice cube if she sat on it. She was that mad, that hurt, that uncertain.

Why was her husband still sitting there like a lump, the

perfect picture of a man guilty of cheating on his wife. Had he tried to kill her, too?

Please, let it not be so... Say something!

He hadn't even said he loved her, not once in this horrible conversation. Of course, she hadn't either, but she had an excuse. She was the target of a killer.

"Are you having an affair with Antonia?"

There. She didn't have time for lies. They had both ripped the fabric of their marriage apart. It lay on the floor between them in tatters. All she wanted now was the truth.

Is that so?

Her face flushed. She felt so hot she might jump up and ditch her skirt. She was lying to herself. Something she never thought she'd do. She wanted more. She wanted to turn back the clock to... *When?*

Before Sharon came.

The thought blazed through her like a comet, but she didn't have time to dwell on it. Benjamin was leaning across his desk, his face earnest and sweating.

He'd hurt her, and she couldn't even bear to look at him.

"Jen, look at me."

"All right." She faced him once more, but it seemed she was now seeing him from a distance, through water, as if both of them were drowning, and he was slowly drifting away from her.

"I am *not* having an affair with Antonia. I have never even kissed her. Though lately... I've been tempted."

His confession stung so hard she almost bent double. How had that happened? Temptation was almost as dangerous to a committed relationship as actually straying.

"I don't believe you." *Four hateful words.* She'd never imagined saying them to her own husband.

"It's the truth."

Maybe. Maybe not. Jen could no longer tell.

"Ask her to come into the office so I can hear her side of the story."

"She's not here."

"How convenient for you." Jen hated barbs, and here she was, taking aim at her husband.

He picked up a pencil and squeezed it so hard he broke it in half. "It's not like that, Jen. She turned in her resignation today. She was so upset, I told her to go home. She's working from there today, and will probably do so for most of her notice."

Shock held her speechless. Was Antonia leaving because she couldn't have Benjamin, or because she *had* and the guilt was tearing her apart? Before she went after a married man, she'd seemed like a nice young woman who enjoyed living in the Sunshine state.

"Did she give a reason why she resigned?"

"She only said that she was ready for a change." Ben wrote something on his notepad and passed it across the desk, his feelings masked behind a neutral expression he might have used with an errand boy. "Here's her address if you want to talk to her. I'm sure she'll be willing."

What if he was telling the truth? What if he wasn't the one trying to kill her? A small glimmer of hope tried to push its way past the debris of a once-wonderful marriage she and Benjamin had torpedoed.

"She's really a nice young woman," he added.

"I've always thought so until someone decided to muddle my mind with diphenhydramine and poison me with blueberries."

Pain flashed across his face. Or was it guilt?

"You think it was... deliberate?"

"It had to be. I don't use sleeping pills, and I would never have ingested either of those toxins accidentally."

His face registered shock, and it took him a few minutes to get himself back under control.

"That's attempted murder," he said. "I don't know how I could have missed something like this, except I've been so... preoccupied. I think we should call in law enforcement. If Matt comes after Sharon, we can protect her."

Benjamin's good heart was one of the things Jen had always admired about him. She was happy to catch a glimmer of his goodness, to remember, if only for a moment, that this was the man she once loved.

Once? Or still? She touched her gold bracelets for reassurance.

"Let's give this more time." Sharon had been adamant, and Matt had already proved his vengeful nature. Jen would never forget her bloodied cottage. "If I haven't found answers in the next couple of days, I'll agree to call the law."

"Fair enough. Sharon is fragile, and she had another scare this morning."

"Matt?"

"No, not this time. A tornado hit Tupelo last night, and she thought her family had been killed. After I saw the news, I called her. It turns out they're okay."

Jen was grateful for the relief of talking about ordinary things. But deep inside, the lacerations inflicted by the accusations they'd hurled were bleeding. "Poor Sharon. Maybe you should pick up the children at school today. Or I could ask Annie."

"She said she wants to. She needs to stay busy."

That had always been one of Sharon's coping mechanisms, and a good one, at that. Stay busy. Focus on helping others instead of pitying yourself. Jen was proud of her.

"I agree. It's good to keep her mind occupied with ordinary things. She knows Tommy has a swim lesson after school, right?"

"Yes. She said she would probably take them to get ice cream afterward, but would have him back by four."

Jen glanced out the window. The beautiful weather made reports of an imminent hurricane seem like the ravings of a madman.

Oh, but the birds. Seagulls had gathered, too far inland to be natural, and were wheeling and screaming in a frenzy that made Jen feel as if her heart were being ripped out.

"Jen. What's wrong? You're white as a sheet."

Everything is wrong. She just couldn't put her finger on it. "Maybe we ought to call Maria and cancel the lesson."

"The latest weather report shows the hurricane veering westward, toward Louisiana. If it makes landfall around New Orleans or anywhere beyond, we'll get tropical storm winds and rain, but nothing like the impact from a cat four." Benjamin picked up his pen and doodled on a note pad, his way of thinking through a problem. Finally, he said, "I want to be the one to bring up my obsession with work. I know it's on your mind, and I know it has driven a wedge between us. Something I deeply regret."

There it was. The bull in their china shop.

"Keep talking," she said. "I'm listening."

"Two days after you flew to Colorado last fall, Magna Medical set plans in motion for a hostile takeover of Turner Medical Solutions."

The news took Jen's breath away. "Why haven't you told me?"

"I felt like a failure. I felt that if Dad had been here, this would not be happening. I've spent every waking minute since then trying to find a way to prevent it." He paused to let the scope of his problem sink in. "As head of legal, Antonia is front and center in this fight. She and I have kept our meetings secret, so our employees won't feel that their jobs are threatened and leave the company. A massive walkout would be disastrous."

"Your only failure was in not trusting me to support you in this, Benjamin."

"I had to almost lose you in order to remember that, Jen."

Her husband sat quietly, watching her. He hadn't studied her that closely in a very long time. It felt gratifying and unsettling at the same time.

"Do you have a solution to the takeover?" she asked.

"I think so. It's called the poison pill."

Jen knew what he meant—she had read about it. Essentially it put in place a provision that would block the accumulation of stocks by an outsider intent on a hostile takeover. If the outsider tried to buy more than a set percentage of the outstanding shares, the company would distribute free or deeply discounted shares to all its shareholders except the buyer who triggered the provision, making the hostile outsider's stocks virtually worthless.

"What happens to this company impacts the children as well as me. Will you keep me in the loop from now on?"

"I promise I will. No more secrets."

What about the pills Annie found hidden in your office?

Shame could explain that little secret. For Jen, the important thing was not who hid the pills, but who had tried to kill her. Her instinct as well as her training in reading a person's expressions and body language said Benjamin was not the culprit.

She left his office without fanfare, no hugs or signs of affection, no small talk about ordinary things they used to find so easy, just a quick parting of two people who had severed the bond Jen once considered unbreakable.

I can fix this.

She could. And she would.

But being determined was no guarantee of success, in spite of the pop-psychology books that would have you believe otherwise.

Jen squared her shoulders and marched off to find Annie and Gran in the cafeteria, having a cup of tea. Her sister had chosen a table in a small alcove, separated from the other diners to give them privacy. A small metal pot of hot water and the tea bags were still on the table. Having her family here with this ritual was so comforting, Jen felt her worries melting as if she were growing a new skin, becoming the strong, optimistic dreamer of her youth.

Her sister got up to hug her and whisper in her ear, "You are a rock star. I see it in the air all around you."

"Thanks, Annie." Jen sat in a chair next to Gran, who squeezed her hand. "Sharon's picking up the children, so we have the rest of the afternoon to do what we want. Tea looks good."

"Annie ordered it this way so you can have a cup without worrying. Tell us everything Benjamin said. If he didn't behave himself, I'll go up there and talk some sense into him."

"Oh, how I've missed being home!" Annie's smile lit candles in Jen's bruised heart. As long as she had sisters, she was blessed. "Tell us only what we need to know, Jen."

"Bottom line... I don't believe my husband is trying to kill me, but we're going to Antonia's house to find out if she is."

FIFTY-SEVEN
ANTONIA'S APARTMENT

Giving up both the job and the man she loved felt like the end of the world. But Antonia knew it was not.

She would recover and move on. She was young, and her entire life was ahead. She would list herself with a headhunter. Find a job in another city. Another state would be even better. She would get another apartment, make new friends, avoid married men as if they were the plague.

But logic had nothing to do with the heart. She had ripped hers in half, knocked a hole that would take months to repair. She stomped around her apartment, barefoot, crying and kicking furniture—but only the soft-sided pieces. She had no intention of injuring herself.

She was Sicilian, prone to dramatics, immune to quiet grieving, and comforted by the Big Moment, the plush robe she hugged around herself, even the noisy sobbing that turned her eyes and her nose red.

Anyone looking through the window might even say she was enjoying herself. Unaware of the three women standing downstairs, determined to put her on the hot seat, she jumped when the buzzer sounded.

Benjamin! He had come to apologize, to reject her resignation, to tell her that he could not go forward with his wife or live without her.

Such is the lovesick mind.

Furious at herself for sliding backward so quickly, she wiped her face with a wrinkled tissue in her pocket and pressed the intercom.

"Who's there?"

"It's Annie." Relief swept through her, only to be brought up short by four little words. "Can we come up?"

"Who is *we*?"

"My grandmother and my sister, Jen. It's very important that we talk to you."

A vision of Benjamin's wife being hauled off on a stretcher made a terrible day even worse. She didn't owe them a thing.

Don't you?

Her conscience twinged her. And her curiosity stirred.

"Come on up."

Antonia braced herself, but nothing could prepare her for the sight of the three Logan women, shoulder to shoulder, fierce warriors fighting the same battle. And she didn't have a big stick.

"Have a seat." She waved her arm to indicate the lovely sofa she would take with her when she left, the comfortable chairs that felt like getting a hug when you sat down. Those would go, too. She made no apologies for her bathrobe or the state of her face, wrecked by grief. This was *her* home. She was in charge. "What can I do for you?"

Annie spoke first. They must have agreed on it. And why not? Hers was the soothing language of cathedral bells in Italy, stirring the air, setting the tops of cypress trees dancing. Antonia had only been there once to visit her Delgado relatives still living in the homeland. But Annie's voice made her want to go again, ignited a longing in her for peace and beauty and amoré, perhaps known only by her people.

Annie's questions about her relationship with Benjamin were asked in such a persuasive way, she found herself eager to tell the truth, bare her soul. Even to erase the pain and uncertainty she saw on Jen Turner's face.

"Did I love Benjamin?" Antonia tucked her legs underneath her and settled into her truth. "I did. I built him up in my mind, convinced myself he was so unhappy he needed me to rescue him. I made up excuses to be with him, invented work to keep him at my side."

Jen turned as pale as the oleander Antonia had put in vases on her mantel to bring a touch of spring inside.

"Did the two of you have an affair?"

For a moment, hope perched in Antonia's soul, that little thing with feathers from the Emily Dickinson poem she loved so well. Depending on what she said, and how she said it, she might demolish Jen and still win Benjamin back.

Her own selfishness mocked her. She knew the difference between healthy hope and stupid desire. Her mother, her grandmother, and all the aunts had taught her.

"No." She sighed. One word brought relief. Antonia could look herself in the mirror again. "In spite of my efforts and my own desire, your husband remained faithful to you. There was never any reason for you to threaten to kill me because of him."

The shock on Jen's face, on the faces of all three women, looked so genuine, Antonia whipped out her cell phone to show them the two hateful text messages. They were both so old the dates had dropped off, but one of them was unmistakably from Jen's phone.

"I wouldn't do that. I always speak my mind, face to face." Jen's denial was strong, but she was known for being forceful. Her face was a careful mask. "When did you get the one from my phone?"

Dates and times were easy for Antonia to remember. Any attorney good at her job can pull up details as if her mind were a computer. After she reeled them off, the grandmother, Victoria Logan, was the first to respond.

"That was the evening I arrived."

"Precisely," Jen said. "At the exact time the text came from my phone, the whole family was in the pool room, enjoying Gran's arrival."

Something flickered briefly across Jen's face. Guilt? Doubt? Suspicion? She was better at keeping her thoughts to herself than the clients Antonia dealt with. Could Dr. Turner hide a lie with the same ease?

"Maybe you sent the text to yourself?" Jen asked. "Were you in my house when I was sick?"

How neatly Benjamin's wife turned the tables on her. When Antonia had set out to take her husband, she had made a grievous mistake, unconscionable for an attorney. She had underestimated her opponent.

"Yes. I brought soup, but it was after this text came in. I was also there the day you left in an ambulance. But I can swear to you that I wish you no harm, and I did nothing to harm you... except try to steal your husband."

Jen's next volley of accusations shocked Antonia. No wonder such a strong woman had been crumpling. Whoever had been in her house, whispering in the dark and putting toxic allergens in her food had surely wanted her gone. But the culprit was not Antonia. If a Delgado made an enemy of you, you would know about it, face to face, toe to toe.

She made a strong case that she had done nothing Jen tried to pin on her. The clincher for Ben's wife was her closing argument.

"If necessary, I can prove my innocence in a court of law."

After they left, Antonia poured herself a glass of wine. Never mind that it was early afternoon. She curled onto her sofa and pulled a cozy throw over her legs. Stress always chilled her. What an awful, horrible, wretched day. But cathartic. And even a bit hopeful.

But there was something magical about Annie. Under other circumstances, they might have been friends.

Maybe, someday, Antonia could explore that option. But for now, she had to burn bridges. Moving to another city wouldn't be enough for her. She couldn't be close enough to Jen to risk running into her in shopping malls and beaches and public events. Reminders of past mistakes were the death of happiness. She couldn't be close enough to Benjamin to drive by his house in a moment of weakness, just to check things out. Longing for the impossible was a recipe for despair.

She had to move to another state. She had to forget the Turners.

FIFTY-EIGHT

Annie's blue rental car parked outside Antonia's apartment was deceptive. For a moment, Jen could believe the last couple of weeks were a bad dream, and she was in the midst of an ordinary spring where seeing a convertible with the top down on a warm spring day in Gulf Breeze meant flying kites on the beach and eating ice cream from the food trucks with their colorful awnings.

Her sister slid behind the wheel, and she sat into the passenger side so she could issue directions.

"Do you believe her?" Gran said, as she settled into the backseat.

"I do," Jen said.

"I didn't pick up any signals of danger in her apartment. Only harmony," Annie added. "Where to next, Jen?"

"I want a good bath and a change of clothes before the children get home from school, and I want to talk to Nancy and Dal."

Gran sniffed. "If you ask me, that housekeeper is capable of anything. She told me I was interfering in *her kitchen,* as if I had rolled off a watermelon truck. I was standing there, big as you please, in my very own granddaughter's kitchen. And house, too. I gave her a piece of my mind. I wouldn't be surprised if she's waiting behind the door with her butcher knife out to slit somebody's throat."

"I don't know what to think about her right now, but considering the rift between you two, maybe it would be best if you and Annie aren't there when I question her."

"Suit yourself. But I'll be close by if you need me. Nancy Park has certainly met her match."

Jen wrapped the support of her family around herself like a hug. As they approached her house in Peake's Point, she remembered the day she and Benjamin had first discovered it was for sale, a rare occurrence in a small, gated community hemmed in by water with no place to grow. The two-acre lot with plenty of space for gardens excited him, but it was the strict security that attracted her.

While Jen's childhood had appeared idyllic to an outsider, she had never felt completely safe. The mystery and mercurial moods of Delilah dominated her life, took up so much space and energy that Jen built a tough outer shell to protect herself. It had taken her years to rid herself of the shell, and now it was back, a barricade against those she had once trusted most.

As Annie parked the car, a herring gull screamed through the air and passed over their heads, his shrieks ear-splitting, and his intimidating posture almost comic in such a small bird. He wheeled and made another pass, coming so close to Jen she could see the message in his yellow eyes.

The worst is yet to come.

Gulls don't threaten unless they think their young or their colony is in danger, and they certainly don't leave the waterfronts to appear in pristine neighborhoods where there is not a dropped chicken bone, or a spilling-over garbage can in sight for them to scavenge.

"Jen?" Annie reached for her hand as the gull lifted beyond the treetops and headed back toward the sea. "What's wrong?"

"Everything."

"What did you see?"

"That's the horrible thing. I don't know..." She gathered her things. "You'd better put the top up, Annie. You don't want to see what an angry seagull can do to the inside of this car."

Inside the house, Jen headed to her bedroom while Annie and Gran detoured by the kitchen, with Gran remarking on the way that she was going to have tea, no matter what Nancy said or did.

Jen tossed her clothes into the hamper and climbed into the shower to let the hot water wash away the stench of the hospital and the sting of betrayal. Then she dressed, slid on her gold bracelets, and went downstairs to find Nancy.

Surprisingly, Nancy immediately wrapped her arms around Jen. When she let go, there were tears in her eyes. Quite the change from her prickly attitude of the past few days.

"I can't believe you had to go to the hospital in an ambulance." Nancy wiped her eyes with the hem of her apron. "Dal and I didn't sleep a wink last night. What on earth happened?"

"You don't know?"

Her defenses went up. "Why would I?"

"I thought maybe Annie told you. Or Benjamin called to let you know."

"No, no. Nothing like that. We've been completely in the dark."

Truth or cover story? If she was guilty, she was doing a fine job of acting innocent. It struck Jen that despite all the years Nancy had worked for her, she knew very little about her and her husband. Her work history was stellar. She and Dal had run a small sandwich shop until they could save enough money to build his landscape business. Then Nancy had closed the shop and worked at various jobs—two different day care centers, a school lunchroom, and several nanny positions—until she came to work for Jen.

She had no children, and occasionally spoke about knitting a sweater or a throw for a cousin or a friend, but Jen had no idea if she went to church or enjoyed theater or shared Dal's love for gardening. She was just Nancy, quiet, efficient, uncomplaining, and loyal... until she wasn't.

"Did you put a bottle of blueberry juice concentrate in the garbage after the party?" Jen asked.

"Goodness, no! We don't keep that stuff around here. It would kill you!"

"Well, it almost did..."

Nancy gasped and covered her mouth with both hands. "That's like something out of the movies."

"Worse. It's real. I believe that whoever tried to kill me also took my things so I would think I was losing my mind. Do you have any idea who might have done that?"

Nancy clamped her mouth as if opening it would release a flood of damaging information. Jen waited her out. Nothing good or reliable could come of force. She'd had years of practice to learn that truth.

"Dal and I have talked. He has something he wants to say to you."

"Is he in the greenhouse?"

"Yes, but he doesn't like people coming there." Nancy stood up and took off her apron. "Wait right here, and I'll bring him to you."

The wait seemed to go on forever. The kitchen clock inched past three, and Jen wondered if Sharon would bring the twins straight home or go for ice cream. Personally, she wanted them here, under her roof, but it was too late to call Sharon now without creating a scene, probably from Marianne. She would see the change of plans as Jen trying to control her. Best to let the whole thing slide. They would be home by four.

Dal walked into the kitchen and sat in the chair opposite her. As usual, his face gave away nothing.

"Dal." Jen nodded her acknowledgment, then waited for him to speak.

"I saw something I think you should know about," he said. "The night of the party."

"What party?"

"The open house. I was in the greenhouse. I saw you cutting azaleas and hibiscus. Then you dropped your basket and headed toward the beach."

"Did you see me cutting oleander?"

"I saw someone cutting oleander, but it wasn't you."

Relief flooded Jen. "Who was it?"

"I don't know. It was someone with long, dark curly hair, wearing a red caftan like you wear. Except your gold bracelets were missing. You had just gone to the beach so I knew you couldn't be two places at the same time."

Images flashed through Jen's mind. Sharon taking the basket with oleander inside. Sharon suggesting Nancy cut it. Sharon in the house, everywhere, all the time.

Fear shot through her. The clock on the wall said three-thirty. She reached into her pocket then realized her phone was in her purse, in the bedroom. She tore upstairs and punched in the number.

"Pick up, Sharon. *Pick up!*"

The phone went to voicemail. Jen immediately dialed Tommy, then Marianne, both with the same result. No answer. Her hands shook as she pulled up the tracking app for her children's phones.

There. They were in downtown Gulf Breeze at Mac's Ice Cream Parlor, just as Sharon had said. She adored the children, and wouldn't harm a hair on their heads. She'd been Jen's best friend for years, loyal and caring, helpful in every way.

And so wounded, physically, mentally, and emotionally.

There was a movement outside Jen's window, the flicker of wings. The great blues were back, their message as ominous as the gigantic shadow of their wings.

DANGER. DANGER.

Jen bolted back downstairs, screaming Annie's name.

Her sister and her grandmother came running from the direction of the pool room, Gran huffing to keep up with Annie.

She arrived with her cropped gray hair sticking up in every direction like the feathers of an angry bird. "If Nancy has harmed one hair on your head, she'll have me to deal with."

"It's not Nancy. It's *Sharon!*" Jen told them what she had learned, and Gran sank into a turquoise chair tucked into the corner. Beyond her, the two great blues still hovered at the window.

"Are the twins still at the ice cream shop?" Annie leaned over Gran, checking her pulse under the guise of holding her hand. "Check the app again, Jen."

Though the hands on her watch inched toward four, time seemed to stand still. Jen checked the app again, just to be sure.

"They're still there."

"Good. We can drive to the ice cream shop just to make sure while Gran waits here to catch her breath."

"I'm not an old lady who needs coddling. I'm going with you."

"Wait a minute." Options raced through Jen's mind—Sharon's history, their long friendship, her interaction with the twins. "We don't know anything for sure yet, only what Dal and Nancy told me. If Sharon is the one who has tried to get rid of me, I don't want to trigger her, especially while she's with Tommy and Marianne. People over the edge are extremely dangerous."

"What do you want to do?" Annie asked her. "Name it, and I'll be right at your side."

"Sharon will be back in about twenty minutes. Until then, I'm counting on her love for the children to keep them safe."

"I know you love her and want to believe in her, but that's not enough." Annie walked over and slid her arm around Jen's shoulder. "But we need to find out who Sharon really is."

"I know. Follow me."

Jen raced out the door, memories of Sharon flooding her mind like demons. Sharon's love of theater, her talent for acting, her ability to fool people into believing anything she wanted them to, including that she was a rich Delta plantation owner's daughter instead of the impoverished daughter of a hill country woman who taught her to scrap and fight for everything she wanted.

What if Sharon is the person who wants me dead?

FIFTY-NINE
THE COTTAGE

As Jen raced toward the guest cottage, only Annie, matching her step for step, kept her from falling apart. *Glorious warrior Annie*. Her sister, her friend, her rock.

It looked peaceful with the late afternoon sun glinting off the windows and turning the once-bloody porch into a tranquil study in buttery yellow. It was not the sort of place you would imagine harboring anything bad.

Still, as Jen slid her key into the lock, she noticed the white oleander creeping around the corner of the porch and spilling across the railings as if it had magically grown in tandem with the evil that had recently overtaken her haven. She pushed open the door, and Annie followed her inside.

Though everything looked the same, something tugged at Jen with the force of an ocean undertow. The bright yellows and sea blues of the chairs and cushions in the front room no longer felt welcoming. With the shutters closed and the shadow of oleander creeping inside, they had taken on the sinister quality of a horror movie at midnight.

Annie noticed, too, and wrapped her arms around herself,

the age-old gesture of self-protection. "Has it always been this... *creepy?*"

"No. It's usually a cheerful place."

"Not anymore." Her sister glanced around, growing apprehension blooming across her face. "Something is terribly wrong. Your guest cottage is telling a very scary story."

Annie was never wrong. Jen's own fear ratcheted up.

"Come on. Let's find out what it is."

They hurried from room to room, searching through every drawer and closet. When they got to Sharon's bedroom, the ominous feeling was so strong, both of them shivered. Spurred by the awful knowledge from their gifts and a growing fear for the children, they ransacked both the bedroom and the ensuite.

"There's nothing in here." Jen sank to the edge of the bed, knocked flat by disappointment and terror mixed with a tiny rush of relief. "I don't know who Dal saw in the garden, but it wasn't Sharon."

"Wait a minute." Annie was standing in the doorway to the closet, as watchful as if she were in a thicket filled with poisonous snakes and landmines that would blow your legs off.

She dragged Sharon's suitcase into the middle of the floor, and Jen leaped off the bed. When Annie picked the lock with a hair pin and lifted the lid, they both gasped. A long, dark wig, almost identical to Jen's hair, rested atop a square of folded cloth. Red. Annie unfolded it, and there lay a caftan so similar to Jen's you wouldn't have been able to tell the difference if you were watching out the kitchen window, as Nancy had been.

Unaware of the tears streaking down her face, Jen knelt on the floor beside Annie. When she picked up the wig, a memory ambushed her, almost took her breath away. The dark hair in Sharon's brush.

She jumped up and rushed to check the ensuite again with Annie right behind her. Minutes earlier, she had removed every item from the drawers, but she had left Sharon's large makeup case zipped and untouched. The cell phone was tucked in the bottom underneath a mind-boggling pile of cosmetics.

Tension electrified both of them. As Jen grabbed it, a horrible premonition shivered through her.

"Is it locked?" Annie peered over her shoulder, the comfort of her as dear as a mother's touch.

"I don't know..." Jen's fingers fumbled.

"Here, let me do it."

"No! I've got this."

Breathe. Just breathe.

Thankfully, the phone finally lit up, both charged and unlocked.

Jen scrolled through the texts. And there they were—the threatening texts Sharon's husband sent after she left Eutaw. According to the timeline, the texts had been sent from this phone while Sharon was in this very cottage.

She sent them to herself.

Comprehension and horror collided in Jen. "Why does she have Matt's phone?"

"Jen, she's got the children!" Annie yelled.

They both leaped up and raced toward the main house. Sharon's car was not in the driveway, nor was Maria's. They burst through the kitchen door, breathless. Dal was no longer there, but Nancy and Gran sat at the table like two old friends, sipping a cup of tea and listening to the afternoon news.

"The body count is rising from the tornado that hit Mississippi, the worst in its history. Twenty-six are now confirmed dead, and first responders are still searching in Amory, Wren, and Rolling Fork."

Pictures of the disaster rolled across the TV screen. And then... the picture of water, meandering and deep. A river. The Tombigbee, the caption said, in Eutaw, Alabama.

"In other news, the body of a man pulled from the river has been identified as Matt Jones ..."

"Sharon's husband!" Fear pulled the color from Annie's face. "Blood in the water..."

As if the TV reporter had heard her, he said, "Cause of death was initially thought to be a drowning, but autopsy reports show a blow to the head with a blunt object. Foul play is suspected."

"It was Sharon." Gran set her teacup in the saucer. "I know it in my bones."

"I never did like her," Nancy said.

The clock on the wall inched past four, but Jen didn't notice. She couldn't move, could barely think. Her arms and legs were made of lead, her feet attached to the floor as if someone had sealed them there with a blowtorch.

"No, not this." Jen's voice wobbled with uncertainty and sheer terror. "Sharon couldn't have done it. She's afraid of water."

"The cottage tells a different story." Her sister's reminder and the fear in her voice brought Jen to her senses. "She's a dangerous, unhinged woman."

She should have seen what was happening to Sharon. She should have pieced the puzzle of her friend together long before now. She had failed her, failed them all.

The news had moved on to the hurricane that would come ashore somewhere westward by nightfall, but Jen's terror for her children was so total she felt as if she had already been carried off by the eye. Everything was broken. *Gone.* She was swirling in a mass of debris, her footing vanished. Nowhere to land.

"Jen!" Annie yelled. "The clock!"

It was five minutes past four. Where was Sharon? For that matter, where was Maria? She was never late for Tommy's swim lesson without calling.

Galvanized, Jen checked her children's tracking app once more, and her face registered her shock. "Still at the ice cream parlor?"

"They can't be." Annie grabbed her arm. "Come on. Let's go!"

"Not without me!" Gran grabbed her truck keys out of her pocket.

They all raced out of the kitchen with Nancy yelling after them, "Be careful. That storm's coming!"

The window in the den was dark with the blur of wings from the great blues and the angry waves beyond crashing against the shore, riled up by the clashing of wind currents and overheated by warm tropical water. Signs of danger bombarded Jen from every direction. Adding to her horror was the knowledge of what a woman of Sharon's precarious mental state could do.

Even murder.

Jen skidded on the newly waxed floor. "Gran, you don't have to come." She couldn't bear it if something awful happened to her, too. "Annie and I can handle this."

"Yes, I do. You're going to need somebody meaner than Annie. And I'm just the ticket." On the way out the door she grabbed her cowboy hat and rammed it on her head. "Hop in my truck. I'm driving. Nobody gets in the way of this big, bad Ram."

"You don't even know the way," Annie cried.

"Yes, I do. I saw it on the way to the beach. You and Jen plan the attack while I drive." She slid behind the wheel, Jen jumped into the backseat of the mega cab, and Annie rode shotgun. "Hold onto your hair."

SIXTY

THE ICE CREAM SHOP

Heads turned as they roared out of Peake's Point and barreled along the Gulf Breeze Parkway. Rising to a crisis was the Logan way. Jen alternated between frantically calling Sharon and the twins, while Annie provided encouragement to their grandmother, who had the fierce look she used to get when she saddled up and set off across the range to round up lost livestock, the lifeblood of the ranch.

"You've got this, Gran." When Victoria Logan blasted her horn at a car trying to cut in front of her from a side road, Annie dug deep to find her warrior-self tucked amidst her living-in-another-world creativity. "That's it! Keep going! The sign is just up ahead on the right."

Gran screeched into the parking lot, came to a teeth-jarring halt, and they all bailed out of the truck. Fear threatened to buckle Jen's legs. She had never been more grateful to have her stormtrooper family with her. She burst through the door of the ice cream shop, screaming her children's names.

Startled women glared at her, and children dropped their ice cream spoons to gawk. Kids were scattered among tables throughout the shop, blonds and brunettes and redheads of all ages. But no Tommy. No Marianne. And no Sharon.

Jen glanced toward the bathroom, hoping to see them emerge. Where were they?

Panic clawed at her, and she was unaware of tears streaking down her cheeks until Annie handed her a tissue. There was a tired-looking woman with her sister, late fifties, brown hair streaked with gray, lipstick chewed off, and makeup settled into the grooves beside her mouth and above the kindest brown eyes Jen had ever seen. She had a dark stain on her blue bibbed apron. Chocolate? Raspberry? Cherry?

"Jen, this is Mabel Satterfield, the shop's manager. She's going to help us."

My sister. My rock. She couldn't talk, couldn't walk. Annie linked arms and did it all for her.

"Come with me." Mabel gave Jen a sad-looking smile then led them into a small office with only two chairs. "Sit here, sweetheart." She turned to Victoria. "You, too, hon."

Fear ripped through Jen. This couldn't be good. Mabel offered too much sympathy, as if she were comforting the bereaved.

Annie stood close to Jen, a hand on her shoulder. "I showed her the twins' photographs. They were here."

Were. Terror seized Jen's heart.

"They were sitting at a table near the back window with a real pretty woman," Mabel said. "All three of them laughing and having the best time. You couldn't help but notice them."

That word again. *Were.* Jen swallowed her scream, found a part of herself that had not reverted to the primitive. "The tracking app on my phone shows that my children are still here."

"Oh, hon, after they left, I found these on the seat at their table." When she took two cell phones from a drawer and slid them across her desk, despair swamped Jen, threatened to topple her. "I expected them to turn around and come back looking for their phones. If I had known what your sister told me, I'd have tried to call their ICE numbers."

"You did the best you could, Mabel, and we're grateful." Annie was cool under pressure, but her own fear showed in the way her ocean eyes darkened from turquoise to green. "Was the woman blond?"

"Yes, she had the kind of hair I always wanted..."

Jen seemed to be on a faraway planet, listening to her sister talk for her while she sat mute, her mind aware of only one thing. She was in the middle of a mother's worst nightmare.

"When did they leave?" Annie asked.

"At least forty-five minutes ago. They didn't stay long, just till the woman finished her coffee, and the kids went to the bathroom. The children took their ice cream with them."

Gran slipped from the room. No grandmother should have to hear the kind of news Mabel just delivered.

Jen pictured it, the twins oblivious to danger, happy to be with the woman they had elevated to the same status as their beloved aunts, Annie and Rachel. Something fierce rose in her, a mama eagle with strong wings to carry her young, sharp talons to defend them, and eyes to see them for miles. Sharon was stealing her children away as surely as a marauding eagle, bearing them off to her home in Alabama.

She gave Annie a look of gratitude and a thumbs-up sign before asking Mabel, "Did you hear them say where they were going?"

"Not exactly. I heard the woman tell the children that you were still in the hospital and their dad had asked her to take them on a big adventure to help take their minds off their poor, sick mother."

A new horror seized Jen. Her children were in the hands of a master manipulator.

"Were they upset? Scared? How did they seem to you?"

"Not to upset you or anything, but they seemed happy. I've never seen a teenager yet who wasn't glad for a reason to be out of school."

The daunting task ahead hit Jen. She closed her eyes to gather strength while Annie stood at her side, squeezing her hand.

Gran came back into the room. "I've just talked to Benjamin. He'll meet us at the house. He said to tell you, 'we'll find them.'"

But Jen wasn't swayed by false promises.

Danger screamed at her from every direction—the darkening sky thick with storm clouds, the wind that had picked up speed and whistled around the small ice cream shop, the colony of seagulls riding the currents and screaming, even her own experience with patients slowly coming unhinged.

With cold dread she realized she might never see her children again.

SIXTY-ONE

THE ROAD NORTHWARD | DESTINATION UNKNOWN

Sharon had always dreamed of taking a road trip with her children, and now it was happening. Her only regret was that she hadn't had a chance to pack her makeup. It would be nearly impossible to duplicate the products in her makeup bag, some of the brands she had picked up in stores that were now closed, and many of her favorite lipstick colors had been discontinued.

Forget about her clothes; they were easy to replace. Ben would be so grateful to her for taking care of the children, he would buy her an entirely new wardrobe. She smiled, remembering his text.

> *Maria Ramos had to cancel swim lessons today because of a family emergency. When you pick up Tommy and Marianne at school, let him know the four o'clock lesson is off. The three of you can have some fun while Jen is recovering from her allergic reaction. You deserve it after the scare you had this morning. I'm glad your family is safe. See you this evening.*

She was doing Ben an enormous favor. Jen, too. *Poor thing.*

She needed a break after all the terrible things that had happened to her. She needed a friend like Sharon.

She adjusted the rearview mirror to check on the twins. They were plugged in to their iPads, playing games, both of them oblivious to the fact that she had slipped their cell phones from their backpacks and left them at the ice cream parlor. She didn't need any nosey posies tracking her.

Sharon hummed "Somewhere Over the Rainbow." It felt amazing to be making her own dreams come true.

This moment was grand, and this evening would be even better. Just the two of them, Ben and Sharon, holding hands by a campfire while the children were inside the tent, asleep after a day of fun.

Sharon decided camping would be just the ticket. She knew the woods as well as she did the inside of Belks' department store. Grew up in them. The trashy little girl from the wrong side of the tracks playing in the woods with rag dolls and stick horses because her mama couldn't afford real toys. Well, no more rag dolls for her, thank you very much. She was coming up in this world. Moving on. Taking charge.

Once she crossed the state line into Alabama, she would buy everything she needed for her family's camping trip and put it on her credit card. No drunken, fast-fisted husband to discover a credit card trail.

That day came to her, unbidden. That last, awful day in Eutaw.

She turned on the car radio to drown out the memories, but the music was a country station, playing an oldie by Tammy Wynette. As if Sharon were under some kind of mind-control, she turned the music up louder while events of that day screamed through her...

* * *

The boat rocked under the weight of her drunken husband, and Sharon thought she was going to tilt over the side before they left the dock. End of plans. End of Sharon.

The picnic basket was so heavy, Matt had to lean over and help her get it aboard. And why not? Forget the two bottles of sauvignon blanc she had showed her husband. She had put enough wine in there to keel over an elephant.

They finally got settled into the boat with Matt at the helm. The outboard motor purred to life, and he navigated out of the backwaters and into the main channel of the river.

"Where to, Sharon?"

"Pick your favorite spot, darling. This is a celebration of our fresh start."

"You've got it, baby."

The boat glided downriver underneath a sliver of moon half-hidden by gathering clouds. Rain was coming. Sharon could feel it in the heaviness of the air, taste it in the charged weather front moving slowly into Eutaw.

Perfect.

They rounded a bend where the oak trees and loblolly pines on the protrusion of land seemed to be floating in the water. This was Matt's favorite fishing spot. The roots of ancient trees and the shade of massive branches created a cool, shadowy underwater world for the big channel catfish, his favorite river catch.

He cut the motor, and the boat swayed on the waves, as gentle as the motion of the cane-bottomed rocking chairs that grace every front porch in the Deep South. Sharon could almost believe she was a child again, sitting in the porch swing with her legs dangling while her mama rocked back and forth, shelling peas.

"I hope that fried chicken is as good as it smells." Matt's voice broke the spell, jerking her back to the reality that her life depended on controlling every detail of the picnic.

"You won't be disappointed. Turn on some music, sweetheart, and let's make this a moment to remember."

"Now, you're talking."

He turned on Tammy Wynette. Of course he did. "Stand By Your Man." His mantra. Her call to battle.

The country singer had been gone from this earth for so long, her opinions were no longer relevant, certainly not those on love and marriage. Wynette grew up in the era when the subservient June Cleaver from the *Leave it to Beaver* TV show was the role model for housewives.

Sharon had no intention of being a Tammy Wynette. She had much bigger plans for her man, and that did *not* include standing by him.

Hugging her big secret to herself, she served up fried chicken and all the trimmings with the elegant manners of a woman born to wealth. Most of them she had learned from Jen. Sharon was a quick study. It was one of her many gifts.

Another was in judging her opponent. Matt's mellow mood could turn in a moment. He could explode because the fried chicken was too crisp, the rolls had gone cold, or she said something to displease him. Every move she made counted.

"I'll pour the wine if you make a toast. You're so much better at it than I am." She flashed her best beauty pageant smile. Would appealing to his ego work one more time? That's all she needed. Just one.

"Of course, I am, baby. It's a man's job." He winked at her. "It will be a good one."

He propped forearms on his knees and bent over, deep in thought, and she seized her chance to slip a tiny foil packet from her pocket and dump the contents into his wine. She hummed as she stirred it with her finger. Let him think she was happy. Let him believe she was sorry for every transgression he had imagined while she doctored his drink with sleeping pills crushed into a fine powder.

If the information on the internet was accurate, it would be just enough to knock him out. She didn't want to kill him.

At least, not this way.

"I've got it!" His shout unnerved her, and she almost dropped the wine.

She mentally slapped herself back into shape, handed him a glass, and lifted her own. "Ready when you are."

His drunken attempt to clink his glass to hers missed by several inches. She tapped the side of the boat with her knuckles, and it made a clunking sound, nothing like crystal striking crystal. Matt never noticed the difference.

"Here's to us, baby," he said. "Long may we wave!"

She waited for more. When it didn't come, Matt scowled at her.

"Aren't you going to say something, Sharon?"

"Of course." She lifted her glass. "Cheers." His scowl deepened, and she struggled to regain lost ground. "That was a great toast. Just splendid, really. One for the books."

"I couldn't tell by your reaction." He chugged back his wine. "Long may we wave... like the American flag, you know. Indi... indest... indis-something. You know, undivided? Can't be separated."

His voice was slurring heavily now. Were the pills working that fast?

"That's the perfect toast for a fresh start." She refilled his glass, and he gulped it down. "There's more where that came from, darling."

He held out his glass. For a moment, it hovered between them, a tiny goblet that might salvage the rapidly deteriorating evening. Suddenly, he swore and flung the glass into the river.

"Are you trying to get me drunk?"

His words slurred so badly she could barely understand him. He jumped up, and the boat tilted under the sudden shifting of weight. Sharon almost toppled overboard.

"No, sweetheart. I'm trying to have a nice picnic on the river with my husband. Won't you sit down and have some fried chicken? You haven't even touched it."

He narrowed his eyes to evil slits. "What did you put in it? Arsenic?"

Oh, help.

Sharon's control slipped. He was staring at her as if he could read every thought in her mind. Suddenly, his expression changed as comprehension began to dawn.

"You *did!*" he shouted. "I should have known something was wrong when you started tossing round the *sweethearts* and *darlings*."

As if he had shouted down the elements, the first drops of rain dimpled the water and pattered against the boat. It dampened her hair and slickened the seat. Thunder rolled. The rain was just getting started. Before long, it would be coming down in a deluge that would turn the food to mush and transform the Tombigbee from the perfect place for a picnic into a raging river taking its revenge on anybody foolish enough to be out in a boat. It would even drown out Tammy Wynette. No sacrifice there.

"Matt, sit down before you turn over the boat!"

"Do you think you can tell me what to do?" His speech was slowing, and he was swaying like a sheet in a gale. "I'll teach you a lesson you'll never... *ffff*."

He lunged at her, arms outstretched, hands clutching at her throat. The body blow knocked both of them to the bottom of the boat. His hands tightened, and she struggled to breathe.

No. Not like this.

Sharon fought to free herself, but Matt was far stronger than she had imagined he would be, even dog-drunk and addled with pills.

"Please... stop." Her voice was a mere squeak. "You're hurting me."

The rain came harder, and she felt the world going black.

Just before it disappeared altogether, Matt sagged and the pressure on her throat stopped. Sharon lay under his weight, feeling the blessed rain on her face as it mingled with her tears.

I'm alive sang through her mind like one of her mama's favorite hymns. She pushed and shoved until Matt rolled off her. She had no idea how long the effect of alcohol and sleeping pills would last, and she didn't intend to linger around long enough to find out.

She crawled toward her seat and found the baseball bat she had secured underneath earlier that evening, carefully wrapped in a beach towel. In case Matt looked, or if he was sober enough to see.

Planting her feet apart for balance, she stood up and hefted the bat. Her mind took her back to the scraggly vacant lot behind the shack where she grew up, the yells of the neighborhood kids as she hefted the bat and waited for the ball.

"Hit it, Sharon. Hit a homer."

She was good at baseball. So were all kids on the wrong side of the tracks in a town that paid them no more attention than the stray cats wandering the alleys. Sandlot baseball was all they knew. Cheap entertainment. No uniforms required. No shoes, either.

She dug her toes into the sand and swung the bat. It connected to the target with a loud crack. The ball sailed over the broken-down fence. She had hit a homer. But it wasn't a *ball*...

It was Matt's skull, cracked like a ripe watermelon. She would never forget the sound. She would have nightmares about it.

But, *oh,* she was *free*... if she worked fast.

The power of terror surged through Sharon, the same kind that gave a mother strength to lift a car off her child, and she rolled Matt overboard. If she got lucky, he wouldn't be found until his body floated downriver all the way to Demopolis,

Alabama, where the Tombigbee converged with the Black Warrior River into the massive Demopolis Lake. A fisherman's paradise. A place where any unlucky fisherman might get drunk and topple over the side of his boat, never to be seen again. Even if someone discovered him, he might have been in the water so long he became bait for the numerous scavengers in the water. He might even have been dinner for an alligator.

All these things went through her mind as the downpour combined with the swelling river carried Matt's body under. Under the veil of rain and darkness, the scene played through her mind like menacing film noir. Dark music screamed through her, Bach's "Toccata and Fugue in D Minor," the organ ominous, the strings clashing with the brass like enemies engaged in mortal combat.

For a moment, she stood in the middle of the boat, teetering on the edge of panic. If she fell over that cliff, all was lost. She might as well have stayed in her dry house and let Matt beat her to death. Her mama's beloved voice echoed to her from her childhood. *Sharon, you are stronger than the bullies at school. You are not trash. You are worthy.*

"I *am* worthy." The wind carried off her words, and they howled back at her through the gathering storm. She had to hurry. She would never get out of the river alive if she kept standing in the boat in a puddle of blood.

She threw the bat into the river then grabbed the empty wine bottles she had stowed in the picnic hamper and flung them all over the bottom of the boat. *My goodness! No wonder that man fell and bashed his head on the side of the boat then toppled overboard. Look how much he had to drink.*

She smashed Matt's pill-laced wine glass against the side of the boat and let the shards fall into the river. Then she flung her plate and plastic cutlery into the swells. In this kind of weather, they would probably be all the way to Demopolis by morning. Even if they got trapped in the underwater caverns where fish sheltered, they would be just another blight left behind by careless tourists.

She stood a moment longer, staring at the spot where Matt went down, as if he might rise out of the river to take his revenge. Then she started the outboard motor.

Her shoes! Sharon killed the motor and threw her bloody flipflops into the river. They were pink plastic, the kind of beach shoes anybody could buy for five dollars at any Walmart or dollar store in the Deep South.

Satisfied, she started the engine again and navigated the boat back upriver as close as she dared to their secluded backwater dock. She had to leave the boat in deep water so it would drift away from the house.

Thunder provided booming sound effects, and the wind picked up speed as rain pounded around her in thick sheets that almost obscured the shoreline. When she got her bearings, she cut the motor and dived overboard. The river sucked her in, and the cold, dark water stole her breath. For a moment she was a little girl again, terrified of drowning, screaming as she fought toward the surface.

Don't fight the water. Relax and let it help you stay afloat.

That was Matt's voice, coming to her as clear as if he had drifted up beside her to give her one last swimming lesson. She shot to the surface and gulped in rainwater and fresh air. Then she swam for shore while the river washed away the blood from her hands and feet and clothes.

Are you washed in the blood? The ancient hymn went round and round her mind like a stuck 45 on Mama's old record turntable.

Where was she? Was she even swimming in the right direction?

She could barely see her surroundings. Doubt clouded her judgment. Where was her house? Where were the lights she'd left glowing?

Keep going, Sharon. Never give up.

Her mama's voice again. Sharon renewed her strength. Lightning split the sky. And there they were, the lights from her house, burning through the gloom. With a burst of adrenaline, she powered toward home. When she came ashore, she collapsed into the river silt and wet grass and lay there, sobbing.

It was over. Matt was gone. In the end, the man who had become her worst enemy was the one who saved her—the woman afraid of water, swimming out of a river in the middle of the night in a thunderstorm all because her abusive husband taught her how…

* * *

"Aunt Sharon?" Tommy's voice brought her back to the car, back to a future devoid of Matt and constant fear. "Where are we going?"

"Camping. Is that all right with you guys?"

"Wow!" Tommy shouted. "Neat!"

"No more math tutor." Marianne gave her brother a high five. "Aunt Sharon, you're the *greatest*!"

She really was, wasn't she? Jen would be so proud.

SIXTY-TWO

THE TURNER HOUSE

Benjamin's world had finally fallen apart.

The hurricane, dubbed Carol by meteorologists, made landing just west of New Orleans, wreaking havoc not only on the City of Romance but on every town, boat landing, and body of water in a massive radius in all directions from the eye. In Gulf Breeze, Florida, crashing waves, howling wind, and lashing rain announced the category four storm's far-reaching power and fury.

It matched the darkening terror that washed over Benjamin, turning the gathering in his kitchen into a somber tableau of disbelief and guilt.

Nobody had seen Sharon's breakdown coming, nobody had guessed that she was spinning a web of lies. Not his wife, whose love for her friend had clouded her professional ability, not Annie and Victoria, flanking Jen's chair like two fierce goddesses of ancient legend, not Nancy, sagging against Dal like a rag doll without her stuffing. And certainly not Benjamin, who had lived in his own head for so long he had failed in the most basic duty of a father, to protect his children.

The only person in the room who had guessed that Sharon

was not all she seemed was Clint Brown, who sat at the head of the table letting his cup of coffee go cold.

"I got the results of the fingerprints I sent for analysis only minutes before I saw Matt's body being dragged from the river. Sharon's prints were all over the bottle of blueberry juice concentrate that nearly killed Jen. And *only* hers."

His wife's color was too high, but she was not falling to pieces. Just the opposite. She had that stubborn, take-charge look he had seen in every crisis of their married life. He had never admired her more. It came as a sort of shock to him that he had also never loved her more. His foolish, secret obsessions mocked him.

"I should have listened to you, Clint." Jen wore her hard-won calm like a shawl. "I should have called law enforcement a long time ago. What do we do?"

Clint glanced at the clock on the kitchen wall. Five o'clock. Dark was coming, the storm was threatening to turn into something even more fierce, and no one had a clue where Sharon was headed with Tommy and Marianne.

"We call the law to set up roadblocks and a search headquarters here, we notify Amber Alert, and we call in a TV news crew to spread the word."

"What about a reward?" Benjamin toyed with his coffee cup, unsure of nearly every aspect of his life, even his ability to help find his children. "Do you think that will help?"

"The short answer is yes," Clint told him. "The longer answer is that a reward will also bring in fake leads from kooks hoping to collect."

"We'll just set up more phones." Jen jutted out her chin, determined. "The reward money might be the only thing that leads us to Tommy and Marianne. Take care of everything, Clint." She stood up and marched toward the back door.

Had his wife lost it, after all? Benjamin hurried after her. "Where are you going?"

"I'm going to the beach to scream, and then I'm going to find my children."

"But Jen, it's pouring out there!"

She kept walking. Didn't even look back. Their marriage had come to that.

He headed after her, saying over his shoulder to Clint. "Call me when you need us."

Rain soaked through his clothes, but Benjamin didn't care. He caught up with his wife halfway down the path to their private beach. He didn't try to hold her hand. That was one of the many easy privileges he had tossed away with his carelessness and secrets.

The water looked as angry as he felt. Dark and surly. Bashing the shore with white-furled waves with a relentless intent that shredded his nerves. Sea oats tickled his ankles, and his feet sank into the sand. What was he going to do?

"I should have been more careful." Pain was an anvil, chipping away at his heart. "I should have been paying attention."

"Yes, you should." Jen's glance slid across his face, and then she turned toward the water. She looked stoic. Her hair was hanging in wet tangles around her face. Her gold bracelets silent as she stood, rock-like, facing the stormy sea as if it might magically spit back their children. "This is about the children, not you. I think she will head north, to the place she has always loved. Alabama."

"To Eutaw?"

"No. She's too smart for that. She probably heard the news about the recovery of Matt's body." Jen's voice hitched. When she hugged herself for comfort, Benjamin felt shamed. "I think she killed him. Considering everything I know, it's the only thing that makes sense. She won't go anywhere near the crime scene."

"Where, then?"

"That's just the thing. I don't know..." She broke then,

shoulders heaving, crying without sound. The rain intensified, matching her grief.

"Jen?" He reached for her.

"*Don't!*" She shrugged him off and struggled for control. Finally won. "If she's heading to Alabama, she could go straight up Highway 97N to Atmore and keep going in that direction so she could hide somewhere in the hills among thousands of wooded acres. Or she might veer toward Birmingham and lose herself and our children in the maze of the city."

"I wish I could turn back time, Jen..."

Regret flitted across his wife's face. Regret. Sorrow. Loss. Terror. All the emotions he was feeling.

"So do I, Benjamin. I brought her into our lives, and let my friendship cloud my judgment." She faced the sea again, gathering strength from its fury. The wind snapped a branch in a tree nearby, but she didn't even flinch. The burden of a mother mourning her stolen children blocked out the external. Finally, she turned to him, her face set. "We have to focus on now."

His final secret weighed heavily on him. He wasn't as strong as Jen, and probably never would be. Courage wasn't in his DNA.

"The sleeping pills you found in my office," he said, and she whipped around to face him. "I borrowed them from Sharon."

"I didn't find any in the cottage or the guest room she used in our house."

"She keeps them in her purse."

Jen almost vibrated with fury. "If you had told me this earlier, I might have guessed she was doctoring all that tea she made for me. None of this might have happened."

She turned and stormed toward the house.

"Jen, where are you going?" he called after her, but she kept on going.

The wind caught her reply and slapped it in his face. "I'm going to find my children."

SIXTY-THREE

THE RAMOS HOUSE | THOMASVILLE, ALABAMA

When the television station interrupted their regular program with a news flash, Maria Ramos was in her mother's kitchen in Thomasville, Alabama, making chicken noodle soup for her parents. Her dad had broken his leg falling off a ladder while he cleaned the gutters, and the soup was her mother's cure for everything. They liked it spicy, and she had instructed Maria not to skimp on the garlic salt.

"Two children are missing from their home in Gulf Shores," the TV reporter said, while their photos flashed across the screen. "They are twins Tommy and Marianne Turner."

Maria nearly dropped the spice jar into the soup. While the reporter went on and on, describing the twins and what they were wearing when last seen, she set the garlic salt down and turned up the volume.

"They are believed to be with this woman, Sharon Clark Jones, who is currently being sought for questioning over the death of her husband, Matt Jones, of Eutaw, Alabama."

Sharon's photo was a beauty queen shot. She had the kind of natural good looks Maria aspired to but would never have. But it wasn't her looks that set Maria off; it was her own suspicions. *Someone* had rammed a nail into her tire, causing the blowout that could have killed her, and she had always suspected Sharon. That woman had looked daggers at Maria the night of the Turners' open house. And she was clearly interested in Dr. Turner's husband. Jen must have been wearing blinders not to see it.

"If you have any information leading to the whereabouts of Sharon Jones or Tommy and Marianne Turner, call one of these numbers." The numbers flashed across the screen while Dr. Turner and Benjamin came on the set. He appeared to be shell-shocked, a walking bundle of anxiety. Even the cool-headed Jen Turner seemed rattled.

Mesmerized, Maria listened to their plea for help finding their children. She was already reaching for her cell phone when the reporter's next words electrified her.

"The Turners are offering a reward of one million dollars to anyone providing information that leads to the safe recovery of their children."

As the TV went back to their regular program, Maria grabbed her phone. She didn't bother calling the numbers on the screen. Those phones would be busy with everybody and his dog trying to collect the reward. She called Dr. Turner's direct number.

"Hello?" Jen's voice was drenched with her pain.

"Dr. Turner, this is Maria Ramos. I saw your children."

There was such a long beat of silence, Maria thought she'd lost the connection. Then Jen came back on.

"I've put you on speaker phone, Maria. Benjamin is here, along with Clint, our head of security. The city police and the Santa Rosa Sheriff's Department are also here. Okay?"

"Yes. I understand."

She could hear the murmur of voices in the background. "Where did you see them and what time?"

"This afternoon, right about five, at the Walmart in

Thomasville, Alabama. I was in their pharmacy getting pain killers for my dad, and I saw them."

"Maria, hold on a minute." There was another flurry of activity on the other end of the line, more conversation.

Many of the voices she didn't recognize, but she had met the Turners' security guard and knew his voice. "She's taken them across state lines," he said. "Call the FBI field office in Mobile."

"Listen." Jen sounded more like herself. "Did you hear Sharon or the twins say where they were going?"

"No, but Sharon was filling the cart with a tent and camping gear."

There was an explosion of activity at the other end of the line. Clint shouting, "We'll need air scent dogs!" Benjamin was calling for the company helicopter. Someone else yelling out the weather report for south and central Alabama.

"Maria, I'm back." Jen sounded breathless. Fatigue, excitement, or fear? It was impossible to tell over the phone. "You're still on speaker, but you can talk frankly. Everybody here is grateful for your information."

"Thanks. I wish I could do more. Tommy's a great kid."

"Tell me about my children. How did they look? Were they scared? Did Sharon seem threatening to them? Anything you can tell me will help."

"I can tell you everything."

Maria had the gift of photographic memory. The scene from Walmart unfolded in Technicolor. As she talked to Jen, she was transported back to the sporting goods aisle, seeing it all over again...

* * *

Sharon wore mismatched pumps and a wrinkled suit, and her hair was unkempt, which was surprising since Maria had never seen her looking less than perfect.

The twins stood on either side of her, checking out sleeping bags. A pair of cheap white, adult-sized tennis shoes, a flashlight, and a large pack of wipes lay in the bottom of Sharon's shopping cart tucked behind a sixteen-pack of bottled water. Piled on top were two pairs of blue jeans, a black sweatshirt, and two black tee shirts with the tags showing, all in adult size small. The basket held mustard, a box of matches, a bag of buns, two packs of hot dogs, paper towels, a box of graham crackers, a bag of marshmallows, and four chocolate bars.

They were going to make s'mores, over a campfire. Maria had been a Girl Scout. She knew these things. But who was the fourth chocolate bar for?

"The sky's the limit, guys," Sharon said. "Choose any sleeping bag you want. This is your great adventure."

Her eyes were too bright, and her voice had the edge of the kids Maria had seen high on marijuana. Nothing about this scene was normal. Why were the Turner twins with Sharon in Alabama planning a camping trip on a school night?

She tucked her dad's prescription into her purse and edged closer. Remaining hidden was never a problem in Walmart. Everywhere she looked, merchandise was piled on shelves higher than her head.

Sharon added camping cookware and a lantern to the teetering pile of merchandise before she left to fetch another shopping cart for the pop-up tent, camping blankets, and a small cooler.

"Aunt Sharon." Marianne tugged her sleeve. "I can't find my phone. Can I borrow yours to call Dad?"

"Why, sweetie? You'll see him tonight."

"I just wanted to make sure he knows where to find us."

"I already took care of everything, honey. You don't have to worry about a thing. Your mom needs some peace and quiet, and we're doing her a big favor. Just think of all the fun the four of us will have when your dad gets here."

Maria found the whole thing odd, but if Benjamin sanctioned the trip, he must have a good reason. He was a careful man and a good father.

Still, Maria felt uneasy as she headed to the grocery aisle to pick up the makings for supper. When she got back to checkout, she saw the twins, standing beside the door to the restrooms, holding onto two carts filled with bagged merchandise. Sharon emerged from the ladies' room wearing jeans, a black tee shirt, and white tennis shoes...

* * *

"Sharon said Benjamin knew about the camping trip?" Jen's voice brought Maria back to the reality of soup on the stove and her own failure.

"Yes. That's why I didn't call you or Benjamin in the first place. I thought you knew." Her guilt would play havoc with her sleep. Probably for a very long time, especially if they didn't find the twins.

"None of this is your fault."

"Something felt off about the whole camping thing, especially with the storm coming. I should have followed them out the door to see which way they went, or at least said something to Sharon. I'm so sorry, Dr. Turner."

"Listen, you did the right thing. When we find the twins, you'll be a hero."

"I don't feel like one. I feel like a fool."

"Sharon fooled all of us. When this is over, come to my office, and we'll sort it all out. Okay?"

"Thank you. I sure hope you find them."

Maria turned the burner under the soup to low then went to find her Rosary beads.

SIXTY-FOUR

SOUTH ALABAMA | LOCATION UNKNOWN

Oblivious to the rain slashing the windshield, the twins whispering in the backseat, and the storm she had unleashed in the Turner mansion—fury and confusion, scent dogs and law enforcement, FBI vans and search helicopters—Sharon took the turnoff to the back roads she knew so well.

She was instantly sheltered by the canopies of hundred-year-old oaks and towering pines. Tangles of wisteria and wild Carolina jasmine intertwined, creating curtains of purple and yellow, mysterious in the lengthening shadows and swaying in the wind kicked up by the massive hurricane battering the Gulf coast all the way from Louisiana to Florida and inland for hundreds of miles.

Though Sharon could feel the steering wheel in her hands and a tag she had forgotten to remove from the neck of her Walmart shirt, she was mentally no longer in the car. In her mind, she was back in Gulf Breeze, lacing her best friend's tea with crushed sleeping pills. Just enough to make her rest. Jen worked too hard. She deserved to rest.

Sharon had to take care of that pack of vultures around her BFF, too. It was too bad the nail she'd rammed into the slut

Maria's tire didn't take her out of the picture. At least she'd got the message. She backed off Jen's husband.

His legal assistant had presented a greater challenge. But Sharon was undaunted. And far too clever for the Italian siren. What a laugh. Cut Antonia's hair short, and she would pass for a boy.

All it took to shatter her plans to be the future Mrs. Turner were a couple of threatening text messages and a perfect imitation of the Italian siren's voice, thanks to Sharon's training in theater. It had been almost laughably easy to wrangle her way into the mansion, and even easier to use the intercom late at night, while Ben was sleeping, to send a warning to Jen.

Her dearest friend deserved to see Antonia's true colors. Jen was too stubborn to listen to reason, and always had been. Whisperings in the night had done the trick, though.

Some people might think her a monster for killing Marianne's hamster, but she'd done the child a favor. *Really*. She needed to learn to help people who deserved it instead of spending all her time with a silly animal who could do nothing but run in circles inside a cage.

But Sharon wasn't done yet. Not by a longshot. Poor Jen had been on the treadmill of taking care of everybody else for so long, she had no idea she needed to step aside and take care of herself for a while. It was up to Sharon to give Jen exactly what she needed, even if it meant making her think she was going crazy so she could recuperate in a quiet institution. Ben could afford the very best for her, and they could all get on with the lives they were meant to lead.

Someday, Jen would thank her. She pictured the two of them together, sitting side by side, their feet in the sand, laughing at how Sharon had saved them all, really.

The curve in the road appeared suddenly, and the gap between two leaning, weathered fence posts trying to hold up a falling-down barbed wire fence. Everything was different from the way Sharon remembered it. Especially in the driving rain. Older. Shabbier. The forest beyond, overgrown and forbidding. The wind bending trees and snapping branches. Howling like a coyote set to tear your throat out.

Still, she made the turn between the fence posts. The car shook in the deep, muddy ruts, rattling her teeth and causing the twins to yelp.

Were they going to be trouble? Sharon hoped not. She'd hate to have to discipline them.

Marianne leaned over the seat to tap her on the shoulder. "This is creepy. I don't want to camp here."

"Beggars can't be choosers." How many times had Mama said that? About a million. Not in a mean way, either. She had tried hard to teach Sharon about the realities of living in poverty, the sacrifices you have to make.

"It's getting too dark to see in the woods." Tommy sounded scared. *Too bad.* "Why don't we go to a motel and wait until Dad gets here to set up camp?" He was more diplomatic and far easier than his sister. Sharon hoped her first child with Ben would be a boy, just like his older brother, except with her blond hair.

"Don't worry. I've camped here many times, I know what I'm doing." The rain lashed against the windshield, turning Sharon into a liar. *Let it storm.* Who cared? She had more important things to think of than the weather. She had been so busy taking care of Jen, she'd hardly had a minute to think of herself. "We're not going to let a few raindrops stop us."

The lake appeared suddenly, gloomy and brooding in the creeping darkness and increasing rain. Sharon skirted around it on an overgrown trail that was rapidly turning to mush. The wheels of her car spun, but she found traction on the fallen debris and pine needles and wound her way deep into the forest.

She parked the car under the shelter of a towering oak. Rain picked up speed, pounding the roof like giant hands trying to get inside to snatch her kids away. There went the s'mores and songs around the campfire. There went holding hands with Ben in the moonlight.

"What are we going to do?" Marianne sounded whiney. She had a lot to learn about survival. You had to take the bad with the good. You had to learn to rise above it.

The rain brought back memories of swimming for her life in the lake while Matt floated somewhere behind her, his head bloody and his fists forever stilled. She shivered, struggling to regain control. Surely, that was self-defense, wasn't it?

She was a survivor, an actress, a woman who deserved better than the sorry hand the past had dealt her. Invisible whispered in her ear, suggesting unspeakable things, even killing the children so she could have a fresh start with Ben.

If Sharon didn't take back control, that's exactly what Invisible would do. She argued with Invisible. *Ben loves the children. He would hate me if I did that.* Sharon listened for Invisible's snarky comeback. When it didn't come, Sharon shrugged her off and made herself as perky as coffee brewed in the dented coffee pot her mama put on the stove every morning at five o'clock.

"I'll tell you what. The two of you stay in the car, while I set up the tent."

"It's pouring rain! And I'm hungry." Marianne was close to tears. Of course she was. She was pampered. She'd never had a single hardship in her life.

Kill her, Invisible said.

It would be easy. Leave them in the woods and drive off. The storm and Mother Nature would take care of the rest. There were cougars in these woods big enough to eat both kids in one meal.

"A little rain never hurt anybody," Sharon told Marianne. She needed time to think. "Go ahead and open the snack crackers. The chocolate bars, too, if you like. I'll have the tent up in just a jiffy."

She bailed out of the car before the twins could launch another protest. The wind jerked the car door out of her grasp, and the pine boughs, heavy with rain, dumped water over her head. Ben would appreciate the sacrifices she was making for them. Someday, she and Jen would laugh about this, too.

The twins pressed their faces to the window, boggle-eyed and uncertain. She gave them a jaunty wave.

See how nice I am? See how I'm going to take care of you?

Sharon trudged around the car and dragged the tent from the trunk to the huge magnolia tree nearby. Rain drenched her hair and clothes, made walking treacherous. But it was relatively dry underneath the tree, the waxy leaves serving as nature's umbrella. It took her only minutes to rip into the box and set up the pop-up tent. She was tempted to crawl inside and wait for the rain to slack. The kids would be fine in the car. They had all the food and no cell phone. Thankfully, Sharon had thought to put hers in the pocket of her blue jeans.

But she knew Ben was coming. She had to get everything ready before she called to let him know where they were. She hoped he would be as thrilled as she was that they were starting their life together in a memorable way.

It hit her suddenly and with great clarity that she should make a photograph album. Something they could all enjoy. Even Jen.

Sharon whipped out her phone and stepped back to get a good view of the tent in the rain. It would make a great first picture. In the morning she would pose all four of them in front of the tent and let Ben take a selfie.

Unless she decided to do what Invisible had suggested… and then Ben would comfort her. He hated tears and would do almost anything to stop them.

Picture first. Then decide.

She bent over her cell phone, squinting to see the screen through the driving rain. She had expected the view to look like something out of *National Geographic*, artistic and appealing, raindrops sparkling as if the elements were blessing her union with Ben. Instead, the tent looked shrouded and uninviting. Soggy and unappealing. It filled too much of the frame.

She stepped backward for a wider angle, and her tennis shoes slipped in the mud. Sharon fought for purchase, pinwheeling her arms. Her phone flew out of her hand and sailed off into the darkness. But that was the least of her worries. She was still sliding.

Sharon grabbed at bushes that broke off in her hands, fought to check her momentum by latching onto one of the tree trunks flying by. Limbs tore at her clothing, her hair, her skin. This couldn't be happening to her. Not now. Not when she was on the brink of having her dream life.

She fought for solid ground.

I will not die!

SIXTY-FIVE
THE TURNER HOUSE

The moment was surreal to Jen.

Maria's phone call galvanized the search team in Gulf Breeze as well as Alabama's law enforcement network. The FBI field office in Mobile dispatched a helicopter to Thomasville; Clint called in a handler with the best air scent dog in the South; the local Thomasville police roared toward Walmart to secure the area, and the team from the Gulf Breeze police and the Santa Rosa Sheriff's Department continued to man the phones and monitor the situation from the command center in the dining room of the Turners' mansion.

Benjamin and Clint watched for the Turner company helicopter, worrying whether the worst of the storm would hold off long enough for them to fly out. Gran and Nancy were in the kitchen, trying to outdo each other. They had the coffee pot going and were making sandwiches for the team who would stay behind.

Jen stood apart, holding her children's clothing as if she cradled her own aching heart. A perfect storm of events had created a nightmare beyond her imagining. Still fighting off the effects of the toxins Sharon had given her, she forced herself not to wobble as she headed toward her port in the storm, clutching the tee shirts her children had worn the day before.

Annie sat with her eyes closed in the turquoise chair in the quiet corner Sharon had once used to separate herself from the crowd. Jen sank down beside her sister, every fiber in her being wishing she could turn back the clock. The great blues were back, haunting the window beyond and casting shadows over the sisters huddled in the same chair, their arms around each other, their heads close.

"Annie?" Jen's voice was a mere whisper, as if sound might make the situation worse. "What do you see?"

"A forest..." Her sister's faraway look telegraphed she was in the midst of a waking dream, absorbing the warning like a sea sponge.

"Like the one you saw when Rachel was taken?"

"No. It's greener, with water everywhere. The storm, but a lake, too, I think..."

"Jen!" Benjamin called to her. "The chopper's here. We have to hurry and get ahead of the storm."

Jen was desperate, torn. "Do you see the children?"

"No, but I feel fear everywhere in that forest. Go, I'll handle things here."

"Jen, we *have* to go." Benjamin slid his arm around her, leaning close to cajole as if she were one of her own children. "Come now. The pilot's waiting to take off."

She was borne off, into wind and rain, into the belly of a giant silver bird waiting on their massive lawn, a grieving mother barely aware of her surroundings and the talk that swirled around her.

Can we make it?

The wind was not a factor yet. The worst of the storm hadn't reached the Florida Panhandle and south Alabama.

Pray that it doesn't.

. . .

The Walmart parking lot in Thomasville was filled with flashing blue lights from the police cars, strobes of bright white from searchlights, and patches of yellow from the lights inside the store. Intermittent streaks of lightning split the sky, blinding white and dangerous. Particularly to those inside the Turner helicopter. They were a flying magnet, caught by the very thing they had hoped to avoid.

"Can you land?" Clint shouted to be heard in the cockpit above the roar of wind and blades.

"I've done it under worse conditions." The pilot, a veteran of two wars, was instrument-rated. He had once landed his chopper in a storm where lightning—hotter than the sun—hit the ground so close to him it vaporized the earth and a cloud of dust mushroomed at the site of the strike.

Rain pelted the tarmac and pounded the helicopter as it set down in the makeshift landing pad cordoned off by the local police.

Gawkers in rain slickers lined up behind police barricades, their curiosity overcoming common sense as they braved the storm. Some of them held umbrellas. Many were filming with cell phones.

The scene made Jen sick to her stomach. And the worst was yet to come. She knew this. She'd seen these tragedies unfold many times, had marched into the aftermath to help families pick up the pieces.

Let this not be a tragedy. Please.

"Let's get you inside." Clint helped Jen from the helicopter, shielding her from the rain and the crowd as they raced toward the building. Benjamin kept step beside them.

The store was controlled chaos. Local police as well as FBI special agents questioned employees and shoppers, searching for any clue. As Jen wove through the crowd, she heard them ask the same question, over and over. "Did you hear or see anything from this woman or these children that might lead us to them?"

Every time a photo of her children was flashed in front of a stranger, she felt the terror of a mother with missing children. Except for the low buzz of conversation, there was an eerie sort of hush over the store, as if everyone had stayed for a funeral and was mourning the dead.

She held herself together by sheer force of will. When Clint excused himself and slipped away, Benjamin reached for her hand. Jen was surprised by the small comfort, finding it gave her hope.

"Are you okay?" He wore his own grief in the deep lines etched around his mouth, as if sorrow had taken up permanent residence.

"I'm holding on." She could feel the tremor that snaked through him, but she had nothing left to give. Dr. Jen Turner with her reassurances and textbook solutions had vanished and left behind this empty shell.

When Clint came back, he brought a fit, dark-haired young man with deeply tanned skin who looked as if he might have returned from winning a triathlon in Hawaii. He was holding the leash of a large black Labrador retriever.

Clint introduced them as Sammy Wayfield, handler, and his air scent dog, Bullet. "As soon as this weather lets up, and we can pinpoint where they might have gone from here, they'll find Sharon and the children."

The young man tipped the Alabama baseball cap he was wearing. Jen almost expected to hear him say, *Roll, Tide*. "Won't the rain wash their trail away?"

"Don't worry about a thing, Dr. Turner," the young man told her. "Air scent dogs don't use a trail on the ground. They pick up scents left behind in the air. Flakes of skin, pieces of hair, bodily gases. And it doesn't have to be fresh, either. I just can't risk Bullet in the middle of a thunderstorm."

Her heart wrenched when she handed over her children's tee shirts. She felt as if they were being ripped away from her, all over again. "My scent will be on there, too."

"Not to worry. Bullet can smell you, standing right here. He knows the difference."

A magical dog. Another time, another place, she would have been enchanted. But the reality of an FBI special agent approaching her torpedoed all thought of anything except her growing urge to sink to the floor, howling, and the somber look on his face.

His badge identified him as Special Agent Jim Sanders. "The clerk who checked them out found this on the floor under the credit card machine."

The item he handed her was the dog tag Tommy's coach had given each boy on the team last year after they won the regional swim meet. The engraved words split Jen's heart in two —*Thomas Finn Turner, Gulf Breeze Swim Champion*. Neither the clasp nor the chain was broken.

She clutched it to her chest. "He left it there deliberately. He must have guessed something was wrong."

She shut her mind to all the things that could happen to her children in a storm in the middle of nowhere with a woman who had killed her own husband. She'd seen those horrible stories play out in her own practice. If her thinking turned down that path, she might collapse.

Suddenly Clint was back. "We've got a room set up for you and Benjamin to wait while we process the scene." He led them to a small conference room filled with comfortable padded chairs, a large table spread with deli trays, and a pot of coffee with Styrofoam cups and an array of flavored creamers sitting on a corner cabinet. "While we're working the store, Sammy will let Bullet imprint the scents then take the dog into the parking lot to see if we can find anything. We'll let you know the minute we have something to report."

Jen nodded, too full of emotion to speak. The door closed behind him, and the deepest silence descended on them, one heavy with fear and regret. For a while, they sat paralyzed while the clock on the wall ticked off the hours and minutes their children had been missing. Would it turn into days, months, years?

She closed her eyes, hoping to shut out the unthinkable.

When she heard her husband moving about, pouring two cups of coffee, she dared open her eyes, clinging to normal. He added cream to hers.

"We should eat something," he said.

"I know."

They both looked at the ham and salami, cheese and crackers, carrot sticks and broccoli as if it had grown fur and claws and might bite their hands off if they reached for it. The storm picked up speed. Wind and rain pounded the building, thunder rattled the window set high up on the wall above a door that would lead outside but felt like it might lead straight to the most unimaginable nightmare a parent could ever have.

Time marched on. Clint returned to tell them that Sammy's dog had tracked the scent all the way to the front of the parking lot.

"He's taken the dog to a motel now to rest so they'll both be fresh to track as soon as we can figure out where she might have set up camp," he said. "Video footage from cameras in the parking lot show she headed north, which we already suspected."

"She can't camp in this weather," Benjamin said. "Nobody can. She'll get a motel somewhere."

"We're already checking area motels," Clint said. "I can assure both of you, we're checking every angle."

"Thanks, Clint," Benjamin plucked ham and cheese off the tray and handed it to her. "You have to eat, Jen."

Maybe she could later. As she set the food on a paper plate

and shoved it aside, she dug deep for courage. *You have the knowledge to help. USE IT!*

"Everybody is assuming Sharon is logical." *There.* She could do this. She *must*. For her children. "She hasn't been logical since she got to Gulf Breeze." While Jen sat in that dreary room in a place she would forevermore hate, all the pieces of the puzzle had fallen into place... and her own culpability in not recognizing it sooner. "Sharon is suffering from cognitive dissonance. It's a common coping tool of the abused. The mind splits. She can believe two opposite things at once. No logic whatsoever."

The thought of her children in the hands of someone out of touch with reality almost bent her double. She clawed her way back to courage.

"The manager of the ice cream shop overheard her telling Tommy and Marianne that they were going on a big adventure," she added. "That's what Sharon believes, in spite of the storm. She bought the gear, so she'll try to camp."

In the midst of a lightning storm with all manner of poisonous snakes and wild animals seeking higher ground and shelter.

Terror caught hold of Jen and wouldn't let go.

SIXTY-SIX

SOUTH ALABAMA | LOCATION UNKNOWN

Blackest night closed around the car, and the wind battered against the roof and the windows as if it were trying to get inside to suck the two huddled on the back seat into a witch's maw. Marianne was crying, but Tommy felt the responsibility of being the only one left in the deep woods who could get them to safety.

But how? He pinched himself so the pain would keep him from crying, too. Aunt Sharon had gone weird, and maybe even worse. He'd seen that in Walmart when he realized both his and Marianne's phones were missing. He wished he'd done more than leave a clue behind. He wished he had grabbed his sister's hand and run when he had the chance.

Aunt Sharon hadn't come back from setting up the tent. Had she left them to die in the woods? Did a rattlesnake bite her? Had some depraved backwoodsman, like those in the TV horror shows he enjoyed watching, sneaked up and carted her off somewhere? He thought he'd heard a scream out there, but in the thunderstorm, he couldn't be certain.

"Tommy, what are we going to do?"

"I'm going to get her phone and call Dad."

He scrambled into the front seat where Aunt Sharon had left her purse. Her phone wasn't there. He searched everywhere, the car pockets, under the seats.

He swallowed the lump in his throat. He couldn't cry, not now. "I can't find it."

"Grab her keys! You can figure out how to drive us out."

That pig trail they had come on would be a muddy mess. "In this storm?"

"If you won't do it, I will!"

He dug around in Sharon's purse, and even turned it upside down and pawed through the contents that spilled onto the seat. A flash of lightning showed the scary truth.

"She took the keys." In the middle of trying to be the brave twin, all he wanted to do was run to his parents for protection.

"We can walk out."

"And go *where*? We could get so lost in these woods nobody would ever find us."

His sister kicked the seat and pounded the door with her fists. She never suffered in silence. He envied her. He wished kicking something would make him feel better. His gut had warned him that going off on a school night was wrong. Dad would have told him the plans. He was not the kind of parent who did things on the spur of the moment. Neither was Mom. Tommy had often wished they would back off, but tonight he realized that what he saw as control was their way of keeping him and his sister safe.

He longed for that safety now. His parents would be searching. He knew they would. He wanted to curl up on the seat and wait for them to find him. But how would they know where to look? Even he didn't know where they were.

Marianne was up on her knees in the backseat, peering anxiously out the window. "The storm's passing over us."

She was right. Any kid living on the coast, especially a swimmer like him, knows when a storm had spent its fury.

"I'm going to find Aunt Sharon." He hoped he sounded braver than he felt.

"But we don't know what's out there in the dark!"

"She bought a flashlight, and I'll stick close to camp." He had visions of every horrible thing he'd seen in movies of people lost in the woods. He didn't want to go out there in the dark.

You can't just sit in the car and wait to die.

He pushed the button to pop the lid of the trunk where Sharon had stashed the Walmart purchases.

"I'm going with you."

They bailed out of the car, and darkness closed around them like a damp blanket. Tommy grabbed his sister's hand and held on. He felt like an explorer on another planet. A *scary* one.

Water dripped from branches heavy with rain. Mists swirled in the air, dampening their hair, their skin, their clothing. The night vibrated with stirrings and whisperings and groanings that shivered him from head to toe. Unfamiliar sounds. Threatening sounds. Who knew what waited for them?

The beam of his flashlight caught the tent, erected under a giant magnolia tree. "Aunt Sharon," his sister called, but there was no answer. He called out, too, but the only thing they heard was the echo of their own voices.

They crawled inside the tent and sank onto the floor. It was dry inside, protected only by thin walls and a zippered door from whatever lay in the vast forest around them. But Aunt Sharon's cell phone and car keys were nowhere in sight. The only sign she had even been inside the tent was a smear of muddy footprints.

Marianne leaned her head on her knees, her shoulder shaking. He wanted to cry, too, but what good would it do?

"If you want to, you can stay here while I search."

"No." She jerked upright. "I'm not about to sit here like a crybaby. Let's go. She has to be around here somewhere."

They held onto each other, moving cautiously, following the

beam of light that cut through the thicket. The spongy forest floor became muddy and slick. Dangerous. The edge of the ravine came suddenly into view. He swept the light over the deep canyon. If they fell, they would die.

Marianne screeched and lost her footing.

He dropped the flashlight to grab her with both hands. Now, both of them were sliding.

"Hang on!" He dropped to the ground and dug in. A small, sturdy bush pressed against his right leg, and he hooked his foot around it, anchoring himself. Together, they inched backward, bellies in the mud.

Finally, the mud gave way to fallen leaves and forest debris. They stretched out, panting. Safe. At least for the moment.

"I found something," his sister said.

"What is it?"

"I think it's a cell phone."

"Does it work?"

"I don't know." He could hear her in the dark, feel her frantic movements. "Come on, come on, come *on*."

Suddenly they heard a piercing scream.

Was it animal or human?

Tommy reached for Marianne, and they huddled together, trembling. Something horrible was out there in the dark. Watching. Waiting.

SIXTY-SEVEN

THE MOTEL | THOMASVILLE, ALABAMA

Jen startled awake. The luminous dial on the cheap bedside clock pointed to three o'clock. Reality flooded her with the shock of a category five hurricane. She was in a motel in Thomasville, Alabama, and her children were missing.

That she had slept at all was a miracle. Benjamin lay beside her, flat on his back, his mouth open as he snored. He was exhausted. Both of them were. She walked to the window, pulled back the heavy tweed curtain, and looked out into a rain-washed parking lot where streetlights illuminated the FBI van, the pickup truck owned by the dog handler, the rental car they could use as they wished, the police cruiser that had carried them from Walmart. Dubbed by law enforcement as *the last known location*.

Her cell phone rang. She bumped her shin as she raced around the bed and grabbed it. It was Sharon's number.

"Mom?"

Jen sank to the mattress, undone by the sound of her daughter's voice.

"Can you come get us?"

"Benjamin! Wake up. It's Marianne!" He shot straight up, galvanized by the sound of his daughter's voice on speaker.

"*Where?*" He was simultaneously grabbing for his pants and his cell phone.

"I don't *know!*" Jen's hand shook so hard she could barely hold onto her phone. "Marianne, where are you? Is Tommy with you?"

"Here... Let him tell you."

Static shuddered through the line, shattering Jen's nerves while Benjamin hobbled around the room, his pants half on as he simultaneously called Clint and unlocked the door.

Jen wanted to shake her phone, throw it against the wall and herself with it, fall onto her knees and beg. "Please," she whispered, a desperate, unspoken prayer.

An eternity later, her son's voice came through.

"Mom, this phone is barely working. We're in the woods not too far from Walmart in Thomasville. About twenty minutes or so. Aunt Sharon said she had camped here before."

Memories spun through her, the stories Sharon had shared, every detail now crystalized in her mind as the FBI walked through the door with the dog handler.

"There're in Pine Hill, Alabama!" she shouted. "On Champion land. Sharon's mother grew up there and Sharon's Aunt Priscilla still lives there... is Sharon with you?"

"No. We don't know where she is... Mom... there's something awful out there in the woods. Can you come get us?"

His voice! So small and scared...

"Hang on, Tommy. I'm coming. *All* of us are."

She didn't even know if he heard. The static was terrible, and suddenly Sharon's phone went dead. Jen threw on her clothes, grabbed her purse and the keys to the rental car, then streaked to the door.

"Jen, what on earth are you doing?"

"Going to get my children. And don't you *dare* try to stop me!"

"We're *all* going. Wait for Clint. The entire team will be ready to leave in fifteen minutes."

"Tommy and Marianne might not *have* fifteen minutes! *You* wait for Clint. Show him the way. I'm gone."

She barreled out of the room with Benjamin calling after her. "Don't do anything until we get there. You hear me, Jen? Sharon's *dangerous*."

How well I know.

Jen skidded on the wet parking lot, almost fell flat on her face before she got to the rental car. Her hands shook so hard she had to try twice before she clicked the correct button to unlock the car.

Keyless cars are a royal pain.

As she tore out of Thomasville and hung a hard left on Highway 43 it was easier to cast aspersions on keyless cars than to imagine what might be happening to her children twenty minutes away on a winding, twisting road that seemed it might be leading straight to perdition.

Rain slashed her windshield, but Jen kept her foot hard on the accelerator. She'd learned to drive in the Rocky Mountains. She'd navigated the sharp curves and dangerous inclines of Pikes Peak. She'd do *anything* to save her children, even drive with the speed of a NASCAR racer.

In the wee hours, she had the road to herself. No sign yet of the rescue caravan she had no intention of waiting for.

After an endless *forever,* Jen spotted the leaning posts, the familiar giant pine tree towering beyond. She slammed on her brakes and skidded as she made a sharp turn into deep woods beyond the gap of a sagging fence.

This is it.

Her children were somewhere in that forbidding tangle of

forest and twisted brambles, that hellish, storm-tossed landscape where a madwoman held them captive.

I'm coming!

She saw Sharon's car up ahead, and her heart almost stopped. Her children were not inside.

Jen's tires spun in the muddy ruts, failing to catch traction. The harder she tried to get out, the deeper her wheels sank. She barreled out of the car, slipping and sliding, instantly soaked as she screamed for her children.

There was no answer. Only the awful quiet of a gloomy forest that had swallowed them whole. Frantic, not knowing which way to turn, Jen stumbled through the dark over fallen logs and bushes so thick she had to fight her way out. Fear spurring her on, she plowed toward the spot she vaguely remembered as Sharon's childhood campsite.

"Marianne! Tommy!" she bellowed. "It's Mom! I've come to get you!"

"*They're mine!*" Sharon's scream came back to her, striking an awful fear Jen hadn't known was possible. "*You'll never have them back!*"

Afraid any response would tip her over the edge, Jen bulldozed through the mud and muck and horror, indestructible as a Sherman tank and twice as deadly. No fury on heaven or earth can match a mother fighting for her children.

She came upon them suddenly—Sharon, a rain-soaked Medusa, brambles sticking out of her hair like vipers, her arms wrapped tightly around Marianne and Tommy, both mud-soaked and scared.

My children are alive! Jen's knees nearly buckled with relief.

Her son opened his mouth to speak then gave his captor a terrified look that told its own story of intimidation and terror. Marianne was sobbing silently, her shoulders heaving, tears mixing with rain that streaked down her muddy cheeks.

"Stand back, Jen, or I'll kill them both."

"Sharon." Tamping down her terror, Jen reached toward her, palms up. Sometimes calling patients by name—a signal that they are *seen*—calmed them, especially when accompanied by the age-old gesture of conciliation and peace.

Not today. Her glare was pure evil.

"You don't want to do this. Benjamin is on the way."

"Ben's coming?" Sharon brightened, even fluffed up her hair. It was both heartbreaking and horrifying.

"He'll be here any minute." Jen listened for the sound of vehicles, the baying of the air scent dog. Even tires spinning in the mud. Anything at all to announce she didn't have to do this alone. "Why don't we all go and wait for him in the car where it's dry and warm?"

Suddenly a black panther appeared on the other side of the ravine, ghost-like, staring at Jen with burning yellow eyes. A big cat not native to Alabama. Spoken of only in whispers, and kept alive in local legends.

Danger. His warning clanged through her as he slunk away.

Sharon's rigid posture and furious face screamed it even louder.

"You are trying to *trick me!*" Releasing her hold on the children, she lunged.

"*Run!*" Jen screamed, bracing for the attack.

"They're *mine!*" Sharon came in low, her shoulder ramming into Jen's solar plexus, knocking her breath out and pushing her backward.

Jen scrambled to find purchase in the mud. Grabbing a handful of hair, she jerked so hard Sharon spun in her tracks.

"Oh *no,* they are not!"

Sharon lost her footing, but she kept a vise grip on Jen as the two of them twisted in a macabre dance through the mud and mire. The deep chasm of the ravine yawned so close, Jen felt rocks underfoot tearing loose, heard them banging their way down the sheer walls to the bottom.

"Mom!" Tommy yelled, his footsteps pounding their way,

"Stay back, Tommy! Stay *back*!"

The rocks moved now with a force of their own. Jen felt herself slipping, imagined the two of them, forever entangled, crashing into the deep ravine below.

She shoved.

Suddenly. A scream. And the long, slow tumble to the lethal boulders at the bottom.

SIXTY-EIGHT

PINE HILL, ALABAMA

Thirty minutes after Jen left, Benjamin was in the lead car of the rescue caravan streaking toward Pine Hill. It was more than just the name of the town; it was the description. In the predawn hours, the heavily forested hills looked medieval.

A hilly, winding two-lane road divided the Champion homestead from the land used for hunting and fishing, traipsing the hills finding forest treasures, camping under the canopies of hundred-year-old trees. It was just as Sharon had described her family's home. Would she be alive to know her dangerous journey had come to an end?

Would his wife? Benjamin's heart hurt just thinking how many ways he had failed Jen. He should have gone with her to find the children and let Clint and the FBI use their vehicles' navigation systems.

What if she was hurt? What if she got there too late and his entire family now lay dead somewhere in the middle of this forbidding landscape?

The caravan came to a halt on the side of the road where a gap in the fence showed tire tracks.

"You should wait in the car." Clint was following correct protocol, but also being kind.

"I have no intention of waiting." *Not anymore.* "Jen and the children need me."

"All right. But stay at the back and let us do our job."

Ben made no promises.

There was a flurry of activity as law enforcement and the search and rescue handler bailed from their vehicles, armed and grim. Benjamin never thought he'd live to see his children as victims requiring such a massive show of force and firepower. He moved into the lineup, matching steps with Clint.

Bullet, the miracle dog, picked up the scent as soon as his feet hit the ground. Benjamin had been on plenty of hunts with his dad and the rest of his Southern family. He knew the bugling of hound dogs as they caught the scent of prey. Retrievers don't bugle. Bullet didn't even bark as he streaked into the forest with his handler and the FBI right behind him.

"Why isn't the dog barking?" he asked Clint.

"He's trained that way."

The dog's path was sure and steady, leading them past the cars—Sharon's and the rental Jen took—both empty.

Benjamin's dismay was total. "Jen didn't wait."

"I didn't think she would." Clint put a reassuring hand on his shoulder. "We'll find them."

Dead or alive?

He was so heavy with fear, he could barely put one foot in front of the other. Brambles grabbed at him. Limbs freshly broken by the storm and old logs rotted through impeded his progress. He stumbled, a grieving, regretful man at home among polished floors and sparkling chandeliers whose wealth meant nothing compared to his loss.

Suddenly, there was a bark. The dog was standing, wagging his tail at the three people, mud-caked and tear-soaked, huddled on the edge of a ravine.

"Jen!" Benjamin raced to her, knelt and wrapped his arms around his wife and his children, his gratitude and relief so deep he was speechless.

"Where's Sharon?" Clint asked.

"Down there." Jen nodded toward the ravine, and the team set about their grim task of retrieving her.

"Let's go." His children didn't need to watch that. Nor did Jen.

He reached for her. A peace offering. A bridge to the future. Jen nestled her hand in his, and they headed toward the car, not saying a word, not even when the sun glowed over the eastern horizon, burning away the darkness and spilling rosy light into the sky. He saw that as a symbol of their marriage. He and Jen would put the past behind them and walk into the light. Together. Just as they always had.

Bracketed by Marianne and Tommy, all of them with arms linked, they were a circle. A family. Just as they should be.

They were almost at the car when a sound behind them made Jen turn around, her face an open book he could read.

In the distance, she saw two agents bearing a stretcher. Sharon.

Her enemy. Her friend.

SIXTY-NINE

THE TURNER HOUSE

Back in Gulf Breeze, Jen and Benjamin kept the children out of school for two days, giving themselves time to decompress, to heal, and to process everything that had happened. Gran and Annie, with their big personalities and giving hearts, made their journey back to normal easier.

As if nature itself wanted to apologize, the sun and balmy weather turned Gulf Breeze into the paradise they had all taken for granted until they almost lost it.

Jen saw an incoming text from Clint. She leaned across the chaise-for-two and told her husband her plans, then slipped from the pool room where their children romped in the water with Gran, resplendent in a swimsuit she had brought from Colorado. It appeared to be a faded relic from the seventies, but knowing Victoria, it could be something she found at a thrift store. She did love to pinch a penny.

Jen smiled as she slipped into the quiet kitchen. Annie was there, already pouring two cups of tea and stacking pastries onto two plates.

"How did you know I needed this?"

"Because I know and love you." Annie pressed cheeks with

Jen then carried the tea tray to the table. "It's all going to be okay."

Jen bit into a cream-cheese filled pastry, her favorite. She was glad she'd given Nancy and Dal a week off. Before they left, Nancy filled the refrigerator with casseroles and pastries, and Dal cut the white oleander to the ground. She was glad it was gone.

"I got a text from Clint."

"Find out what he knows, and then we can relax and enjoy our teatime."

Jen punched in her security guard's number and put him on speaker. "Clint? What's up?"

"Sharon has been charged with kidnapping and the murder of her husband."

"I'll go to the hospital to see her."

"I don't advise it."

"I know you don't. And I don't ever want to be without your assistance and your advice."

He chuckled. "That part's debatable."

"Maybe. But you know I have to see her. She was my friend, and she's still my patient."

Annie leaned closer to the phone. "She won't be alone, Clint, and I'm not going to let her go barreling off without first taking a minute for herself."

"Good. Keep her out of trouble."

"I intend to." Annie bit in her own strawberry cream-filled pastry then leaned back, sighing. "Heavenly. I'm going to pack a few of these for the drive over to New Orleans."

That bombshell got Jen's attention. "When did you plan this? Are you going to find out about Mom's people?"

"Unearth her secrets after all these years? No. My agent booked an art lecture."

Suddenly two great blue herons darkened the kitchen

window, their wingspan turning the kitchen to a shade resembling the inside of a coffin. Jen felt the color leave her face.

"Jen?" Annie leaned over and squeezed her hand. "What's wrong? Are the children still in danger from Sharon?"

"No. It's you, Annie. New Orleans holds danger for you. Please, don't go."

"I have to. But I *promise you* I'll watch my back, and I won't stay a minute longer than I have to." Annie bustled about, rinsing their teacups. "Let's go to the hospital and finish this business with Sharon. I'm driving."

Her sister was strong, efficient, powerful, but *still*, as they climbed into her snazzy convertible, Jen felt nature's warning for her sister like a toothache.

* * *

An armed guard stood outside Sharon's hospital room, a sober reminder that the woman inside was considered a criminal. Jen showed her ID.

"I'm Dr. Jennifer Turner, Sharon's psychologist. And this is my sister, Annie."

"Go right in, Dr. Turner."

She paused to center herself. Besides almost losing her children, facing the woman who was her enemy as well as her patient and her former friend was the hardest thing she had to do.

"I'm with you." Annie linked arms, and Jen pushed open the door.

Sharon was alone in the bed, small and fragile-looking, her face bruised and swollen from the rocks at the bottom of the ravine, her broken left arm in a sling, and her shattered left leg in a cast suspended over the mattress. Her blue eyes widened at the sight of Jen.

"I knew you would come. They say I murdered Matt and

kidnapped your children. That can't be right. I've only ever *loved* you." Her voice broke on a sob. "That's not right, is it?"

Jen vibrated with the urge to scream at her then turn on her heel and run. Instead, she pulled a chair next to the bed, and Annie moved to stand right behind her, a hand on her shoulder. She drew enough strength from her sister's loving support to set her own feelings aside long enough to be the psychologist Sharon needed.

"That's not the whole story. When a woman is battered the way you were, her mind splinters apart so she has a hard time knowing what is real and what is not. That happened to you."

She explained cognitive dissonance in layman's terms, and saw the dawning of both comprehension and terror in Sharon's face.

"That's why you could love me and want me to disappear at the same time." *And that's why I can sit here explaining things to you without giving in to a mother's awful rage at what you did.* "That's why you could scheme to take everything that belonged to me and even try to poison me while you were also taking good care of me."

"That's so awful." Tears spilled down Sharon's cheeks. "I can't believe I did that. I'm so sorry."

"It wasn't you. It was a woman with a battered body and a broken mind."

She went quiet, giving Sharon time to process a reality that was vastly different from the way her troubled mind had imagined it. Sunlight flooded the room through the window, and not a single seagull or heron marred the peace of a sky so vast the blue seemed to go on forever. The nightmare with Sharon was almost over. All it needed now was a proper ending.

"Jen? Am I going to prison?"

"No, you are not a criminal. You're a victim."

"You'll help me, won't you?"

"No." Jen was unmoved by the tears that pooled in Sharon's

eyes. She'd done her professional duty. It was over. "You tried to murder me and steal my children. You put my entire family in danger. I will never help you again."

"But... what's going to happen to *me?*"

It occurred to Jen with great clarity that, mentally unstable or not, Sharon had *always* been concerned only for herself. Jen had let their history create a friendship that was as one-sided as it was dangerous. The mother in her wanted this woman to suffer as much as she and her family had, but her training as a psychologist wouldn't let her be that hard-hearted and mean. Not to mention her upbringing by Victoria Logan.

"Your family will get a good lawyer who'll use your mental condition to get you into an institution where you'll likely serve all your time."

"But you'll come to see me there, right? You'll help me get well?"

Weeks ago, the edge of desperation in Sharon's voice would have spurred her to offer help.

"No, I will never see you again."

"But, Jen, I *need you...*"

"You need help, but it won't come from me."

"You don't *mean* that."

Jen sighed. Sharon had always been able to cajole her and charm her. She was never going to understand a *nice* explanation.

"I mean every word. Make no mistake about it." She leaned closer, her expression as fierce as her heart. "And if you ever try to come near me or my family again, you will regret it until the day you die."

Finally, understanding and regret opened the floodgates of Sharon's sorrow. Racked by agony and sobs, she bowed her head while Jen and Annie marched from the room, arms linked, sisters and *true* best friends.

Outside, the air felt clean, washed by rain and the tears Jen didn't even know were coursing down her cheeks until her sister reached up to wipe them away.

"It's finally over." Jen let the horrors of the past few weeks slide away, like shedding a coat she no longer needed.

"I *know*. This calls for a celebration." Annie slid behind the wheel of the convertible and let the top down.

"Tea?" Jen slid into the passenger seat, her sudden lightness of heart a stark reminder of how narrowly she had escaped from the woman she'd believed to be her friend.

"Not tea." Annie flashed a dazzling smile. "A margarita, maybe, with a CD of Jimmy Buffett playing the beach songs we love."

"I know just the place." Jen sent Benjamin a text then directed her sister toward Shaggy's Bar and Grill.

Within minutes, they were sitting in the sunlight on Shaggy's porch facing the now-calm blue waters of Santa Rosa Sound, celebrating as only the tightly knit Logan sisters could.

Annie lifted her margarita and clinked glasses. "To us."

"To us." It was the perfect toast in what would have been the perfect moment if Jen hadn't noticed the great blues drifting by, their warning for Annie as ominous as the sound of a bell tolling.

Not my sister, Jen vowed. *Not while I have breath.*

She turned her attention back to Annie. As long as they had each other—and Rachel—the Logan sisters would not only survive; they would triumph.

A LETTER FROM PEGGY

Dear reader,

Thank you so much for reading *Taken in the Dark*. If you want to keep up to date with all my latest releases, just sign up at the following link. Your email address will never be shared and you can unsubscribe at any time.

www.bookouture.com/peggy-webb

It was such fun to be with the Logan sisters again as I created Jen's story. I adore them, and I particularly love the setting. It was inspired by a wonderful visit with my son, who lives in Florida. He enjoys taking me on big adventures, and one of them was across 3-Mile Bridge to Gulf Breeze, Florida. I fell in love with the historic leaping marlin sign, Shaggy's Bar and Grill, and the iconic Gulf Breeze Bait and Tackle Shop. You'll visit them all in *Taken in the Dark*.

I hope you loved the chilling and yet mystical world of the Logan sisters as much as I enjoyed creating it. If you did, I would be very grateful if you could write a review. I'd love to hear what you think, and your feedback helps new readers to discover one of my books for the first time.

To loyal fans who have been with me through the years and to new fans who have joined me on this thrilling writing journey with Bookouture—my heartfelt thanks!

I love hearing from you! Do stay in touch on my social

media pages, my new YouTube channel, and my website. My regular FB page is chock full of fun posts, including my music videos. Though I've been writing for many years, my author FB page is new, so bear with me while I populate it with good stuff and good friends. You'll find my blog with insider info on my website, and some surprises, too!

Thank you so much for being such amazing, supportive readers!

Peggy Webb

www.peggywebb.com

- facebook.com/peggywebbauthor
- instagram.com/peggy.webb.92
- youtube.com/@PeggyWebbOnPageAndPiano

ACKNOWLEDGMENTS

Deepest gratitude goes to my wonderful editor, Jess Whitlum-Cooper. I don't know how you climb into my mind to understand every nuance of my characters and my story, but you somehow perform that magic trick with every Logan Sisters thriller! I can't thank you enough for your patience, your skill, and your commitment to making *Taken in the Dark* the best it could be! I am blessed.

To my publisher Ruth Tross for amazing support, Noelle Holton for brilliant marketing, and the entire team at Bookouture whose expertise, dedication, and respect for authors and our stories brought *Taken in the Dark* to life and to bookshelves —*thank you!*

To my son, Trey Webb, for taking me across 3-Mile Bridge on a *big adventure* that sunny day in Florida where I had an amazing time *and* discovered the setting for this story—I love you every moment of every day! I think I owe you the moon for answering a million questions about the various bays that surround the peninsula and the marine life there. Just don't ask me to cross the water in your kayak!

Also, a big thank you to the Chamber of Commerce and the good people in Gulf Breeze, Florida, for the wealth of insider information that helped me bring the setting alive for you.

As always, my wonderful children and grandchildren in Florida and New Hampshire have loved me and cheered for me through the entire process of writing *Taken in the Dark*.

Hugs to all!

Peggy

PUBLISHING TEAM

Turning a manuscript into a book requires the efforts of many people. The publishing team at Bookouture would like to acknowledge everyone who contributed to this publication.

Audio
Alba Proko
Melissa Tran
Sinead O'Connor

Commercial
Lauren Morrissette
Hannah Richmond
Imogen Allport

Cover design
Eileen Carey

Data and analysis
Mark Alder
Mohamed Bussuri

Editorial
Jess Whitlum–Cooper
Imogen Allport

Proofreader
John Romans

Marketing
Alex Crow
Melanie Price
Occy Carr
Cíara Rosney
Martyna Młynarska

Operations and distribution
Marina Valles
Stephanie Straub

Production
Hannah Snetsinger
Mandy Kullar
Jen Shannon

Publicity
Kim Nash
Noelle Holten
Jess Readett
Sarah Hardy

Rights and contracts
Peta Nightingale
Richard King
Saidah Graham

www.ingramcontent.com/pod-product-compliance
Lightning Source LLC
LaVergne TN
LVHW041618060526
838200LV00040B/1337